Primary Command

Jack Mars

Jack Mars is the USA Today bestselling author of the LUKE STONE thriller series, which includes seven books. He is also the author of the new FORGING OF LUKE STONE prequel series, comprising three books (and counting); and of the AGENT ZERO spy thriller series, comprising six books (and counting).

ANY MEANS NECESSARY (book #1), which has over 800 five star reviews, is available as a free download on Amazon!

Jack loves to hear from you, so please feel free to visit www.Jackmarsauthor.com to join the email list, receive a free book, receive free giveaways, connect on Facebook and Twitter, and stay in touch!

Books by Jack Mars

LUKE STONE THRILLER SERIES

ANY MEANS NECESSARY (Book #1)

OATH OF OFFICE (Book #2)

SITUATION ROOM (Book #3)

OPPOSE ANY FOE (Book #4)

PRESIDENT ELECT (Book #5)

OUR SACRED HONOR (Book #6)

HOUSE DIVIDED (Book #7)

FORGING OF LUKE STONE PREQUEL SERIES

PRIMARY TARGET (Book #1)

PRIMARY COMMAND (Book #2)

PRIMARY THREAT (Book #3)

AN AGENT ZERO SPY THRILLER SERIES

AGENT ZERO (Book #1)

TARGET ZERO (Book #2)

HUNTING ZERO (Book #3)

TRAPPING ZERO (Book #4)

FILE ZERO (Book #5)

RECALL ZERO (Book #6)

Primary Command

The Forging of Luke Stone—Book #2 (an Action Thriller)

Jack Mars

Table of Contents

Chapter One

June 25, 2005
1:45 p.m. Moscow Daylight Time (5:45 a.m. Eastern Daylight Time)
130 Nautical Miles East-Southeast of Yalta
The Black Sea

"I'm sick of waiting," the fat sub pilot said to Reed Smith. "Let's do this already."

Smith sat on the deck of the *Aegean Explorer*, a beat-up old fishing trawler that had been retrofitted for archaeological discovery. He was smoking a Turkish cigarette, drinking a can of Coke, and soaking up the warmth of the bright day, the dry salty feeling of the air, and the call of the seagulls that congregated in the sky around the boat.

The midday sun had crested above their heads and was now starting to creep to their west. The science crew was still inside the pilot house of the trawler, pretending to make calculations concerning the whereabouts of an ancient Greek trading vessel resting in the mud 350 meters below the surface of this beautiful blue sea.

All around them was wide open water, the waves shimmering in the sun.

"What's the rush?" Smith said. He was still nursing a hangover from two nights before. The *Aegean Explorer* had been docked for several days in the Turkish port of Samsun. With nothing else to do, Smith had sampled the local nightlife.

Smith liked to live in airtight compartments. He could be out drinking and partying with prostitutes in a strange city, and never once think about the people in other places who would kill him if given a chance. He could sit on this deck, enjoying a smoke and the beauty of the waters surrounding him, and never once think about how, in a little while, he would be tapping into Russian communications cables one hundred stories below the surface of those waters. And living in compartments meant he didn't enjoy people who were constantly thinking, anticipating, sifting through the contents of one compartment and putting them in another. People like this sub pilot.

"What kind of archaeology team dives in the middle of the afternoon?" the pilot said. "We should have gone down in the morning."

Smith didn't say a word. The answer should be obvious enough.

The *Aegean Explorer* worked the waters, not just of the Aegean, but also the Black Sea and the Sea of Azov. By all appearances, the *Explorer* was looking for shipwrecks left behind by long-dead civilizations.

The Black Sea in particular was an excellent place to search for wrecks. The water here was anoxic, which meant that below 150 meters there was almost no oxygen. Sea life was sparse down there, and what little there was tended toward the anaerobic bacteria variety.

And what that meant was objects that fell to the sea floor were very well preserved. There were ships down there from the Middle Ages in which modern divers had found crew members still dressed in the clothes they were wearing when they died.

Reed Smith would like to see something like that. Of course, it would have to wait for another time. They weren't here to dive a shipwreck.

The *Aegean Explorer* and its mission was a lie. Poseidon Research International, the organization that owned and manned the *Aegean Explorer*, was also a lie. Reed Smith was a lie. The truth was, every man on board this ship was either an employee of, an elite covert operator on loan to, or a freelancer temporarily hired by the Central Intelligence Agency.

"*Nereus* crew, load up," a flat voice said over the loudspeaker.

The *Nereus* was a tiny, bright yellow submarine—known in the trade as a submersible. Its cockpit was a perfectly round acrylic bubble. That bubble, as fragile as it appeared, would resist the pressure at a depth of a thousand meters—pressure one hundred times that at the surface.

Smith pitched his smoke into the water.

The two men moved toward the submersible. They were joined by a third man, a wiry, muscular guy in his twenties, with a deep scar on the left side of his face. He had a jarhead haircut. His eyes were razor sharp. He claimed to be a marine biologist named Eric Davis.

The kid had special ops written all over him. He had hardly spoken a word the entire time they'd been on the boat.

The bright yellow *Nereus* squatted on a metal platform. Looking like a friendly robot from a science fiction movie, it even had two black metal robot arms reaching from the front of it. A heavy crane loomed above from the deck of the trawler, ready to lift the *Nereus* into the water. Two men in orange jumpsuits waited to hook the *Nereus* to the thick cable that it would be suspended from.

Smith and his two crewmates mounted the stairs and climbed, one at a time, through the main hatch. The special ops kid went first, as he would sit in the back. Then the pilot went in.

Smith went in last, easing into his co-pilot chair. Directly in front of him were the controls to the robot arms. All around him was the clear bubble of the cockpit. He reached up and pulled the hatch shut behind him, turning the valve to seal and lock it.

He was shoulder to shoulder with the thick pilot, Bolger. The glass of the cockpit was not more than a foot from his face, and six inches from his right shoulder.

It was hot inside this orb, and getting hotter.

"Cozy," Smith said, not enjoying the feeling any more than he had when he was in training for this. A claustrophobic wouldn't last three minutes inside this thing.

"Get used to it," the pilot said. "We're going to be in here awhile."

No sooner had Smith sealed the hatch than the *Nereus* lurched to life. The men had hooked it to the cable, and the crane lifted it toward the water. Smith looked behind them. One of the men in the orange jumpsuits was riding on the *Nereus*'s narrow outside deck. He held onto the cable with one thick-gloved hand.

In a moment, they were out over nothing, two stories in the air. The crane lowered them to the water, the green fishing trawler looming above them now. A Zodiac appeared with one man aboard, moving fast. The man on the outside deck busied himself releasing the cable straps and then stepped into the Zodiac.

A voice came over the radio. "*Nereus,* this is *Aegean Explorer* command. Initiate tests."

"Roger," the pilot said. "Initiating now." The man had an array of controls in front of him. He pressed a button on top of the joystick he held in his hand. Then he began to flip switches, his meaty left hand moving from one to another in fast succession. His right hand stayed on the joystick. Cool, oxygenated air began to blow into the tiny module. Smith took a deep breath of it. It felt so nice on his sweaty face. He'd been starting to overheat there for a minute.

The pilot and radio voice exchanged information, talking back and forth as the sub rocked gently forward, then backward. The water bubbled and rose all around them. In a few seconds, the surface of the Black Sea was just above their heads. Smith and the man in the back remained quiet, letting the pilot do his thing. They were nothing if not complete professionals.

"Initiate silent running," the voice said.

"Silent running," the pilot said. "See you tonight."

"Godspeed, *Nereus.*"

The pilot did something then that no civilian submersible pilot looking for a shipwreck would ever do. He switched the radio off. Then he switched his locator beacon off. His lifelines to the surface were cut.

Could the *Aegean Explorer* still see the *Nereus* on sonar? Sure. But the *Explorer* knew where the *Nereus* was. In a little while, even that wouldn't be true. The *Nereus* was a tiny dot in a vast sea.

For all intents and purposes, the *Nereus* was gone.

Reed Smith took another deep breath. This must be the thirtieth time he had gone below the surface in one of these things, in training and in the real world, but he still couldn't get over it. Just fifteen feet down and the sea became bright blue as the sunlight from the surface was scattered and absorbed. On the color spectrum, red was absorbed first, casting a blue patina over the undersea world.

It became bluer and darker as the sub sank through the depths.

"It's beautiful," Eric Davis said from behind them.

"Yes, it is," the pilot said. "I never get tired of it."

They dropped through the blue into deep, still darkness. It wasn't complete, though. Smith knew that a small amount of light from the surface still reached them. This was the twilight layer. Below them, even deeper, was midnight.

The black enveloped them. The pilot didn't turn his lights on, navigating with his instruments instead. Now there was nothing to see.

Smith allowed himself to drift. He closed his eyes and took a deep breath. Then another. And another. He let the hangover take him. He had a job to do, but not yet. The pilot, Bolger, would tell him when his time came. Now he just floated in his mind. It was a pleasant sensation, listening to the hum of the engines and the occasional soft murmuring of the two men in the capsule with him, as they made small talk about one thing or another.

Time passed. Possibly a long time.

"Smith!" Bolger hissed. "Smith! Wake up."

He spoke without opening his eyes. "I'm not asleep. Are we there yet?"

"No. We have a problem."

Smith's eyes popped open. He was surprised to see near total darkness everywhere around him. The only lights came from the red and green glow of the instrument panel. *Problem* was not a word he wanted to hear hundreds of meters below the surface of the Black Sea.

"What is it?"

Bolger's stubby finger pointed at the sonar display. Something big was on there, maybe three kilometers to their northwest. If it wasn't a blue whale, which it almost certainly was not, then it was a ship of some kind, probably a submarine. And there was only one country Smith knew of that operated real subs in these waters.

"Aw hell, why did you turn the sonar on?"

"I had a bad feeling," Bolger said. "I wanted to make sure we were alone."

"Well, clearly we're not," Smith said. "And you're advertising our presence."

Bolger shook his head. "They knew we were here." He pointed at two much smaller dots, behind them to the south. He pointed at a similar dot ahead and just to their east, less than a kilometer out. "See these? Not good. They're converging on our location."

Smith ran a hand over his head. "Davis?"

"Not my department," the man in the back said. "I'm here to rescue your asses and scuttle the sub in case of a system malfunction or pilot error. I'm in no position to engage an enemy from inside here. And at these depths I couldn't open the hatch if I wanted to. Too much pressure."

Smith nodded. "Yeah." He looked at the pilot. "How far to the target?"

Bolger shook his head. "Too far."

"Rendezvous spot?"

"Forget it."

"Can we evade?"

Bolger shrugged. "In this? I guess we can try."

"Take evasive action," Smith nearly said, but he didn't get the chance. Suddenly, a bright light came on directly in front of them. The effect in the tiny capsule was blinding.

"Turn it around," Smith said, shielding his eyes. "Unfriendlies."

The pilot sent the *Nereus* into an abrupt 360-degree spin. Before he could finish the maneuver, another blinding light came on behind them. They were surrounded, front and back, by submersibles like this one. Like this one, except Smith was familiar with the enemy submersibles. They'd been designed and built back in the 1960s, during the era of pocket calculators.

He nearly punched the screen in front of him. Dammit! None of this even took into account that large object further out there, probably a hunter-killer.

The mission, highly classified, was going to be a dead loss. But that wasn't the worst of it. Not even close. The worst of it was Reed Smith himself. He couldn't be captured, not at any cost.

"Davis, options?"

"I can scuttle with the team inside here," Davis said. "But personally, I'd rather let them have this hunk of junk and live to fight another day."

Smith grunted. He couldn't see a thing. And his only choices were to die inside this bubble, or... he didn't want to think about the other choices.

Terrific. Whose idea was this again?

He reached down to his calf and opened the zipper on his cargo pants. There was a tiny, two-shot Derringer taped to his leg. It was his suicide gun. He ripped the tape off his calf, barely feeling it as the hair was torn away. He put the gun to his head and took a deep breath.

"What are you doing?" Bolger said, alarm rising in his voice. "You can't fire that in here. You'll blow a hole in this thing. We're a thousand feet below the surface."

He gestured at the bubble all around them.

Smith shook his head. "You don't understand."

Suddenly, the special ops kid was behind him. The kid wriggled like a thick snake. He had Smith's wrist in a powerful grip. How did he move so fast in such a tight space? For a moment, they grunted and wrestled, barely able to move. The kid's forearm was around Smith's throat. He banged Smith's hand against the console.

"Drop it!" he screamed. "Drop the gun!"

Now the gun was gone. Smith pushed down with his legs and wrenched himself backward, trying to shake the kid off of him.

"You don't know who I am."

"Stop!" the pilot shouted. "Stop fighting! You're hitting the controls."

Smith managed to slip out of his seat, but now the kid was on top of him. The kid was strong, immensely strong, and he forced Reed down between the seat and the edge of the sub. He wedged Reed in there and pushed him into a ball. The kid was on top of him now, breathing heavily. His coffee breath was in Reed Smith's ear.

"I can kill you, okay?" the kid said. "I can kill you. If that's what we need to do, okay. But you can't fire the gun in here. Me and the other guy want to live."

"I got big problems," Reed said. "If they question me … If they torture me …"

"I know," the kid said. "I get it."

He paused, his breath coming in harsh rasps.

"Do you want me to kill you? I'll do it. It's up to you."

Reed thought about it. The gun would have made it easy. Nothing to think about. One quick pull of the trigger, and then … whatever was next. But he enjoyed this life. He didn't want to die now. It was possible that he might slip the noose on this. They might not discover his identity. They might not torture him.

This could all be a simple matter of the Russians confiscating a high-tech sub, and then doing a prisoner swap without asking a lot of questions. Maybe.

His breathing started to calm down. He never should have been here in the first place. Yes, he knew how to tap into communications cables. Yes, he had undersea experience. Yes, he was a smooth operator. But …

The inside of the sub was still bathed in bright, blinding light. They had just given the Russians quite a show in here.

That in itself was going to be worth a few questions.

But Reed Smith wanted to live.

"Okay," he said. "Okay. Don't kill me. Just let me up. I'm not going to do anything."

The kid began to push himself up. It took a moment. The space in the sub was so tight, they were like two people knocked down and dying in the crush of the crowds at Mecca. It was hard to get untangled.

In a few minutes, Reed Smith was back in his seat. He had made his decision. He hoped it turned out to be the right one.

"Turn the radio on," he said to Bolger. "Let's see what these jokers have to say."

Chapter Two

10:15 a.m. Eastern Daylight Time
The Situation Room
The White House, Washington, DC

"It seems that it was a poorly designed mission," an aide said. "The issue here is plausible deniability."

David Barrett, nearly six feet, six inches tall, stared down at the man. The aide was blond with thinning hair, a touch overweight, in a suit that was too big at the shoulders and too small around the midsection. The man's name was Jepsum. It was an unfortunate name for an unfortunate man. Barrett didn't like men who were shorter than six feet, and he didn't like men who didn't keep themselves in shape.

Barrett and Jepsum moved quickly through the hallways of the West Wing, toward the elevator that would take them down to the Situation Room.

"Yes?" Barrett said, growing impatient. "Plausible deniability?"

Jepsum shook his head. "Right. We don't have any."

A phalanx of people strode with Barrett, ahead of him, behind him, all around him—aides, interns, Secret Service men, staff of various kinds. Once again, and as always, he had no idea who half these people were. They were a tangled mass of humanity, zooming along, and he stood a head taller than nearly all of them. The shortest of them could be a different species from him altogether.

Short people frustrated Barrett to no end, and more so every day. David Barrett, the president of the United States, had come back to work too soon.

Only six weeks had passed since his daughter Elizabeth was kidnapped by terrorists and then recovered by American commandos in one of the most daring covert operations in recent memory. He'd had a breakdown during the crisis. He had stopped functioning in his role, and who could blame him? Afterward, he had been wrung out, exhausted, and so relieved Elizabeth was safe that he didn't have the words to fully express it.

The entire mob moved into the elevator, packing themselves inside like sardines into a can. Two Secret Service men had entered the elevator with them. They were tall men, one black and one white. The heads of Barrett and his protectors loomed over everyone else in the car like statues on Easter Island.

Jepsum was still looking up at him, his eyes so earnest he almost seemed like a baby seal. "...and their embassy won't even acknowledge our communications. After the fiasco at the United Nations last month, I don't think we can anticipate much cooperation."

Barrett couldn't follow Jepsum, but whatever he was saying, it lacked forcefulness. Didn't the president have stronger men than this at his disposal?

Everyone was talking at once. Before Elizabeth was kidnapped, Barrett would often go on one of his legendary tirades just to get people to shut up. But now? He just allowed the whole mess of them to ramble, the noise from the chattering coming to him like a form of nonsensical music. He let it wash over him.

Barrett had been back on the job for five weeks already, and the time had passed in a blur. He had fired his chief of staff, Lawrence Keller, in the aftermath of the kidnapping. Keller was another short stack—five foot ten at best—and Barrett had come to suspect that Keller was disloyal to him. He had no evidence of this, and couldn't even quite remember why he believed it, but he thought it best to get rid of Keller anyway.

Except now, Barrett was without Keller's smooth gray calm and ruthless efficiency. With Keller gone, Barrett felt unmoored, at loose ends, unable to make sense of the onslaught of crises and mini-disasters and just plain *information* he was bombarded with on a daily basis.

David Barrett was beginning to think he was having another breakdown. He had trouble sleeping. Trouble? He could barely sleep at all. Sometimes, when he was alone, he would start hyperventilating. A few times, late at night, he had found himself locked in his private bathroom, silently weeping.

He thought he might like to enter therapy, but when you were president of the United States, engaging with a shrink was not an option. If the newspapers got hold of it, and the cable talk shows ... he didn't want to think about that.

It would be the end, to put it mildly.

The elevator opened into the egg-shaped Situation Room. It was modern, like the flight deck of a TV spaceship. It was designed for maximum use of space—large screens embedded in the walls every couple of feet, and a giant projection screen on the far wall at the end of the table.

Except for Barrett's own seat, every plush leather seat at the table was already occupied—overweight men in suits, thin and ramrod-straight military men in uniform. A tall man in a dress uniform stood at the far head of the table.

Height. It was reassuring somehow. David Barrett was tall, and for most of his life he had been supremely confident. This man preparing to run the meeting would also be confident. In fact, he exuded confidence, and command. This man, this four-star general ...

Richard Stark.

Barrett remembered that he didn't care much for Richard Stark. But right now, he didn't care much for anyone. And Stark worked at the Pentagon. Maybe the general could shed some light on this latest mysterious setback.

"Settle down," Stark said, as the crowd the elevator had just expelled moved toward their seats.

"People! Settle down. The president is here."

The room went quiet. A few people continued to murmur, but even that died out quickly.

David Barrett sat down in his high-backed chair.

"Okay, Richard," he said. "Never mind the preliminaries. Never mind the history lesson. We've heard it all before. Just tell me what in God's name is going on."

Stark slipped a pair of black reading glasses onto his face and looked down at the sheets of paper in his hand. He took a deep breath and sighed.

On screens around the room, a body of water appeared.

"What you're seeing on the screens is the Black Sea," the general said. "As far as we can tell, about two hours ago, a small, three-man submersible owned by an American company called Poseidon Research was operating deep below the surface, in international waters more than one hundred miles southeast of the Crimean resort of Yalta. It appears to have been intercepted and seized by elements of the Russian Navy. The stated mission of the sub was to find and mark the location of an ancient Greek trading vessel believed to have gone down in those waters nearly twenty-five hundred years ago."

President Barrett stared at the general. He took a breath. That didn't seem bad at all. What was all the hubbub about?

A civilian submarine was doing archaeological exploration in international waters. The Russians were rebuilding their strength after a disastrous fifteen years or so, and they wanted the Black Sea to be their own private lake again. So they got irritated and overstepped. All right. Lodge a complaint with the embassy and get the scientists back. Maybe even get the sub back, too. It was all a misunderstanding.

"Forgive me, General, but this sounds like something for the diplomats to work out. I appreciate being kept informed of developments like this, but it seems like it's going to be easy to skip the crisis on this one. Can't we just have the ambassador—"

"Sir," Stark said. "I'm afraid it's a bit more complicated than that."

It instantly annoyed Barrett that Stark would interrupt him in front of a room full of people. "Okay," he said. "But this better be good."

Stark shook his head and sighed again. "Mr. President, Poseidon Research International is a company funded and run by the Central Intelligence Agency. It's a front operation. The submersible in question, *Nereus*, was masquerading as a civilian research vessel. In fact, it was on a classified mission under the aegis of both the CIA Special Operations Group and the Joint Special Operations Command. The three men captured include a civilian with high-level security clearances, a CIA special agent, and a Navy SEAL."

For the first time in more than a month, David Barrett felt an old familiar sensation rising within him. Anger. It was a feeling he enjoyed. They sent a submarine on a spy mission in the Black Sea? Barrett didn't need the map on the screen to know the geopolitics involved.

"Richard, pardon my French, but what in the hell were we doing with a spy submarine in the Black Sea? Do we want to have a war with the Russians? The Black Sea is their backyard."

"Sir, with all respect intended, those are international waters open to navigation, and we intend to keep them that way."

Barrett shook his head. Of course we did. "What was the sub doing there?"

The general coughed. "It was on a mission to tap into Russian communications cables at the bottom of the Black Sea. As you know, since the collapse of the Soviet Union, the Russians lease the old Soviet naval port at Sebastopol from the Ukrainians. That port was the mainstay of the Soviet fleet in the region, and serves the same purpose for the Russian Navy. As you can imagine, the arrangement is an awkward one.

"Russian telephone lines and computer-based communications cables run across Ukrainian territory in Crimea to the border with Russia. Meanwhile, tensions have been rising between Russia and Georgia, just to the south of there. We are concerned a war could break out, if not now, then in the near future.

"Georgia is very friendly with us, and we'd like for both them and Ukraine to join the NATO alliance one day. Until they do join NATO, they are vulnerable to a Russian attack. Recently, the Russians laid communications cables along the sea floor from Sebastopol to Sochi, completely circumventing the cables that run across Crimea.

"The mission of the *Nereus* was to find the location of those cables, and if possible, tap into them. If the Russians decide to attack Georgia, the fleet at Sebastopol is going to know in advance. We're going to want to know that, too."

Stark paused.

"And the mission was a total failure," David Barrett said.

General Stark didn't fight it.

"Yes, sir. It was."

Barrett had to give him credit for that. A lot of times, these guys came in here and tried to spin shit into gold right in front of his eyes. Well, Barrett wasn't having it anymore, and Stark got a couple of points for not even trying.

"Unfortunately, sir, the failure of the mission is not really the major issue we're facing. The issue we need to deal with at this time is that the Russians have not acknowledged they've taken the sub. They also refuse to respond to our inquiries as to its whereabouts, or to the conditions faced by the men who were on board. At the moment, we're not even sure if those men are alive or dead."

"Do we know for a fact that they took the sub?"

Stark nodded. "Yes, we do. The sub is outfitted with a radio locator beacon, which has been turned off. But it is also outfitted with a tiny computer chip that broadcasts its location to the satellite global positioning system. The chip only works when the sub is at the surface. The Russians appear not to have detected it yet. It's embedded deep within the mechanical systems. They will have to take the entire sub apart, or destroy it, to render the chip inoperable. In the meantime, we know they've raised the sub to the surface, and have taken it to a small port several miles south of Sochi, near the border with the former Soviet state of Georgia."

"And the men?" Barrett said.

Stark half nodded and half shrugged. "We believe they're with the ship."

"No one knows this mission took place?"

"Just us, and them," Stark said. "Our best guess is there may have been a recent intelligence leak among the mission participants, or within the agencies involved. We hate to think that, but Poseidon Research has operated out in the open for two decades, and there has never been any indication that its security was breached before."

An odd thought occurred to David Barrett then.

What's the problem?

It was a secret mission. The newspapers didn't know anything about it. And the men involved well knew the risks they were taking. The CIA knew the risks. The Pentagon brass knew the risks. On some level, they must have known how foolish it was. Certainly, no one had asked the president of the United States for permission to carry out the mission. He was only hearing about it after disaster had struck.

That was one of his least favorite aspects of dealing with the so-called intelligence community. They tended to tell you things after it was already too late to do anything about them.

For an instant, he felt like an angry dad who has just learned his teenage son was arrested for vandalism by the local town cops. *Let the kid rot in jail for the night. I'll pick him up in the morning.*

"Can we leave them there?" he said.

Stark raised an eyebrow. "Sir?"

Barrett looked around the room. All eyes were on him. He was acutely sensitive to the two dozen pairs of eyes. Young eyes in the back rows, wizened eyes with crow's feet around the table, owlish eyes behind glasses. But the eyes, which normally showed such deference, now seemed to look at him with something else. That something might be confusion, and it might be the beginning of…

Pity?

"Can we leave them there, and quietly negotiate their release? That's what I'm asking. Even if it takes some time? Even if it takes a month? Six months? It seems like negotiations would be one way to avoid yet another incident."

"Sir," the general said. "I'm afraid we can't do that. The incident has already happened."

"Right," Barrett said.

And just like that, he snapped. It was quiet, like a twig snap. But he'd had enough. The man had contradicted him one time too many. Did he even realize who he was speaking to? Barrett pointed at the general with a long finger.

"The horse is already out of the barn. Is that what you're telling me? Something has to be done! You and your shadow puppets made a stupid play, out on the edge all by yourselves, and now you want the official, popularly elected government to bail you out of your mess. Again."

Barrett shook his head. "I'm sick of it, General. How does that sound to you? I can't stand it anymore. All right? My instinct here is to leave those men with the Russians."

David Barrett scanned the eyes in the room again. Many of them were looking away now, at the table in front of them, at General Stark, at shiny reports bound with plastic ring binders. Anywhere but at their president. It was as if he had made a particularly ripe-smelling boo-boo in his pants. It was if they knew something he didn't know.

Stark instantly confirmed the truth of that.

"Mr. President, I wasn't going to bring this up, but you leave me no choice. One of the men on that crew has had access to intelligence of the most sensitive nature. He has been an integral part of covert operations on three continents for more than a decade. He has encyclopedic knowledge of American spy networks inside Russia and China for starters, not to mention Morocco and Egypt, as well as Brazil, Colombia, and Bolivia. In a few cases, he established those networks himself."

Stark paused. The room was dead quiet.

"If the Russians torture this man during interrogation, the lives of dozens of people, many of them important intelligence assets, may as well be forfeit. Worse than that, the information those people have access to will in turn become transparent to our opponents, leading to even more deaths. Extensive networks, which we've spent years building, could be rolled up in a short period of time."

Barrett stared at Stark. The gall of these people was breathtaking.

"What was that man doing in the field, General?" Acid dripped from every word.

"As I indicated, sir, Poseidon Research International had been operating for decades under no obvious suspicion. The man was hiding in plain sight."

"Hiding…" Barrett said slowly. "In plain sight."

"That's what it's called, sir. Yes."

Barrett said nothing in response. He just stared. And Stark finally seemed to realize that his explanations were not nearly good enough.

"Sir, and again this is with all respect due, I had nothing to do with the planning or execution of this mission. I didn't know anything about it until this morning. I'm not part of Joint Special Operations Command, nor am I employed by the Central Intelligence Agency. I do, however, have complete faith in the judgment of the men and women who do…"

Barrett waved his hands over his head, as if to say STOP.

"What are our options, General?"

"Sir, we have only one option. We need to rescue those men. As fast as we can, if possible before interrogations begin. We need to scuttle that sub as well, and that's crucial. But this one individual… we need to either rescue him, or eliminate him. As long as he's alive and in Russian hands, we have a potential disaster unfolding."

It was a moment before David Barrett spoke again. The general wanted to rescue the men, which suggested a secret mission. But the reason they were captured in the first place was a security breach. There's been a security breach, so let's plan more secret missions? It was circular thinking at its finest. But Barrett hardly felt the need to point that out. Hopefully, it was clear to even the numbest imbecile in this room.

An idea occurred to him then. There was going to be a new mission, and he was going to assign it, but not to the CIA or the Pentagon. They were the ones who had brought this problem about in the first place, and he could hardly trust them to resolve it. It would be stepping on toes to give the job to someone else, but it was clear that they had brought this on themselves.

He smiled inwardly. As painful as this situation was, it also presented him with an opportunity. He had the chance here to seize some of his power back. It was time to take the CIA and the Pentagon, the NSA, the DIA, all of these well-established spy agencies, out of the game.

Knowing what he was about to do made David Barrett feel like the boss again, for the first time in a long while.

"I agree," he said. "The men should be rescued, and as quickly as possible. And I know exactly how we're going to do it."

CHAPTER THREE

10:55 a.m. Eastern Daylight Time
Arlington National Cemetery
Arlington, Virginia

Luke Stone stared down the trench at Robby Martinez. Martinez was screaming.

"They're coming through on all sides!"

Martinez's eyes were wide. His guns were gone. He had taken an AK-47 from a Taliban, and was bayoneting everyone who came over the wall. Luke watched him in horror. Martinez was an island, a small boat fighting a wave of Taliban fighters.

And he was going under. Then he was gone, under the pile.

It was night. They were just trying to live until daybreak, but the sun refused to rise. The ammunition had run out. It was cold, and Luke's shirt was off. He had ripped it off in the heat of combat.

Turbaned, bearded Taliban fighters poured over the sand-bagged walls of the outpost. They slid, they fell, they jumped down. Men screamed all around him.

A man came over the wall with a metal hatchet.

Luke shot him in the face. The man lay dead against the sand-bags, a gaping cavern where his face had just been. The man had no face. But now Luke had the hatchet.

He waded into the fighters surrounding Martinez, swinging wildly. Blood spattered. He chopped at them, sliced them.

Martinez reappeared, somehow still on his feet, stabbing with the bayonet.

Luke buried the hatchet in a man's skull. It was deep. He couldn't pull it out. Even with the adrenaline raging through his system, he didn't have the strength left. He yanked on it, yanked on it... and gave up. He looked at Martinez.

"You okay?"

Martinez shrugged. His face was red with blood. His shirt was saturated with it. Whose blood? His? Theirs? Martinez gasped for air and gestured at the bodies all around them. "I've been better than this before. I can tell you that."

Luke blinked and Martinez was gone.

In his place were row upon row of plain white gravestones, thousands of them, climbing the low green hills into the distance. It was a bright day, sunny and warm.

Somewhere behind him, a lone bagpiper played "Amazing Grace."

Six young Army Rangers carried the gleaming casket, draped in the American flag, to the open gravesite. Martinez had been a Ranger before he joined Delta. The men looked sharp in their dress greens and their tan berets, but they also looked young. Very, very young, almost like kids playing dress-up.

Luke stared at the men. He could barely think about them. He took a deep breath. He was beat. He couldn't remember a time—not in Ranger school, not during the Delta selection process, not in war zones—when he had been this tired.

The baby, Gunner, his newborn son... wouldn't sleep. Not at night, and hardly in the day. So he and Becca weren't getting any sleep, either. Also, Becca couldn't seem to stop crying. The doctor had just diagnosed her with postpartum depression, complicated by exhaustion.

Her mom had come out to the cabin to live with them. It wasn't working. Becca's mom... where to begin? She had never held a job in her life. She seemed baffled that Luke left every morning to make the long commute to the Virginia suburbs of Washington, DC. She seemed even more baffled that he didn't reappear until evening.

The rustic cabin, beautifully situated on a small bluff above Chesapeake Bay, had been in her family for a hundred years. She had been going to the cabin since she was a little girl and now acted like she owned the place. In fact, she did own the place.

She was making noises that she, Becca, and the baby should relocate to her house in Alexandria. The hardest part for Luke was that the idea was beginning to seem sensible.

He had started to indulge fantasies of arriving at the cabin after a long day, the place dead silent. He could almost watch himself. Luke Stone opens the old humming refrigerator, grabs a beer, and walks out to the back patio. He's just in time to catch the sunset. He sits down in an Adirondack chair and…

CRACK!

Luke nearly jumped out of his skin.

Behind him, a seven-man team of riflemen had fired a volley into the air. The sound echoed across the hillsides. Another volley came. Then another.

A twenty-one-gun salute, seven guns at a time. It was an honor that not everyone merited. Martinez was a highly decorated combat veteran in two theaters of war. Dead now, by his own hand. But it didn't have to be that way.

Three dozen servicemen stood in formation near the grave. A smattering of Delta and former Delta operators stood in civilian clothes further away. You could tell the Delta guys because they looked like rock stars. They dressed like rock stars. Big, broad, in T-shirts and blazers, khaki pants. Full beards, earrings. One guy had a wide, closely cropped Mohawk hairdo.

Luke stood alone, dressed in a black suit, scanning the crowd, looking for something he expected to find: a man named Kevin Murphy.

Near the front was a row of white folding chairs. A middle-aged woman dressed in black was comforted by another woman. Near her, an honor guard made up of three Rangers, two Marines, and an Airman carefully took the flag from the casket and folded it.

One of the soldiers lowered to one knee in front of the grieving woman and presented the flag to her.

"On behalf of the president of the United States," the young Ranger said, his voice breaking, "the United States Army, and a grateful nation, please accept this flag as a symbol of our appreciation for your son's honorable and faithful service."

Luke looked at the Delta guys again. One had broken away and was walking alone up a grassy hillside through the white stones. He was tall and wiry, with blond hair shaved close to his head. He wore jeans and a light blue dress shirt. Thin as he was, he still had broad shoulders and muscular arms and legs. His arms seemed almost too long for his body, like the arms of an elite basketball player. Or a pterodactyl.

The man walked slowly, in no particular hurry, as though he had no pressing engagements. He stared down at the grass as he walked.

Murphy.

Luke left the service and followed him up the hill. He walked much faster than Murphy did, gaining ground on him.

There were a lot of reasons why Martinez was dead, but the clearest reason was he had blown his own brains out in his hospital bed. And someone had brought him a gun with which to do it. Luke was about one hundred percent sure he knew who that someone was.

"Murphy!" he said. "Hold on a minute."

Murphy looked up and turned around. A moment ago, he had seemed lost in thought, but his eyes had come instantly alert. His face was narrow, birdlike, handsome in its own way.

"Luke Stone," he said, his voice flat. He didn't seem pleased to see Luke. He didn't seem displeased. His eyes were hard. Like the eyes of all Delta guys, there was a cold, calculating intelligence in there.

"Let me walk with you a minute, Murph."

Murphy shrugged. "Suit yourself."

They fell into step with each other. Luke slowed down to accommodate Murphy's pace. They walked for a moment without saying a word.

"How are you doing?" Luke said. It was an odd nicety to offer. Luke had gone to war with this man. They had been in combat together a dozen times. With Martinez gone, they were the last two survivors of the worst night of Luke's life. You would think there'd be some intimacy between them.

But Murphy didn't give Luke anything. "I'm fine."

That was all.

No "How are you?" No "Did your baby come?" No "We need to talk about things." Murphy was not in the mood for conversation.

"I heard you left the Army," Luke said.

Murphy smiled and shook his head. "What can I do for you, Stone?"

Luke stopped and gripped Murphy's shoulder. Murphy faced him, shrugging Luke's hand off.

"I want to tell you a story," Luke said.

"Tell away," Murphy said.

"I work for the FBI now," Luke said. "A small sub-agency within the Bureau. Intelligence gathering. Special operations. Don Morris runs it."

"Good for you," Murphy said. "That's what everybody used to say. Stone is like a cat. He always lands on his feet."

Luke ignored that. "We have access to information. The best. We get everything. For example, I know you were reported AWOL in early April and were dishonorably discharged about six weeks later."

Murphy laughed now. "You must have done some digging for that, huh? Sent a mole in to examine my personnel file? Or did you just have them email it to you?"

Luke pressed on. "Baltimore PD has an informer who's a close lieutenant of Wesley 'Cadillac' Perkins, leader of the Sandtown Bloods street gang."

"That's nice," Murphy said. "Police work must be endlessly fascinating." He turned and started walking again.

Luke walked with him. "Three weeks ago, Cadillac Perkins and two bodyguards were assaulted at three a.m. while entering their car in the parking lot of a nightclub. According to the informer, just one man attacked them. A tall, thin white man. He knocked the two bodyguards unconscious in three or four seconds. Then he pistol-whipped Perkins and relieved him of a briefcase containing at least thirty thousand in cash."

"Sounds like a daring white man," Murphy said.

"The white man in question also relieved Perkins of a gun, a distinctive Smith & Wesson .38, with a particular slogan engraved in the grip. *Might Makes Right.* Of course, neither the attack, nor the theft of the money, nor the loss of the gun was reported to the police. It was just something this informer talked about with his handler."

Murphy was not looking at Luke.

"What are you telling me, Stone?"

Luke looked ahead and noticed they were approaching the John F. Kennedy gravesite. A crowd of tourists stood along the edge of the two-hundred-year-old flagstones and snapped photos of the fire of the eternal flame.

Luke's eye wandered to the low granite wall at the edge of the memorial. Just above the wall, he could see the Washington Monument across the river. The wall itself had numerous inscriptions taken from Kennedy's inaugural address. A famous one caught Luke's attention:

ASK NOT WHAT YOUR COUNTRY CAN DO FOR YOU …

"The gun Martinez used to kill himself had the inscription *Might Makes Right* on the grip. The Bureau traced the gun and discovered it had previously been used to commit two execution-style murders believed to be associated with the Baltimore drug wars. One was the torture killing of Jamie 'Godfather' Young, the previous leader of the Sandtown Bloods."

BUT WHAT YOU CAN DO FOR YOUR COUNTRY.

Murphy shrugged. "All these nicknames. Godfather. Cadillac. Must be hard to keep track of them."

Luke kept going. "Somehow, that gun found its way from Baltimore all the way south to Martinez's hospital room in North Carolina."

Murphy looked at Stone again. Now his eyes were flat and dead. They were murderer's eyes. If Murphy had killed one man before, he had killed a hundred.

"Why don't you get to the point, Stone? Say what's on your mind, instead of telling me some children's fable about drug lords and stickup men."

Luke was so angry he could almost punch Murphy in the mouth. He was tired. He was aggravated. He was heartbroken by Martinez's death.

"You knew Martinez wanted to kill himself…" he began.

Murphy didn't hesitate. "You killed Martinez," he said. "You killed the whole squad. You. Luke Stone. Killed everyone. I was there, remember? You took a mission you knew was FUBAR because you didn't want to countermand an order from a maniac with a death wish. And this was…for what? To further your career?"

"You gave Martinez the gun," Luke said.

Murphy shook his head. "Martinez died that night on the hill. Just like everybody else. But his body was too strong to realize that. So it needed a push."

They stared at each other for a long moment. For an instant, in his mind's eye, Luke was back in Martinez's hospital room. Martinez's legs had been shredded, and could not be saved. One was gone at the pelvis, one below the knee. He still had the use of his arms, but he was paralyzed from just below his ribcage down. It was a nightmare.

Tears began to stream down Martinez's face. He pounded the bed with his fists.

"I told you to kill me," he said through gritted teeth. "I told you…to…kill…me. Now look at this…this mess."

Luke stared at him. "I couldn't kill you. You're my friend."

"Don't say that!" Martinez said. "I'm not your friend."

Luke shook the memory away. He was back on a green hill in Arlington, on a sunny early summer day. He was alive and mostly well. And Murphy was still here, offering his version of a lecture. Not one that Luke wanted to hear.

There was a crowd of people all around them, looking at Kennedy's flame and quietly murmuring.

"True to form," Murphy said. "Luke Stone has failed upward. Now he finds himself working for his old commanding officer at a super-secret civilian spy agency. They got nice toys there, Stone? Of course they do, if Don Morris is running it. Cute secretaries? Fast cars? Black helicopters? It's like a TV show, am I right?"

Luke shook his head. It was time to change the subject.

"Murphy, since you went AWOL, you've committed a string of solo armed robberies in Northeast cities. You've been targeting gang members and drug dealers, who you know are carrying large amounts of cash, and who won't report…"

Without warning, Murphy's right fist flew outward. It moved like a piston, connecting with Luke's face just below his eye. Luke's head snapped back.

"Shut up," Murphy said. "You talk too much."

Luke took a stumble step and crashed into the person behind him. Nearby, someone else gasped. The sound was loud, like a hydraulic pump.

Luke went several steps backward, pushing through bodies. For a split second, he had a familiar floating sensation. He shook his head to clear the cobwebs. Murphy had tagged him a good one.

And Murphy wasn't done. Here he came again.

People streamed by on both sides, trying to get away from the fight. An overweight woman, well dressed in a beige skirt and jacket ensemble, fell to the flagstones between Luke and Murphy. Two men rushed to help her up. On the other side of this little pile, Murphy shook his head in frustration.

To Luke's right was the low chain barrier that separated visitors from the eternal flame. He stepped over it, onto the wide cobblestones and out into the open. Murphy followed. Luke shrugged out of his suit jacket, revealing the shoulder holster and his service gun underneath. Now someone screamed.

"Gun! He's got a gun!"

Murphy gestured at it, a half-smile on his face. "What are you gonna do, Stone? Shoot me?"

The crowd of people flowed down the hill, a mass exodus of humanity, moving fast.

Luke unfastened the holster and dropped it to the cobblestones. He circled to his right, the eternal flame of the John F. Kennedy grave just behind him, the flat grave markers of the Kennedy family in front of him. In the far distance, he caught another glimpse of the Washington Monument.

"You sure you want to do this?" Luke said.

Murphy stepped across the face of one of the Kennedy gravestones.

"There's nothing I would rather do."

Luke's hands were up. His eyes honed in on Murphy. Everything else dropped away. He saw Murphy as though the man were bathed in some strange light, like a spotlight. Murphy had the reach advantage by a mile. But Luke was stronger.

He gestured with the fingers of his right hand.

"Then come on."

Murphy attacked. He feinted a left jab, but came in hard with the right. Luke slipped it and delivered his own hard right hand. Murphy pushed Luke's right arm out and away. Now they were close. Right where Luke wanted to be.

Suddenly they were grappling. Luke kicked Murphy's leg out, lifted him high, and brought him down to the ground with a thud. Luke could feel the impact of Murphy's body—the flagstones vibrated with it. Murphy's head bounced off the rough, round stone platform that housed Kennedy's flame.

Most men would be done. But not Murphy. Not a Delta.

His right hand pistoned out again. The fingers tore at Luke's face, trying to find his eyes. Luke pulled his head back.

Now came Murphy's left, a punch. It hit the side of Luke's head. His ears rang.

Here came the right again. Luke blocked it, but Murphy was pushing up off the ground. He launched himself at Luke and they tumbled backward, Murphy on top. The metal canister that held the flame, six inches high, was just to Luke's right.

A breeze blew and the fire was on them. Luke could feel the heat of it.

With all of his strength, he grabbed Murphy and rolled hard to his right. Murphy's back hit the eternal flame. Fire surged all around them as they rolled up and over the top of it. Luke landed on his left side and used his momentum to keep rolling.

He climbed on top of Murphy and grabbed his head in both hands.

Murphy punched him in the face.

Luke shrugged it off and slammed Murphy's head against the concrete.

Murphy's hands tried to push him away.

Luke slammed his head again.

"FREEZE!" a deep-throated voice screamed.

The muzzle of a gun was pressed to Luke's temple. It jabbed him there, hard. In the corner of his eye, Luke saw two big black hands holding the gun, and a blue uniform looming behind them.

Instantly, Luke put his hands in the air.

"Police," the voice said, only slightly calmer now.

"Officer, I'm Agent Luke Stone, with the FBI. My badge is in that jacket over there."

Now there were more blue uniforms. They swarmed Luke, pulling him away from Murphy. They pushed him to the ground and held him face down against the stone. He went as limp as possible, offering no resistance. Hands roamed his body, searching him.

He looked at Murphy. Murphy was getting the same treatment.

Don't have a weapon on you, Luke thought.

In a moment, they pulled Luke to his feet. He looked around. There were ten cops here. At the far edge of the action, a familiar figure loomed. Big Ed Newsam, watching from a modest distance.

A cop handed Luke his jacket, his holster, and his badge.

"Okay, Agent Stone, what seems to be the problem here?"

"No problem."

The cop gestured at Murphy. Murphy sat on the flagstones, arms around his knees. His eyes looked a bit fuzzy, but coming back.

"Who is that guy?"

Luke sighed and shook his head. "He's a friend of mine. Old Army buddy." He cracked a ghost of a smile and rubbed his face. The hand came away bloody. "You know, sometimes these reunions…"

Most of the cops were already moving away.

Luke stared down at Murphy. Murphy was making no effort to get up. Luke reached into the pocket of his jacket and came out with a business card. He looked at it for a second.

Luke Stone, Special Agent.

In the corner was the SRT logo. Under Luke's name was a phone number that would reach a secretary at the office. There was something absurdly pleasing about that card.

He flipped it at Murphy.

"Here, you idiot. Call me. I was going to offer you a job."

Luke turned his back on Murphy and walked toward Ed Newsam. Ed was in a dress shirt and dark tie and had a blazer draped over his shoulder. He was as big as a mountain. His muscles rippled under his clothes. His hair and beard were jet black. His face was young, not a line on his skin.

He shook his head and smiled. "What are you doing?"

Luke shrugged. "I don't really know. What are you doing?"

"They sent me to get you," Ed said. "We've got a mission. Hostage rescue. High priority."

"Where?" Luke said.

Ed shook his head. "Classified. We won't know until the briefing. But they want us ready to move as soon as the briefing is over."

"When's the briefing?"

Ed had already turned and was heading back down the hill.

"Now."

Chapter Four

12:20 p.m. Eastern Daylight Time
Headquarters of the Special Response Team
McLean, Virginia

"Don't worry. You look real pretty."

Luke was in the men's room of the employee locker room. His shirt was off and he was washing his face in the sink. A deep scratch ran down his left cheek. The lower right side of his jaw was red and bruised and beginning to swell. Murph had clocked him a good one along there.

Luke's knuckles were raw and ripped up. The wounds were open, and blood was still running a little bit. He had clocked Murphy a few good ones himself.

Behind him, big Ed loomed in the mirror. Ed had put his blazer back on and was every bit the consummate, well-dressed professional. Luke was supposed to be Ed's superior officer in this job. He couldn't put his own suit jacket back on because it was dirty from when he had thrown it on the ground.

"Let's go, man," Ed said. "We're already late."

"I'm going to look like something the cat dragged in."

Ed shrugged. "Next time do what I do. Keep an extra suit, plus an extra set of office casual, right here in your locker. I'm surprised I need to teach you this stuff."

Luke had put his T-shirt back on and was starting to button up his dress shirt. "Yeah, but what do I do now?"

Ed shook his head, but he was grinning. "This is what people expect from you anyway. Tell them you were doing a little tae kwon do sparring in the parking lot during your coffee break."

Luke and Ed left the locker room and bounced up the concrete stairwell to the main floor. The conference room, as close to state-of-the-art as Mark Swann could get it, was down the end of a narrow side hallway. Don tended to call it the Command Center, though Luke felt that was stretching the facts a bit. One day, maybe.

Nervous butterflies bounced against the walls of Luke's intestines. These meetings were a new thing for him, and he couldn't seem to get used to them. Don told him it would come to him in time.

In the military, briefings were simple. They went like this:

Here's the goal. Here's the plan of attack. Questions? Input? Okay, load gear.

These briefings never went like that.

The door to the conference room was straight ahead. It was open. The room was somewhat small, and twenty people inside would make it look like a crowded subway car at rush hour. These meetings gave Luke the willies. There were endless discussions and delays. The press of people made him claustrophobic.

Invariably there would be bigwigs from several agencies and their staffers milling around, the bigwigs insisting on having their say, the staffers typing into BlackBerry phones, scratching out notes on yellow legal pads, running in and out, making urgent phone calls. Who were these people?

Luke crossed the threshold, followed closely by Ed. The overhead fluorescents were bright and dazzling.

There was nobody in the room. Well, not nobody, but not many. Five people, to be exact. Luke and Ed make it seven.

"Here are the men we've all been waiting for," Don Morris said. He was not smiling. Don didn't like to wait. He looked formidable in a dress shirt and slacks. His body language was relaxed, but his eyes were sharp.

A man stepped in front of Luke. He was a tall and thin four-star, in impeccable dress greens. His gray hair was trimmed to the scalp. There wasn't a stray whisker anywhere on his clean-shaven face—whiskers knew better than to defy him. Luke had never met the man, but he knew him in his bones. He made his bed every morning before doing anything else. You could bounce a quarter off it. He probably did, just to make sure.

"Agent Stone, Agent Newsam, I'm General Richard Stark, Joint Chiefs of Staff."

"General, it's an honor to meet you."

Luke shook his hand before the man moved on to Ed.

"We were very proud of what you boys did a month ago. You're both a credit to the United States Army."

Another man stood there. He was a balding man, maybe somewhere in his forties. He had a large round gut and pudgy little fingers. His suit did not fit well—too tight at the shoulders, too tight around the center. His face was doughy and his nose was bulbous. He reminded Luke of Karl Malden doing a TV commercial about credit card fraud.

"Luke, I'm Ron Begley of Homeland Security."

They also shook hands. Ron didn't mention last month's operation.

"Ron. Good to meet you."

No one said a word about Luke's face. That was a relief. Though he was sure he would hear about it from Don after the meeting was over.

"Boys, won't you sit down?" the general said, waving a hand at the conference table. It was gracious of him, to invite them to sit at their own table.

Luke and Ed took seats near Don. There were two other men in the room, both wearing suits. One was bald and had an earpiece that disappeared inside his jacket. They looked on impassively. Neither man said a word. No one introduced them. To Luke, that meant enough said.

Ron Begley closed the door.

The major surprise here was there were no other SRT people in the room.

General Stark looked at Don.

"Ready?"

Don opened his big hands as if they were flowers opening their petals.

"Yes. This was all we needed. Do your worst."

The general looked at Ed and Luke.

"Gentlemen, what I'm about to share with you is classified information."

"What are they not telling us?" Luke said.

Don looked up. The desk he sat behind was polished oak, wide and gleaming. There were two pieces of paper on it, an office telephone, and an old, battered Toughbook laptop with a sticker on the back of the screen depicting a red spearhead with a dagger on it—the logo of Army Special Operations Command. Don was a clean desk kind of guy.

On the wall behind him were various framed photographs. Luke spotted the one of four shirtless young Green Berets in Vietnam—Don was on the right.

Don gestured at the two chairs in front of the desk.

"Have a seat. Take a load off."

Luke did.

"How's your face?"

"It's a little sore," Luke said.

"What did you do, slam the car door on it?"

Luke shrugged and smiled. "I ran into Kevin Murphy at Martinez's funeral this morning. Remember him?"

Don nodded. "Sure. He was a decent soldier as Delta goes. Bit of a chip on his shoulder, I suppose. How did he look…after you ran into him?"

"Last I saw, he was still on the ground."

Don nodded again. "Good. What was the issue?"

"He and I are the last men standing from that night in Afghanistan. There are some hard feelings. He thinks I could have done more to abort the mission."

Don shrugged. "It wasn't your mission to abort."

"That's what I told him. I also gave him my business card. If he calls me, I'd like you to consider hiring him here. He's Delta trained, combat experienced, three tours that I know of, doesn't wet his pants when the fur starts to fly."

"He's out of the service?"

Luke nodded. "Yeah."

"What's he up to?"

"Armed robbery. He's been taking down drug kingpins in various cities."

Don shook his head. "Jesus, Luke."

"All I ask is you give him a chance."

"We'll talk about it," Don said. "When and if he calls."

Luke nodded. "Fair enough."

Don pulled one of the pieces of paper on his desk closer to him. He slipped a pair of black reading glasses on the tip of his nose. Luke had seen him do this a few times now, and the effect was jarring. Superhuman Don Morris wore reading glasses.

"Now to matters a little more pressing. The things we didn't talk about at the briefing are as follows. This mission comes straight from the Oval Office. The president took it away from the Pentagon and the CIA because he thinks there's a leak somewhere. If the Russians manage to crack open this captured CIA guy, who knows what's gonna come out of him. We are looking at a large potential setback, things need to move very fast, and privately, the president is furious."

"That's why we're on our own?"

Don raised a finger. "We have friends. You're never quite on your own in this business."

"Mark Swann can…"

Don put a finger to his lips. He pointed around the room and raised his eyebrows. Then he shrugged. The message was: let's not talk about what Mark Swann can do. No sense sharing that information with the people in the gallery.

Luke nodded and changed direction mid-sentence. "...get us access to all kinds of databases. Lexis Nexis, that kind of thing. He's a madman with a Google search."

"Yeah," Don said. "I think he's got a subscription to the *New York Times* online. He says he does, anyway."

"Who was the guy from Homeland Security?"

Don shrugged. "Ron Begley? Desk jockey. He worked at Treasury when September eleventh happened. Fraud, counterfeiting. When they created Homeland, he switched over. Seems to be stumbling and fumbling his way up the ladder. I don't think he's a problem for us."

Don stared at Luke for a long moment.

"What do you think of this mission?" he said.

Luke didn't look away. "I think it's a deathtrap, to be honest with you. It scares me. We're supposed to drop into Russia undetected, rescue a bunch of guys..."

"Three guys," Don said. "We're allowed to kill them, if that's easier."

Luke wouldn't even entertain that thought.

"Rescue a bunch of guys," he repeated, "torch a submarine, and get back out alive? That's a tall order."

"Who would you send on it?" Don said. "If you were me?"

Luke shrugged. "Who do you think?"

"Do you want it?"

Luke didn't answer right away. He thought of Becca and baby Gunner, in the cabin just across the Chesapeake on the Eastern Shore. God, that little baby...

"I don't know."

"Let me tell you a story," Don said. "When I was a commander in Delta, a bright-eyed young guy came in. He had just qualified. Came out of the 75th Rangers, like you did, so he wasn't green. He'd been around the block. But he had an energy, this kid, as though it was all new to him. Some guys come into Delta and they're already grizzled as hell at the age of twenty-four. Not this guy.

"I tapped him for a mission right away. I was still going on missions myself in those days. I was deep into my forties by then, and the brass at JSOC wanted to put me out to pasture, but I wouldn't hear of it. Not yet. I wouldn't send my men into places where I wouldn't go myself.

"We parachuted into the Democratic Republic of Congo. Way upriver, out beyond anything resembling law and order. It was a night drop, of course, and the pilot put us in the water. We crawled up out of those swamps looking like we'd all been dipped in shit. There was a warlord up there, called himself Prince Joseph. He called his ragtag militia Heaven's..."

"Heaven's Army," Luke said. Of course he knew the story. And of course he knew all about the new Delta recruit Don was describing.

"Three hundred child soldiers," Don said. "Eight men went up there, eight American soldiers, no outside support of any kind, and put bullets in the brains of Prince Joseph and all his lieutenants. A perfect operation. A humanitarian mission, with no ulterior motives but to do the right thing. Bang! Decapitation strike."

Luke took a deep breath. The night had been terrifying and exhilarating all wrapped into one adrenaline rush of a package.

"The international aid societies came in and did what they could with the children, repatriated them, fed them, loved them, reeducated them to be human again, if that was even possible. And I kept tabs. Many of them eventually made it back to their home villages."

Don smiled. No, he positively beamed.

"In the morning, I lit up a victory cigar along the bank of the mighty Congo. I was still smoking them in those days. My men were with me, and I was proud of every single one of them. I was proud to be an American. But my newbie was quiet, thoughtful. So I asked him if he was all right. And you know what he said?"

Now Luke smiled. He sighed and shook his head. Don was talking about him. "He said, 'All right? Are you kidding me? I live for this.' That's what he said."

Don pointed at him. "That's right. So I'll ask you again. Do you want this mission?"

Luke stared at Don for another long moment. Don was a drug dealer, Luke realized. A pusher. He sold you on a feeling, a rush, that you could only get one way.

An image of Becca holding Gunner again flashed across the screen in his mind. Everything had changed when that baby was born. He remembered Becca giving birth. She was more beautiful in those moments than he had ever seen her.

And they were planning to build a life together, the three of them.

What was Becca going to think about this mission? When he sold her the last one, when she was about to give birth, she had been upset. And that one was an easy sell—just a quick trip to Iraq to arrest a guy. Of course, it turned into much more than that, full-on combat and the rescue of the president's daughter, but Becca had only learned about it after the fact.

Here, she would know the deal going in: Luke was going to infiltrate Russia and attempt to rescue three prisoners. He shook his head.

There was no way he could tell her that.

"Luke?" Don said.

Luke nodded. "Yeah. I want it."

CHAPTER FIVE

3:45 p.m. Eastern Daylight Time
Queen Anne's County, Maryland
Eastern Shore of Chesapeake Bay

"You're home early."

Luke looked at his mother-in-law, Audrey, taking his time, soaking her in. She had deep-set eyes with irises so dark, they seemed almost black. She had a sharp nose, like a beak. She had tiny bones and a thin frame. She reminded him of a bird—a crow, or maybe a vulture. And yet, in her own way, she was attractive.

She was a well-preserved fifty-nine now, and Luke was aware that as a young woman in the late 1960s, she had done some modeling for newspaper and magazine advertisements. As far as he knew, it was the only work she had ever done.

She had been born into an arm of the Outerbridge family, vastly wealthy New York City and New Jersey landowners since before the United States became a country. Her husband, Lance, came from the equally old-money St. John family of New England lumber barons.

As a general rule, Audrey St. John frowned upon work. She didn't understand it, and she especially didn't understand why someone would do the kind of dangerous, dirty work that occupied Luke Stone's time. She seemed continually flabbergasted that her own daughter, Rebecca St. John, would marry someone like Luke.

Audrey and Lance had never accepted him as their son-in-law. They had been a toxic influence on this relationship since well before he and Becca exchanged their vows. Her presence here was going to make it that much harder to talk to Becca about this latest assignment.

"Hi, Audrey," Luke said, trying to sound cheerful.

He had just walked in. He had taken off his tie and unbuttoned the top two buttons of his dress shirt, but so far that was his only nod toward being home. He reached into the refrigerator and came out with a cold beer.

It was full summer now, and the weather was fine. The surroundings here were beautiful. He and Becca were living at her family's cabin in Queen Anne's County. The house had been in the family for over a hundred years.

The place was an ancient, rustic place sitting on a small bluff right above the bay. It was two floors, wooden everything, with creaks and squeaks everywhere you stepped. The kitchen door was spring-loaded, and slammed shut with enthusiasm. There was a screened-in porch facing the water, and a newer stone patio with commanding views right on the bluff.

They had started gradually replacing the generations-old furniture to make the place more suited for everyday living. There was a new sofa and new chairs in the living room. One Saturday morning, by hook or by crook, and by sheer animal will, Luke and Ed Newsam had managed to insert a king-sized bed in the upstairs master bedroom.

Even with those upgrades, the sturdiest thing in the house remained the stone fireplace in the living room. It was almost as if the stately old hearth had been there, looking out over Chesapeake Bay since biblical times, and someone with a sense of humor had built a small summer cabin all around it.

It really was an incredible place. Luke loved it there. Yes, it was far from his office. Yes, if the SRT job really did pan out, and it looked like it was going to, they were going to have to move closer. But for now? Paradise. The ninety-minute commute home didn't seem nearly as bad, just knowing that this was the payoff at the end of it.

He glanced out the window. Becca was on the patio, feeding the baby. Luke would have loved nothing more than to take a seat out there with them, gaze out at the water and the sky, and just sit there until the sun went down. But it wasn't to be. Unfortunately, he had to pack for his trip. And before he even started, he had to do the hardest thing—announce that he was going.

"Did you get punched on the job?" Audrey said.

Luke shrugged. Even though he could feel them well enough, he had almost forgotten the scrape on his cheek and the swollen jaw line. Pain was an old friend of his. When it wasn't excruciating, he could barely feel it. There was almost something comforting about it.

He cracked open the beer and took a slug. It was ice cold and delicious. "Something like that. But you should see the other guy."

Audrey didn't laugh. She made a sort of half-grunt and went upstairs.

Luke was tired. It had already been a long day, with Martinez laid to rest, the fight with Murphy, and everything else. And really, it was just getting started. He intended to be here for an hour before he headed right back to the city again, from there to Turkey, and then, if all the signs were favorable, over to Russia.

He went outside. Becca nursing the baby was like an impressionist painting, her bright red jumper and floppy sun hat against the green grass, and the vast sweep of pale blue sky and dark water. There was a double-mast tall ship replica at full sail in the distance, moving slowly to the west. If he could press STOP and freeze this moment in time, he would do it.

She looked up, saw him there, and smiled. Her smile lit him up. She was as pretty as ever. And a smile was a good thing, especially these days. Maybe the darkness of this postpartum depression was beginning to lift.

Luke took a deep breath, sighed quietly, and smiled himself.

"Hello, beautiful," he said.

"Hello, handsome."

He leaned down and shared a kiss with her.

"How's the baby boy today?"

She nodded. "Good. He slept for three hours, Mom kept an eye on him, and I even got to take a nap. I don't want to promise anything, but we might be turning a corner here. I hope so."

A long pause drew out between them.

"You're home early," she said. That was the second time in the past five minutes someone had said that. He took it as a bad omen. "How did your day go?"

Luke sat down across the small round table from her and took a sip of his beer. As always, he believed that when trouble was brewing, the thing to do was to get right to the meat of it. And if he could get past the worst of it, maybe it would happen too fast for Audrey to come out here and pile on.

"Well, I have an assignment."

He noticed himself fudging. He didn't call it a mission. He didn't call it an operation. What kind of assignment was it? Was he going to interview a local craftsman for the weekly newspaper? Maybe it was a high school science project?

Instantly, she was wary.

Her eyes stared deep into his, searching there. "What is it?"

He shrugged. "It's a diplomatic snafu, really. The Russians took three American archaeologists prisoner, and confiscated their little submarine. They were diving in the Black Sea, looking for the wreck of an old trading ship from ancient Greece. They were in international waters, but the Russians felt they were too close to Russian territory."

Her eyes never wavered. "Are they spies?"

Luke took another sip of his beer. He let out a sound, a short bark of laughter. She was good at this. She'd already had a lot of practice. She went right for the open vein.

He shook his head. "You know I can't tell you that."

"And you're going to go where, and do what?"

He shrugged. "I'm going to Turkey, to see if we can get them released." The statement was true, as far as it went. It also overlooked an entire continent's worth of detail. It was a sin of omission.

And she also knew that. "To see if we can get them released? Who are *we*?"

Now it was a chess match. "The United States of America."

"Come on, Luke. What are you not telling me?"

He sipped the beer again and scratched his head. "Nothing of substance, hon. The Russians are holding three guys. I'm going to Turkey. They want me there because I have experience in the kind of mission that led to this. If the Russians are willing to negotiate, I probably won't even be directly involved."

Behind Luke, the screen door slammed. Becca's eyes looked past him for a second. Dammit! Here came Audrey.

Becca's eyes were suddenly angry. Tears welled up in them. No! The timing couldn't be worse. "Luke, the last time you went abroad, I was almost nine months pregnant. You were going to Iraq to arrest someone, remember? A police job, I think you called it. But it turned out you were going to rescue the president's..."

He raised a finger. "Becca, you know that isn't true. I did go to arrest someone, and the arrest was uneventful..."

That was a lie. Another lie. The arrest was a slaughterhouse.

"...daughter from Islamic terrorists. Your helicopter crashed. You and Ed fought Al Qaeda militants on a mountaintop."

"All of that happened after we were already there."

"I'm not stupid, Luke. I can read between the lines of newspaper reports. The articles admitted that dozens of people were killed. That tells me there was a bloodbath and you were right in the middle of it."

Luke raised his hands a tiny amount, as if she had just pulled the world's tiniest gun on him. The baby was still there, suckling away as if none of this was happening.

"It's an assignment, hon. It's my job. Don Morris..."

Now she raised a finger. "Don't you Don Morris me. I don't even blame Don anymore. If you didn't want to go on these suicide missions, then he couldn't get you to go. It's really that simple."

Now she was crying, the tears pouring down.

"What's going on?" a voice said. The voice was too eager. It sensed blood in the water, and was moving in for the kill.

"Hi, Audrey," Luke said, without even turning around.

Becca stood and handed Audrey the baby. She looked down at Luke, her eyes hard. Her entire body was shaking now from the tears.

"What if you die?" she said. "We have a son now."

"I know that. I'm not going to die. As always, I'm going to be very careful. Even more so now, because of Gunner."

Becca stood there next to her mother, her hands balled up in fists. She looked like a toddler who was about to start shrieking in the middle of the supermarket. Her mother, in contrast, was calm, simpering, self-satisfied. She bounced the baby in her thin, birdlike arms and cooed to him in quiet baby talk.

"It's going to be okay," Luke said. "It's going to be fine. I know it is."

Abruptly, Becca stormed off, up the small hill toward the house. A moment later, the screen door slammed again.

Now Luke and Audrey stared at each other. Audrey had the sharp, predatory eyes of a hawk. Her mouth opened.

Luke raised a hand and shook his head. "Audrey, please don't say a word."

Audrey ignored him. "One day, you're going to come back here and you're not going to have a wife anymore," she said. "Or a house to live in, for that matter."

Chapter Six

8:35 p.m. Eastern Standard Time
The Skies Above the Atlantic Ocean

"Rock and roll," Mark Swann said.

"Hip-hop, son," Ed Newsam said. "Hip-hop."

He held his big hand out across the narrow aisle of the small jet plane and Swann gave him a smooth, slow tap. Then Swann turned his own hand over and Ed appeared to place a few coins in Swann's palm. They had just acted out the whole "gimme five, keep the change" brother man hand jive.

Since the last mission, Newsam and Swann had become unlikely friends.

Luke watched them. Ed lounged in his seat, steely-eyed, huge, neatly dressed in khaki cargo pants and a form-fitting SRT T-shirt. Ed's job was weapons and tactics. Both his hair and his beard were close-cropped and the edges perfectly even. He looked exactly like what he was—no one to mess with.

Meanwhile, Swann looked like anything other than a federal agent. His wore black-framed glasses. His hair was pulled into a long ponytail. He wore a T-shirt that said BLACK FLAG, with a photo of a man diving from a stage into a swarming crowd. He stretched his long legs out into the aisle, an old pair of ripped jeans on his skinny legs, with a pair of bright yellow Chuck Taylors as an obstacle for any passersby. His feet were huge.

The two men had originally bonded over a love of the 1980s rap group Public Enemy, and a similar sarcastic sense of humor.

Now they were bonding over God only knew what. Youthful male energy? Unlimited possibility?

The guys were enjoying themselves, ramping up for another trip to the back of beyond. That was good. These guys needed to be dialed in and razor sharp.

Luke himself didn't feel half as much enthusiasm. He felt exhausted, more emotionally than physically. Of course, he was the only one here with a newborn baby, an angry wife, and a conniving mother-in-law. He was also the only one who had made the three-hour round trip out to the Eastern Shore and back.

Newsam and Swann had gone to Red Lobster instead. It seemed like they might have had a few drinks with their seafood dinner.

"Are you guys ready to work?" Luke said.

Ed shrugged. "Born ready."

"Rock and roll," Swann said again.

The six-seat Lear jet screamed north and east across the sky. The jet was dark blue with no markings of any kind. They'd left from a small private airport west of the city twenty minutes earlier. This could be a corporate plane on a business trip, or a bunch of rich kids off on a European romp.

Behind them and to their left was the last of the early evening sunlight. Ahead and to their right was the onrushing night.

Luke felt like he often felt at moments like this—as though he was plunging into something beyond his understanding. The missions didn't bother him. He was nervous, but not really afraid. He had seen so much combat now that very few things shook his confidence. What he didn't understand was the context.

Why? Why were they doing this? Why did the major players do what they did? Why were there terrorists and terrorist groups? Why were Russia and America, and numerous other countries, always entangled behind the scenes, pulling strings and manipulating the action like puppet masters?

When he was younger, these questions had never bothered him. Understanding geopolitics was not part of his job description. Good guys over here, bad guys over there.

He would deliberately misquote the line from the famous poem "The Charge of the Light Brigade," "Theirs not to reason why, theirs but to do or die." Rather than "theirs," he would make it "ours." For years, he had used it as a motto of sorts.

But now he wanted to know more. It was no longer enough to kill and die for reasons that were never explained. It was possible that Martinez's suicide had finally rammed that home for him.

For the moment, the source of most of his knowledge was a woman nearly ten years younger than him. He glanced back at Trudy Wellington, the science and intel officer, sitting one row behind them.

She was dressed casually in jeans, a blue T-shirt, and pink socks. The T-shirt had two short words across the front, in small white lettering: Be Nice. She had kicked off her sneakers when they got on the plane. She was curled up with a clipboard, a thick file folder, and a bunch of paperwork. She pored through it, marking things with a pen. She had hardly spoken since the plane had taken off.

Sensing Luke staring at her, she looked up with big eyes behind her round red glasses. She was beautiful.

Trudy... what went on inside that mind of hers?

"Yes?" she said.

Luke smiled. "I thought you might want to fill us in on what we're all doing here. They told us next to nothing at the briefing, most of it being classified. Once Don took the mission, he said you would know what was going on by the time we got airborne."

Ed and Swann were watching them now.

"And we are officially airborne," Swann said.

Luke glanced out his window again. The sun was well behind them now, the day fading into nothingness. Hours from now, as they moved further east, the sky would begin to brighten. He checked his watch. Nearly nine o'clock.

"What do you say, Trudy? Ready to school us kids?"

Trudy made a bizarre sort of military salute with her right hand. It was awful. Luke did not glance back at Ed for fear of laughing.

"Ready, captain."

She stood and moved to the forward seat so that the four of them were together.

"I'm going to assume that none of you have any prior knowledge of this mission, the people involved, the current state of our relationship with Russia, or the task placed before us," she said. "It might make this conversation a little longer than necessary, it might not. But it tends to guarantee we're all on the same page. Sound okay?"

Luke nodded. "Good."

"Sounds okay," Ed said.

"It's a long flight," Swann said.

Trudy nodded. "Then let's begin."

She paused, took a deep breath, and looked at the page in front of her. Then she launched into her story.

"Earlier today our time, yesterday their time, the Russians seized the American research submersible *Nereus* from international waters in the Black Sea. The confrontation took place about one hundred forty-five miles southeast of the Crimean resort of Yalta. Yes, where the famous World War Two meeting took place between FDR, Winston Churchill, and Joseph Stalin."

Ed Newsam smiled. "That's some deep history right there."

"FDR?" Swann said. "The guy who got assassinated in, uh… Denver?"

Trudy smiled. She almost seemed to blush. Luke shook his head and almost laughed out loud. Tough crowd for a history lesson.

"*Nereus* was a sitting duck. A Russian destroyer tracked its location from the time it dropped from its mother ship. The destroyer and two smaller ships from the Russian Coast Guard converged on *Nereus*. Once they had it hemmed in, they dropped three bathyscaphes, which surrounded *Nereus* at close quarters, and escorted it to the surface. They also took the crew into custody."

"Who are they?" Luke said.

Trudy sifted through her files and brought a different paper to the top.

"A crew of three. The sub's pilot is forty-four-year-old Peter Bolger, official residence Falmouth, Massachusetts. Graduate of Maine Maritime Academy, class of 1983. Four years in the Coast Guard, honorable discharge 1987, rank of lieutenant. Spent nearly a decade piloting ships for Wood's Hole Oceanographic Institution in Cape Cod, in cooperation with numerous colleges, universities, and aquariums. Hired by Poseidon Research International, November 1996. To the naked eye, this is a civilian who has spent his entire adult life on the water, much of that conducting research. The presence of someone like Bolger is probably meant to give PRI a veneer of reality."

"He'll probably be the weak link when it comes to getting them out," Luke said.

Trudy nodded. "According to his dossier, he is five foot nine, and weighs two hundred thirty or two hundred forty pounds."

"How does he fit in the sub?" Swann said.

Ed shrugged. "Could be all muscle."

Now Trudy shook her head. "It isn't." She held up a photo of Peter Bolger. He wasn't morbidly obese, but he wasn't going to run the hundred-yard dash, either.

"Next," Luke said.

Trudy brought the next sheet to the top.

"Eric Davis, twenty-six-year-old graduate student from the University of Hawaii, on a research fellowship to Wood's Hole. Where do they come up with this stuff? He's really a twenty-eight-year-old Navy SEAL named Thomas Franks. Naval ROTC at the University of Michigan, graduated magna cum laude. Entered the Navy upon graduating, and immediately applied for BUD/S. Tours of duty in Afghanistan and Iraq, one each, as well as classified missions under Joint Special Operations Command. His mission here was to protect the other two men, and to scuttle the *Nereus* in the event of an accident or other mishap. Clearly, he didn't do any of that."

"Clearly," Swann said.

"He's our strongest link," Luke said. "If we get to these guys, and they're alive, it will be good to get a weapon or weapons into his hands. The major danger with Franks is that he may prematurely engineer some sort of escape attempt on his own, or acquire a weapon and come out shooting. Okay, next."

Trudy brought up the last piece of paper. "Reed Smith, thirty-six-year-old mission commander," she said. "A ghost. Total wild card. His true identity and age are Top Secret. I have nothing on him at all, other than he's been employed as a research associate at PRI for the past six months. Where he came from, and what he's been up to, is anybody's guess. He is the man that the CIA and the Pentagon are most concerned about. There are apparently a lot of secrets inside that little head of his."

Swann looked at Luke. "Black ops. I'm surprised he and Franks haven't toppled the Russian government by now."

Luke smiled. "I love your sense of humor, Swann. That's why I let you live."

He looked at Trudy. "I'd like a little context, if you have it. Where they took the *Nereus*, and the Russian state of readiness when ... if ... we go in there."

Trudy nodded. "I have some. The *Nereus* was taken into the holds of an old shipping freighter and has been brought to the Port of Adler, just south of the Black Sea resort city Sochi, and just north of the Russian border with Georgia. They are attempting to hide the *Nereus* and pretend they don't have it. They're acting as though the freighter has made a normal call into port. And at least as of when we left Washington, there was no evidence they've moved the *Nereus* crew to another location. There's been very little action on those docks at all."

"They know we're watching," Swann said.

"That seems to be the case," Trudy said.

"And the rest?" Luke said. "How ready are they?"

Trudy pursed her lips. "I can give you my own theory."

"Tell me," Luke said.

"It's a little involved."

Luke waved a hand. "It's not my bedtime yet."

Trudy nodded. "Vladimir Putin is playing whack-a-mole with debacles of various kinds. The Kursk disaster. The Beslan school massacre. Who knows when that will stop? But in the meantime, he is making progress on numerous fronts. He has cemented his iron grip on the government. The Russian economy, while still a shambles by our standards, is enjoying more prosperity than it's seen in fifteen years, primarily because of high worldwide oil and natural gas prices. Pentagon threat assessments suggest that the military is better funded, somewhat better trained, and the soldiers are getting better pay than they've seen in a long while. They are modernizing some weapon systems, especially ballistic missile systems.

"Russia is on a long, hard road back to its former place in the world. There's no telling if they'll make it. But there's also no doubt that since Putin took over, they are in fact on that road. Previously, they were upside down in a ditch by the side of the road."

"What does this mean to us?" Luke said.

"It means they took that sub to put us on notice," Trudy said. "The Black Sea was indisputably theirs for generations. Except for the Turkish coast, it was a Russian bathtub. We barely even put ships in there for years on end. They're telling us they're back, and they're not going to let us put spy ships in there any time we like."

"Yes, but is it really true?" Luke said. "Are they back? If we go in there and try to rescue those men, are we going to walk into a buzz saw?"

Trudy shook her head, offering the ghost of a smile. "No. They're not back. Not yet. Morale is still low. Command and control is still poor. Corruption is rampant. Lots and lots of infrastructure and equipment are degraded or nonfunctional. With a clever enough plan, and a fast-moving attack, I think you'll catch them flat-footed. I don't say this lightly, but I think we can get the men out of there."

Luke stared at her. He thought of her plan for taking out the renegade American military contractor Edwin Lee Parr and his ragtag militia in Iraq, and her optimistic assessment of the odds of doing so. At the time, Luke had been dismissive of her, her plan, and her assessment.

Then the whole thing turned out very similar to how she had described it. Luke and Ed still had to go in there and do it, but that part was a given.

"Boy, I hope you're right," he said.

Luke had fallen into a restless sleep. His dreams were strange, frightening, and rapidly shifting. A night skydive. As he fell, his parachute wouldn't open. Below him was a wide expanse of dark river. Alligators, dozens of them, watched him fall from the sky. They converged on him. But his leg was attached to a bungee cord. He bounced, a long slow-motion bounce, just above the water, his arms hanging down, the alligators lunging and snapping at him.

Then it was daytime. A Black Hawk helicopter had been shot out of the sky. Its tail rotor was gone, the chopper spinning out of control and coming down hard. Luke ran across a field, an old, empty soccer stadium, toward the chopper. If he could just get there before it hit, he could catch it and save those men on board. But the grass was growing all around him, reaching up, twisting, pulling at his legs, slowing him down. His arms were out, reaching… He was too late. He was too late.

God, the chopper was coming down sideways. Here … it … came …

He bucked awake in the midst of midair turbulence—the plane shuddered, then rode the unsettled air like a roller coaster. Luke glanced around. The lights were out. For a moment, he wasn't sure if he was asleep or awake. Then he noticed the rest of his team, sprawled out unconscious in various parts of the darkened cabin.

He gazed out his window—he couldn't see anything but a blinking light on the wing. Far below, the ocean was vast, endless, and black. The sun was far behind them now, the day long gone.

They'd been flying for hours, and they had more to go.

Hours from now, as they moved further east, the sky would begin to brighten. He checked his watch. Just after midnight back in DC, which meant that in Sochi, it was a little after eight a.m. Morning already.

Watching the clock gave him the sense of events surging out ahead. The Russians could move those men any time they wanted. They could have already moved them during the night.

It was frustrating to be trapped on this plane with the clock ticking.

Luke hadn't gotten much shut-eye, but he knew he wasn't going to fall asleep again. He had a lot weighing on him. The ghosts of the past. Becca and Gunner. The uncertain future of a baby born into a terrible world. This dangerous mission.

He got up, went to the tiny kitchenette at the back of the plane. He passed Ed Newsam and Mark Swann, who were dozing on opposite sides of the aisle from each other. Without turning on a light, he poured half a mug of hot water from the spigot and mixed some instant coffee, black with a touch of sugar. He tasted it. Eh. It wasn't bad. He grabbed an apple Danish wrapped in plastic and went back to his seat.

He turned on the overhead spotlight.

He glanced across the aisle from him. Trudy was asleep, curled into a ball. She was young for this job. It must be nice to know so much at such a tender age. He thought of himself in his early twenties. He'd been like that off-brand superhero, the one made out of granite, whose answer to any problem was to put his head down and run through walls. Not a lot going on upstairs.

He shook his head and looked at the paperwork in his lap. She had given him a ton of useful data. He had satellite imagery of the freighter, including close-ups of the upstairs catwalks and the rooms where the men were thought to be held, and the holds below where the sub was likely hiding.

Luke had to admit that the sub wasn't a major priority for him personally, but he knew that others didn't agree. They wanted that thing destroyed. Okay. If it was possible, and it didn't jeopardize the men, okay. He would do it.

Hmmm. What else did he have? A bunch of stuff. Schematics of the freighter. Maps and satellite imagery of the surrounding city streets, the docks, and the long seawall that protected the port from the Black Sea. Long-view maps and imagery of the entire area, with the sprawling beach resort of Sochi just to the north, the wide open water, and the border with Georgia to the south, tantalizingly close.

So near, and yet so far.

What else? Assessments of troop strength at the port and nearly facilities—best guesses, really. Assessments of first responder capabilities in metropolitan Sochi—good once upon a time, but underfunded and badly degraded now. Assessments of morale—low across the board. The two apocalyptic Chechen wars and the resulting terrorist attacks on civilian soft targets, combined with the Kursk disaster, had heads rolling among the Russian military brass, and the frontline troops in disarray.

Luke didn't doubt it. The shock of September 11, along with repeated setbacks in Iraq and Afghanistan, bad press at home… it had left a lot of people on this side of the fence feeling the same way. American equipment, training, and personnel were generally tip-top, but people were people, and when things went sideways, it hurt.

He let the information wash over him.

Don had promised him more people when he arrived in Turkey, deep cover operatives with local knowledge, fluency in the Russian language, and experience in fast-moving, hard-hitting black ops. Don didn't say where they were coming from, only that they would be the best available. He had promised Luke methods for both him and Ed, moving separately, to enter Russia undetected. He had promised Luke any materials he wanted, within reason—guns, bombs, cars, airplanes, whatever.

A picture began to emerge…

Yeah. He started to imagine the broad outlines of it. In an ideal world… if he got everything he wanted… with the element of surprise… total commitment… and moving at warp speed…

He could see how this just *might* work.

"They used to call me Monster."

Luke stared at Ed. They were the only two awake, sitting in the back seats of the plane. But now Luke was fading. Further up, Trudy was still curled into a ball, and Swann was sprawled out, his long legs crossing the aisle.

The window shades were down, but Luke could see bits of sunlight peeking in along the bottom edges. Wherever they were in the world, it was morning now.

Luke had just laid out the mission to Ed, as he was starting to imagine it. He was thinking he might get a little feedback. Did this part seem possible? Was there a gaping hole he was overlooking? What kind of weapons should they carry? What kind of equipment did they need?

Instead, he got this: "They used to call me Monster."

It was all the answer he needed, he supposed. The man was a monster. If it came to it, he would go at this problem with half a plan and a handful of rusty nails.

"Somehow, that doesn't surprise me," Luke said.

Ed shook his head. He was half asleep himself. "Not because of my size. Because I was so evil. I grew up in Crenshaw, in LA. Four kids, I was the oldest. The closest thing to a grocery store in the neighborhood was a place that sold liquor, lottery tickets, and cans of soup and tuna fish. My mom couldn't keep the lights on sometimes.

"I said, un-unh. It ain't gonna be like this. It's not right we gotta live this way, and I'm gonna fix it. I was out working on the corner at twelve, trying to get that money. I was running with the worst of the worst by fifteen, and I was worse than they were. In and out of juvie. I wasn't fixing anything."

Ed sighed heavily. "Ten of those nights, I could have easily died. People did. I was getting shot at long before I ever saw Iraq, or

Afghanistan, or any of these other classified places I supposedly never went."

He squinted and shook his head. "I came before a judge when I was seventeen. She told me I could now be tried as an adult. I could see real time in big-boy jail. Or I could get a suspended sentence and join the United States Army. Up to me."

He smiled. "What else was I gonna do? I joined. I got to basic, drill sergeant there, name of Brooks, immediately had a hard-on for me. Master Sergeant Nathan Brooks. Didn't like me, and decided he was gonna break me."

"Did he?" Luke said. He had trouble picturing such a thing, but this wasn't the first time he had heard something along these lines. "Did he break you?"

Ed laughed. "Oh yeah. He broke me. Then he broke me again. And again. I've never been broken so bad in my life. He saw me coming a mile away. Made me his personal project. He said, 'You think you hard, nigger? You ain't hard. You ain't even seen hard yet. But I'm gonna show it to you.'"

"Was he a white guy?" Luke said.

Ed shook his head. "Nah. In those days, if a white man called me nigger, I'd have just killed him. He was a down home brother, from South Carolina someplace. I don't know. He broke me right in half. And when he was done, he put me back together again, a little better than before. Now I was something other people up the line could at least work with, make something out of."

He was silent for a moment. The airplane shuddered across a patch of turbulence.

"I never really found the right way to thank that guy."

Luke shrugged. "Well, it's not over. Send him some flowers. A Hallmark card. I don't know."

Ed smiled, but it was wistful now. "He's dead. Maybe a year ago. Forty-three years old. He'd already been in the service twenty-five years. He could have retired any time. Apparently, he volunteered for Iraq instead, and they gave it to him. He was on a convoy that got ambushed near Mosul. I don't know all the details. I saw it in

Stars and Stripes. Turns out he was a highly decorated guy. I didn't know that about him when he was running me into the ground. He never mentioned it."

He paused. "And I never told him what he meant to me."

"He probably knew," Luke said.

"Yeah. He probably did. But I should have said it anyway."

Luke didn't disagree.

"Where's your mom?" he said instead.

Ed shook his head. "Still in Crenshaw. I tried to get her to move out east near me, but she wouldn't hear of leaving. All her friends are there! So me and my sister chipped in and bought her a little bungalow six blocks away from the old rat hole apartment building where we used to live. A chunk of my pay every month goes to paying the mortgage on that thing. Right in the old neighborhood I used to risk my life trying to get her out of."

He sighed heavily. "At least there's food in the fridge and the lights are on. I guess that's all I care about. She says, 'Ain't nobody gonna mess with me. They know you're my son. And you're gonna come see 'em if they do.'"

Luke smiled. Ed did too, and this time the smile was more genuine.

"She's impossible, man."

Now Luke laughed. After a moment, so did Ed.

"Listen," Ed said. "I like your plan. I think we can pull it off. A couple more guys, the right ones..." He nodded. "Yeah. It's doable. I need to catch about forty more winks, and maybe I'll have a few thoughts of my own, some things to add."

"Sounds good," Luke said. "I look forward to that. I'd prefer not to get anybody on our team killed out there."

"Especially not us," Ed said.

Chapter Seven

June 26
6:30 a.m. Eastern Daylight Time
Special Activities Center, Directorate of Operations
Central Intelligence Agency
Langley, Virginia

"It seems the president has lost his marbles."

"Oh?" the old man smoking the cigarette said. It sounded like he had marbles in his throat. His teeth were dark yellow. Receding gums made them long. They seemed to click together when he spoke. The effect was horrifying. "Do tell."

They were deep inside the bowels of headquarters. Most places inside the building, smoking was now off limits. But here in the inner sanctum? Anything was allowed.

"I'm sure you've already heard," Special Agent Wallace Speck said.

He sat across a wide steel desk from the old man. There was almost nothing on the desk. No phone, no computer, not a piece of paper or a pencil. There was only a white ceramic ashtray, filled to overflowing with used cigarette butts.

The old man nodded. "Refresh my memory."

"Yesterday he suggested that the crew of the *Nereus* be left to rot in Russian hands. He said this in front of twenty or thirty people."

"Skip the easy stuff," the old man said. They were in a room without windows. He took a deep drag on his cigarette, held it, and then let loose a plume of blue smoke. The ceiling was at least fifteen feet above their heads, and the smoke drifted upward toward it.

"Well, he walked that sentiment back. But he's cut us and our friends out of the rescue operation, in favor of our new little brother at FBI."

"Skip," the old man said.

Wallace Speck shook his head. The old man looked like hell. How was he even still alive? He'd been chain smoking cigarettes since before Speck was born. His face was like ancient newsprint, turning almost as yellow as his teeth. His wrinkles had wrinkles. His body had no muscle tone at all. His flesh seemed to hang on bone.

The thought gave Speck a brief flashback to eating at a fancy restaurant one time. "How's the chicken tonight?" he said to the waiter. "Beautiful," the waiter said. "It falls right off the bone."

The old man's meat was anything but beautiful. But his eyes were still as sharp as razors, as focused as lasers. They were the only things left.

Those eyes regarded Speck. They wanted the dirt. They wanted the parts that people like Wallace Speck worried about sometimes. He could dig up the dirt, and he did. That was his job. But sometimes he wondered if the Special Activities Center of the CIA wasn't overstepping its mandate. Sometimes he wondered if the *special activities* didn't amount to treason.

"The man has trouble sleeping," Speck said. "It seems he hasn't gotten over the kidnapping of his daughter. He relies on Ambien to sleep, and he often washes his pill down with a glass of wine, or two. It's a dangerous habit, for obvious reasons."

Speck paused. He could give the old man paperwork, but the man didn't want to look at paper. He just wanted to listen. Speck knew that. "We have audiotape and transcripts of a dozen telephone calls to his family ranch in Texas over the past ten days. The conversations are with his wife. In each call, he expresses his desire to leave the presidency, move back to the ranch, and spend time with his family. During three of those calls, he breaks down crying."

The old man smiled and took another deep drag on the smoke. His eyes became slits. His tongue darted out. There was a piece of tobacco there at the tip of it. He looked like a lizard. "Good. More."

"He has a sort of hero worship obsession with Don Morris, our little upstart rival at the FBI Special Response Team."

The old man made a hand motion like a wheel spinning.

"More."

Speck shrugged. "The president has a little dog, as you know. He has taken to walking it on the White House grounds late at night. He becomes angry if he runs across any Secret Service agents while he's out there. A few nights ago, he came across two inside of ten minutes, and threw a temper tantrum. He called the night supervisory office and told them to stand their men down. He no longer seems to grasp that the men are there to protect him. He thinks they're there to annoy him."

"Hmmm," the old man said. "Would he try to run away?"

"I would say it seems implausible," Speck said. "But with this president, you never can tell what he's going to do."

"What else?"

"The political action group has begun to look at options for removal," Speck said. "Impeachment is out because of the split in Congress. Also, the speaker of the House is a close ally of David Barrett's and on the same page with him about most issues. He is very unlikely to pursue impeachment, or allow it to happen on his watch. Removal by the Twenty-fifth Amendment appears to be out as well. Barrett probably isn't going to admit his inability to discharge his duties, and if the vice president attempts to…"

The old man held up his hand. "I get it. Skip. Tell me this: do we have Secret Service agents in nighttime operations on the White House grounds? Men who are loyal to us?"

"We do," Speck said. "Yes."

"Good. Now tell me about the Russia rescue operation."

Speck shook his head. "We have no details. Don Morris is notoriously tight-fisted with information. But the bench isn't deep over there, at least not yet. We can assume he's given it to his two best agents, Luke Stone and Ed Newsam, young guys, both former Delta Force operators with extensive combat experience."

"The ones who rescued the president's unfortunate daughter?"

Speck nodded. "Yes."

The old man smiled. His teeth were like yellow fangs. He could pass for the oldest of vampires, one who hadn't tasted blood in a long, long time. "Cowboys, aren't they?"

"Uh... I think they tend to shoot first, and then..."

"Are we planning to interdict? Derail their operation in some way?"

"Ah..." Wallace Speck said. "It's certainly been on the table as an option. I mean, at the moment we don't have that much..."

"Don't do it," the old man said. "Get out of their way and let it rip. Maybe they'll get themselves killed. Maybe they'll start a world war. Either way, it's good for us. And if David Barrett does anything crazy, I mean really crazy, be ready to swoop in and take control of the situation."

Wallace Speck stood to leave.

"Yes sir. Anything else?"

The old man looked at him with the ancient eyes of a demon. "Yes. Try to smile a little more, Speck. You're not dead yet, so make an effort to enjoy your time here. This is supposed to be fun."

Chapter Eight

11:20 p.m. Moscow Daylight Time (3:20 p.m. Eastern Daylight Time)
Port of Adler, Sochi District
Krasnodar Krai
Russia

"Are they sure they want us to play this concert?" Luke said into the blue plastic satellite phone in his hand. "I think it's going to be pretty loud."

He leaned against an old black Lada sedan, made in Hungary. The boxy little car reminded him of an old Fiat or Yugo, just not as fancy as those. It seemed to be made of welded sheets of scrap metal. It gave off a faint smell of burning oil. The faster it went, the more it seemed to vibrate, like it was coming apart at the seams. Luckily, it was not the getaway car.

Nearby, his driver, a heavyset Chechen named Aslan, was smoking a cigarette and urinating through a chain-link fence. Aslan preferred it if you called him Frenchy. This was because when Chechnya collapsed, he had escaped the Russians by disappearing to Paris for a few years. His three brothers and his father had all died in the war. Now Frenchy was back, and Frenchy hated Russians.

They were in an empty parking lot near the mouth of the Mzymta River. A moist, pungent odor of untreated sewage wafted up from the water. From here, a bleak boulevard of warehouses ran along the waterfront to a small cargo port, guarded by a gatehouse and razor-topped fencing. In the glow of weak yellow sodium arc lamps, he could see men moving around by the gate.

The grand old Communist Party dachas, the new hotels and restaurants, and the glimmering Black Sea beaches of Sochi were just five miles up the road. But Adler was as desultory and depressing as a Russian port should be.

There was a delay as Mark Swann's reedy voice bounced all over the world, from encrypted networks to black satellites, and finally to Luke's phone. Swann's voice trembled with nervous excitement.

Luke shook his head and smiled. Swann was in a penthouse suite with beautiful Trudy Wellington, in a five-star hotel in Trabzon, Turkey. They were supposedly a rich young newlywed couple from California. If bullets started to fly, Swann would be watching it on a computer screen, nearly but not quite live, via satellite. That's why his voice was shaking.

"We are green light," Swann said. "They understand we might get some complaints from the neighbors."

"And the disco ball?"

"Right where we said it would be."

Luke gazed across at a rusty old mid-sized cargo ship, the *Yuri Andropov II*, resting at dock. He mused that an old KGB torture specialist like Andropov must be spinning in his grave that this thing was named after him. It must be somebody's idea of a joke.

The disco ball, of course, was the missing submersible, *Nereus*. Its GPS chip was still pinging from inside one of the holds on that ship.

"And the instruments?" The instruments were the crew of the *Nereus*.

"Upstairs in the closet, as far as we know."

"Aretha? What does she have to say?"

Trudy Wellington's voice came on, just for a second.

"Your friends are already partying on the beach."

Luke nodded. Just south of here was the border with the former Soviet Republic of Georgia. The Georgians and the Russians were currently at each other's throats. Trudy suspected they were going to have a little shooting war one of these days, but hopefully it wouldn't start tonight.

The Georgian beach resort town of Kheivani was right across that border. It was a quiet, sleepy place compared to Sochi. There was a retrieval crew on a dark beach there, waiting to receive the rescued prisoners, if any of this even got that far.

From the beach, the prisoners would be moved away from the border, deeper into Georgia, and then out of the country. Eventually, when they reached a safe place, they would be debriefed about this whole mess.

None of that was Luke's department. By design, he knew nothing about how it would go. Don and Big Daddy Cronin had cooked up that part. Luke didn't even know who was involved. You could cut his fingers off and gouge his eyes out, and he couldn't tell you a thing about it.

"Has the big man joined the band?" Luke said.

Ed Newsam's voice came on. A howl of wind and the roar of heavy engines nearly drowned him out. "He's in the dressing room and ready to get on stage. The sooner the better, as far as he's concerned."

Luke sighed. "All right," he said, and the weight of the decision settled onto his shoulders like a boulder. People were probably about to die. You knew that going in. You just didn't know which ones.

"Let's do it."

"See you in Vegas," Swann said.

"Be sure to catch the fireworks show," Ed shouted. "I hear it's gonna be good."

The call went dead. Luke dropped the satellite telephone to the broken blacktop of the parking lot. He raised his boot and brought it down hard on the phone, cracking the plastic casing apart. He did it again. And again. And again. Then he kicked the shattered remnants through an open runoff drain and into the water.

He still had one more.

He looked up.

Frenchy was there. His face was broad and his skin seemed thick, almost like a rubber mask. His hair was jet black and swooped backward. He was clean-shaven to blend in better with Russian society. Normally, his people had thick beards for Allah.

Frenchy wore a dark, loose-fitting windbreaker jacket over his big body. The night was a little warm for that. His hard eyes stared at Luke.

"Yes?" Frenchy said.

Luke nodded. "Yes."

Frenchy took a deep drag of his cigarette. He slowly exhaled the smoke. Then he smiled and nodded.

"I am happy."

"Fast," Ed Newsam said. He was speaking to no one. This was good because no one would ever be able to hear him.

"Very, very fast."

He stood in the cockpit, his feet bare, hands on the wheel of a boat shaped like a giant wedge. The boat was long and narrow, with a very long bow. At the stern, there were five big 275-horsepower engines. The boat itself only had two seats.

In America, they would call it a Cigarette boat, or a Go Fast. In the days before satellite tracking, drug traffickers in South Florida used these things to outrun the Coast Guard. This boat wasn't packed with cocaine, though.

In the nose of the boat, way up at the bow, was a tiny compartment. That compartment was packed with a small amount of TNT.

Ed ran hard in the night, lights off, bouncing over the swells. His engines roared, a huge sound. The wind howled around him. In front of him, maybe three clicks ahead, was the mostly dark coastline of Georgia. Behind him were the bright lights of Sochi. Sochi was enjoying its post-communist, big money heyday. Expensive boats like this were easy to come by.

In fact, behind Ed and running just as hard, was another speedboat.

That boat was driven by a nutty Georgian daredevil named Garry. Ed couldn't see Garry back there. Garry's lights were also off. And he couldn't hear Garry. There was too much noise to hear anything. But he knew Garry was back there. He had to be.

Ed's life depended on it.

Garry, along with Stone's crazy Chechen driver, Frenchy, had been provided by Big Daddy Bill Cronin. Big Daddy was CIA, and they weren't supposed to involve the CIA in this, but they did it anyway. The danger was that the CIA had sprung a leak somewhere.

"Bill Cronin's paychecks come from CIA," Don Morris had said. "But the man is a law and a world unto himself. If he gives us operators, they won't be talkers. There will be no security breaches. I can assure you of that."

So Garry was back there with Ed's and Luke's and everybody's lives in his hands.

To Ed's left, the east, there was a long stone seawall, jutting far out into the water. It protected a small port area. He ran the length of it, coming at it on a diagonal. He slowed, just a touch, and made the sharp turn in toward land.

He glanced at the sky, scanning for aircraft.

Nothing. All clear.

That seawall was topped with concrete docks. It ran parallel to land, a hundred meters from the shore. The seawall and the shore formed a narrow pass a thousand meters long. At the far end was the cargo ship, the *Yuri Andropov II.*

Ed's job was to punch a hole in it. A hole, maybe a small fire. Enough to cause a distraction, a misdirection. Enough to let Stone and Frenchy sneak onto the boat, release the prisoners, and maybe even scuttle that sub.

The Russians knew the Americans were watching them from the skies. So these docks looked like they had minimal activity. Just an old cargo ship, not too much security, nothing to see here.

But Ed knew there were gun men on those docks. Driving this boat up that pass was going to be running a gauntlet.

He reached the mouth of the pass. He took a deep breath.

"Garry, you better be there."

He opened the throttle all the way. The engines screamed.

The boat burst forward, even faster than before.

Land raced by on either side of him, the seawall on his left, the shore on his right. But he kept his eyes on the prize. He could see it now, the *Andropov*, looming far ahead. It was docked perpendicular to him, showing him its whole length.

"Beautiful."

To his left, men ran along the docks. He saw them as tiny stick figures, moving slow, much too slow.

He ducked way down, already knowing what they would do. An instant later, automatic gunfire ripped up the side of the boat. He felt it more than heard it or saw it. It was altering his course, the thudding impacts of the high-caliber rounds.

The windshield shattered.

The *Andropov* was coming closer, growing larger.

There was an iron bar on the floor. Ed picked it up. One end had a gripping tool, almost like a hand. He placed this onto the steering wheel. He wedged the far end into a metal slot welded onto the floor.

Old school, but it would do the trick. It would keep the boat going more or less straight ahead.

He glanced up. The *Andropov* was big now.

It seemed like it was RIGHT THERE.

"Uh-oh, time to go."

He darted to the right side of the boat, away from the gunfire. He squatted, all the power in his legs, and leapt to his right, over the gunwale. He curled into a ball, like a child doing a cannonball at the local swimming pool.

The boat zoomed away while he was in the air.

Dimly, he had the sensation of falling, falling through the sky. A long time passed. He crashed into the water and for a moment the blackness was all around him. He moved through it like a torpedo, no feeling except the feeling of dark speed.

At first there was a loud roar, and then the muffled sounds of the deep.

For a moment, he thought about floating in the womb, bathed now in warm light. It occurred to him that the beacon light on his life vest had activated. The vest yanked him to the surface, back to the roar and the spray of the boat's wake.

He gasped for air and dove again. For another few seconds, those gunners were going to be looking for him.

After that…

He bobbed to the surface again. Everything was dark—the night, the water, everything.

For a moment he could not see the boat. Then he spotted it. It was moving fast, dwindling, dwindling. It was tiny in the looming shadow of the freighter.

Ed dove below the surface again, to the safety of the darkness.

Luke leaned on the Lada, pretending to smoke a cigarette. Everybody around here smoked, so he figured it might help his disguise. He had tried it a couple of times before in high school but never caught the hang of it. He liked football better.

He took a drag, held it in his mouth for a few seconds, then let the whole mess blow out again. It tasted like smog. He nearly laughed at himself. If anyone was watching, they would see how ridiculous he looked.

He pitched the lit cigarette into the gutter.

The Lada was parked fifty yards from the security gate of the small port. Frenchy was over there at the gate, asking the guards for directions. There was a small knot of men, silhouettes in the fog, shadows thrown by the yellow lamps, talking and laughing through the gate. Frenchy was kind of a funny guy. He could crack anybody up.

Frenchy was smoking effortlessly. Smoke one down to the nub, pitch it, and light another one. That was Frenchy.

Suddenly gunshots rang out. They came from the other side of the wharf. Three hundred yards away, Luke saw the muzzle flashes of the guns.

POP! POP! POP! POP!

Now men were shouting. A man screamed in terror, a high falsetto wail.

Someone opened up with a heavy gun, full auto. Luke could hear the metallic stomp of the rounds being unleashed.

DUH-DUH-DUH-DUH-DUH-DUH-DUH-DUH.

Now the guards were running away from the gate, back toward the action. That was Luke's cue. Just like that, they were in.

But then Frenchy did something unexpected. As soon as the guards turned from him, he had a gun in his hand. He took a two-handed stance and started firing. His shots were LOUD.

BANG! BANG! BANG! BANG! BANG!

He shot the running guards in their backs. They spun to face him, and he shot them in their fronts. Poor guys, they didn't know if they were coming or going.

"Frenchy!" Luke almost shouted, but didn't.

"Dammit!" he said instead.

The man hated Russians. Luke knew that going in. Don knew it. Big Daddy knew it. But no one expected him to start killing Russians the second he got a chance.

Luke reached into the car and pulled out the heavy bolt cutters. He set the incendiary beneath the dashboard for one minute. Then he dashed to Frenchy's side.

"You're my driver! You're not supposed to kill anybody!"

Frenchy shrugged. "Russians," he said. "Cowards."

"You shot them in the back." To Luke the implications of that were clear. Who's the coward around here?

But it wasn't clear to Frenchy. He nodded and smiled. "Yes. I did."

Luke put the clippers to the thick chain looped through the fence links and cut it. He dropped the cutters and shoved the gate open. Now they were really in.

Ba-BOOOOOOOM!

Ahead of them, a massive explosion ripped open the night.

A flash of light appeared. On the heels of that came a sound like boulders rushing downhill. An avalanche. The explosion rent the sky in oranges, reds, and yellows. For a split second, it turned night into day. It was *not* what Luke expected.

The explosion was so big that the ground trembled violently. Luke nearly lost his feet. Everything went sideways. For a moment, he thought the explosion was enough to tear the docks off their moorings. A giant flaming fireball went straight into the sky.

Ed's boat had hit like a torpedo.

That was going to bring people. No doubt about it. Luke pulled his gun out, an MP5. His weapon of choice. *The murder weapon.* He started to run.

Frenchy was several steps ahead of him. The big Chechen reached the first man down, a guard who was trying to crawl forward, and finished him with a shot to the back of the head. BANG. Without pausing, he moved on to the next one. BANG.

Cold-blooded. He had just been sharing a laugh with these guys.

Three guards were still running out ahead of them. It was too late to let them live. Frenchy had scuttled that. Luke sprayed them with the MP5. They all dropped.

Now Luke was moving fast. He blew ahead of Frenchy, left him to clean up the mess. Ahead, the freighter, the *Yuri Andropov II*, was on fire. Oil or gasoline on the surface of the water had also caught. The whole area was fast becoming an apocalypse.

How much TNT had they put in that speedboat?

BOOM! Another explosion went up behind him. The Lada.

A second later, a smaller explosion went up. The Lada's gas tank. Good. That flaming car at the gate would add to the confusion when the cavalry got here.

Luke reached where the freighter was docked lengthwise along the pier. The heat here was already intense, though the fire was on the other side of the boat. Flames ten stories high reached into the night. The fire shouldn't be that…

BOOOOM!

Another long explosion rent the night, ripping out from somewhere inside the freighter. The docks trembled and Luke was nearly knocked off his feet again. The wind from a blast wave hit him.

What the hell was going on?

The ship was secured to the pier with giant shipping chains. Luke strapped his gun to his back, crossed the low barrier along the dock's edge, grabbed a chain, and swung out over the water. He pulled himself, moving like a spider along the shipping chain on a diagonal up to the first deck.

There was no one on this deck. He moved along the catwalk, fast but careful, much like a cat himself. He came to a steel stairway. Gun out again, he moved cautiously to the top. Already, he could hear sirens behind him. Reinforcements were on their way. He'd better make this quick.

He stopped just short of the top of the steps and poked his head over the top. This was the deck. It was loud up here. A clarion bell was shrieking. Across the deck, the fire surged. Men had reached the firefighting equipment and were attempting to put the fire out. They sprayed it with powerful hoses—flame retardant or water, Luke couldn't tell. From the smoke and the flames, all he could really see were vague forms moving through the chaos.

GA-BOOOOM!

Another explosion came, this one from directly beneath the firefighters. The deck erupted upward, and the men flew into the air, their bodies lit up like torches.

Luke stopped. He popped the magazine out of his gun and slipped it into his jacket. It was probably half-full. He pulled out a new forty-round magazine, slid it into the gun, and drove it home with his fist.

He gazed out at the deck. Flames shot through the hole. Burning corpses, ten, maybe twelve, littered the ground.

Ordnance.

The ship was a floating weapons depot. What else would cause these explosions? The Russians had loaded up this old rust bucket freighter with bombs. Was this what they were reduced to? That hadn't been in any intelligence assessment Luke had…

BOOOM!

Another explosion ripped through the ship somewhere.

Now the fire just burned, unchecked, the flames crackling, the heat coming off it in waves. This thing was going to disintegrate. It was going to blow apart. It could happen any time. There wasn't a moment to waste.

"Oh, man."

Luke got up and ran across the deck, through the surge of heat. At the far end was a corridor. He raced along it. There were heavy steel doors on either side.

He stopped, tried the latch on one. It opened. He peeked in, gun raised and ready. There was no one in here.

He moved to the next one. Then the next one. Jesus. There was no one here. Where did they put the prisoners? He started to get a sinking feeling: the Russians had taken the prisoners somewhere else. This whole mission could turn out to be for nothing. Well, next to nothing—they could still destroy the submersible.

He tried another door. It was locked.

He stopped.

"If you can hear me," he shouted. "Stay away from the door!"

He fired into the lock. Once, and the bullet ricocheted and whined off into the night. Twice, and the bullet punched a hole through the mechanism. Three times, and the lock came apart. He pulled the latch.

Three men sat on a low wooden bench. One was short and heavyset with a beard—the sub pilot, according to Luke's information. One was thin like beef jerky—the spy, the prize, the man with the intelligence networks mapped in his brain. The last one was tall, broad, and muscular—the Navy SEAL. The men were blindfolded, and their hands were fastened behind their backs. They were slumped together as though they were asleep…or dead.

"You guys alive?" Luke said.

The SEAL nodded, his head moving sluggishly. He was the only one moving at all.

"American?" he said.

"Yeah," Luke said. "Have the interrogations started?"

The SEAL shook his head, just a bit. "No."

Luke sighed. That was one piece of good news. He glanced down the corridor, both ways. No one was coming yet. Where was Frenchy? It looked like Luke was going to need him to get these guys moving.

"We're here to rescue you. But I suppose that part is obvious."

The SEAL shrugged. "They drugged us, man. Keeps us docile. Nothing is obvious right now."

The water was on fire.

No one had game planned this. There was so much leaked oil and gasoline in this little harbor that the surface of the water was aflame.

Russians!

Ed poked his head up through the inky blackness. He took a deep breath. Ahead of him, the sky was on fire, great up-rushing bursts of orange and red and yellow, black smoke pouring from it. Closer, the bobbing swells were blanketed with red and orange and blue flame, all of it spreading its fingers toward him. All the fire gave an eerie effect—it was almost hard to tell where the sky ended and the water started.

As Ed watched, another explosion ripped open the night.

It was too much. There was no way his boat could have caused all this. There was an inferno going on over there.

To his left, gunfire erupted again. There were men still alive on the seawall. Ed ducked, thinking the gunfire was for him. But below the surface, he heard the rumble of approaching engines. Garry.

Thank God.

He popped up, and here came the boat, moving slow, spotlight scanning the surface of the water. Ed moved to his left, putting the boat between himself and the gunfire coming from the seawall.

"Cut that light!" he screamed. "Cut it! I'm right here!"

The boat pulled up. It was a very different boat from the one Ed had driven. This one was also a fast boat, but it was hung from bow to stern with heavy aftermarket armor. It looked like something out of *Mad Max*. Ed stayed to its starboard side, all the gunfire hitting it on the port side. With the boat going so slow, the gunmen were really clobbering it.

Duh-duh-duh-duh-duh. An automatic gun ripped up the metal.

Small arms fired winged it.

Ding!

Ed climbed the ladder and collapsed over the gunwale. Garry was up ahead, in the small protected cockpit, watching ahead through the slit in the metal.

"Edward!" he said, laughing. "You are alive!"

He was a big bear of a man, bearded, maybe forty years old. His hands were enormous. He looked back and smiled.

"Yes," Ed said. "I'm alive."

"Then man the gun, my friend."

There was a big rear-mounted .50-caliber machinegun surrounded by armor. It could spin on a turret and poke its snout out through the slits in its armor. It was already loaded, but Ed would have to feed it himself, one hand on the trigger, one hand keeping the rounds flowing smoothly.

Ed sighed. "With pleasure."

He crawled to it and slithered up into the turret.

No sooner had he gotten inside than Garry opened the throttle. The boat planed upward and took off toward the towering flames in front of them.

Ed sighted through the turret slit. Men ran along the seawall, shooting at the boat.

Ed opened fire with the .50-caliber.

⚜ ⚜ ⚜

"Frenchy, where the hell have you been?"

The big man loomed out of the dark inferno. His face was red with flames. The reflection of the fire shined in his sweat.

He shrugged. "Killing Russians."

Luke shook his head. Where did they get this guy?

"Can you help me, please?" Luke said.

He had cut the cuffs off the prisoners and roused them from their stupors long enough to get them moving. The SEAL was okay. His eyes were dazed and his balance was off, but he could walk well enough. The other two were zonked. Vacant eyes, mouths hanging half ajar, stumbling footsteps. They didn't seem to understand what was happening. Luke pushed them along in a single file line. He had stopped the convoy at the head of the corridor. In front of them, the deck was burning out of control.

"We need to find another way out," Luke said.

Frenchy pointed the way Luke had just come. "I am on ships very much. That way. New stairwell will be at end of this hall."

Luke's shoulders slumped. The hall was fifty or sixty yards long and might as well have been a mile. Then the stairs down to the water, and the rendezvous with Ed and the Georgian, if that was even happening. How were they supposed to navigate all that?

"We might need to carry these guys," Luke said.

Frenchy shook his head.

"What?" Luke said.

"I have bad back. No one said before we carry men. Not possible."

Luke rubbed his forehead. What kind of commando had Big Daddy given him? The guy was overweight, he smoked, and he had a bad back. He seemed pretty good at killing people, but that was all he did, whether you wanted him to or not. He was a one-trick pony.

Luke pulled out his second satellite phone. He turned it on and waited several seconds while it powered up. Several seconds seemed like several minutes verging on several hours.

"Luke…" Frenchy said.

Luke raised a hand. "I know. I know. Let's get them moving anyway."

Frenchy took control of that. He walked over to the three men, physically turned them around, and started to push them along the hallway. He pushed the pilot too hard and the man fell to the metal deck.

Frenchy looked at Luke and shook his head. He reached down, grabbed the heavyset man around his ample waist, and wrenched him back up to his feet. He let out a long, guttural bark as he did so. It sounded like a bark of agony.

Luke smiled. "And you said you had a bad back."

Luke hit the green button on the phone and it auto-dialed Swann, the signal beaming back and forth across the earth and the stars before finding its mark in Turkey.

A cautious voice came on the line. "Jimi?" It was Swann.

Luke had nearly forgotten. They were supposedly throwing a concert.

"The very same."

"You've got a crowd gathering. It might be time to exit the stage." This was Swann talking in code. It was too late for code. Everything was in motion.

"Where is Ed?"

"The big man?"

"Swann! Cut it out. I don't have time. Okay? The boat is on fire."

Swann was quiet for a long second.

"Yes, I see that it is. That wasn't really the plan. We were just gonna do a hole. Maybe a little bit of fire as a distraction."

"Thanks for the recap, Swann."

Sirens were howling now. Somewhere just below them, someone was screaming. It sounded like agony. The ship trembled again as something rumbled deep in its bowels. Flames made a great whooshing noise as another fireball went up into the sky.

"Where is Ed? If you say *the big man* again, I'm going to kill you when I see you."

A female voice cut in. Trudy.

"Luke! Don't say that!"

"Ed is in the second speedboat," Swann said. "They are en route to your position. They'll arrive at the dock just south of you any minute. My imagery is on a time delay, so they might already be there."

"Tell Ed I need him to come up here."

"No way. The speedboat is under sustained assault from the seawall. A bunch of guys are setting up weapons along the opposite shore. The ship you're on is like the towering inferno. It looks like the whole thing is gonna go. And they're right in its shadow. Also, the harbor itself is on fire. I don't even know how long they can hang out there. There's no way he can get off that boat."

"Swann, if he can't get off the boat, how are we supposed to get on it? I've got the prisoners here, and they're all drugged to the gills. They can barely walk."

There was no answer.

"Swann?"

"I'm thinking."

Luke shook his head, the phone pressed to his ear. "Take your time." They were moving along the hallway, Frenchy pushing, shoving, holding up, and otherwise cajoling two of the prisoners along. The third prisoner, the Navy SEAL, stumbled down the hall under his own power. At times he put his hand along the wall to hold himself up.

Dammit! Luke had been hoping to put a gun in that guy's hands. None of this was going according to plan. From Frenchy suddenly deciding to kill people, to the ship blowing up of its own accord... 100% SNAFU.

They were almost at the stairwell.

"Luke, it's really time to go. There are two helicopters coming in from the northeast now. They'll be above you in seconds. They've massed about ten or twenty vehicles at the front gate."

"What kind of choppers?"

"I don't know. I can't get a good ID. Small. Could be anything. News choppers, police, Spetsnaz. Who knows?"

Luke sighed. "The vehicles?"

"First responders, fire trucks, ambulances, looks like maybe some SWAT guys. More coming. The roads to your location are full of flashing red and blue lights. It's gonna be a traffic jam there in a minute."

"All right. Just tell Ed we're coming down. Tell him be ready to blow out of here. We'll get these guys on the boat somehow. Signing off."

"Luke?" Swann said.

"Yeah?"

"What about the sub?"

Luke looked at the phone. "What about it?"

"You're supposed to scuttle it."

Luke patted the plastic explosives and the blasting caps in the pockets of his cargo pants. He had the tools, but he had no idea how he was supposed to reach the sub and use them.

"Swann, have you seen this place?"

"Yeah. It's on fire. But that doesn't mean the sub is on fire. If the ship goes down, but somehow the sub doesn't burn ... it's a sub, you know what I mean? A little water isn't going to hurt it."

"I always enjoy talking to you, Swann."

Swann hung up the phone.

"We got problems," he said.

"What is it?"

Swann looked at Trudy. Her brown hair cascaded to her shoulders. Her eyes were big and pretty and wide open and concerned behind owlish, bright blue glasses. She wore jeans, a white T-shirt, and pink socks. The T-shirt had a cartoon of a sexy female cat lying on its side, propped up on its elbow, its head resting in its hand. The shirt had one word on it, just below the cat: Meow.

Meow was right. Trudy looked beautiful. Behind her, a giant bay window looked out on the night skyline of Trabzon. They were together in this crazy opulent suite at the top of this hotel, pretending to be rich newlyweds from Marin County. Just two young kids, holed up in bed together for days, ordering in room service.

Swann shook his head to clear it. It was a nice fantasy.

He turned to look at his bank of computer monitors. On two of them, there was nothing but raging fires. On the third, there was a blinking light—the GPS location of the submersible *Nereus* near, but not necessarily within, those flames.

"They've got all kinds of Russian personnel converging on them. Luke has the prisoners with him, but they've all been drugged. They can't walk, apparently. The boat is on fire, and it looks to me like it's probably going to sink. But that might not take out the sub. We need to think of something so Luke can just get out of there."

Trudy pursed her lips. "Thinking out loud here. What if they don't destroy the sub? If they get the prisoners out, that's still a win, right?"

Swann stroked his goatee.

"I don't know. I guess so. But the sub is high tech, super modern, and the Russians are still laboring where the Soviets left off in 1986. I'm sure they'd love to have that thing."

"Can we destroy it from here?" Trudy said.

Swann stared at her for a long moment. It was the million-dollar question.

"I love you," he said.

Her face flushed crimson. "Swann …"

He shook his head. "For your mind. Can we destroy it from here? Maybe. Maybe we can. I have a couple of friends at the National Security Agency. They've got drones flying that border perimeter between Georgia and Russia. I know they do."

He paused, trying to think through the ramifications of a drone strike from Georgian territory into Russia. It was a lot to chew on, and there wasn't a lot of time. Instead, he found himself just imagining a Predator drone, the latest thing in killing machines, flying silently through the night sky.

"We're not supposed to do this, but …"

"Do you think it's a good idea?" Trudy said.

Swann looked at the phone in his hand. He shrugged and started to dial a number.

"The whole thing's already a mess. What do we have to lose?"

"Luke? Luke! Forget the sub! Negative on sub!"

It was almost too loud to hear what Swann was saying.

Luke was crouched in the iron stairwell with the phone to his ear. It was getting hot in here. The ship was burning out of control. It was a firestorm. The reflections of flames flickered on the walls all around him. Every few moments, another piece of unexploded ordnance in one of the cargo holds blew up.

He stared out the doorway at the armored speedboat floating near the dock, catching hell from every direction. Neither Ed nor the Georgian had been able to tie the boat up.

"What?"

"Abort!" Swann screamed. "Abort mission! Escape with prisoners!"

The three American prisoners sat slumped in the stairwell, each clinging to the metal rail. Frenchy was at the doorway, peering around the corner. He cradled an Uzi in his hands. It was raining fire out there.

"What about the sub?" Luke said.

"Forget the sub! We will handle it!"

Who was going to handle it? Swann and Trudy? Well, that didn't make a whole lot of sense, unless they were planning to call in …

"Just get out of there!" Swann shouted. "Just get out!"

… an air strike.

"Get out!" Swann screamed. "Get out!"

Okay. There was no time to talk about the advisability of air strikes in this set of circumstances. If that's what they were going to do, they must have gotten clearance from on high, possibly as high as the Almighty himself.

"Roger!" Luke shouted into the phone.

"Out!" Swann screamed.

Luke hung up.

He peeked outside. There were the ripped and shredded remains of maybe half a dozen men littering the dock. The speedboat had drifted around, giving Luke its port side. He could see Ed inside a small armored booth, the snout of a heavy gun poking out. Ed was feeding the gun with one hand, firing with the other. There had been a delay of several moments while Ed reloaded the gun by himself.

The boat was being hit from the seawall, and from the shoreline to the far opposite side. They were triangulating fire, and the boat was caught in the middle of it.

DUH-DUH-DUH-DUH-DUH...

The metallic clank of Ed's gun cut through the noise. He raked the seawall, trying to finish off the last of the resistance over there. It was a good plan. If he could put a stop to those guys, then the gunfire would be coming from only one direction. Perhaps they could use the boat as a shield, and rush these guys...

zzzZZZZZZZ. Shooop. DING!

Some sort of rocket zipped out of the night, hit the speedboat, and bounced into the air without exploding. Luke and Frenchy both hit the deck instinctively.

Luke looked up at the stairwell. The three men sat there, slack-jawed. They barely noticed the rocket. The SEAL blinked and jerked his head away. That was the best he could do.

Luke sighed. This night was long, and getting longer. He looked out the doorway again. He had a new vantage point now—a worm's-eye view. To their left, flames shot up five stories high. Men, crouched low, were running through those flames.

DUH-DUH-DUH-DUH-DUH-DUH-DUH.

"Frenchy!" Luke shouted. "We gotta get out of here."

He pointed out the doorway at the men taking firing positions further up the dock.

Frenchy looked out. When he saw the men, his body seemed to lose all its air and bonelessly settle to the floor. Further back, men were racing up the opposite stairwell. They were probably going to work their way across the top deck, through that long hallway, and down these stairs. Luke gazed up the narrow empty stairwell.

Any minute now it was going to be full of Russians.

Frenchy rolled over, faced Luke, and unzipped his jacket. That jacket, inappropriate for a warm night like this … Frenchy opened it. Beneath the jacket, he was wearing a heavy leather vest. Luke stared at the familiar outlines of wired up grenades and pipe bombs, the latter probably stuffed with nails, encircling Frenchy's torso.

It was a suicide vest.

Luke shook his head. If he still needed confirmation, here it was. Frenchy was crazy.

"No, no," Luke said. "Don't do that. We'll think of something."

Frenchy slid his Uzi across the floor to Luke.

He smiled. "Boom," he said.

"Frenchy! The boat is right there! All we have to do is make it across this dock, get in the boat, and escape. That's all we have to do!"

Frenchy shook his head. The smile was still on his face, but now it looked very, very sad. "I don't come here to escape. I come to kill Russians. For my brothers. And my father. And my people."

"Frenchy!"

Frenchy pulled himself to his feet. "When boom comes, you go." He gestured out at the speedboat. It had drifted with the swells into the dock. It kept slapping the side of the dock, drifting out a couple of feet, then slapping the dock again. Ed was still raking the seawall. Things had quieted down over there. The boat was between Luke and the opposite shore. Maybe, just maybe …

Frenchy stepped out the doorway, hands held high, and started walking toward the men positioned down the dock.

Luke slapped his forehead. "Ah, no."

He pulled himself to his feet and went over to the men on the stairwell. "Get up!" he shouted at them. "Get up!" He slapped the first one, the CIA spook, across the face. The man looked at him with suddenly fierce eyes.

"Up!" Luke said. He grabbed the guy by the hair and yanked him to his feet. He looked at the Navy SEAL. "You! Get that man up! Let's go!" He pointed at the last in line, the heavyset submersible pilot.

The SEAL nodded groggily and pulled himself up. Then he turned, grabbed the man by his shirt front, and fell backward, pulling the man to his feet.

"Move your ass!" Luke screamed at the SEAL. "Get these men ready! We're bugging out!"

He went to the doorway and raised a STOP hand behind him.

"On my go."

Frenchy walked toward the men, hands high above his head. Even amidst the flames, Luke could see the men sighting on him. Frenchy was shouting something in Russian. Closer, closer, he kept walking toward them.

One of the men shouted something. Frenchy kept walking.

A muzzle flash and BANG!

Frenchy flinched, but kept walking.

A flurry of shots erupted.

BANG! BANG! BANG!

Frenchy jittered and fell to the deck. Luke heard himself groan.

That didn't work.

The Russians came out, guns drawn, moving cautiously. They approached Frenchy. Luke watched, but he couldn't tell if Frenchy was alive or dead. He wasn't moving. His body was just a big lump on the concrete decking.

Things had quieted down. Ed had stopped firing at the seawall. The crackle of gunfire slowed down from the distant shoreline. They were giving a ceasefire over there. They didn't want to hit the men on the dock.

"Wait..." Luke said, very quietly. "Wait..."

He readied the Uzi. Somewhere above him, he heard men running along an iron catwalk. They were coming.

Half a dozen men surrounded Frenchy's body. They didn't touch it. Luke knew this was for fear it was booby-trapped. A man jabbed at him with a rifle.

Then Frenchy blew up.

No warning. Just:

BOOOM!

There was a flash of light. Luke ducked way back. The ground shook beneath his feet. In the initial flash, he saw severed limbs flying. The limbs didn't worry him—it was the nails in the pipe bombs.

He counted to three.

One.

Two.

"Go!" he shouted. "Go! Let's go!"

He darted out onto the dock, rolled to the ground, and opened up with the Uzi. It bucked in his hands, making an ugly automatic blat. From the corner of his eye, he saw the SEAL pushing the other two men in front of him, toward the boat.

Good man. Good man. That guy had roused himself just enough to get it done.

Luke let loose with another burst from the Uzi.

Someone over there was firing back. Bullets rained around him. The shooting was coming from above him, not down the dock. He looked up—there were men on an iron catwalk three stories above his head.

He felt something very sharp, like a wasp sting, in his forearm. For an instant the pain was so blinding he thought he might be having a heart attack. The Uzi slid away from him.

He gritted his teeth. "Ow! Dammit!" He was hit.

Suddenly, the sound of Ed's heavy gun came again.

DUH-DUH-DUH-DUH-DUH-DUH.

The men on the catwalk jittered and jived as Ed sliced them up.

"Stone! Let's go!"

The speedboat's engine roared. A great, churning wake appeared behind it. Luke's ride was leaving.

He pressed up and ran in a low squat. Zing! Another bee sting in his lower right leg. Bullets were flying.

Just ahead, the boat had left the dock. There was a three-foot gap, growing bigger every second. Luke took two giant steps and leapt across the chasm. He hit the gunwale chest high and dragged himself over the lip. He tumbled into the boat.

The other three men were sprawled on the floor with him. The floor was awash in blood. He wasn't the only one who had been hit.

DUH-DUH-DUH-DUH-DUH-DUH-DUH.

Ed was firing everywhere at once.

The speedboat planed upward, the nose riding high. It took off at warp speed. Luke was rolled over and thrown against the stern. He lay just under the big engines, all of them screaming above his head. All he could hear was the noise of the engines.

He glanced up at them. They were each covered in thick steel armor plating.

Well, he had pretty much gone deaf in the last few minutes, so the noise didn't bother him much. And this was as good a place to hang out as any.

He closed his eyes, and for a moment got lost in the sensation of dark speed. He didn't want to think about anything. He didn't want to think about Frenchy, and the bloodbath they had left on the dock. He didn't want to think about the fact that at least one of the prisoners was bleeding and probably shot.

He didn't want to think about what Don Morris was going to say about all this.

He opened his eyes. He *really* didn't want to think about Don Morris right now. And he really didn't want to think about Don's superiors.

There was a helicopter in the sky above their heads, moving fast. A gunman was in the side bay doorway, and the pilot was trying to give him a shot. The chopper had a bright spotlight, shining down on the black water in front of them.

The big Georgian captain of this mongrel was aware of the chopper. All his lights were out. The boat was past the seawall already, entering open water, and he was trying to do a high-speed serpentine. Oh God. All the way to Georgia? There was no way.

Luke looked to the right. More lights in the sky were coming from the north. They were going to be sitting ducks down here.

If possible, he needed to get those men up and under the Georgian's cockpit canopy. It was going to be a tight fit, but…

He moved. "ANHHH!" He was in a lot of pain. For a moment, he had forgotten about that.

The choppers were converging. This was about to get ugly.

"Get up!" he told himself. "Get up!"

A bright light flashed behind him, if possible the brightest one of the entire night. There was a new explosion, very loud, so loud that Luke could barely discern the limits of it. For an instant, it drowned out the roar of the engines.

Luke looked back. The freighter had blown up again.

Had a reserve gas tank been hit? Luke was pretty sure the fuel tanks on that thing had already blown. Suddenly, a battery of missiles screamed out of the sky, hitting the ship again. The explosion was blinding. It was more like six explosions, happening all at once. Luke shielded his eyes to watch it.

"What the…"

The answer came to him an instant later.

"Swann."

Above their heads, the choppers peeled off, looking for whatever had just launched those missiles. The boat was moving so fast that behind them, the explosions began to dwindle into the distance.

Big Ed slithered out from under the steel box surrounding the machine gun. Ed's shirt was torn to shreds. He seemed to be bleeding from everywhere—his hands, his feet, his legs, his upper body. Luke pulled himself from under the engines and sat along the gunwale. Ed dropped down next to him.

"You hit?" Luke said.

Ed shrugged. "I don't know. Can't tell. Probably."

He looked at Luke. "You?"

Luke nodded. "Yeah."

"Bad?"

Now Luke shrugged. "I don't know."

Ed gestured at the former prisoners. The SEAL had pulled himself into a sitting position against the opposite gunwale. He hugged his knees. The other two were still sprawled on the bottom of the boat.

"These guys hit?" Ed said.

Luke nodded. "I think so. It was murder out there. Thick."

"How would you rate this operation?" Ed said.

"Rate it?" Luke said. "Like on a scale of one to ten?"

Ed nodded. "Sure."

Luke nearly laughed. He gazed back at the orange glow on the dark horizon. Absolutely nothing had gone the way he planned it. His original intention was to sneak on board the ship while the Russians were absorbed by the speedboat crash. Sneak in, grab the prisoners, blow the submersible, and muscle their way out on the second speedboat. If they went fast enough, maybe they'd be gone before anyone fired a shot.

No. None of that had happened. And yet, here they were, escaping to Georgia with the prisoners, and the submersible scuttled, to put it mildly.

"I'd rate it International Incident."

Ed laughed. Then Luke did. A fit of the giggles started to overcome them.

The Georgian speedboat driver looked back at them. His face was sweaty and gleaming. He smiled, then raised a large fist into the air.

"Next stop, my home country," he said. "Tonight, we drink!"

Chapter Nine

4:45 p.m. Eastern Daylight Time
The Situation Room
The White House, Washington, DC

"I was told to get those men out," Don Morris said.

He looked around the packed conference room. The place was a forest of eyes, all of them staring right at him. Eyes, eyes, everywhere he looked.

"And the men are out. I was told to scuttle that submersible. It's been destroyed."

Standing along the walls were the young people, the aides, the assistants, their eyes open and staring and concerned, but also serious, ready to punch numbers into their BlackBerries or scribble down notes. Those folks were of no concern to him.

Sitting with him at the oval table in the center were the bigwigs and heavy hitters, several of them military men who had once outranked him, his superior officers, many of them civilians with appointed posts close to the president.

These eyes were angry. They believed they had found their scapegoat, and they had hauled him in here to be raked over the coals.

Well, Don wasn't having it. Not for a minute, none of it. There wasn't a military man at this table who had seen and survived the combat Don had. There wasn't a civilian man or woman who knew the kind of guts, determination, and initiative it had taken to succeed in the operation Stone and Newsam had carried out today.

"You all wanted a Top Secret mission, with the Special Response Team going it alone. You got that. And if you happened to want a mission that punched through and exposed Russian vulnerabilities, you got that, too. In spades."

Was he mad at Stone and Newsam? Was he mad at Trudy Wellington and Mark Swann? You bet he was, and when they got back, he planned to kick their asses up and down the halls of SRT headquarters. But in the meantime, he'd be dipped if he was going to sell out his team in front of twerps like these.

They had his fire up, for sure.

Dick Stark of the Joint Chiefs was standing near the president.

"Don, no one here is looking to blame you for what happened. I think the president, and the rest of the people assembled here, just want to understand what happened out there, and why. Mr. President, would you agree with that?"

Alone among the people in the room, President David Barrett's eyes seemed vacant, unfocused, maybe even dazed. That wasn't good. The United States and Russia were toe to toe right now, and one thing America needed at a time like this was confident, decisive leadership.

The president nodded. "I would, yes."

Don suspected that at this moment, David Barrett would answer nearly any question put to him in the same way.

"Mr. President, would you like a large cheeseburger, medium rare?"

"I would, yes."

"Mr. President, would you say that mole people live deep under the earth?"

Nevertheless, Don softened his stance in deference to the leader of the free world. "Mr. President, the operation took place a short while ago, and in some sense is still in motion, but I'm happy to report on the broad outlines of it, as I understand them."

"Please do," the president said.

Don nodded. He had no PowerPoint display of the operation. He had nothing on paper. He'd given Stone a great deal of leeway to birth it or abort it on the fly, depending how the circumstances looked on the ground. He knew what Stone had pitched him, he knew that it was creative, daring, and dicey as hell. And he gave Stone the green light.

"We infiltrated Russia with four men," Don said. "Two Special Response Team operatives led the operation, the same men who rescued your daughter six weeks ago, Mr. President. I believe those two men may be the best special operators America has in her arsenal. Certainly among the best.

"They went in separately, and were accompanied by a member of the Chechen resistance and a highly regarded Georgian commando, both men combat experienced."

Don paused.

"As we understand it, the Chechen blew himself up with a suicide belt," a man said. He was a thin man with sandy hair in a blue dress shirt and wire frame glasses. "He took out several Sochi policemen. Our using an Islamic extremist in an operation, who himself employs a technique so closely associated with the terrorist atrocities in Beslan and Moscow... well, you can all gauge the optics on that for yourselves."

Don stared at the man. "Who are you, please?"

The man nodded. He didn't look up from the papers in front of him. "Paul Neal, Associate Director, Office of Russian and European Analysis, Central Intelligence Agency."

"Well, Paul Neal, the president asked me to report on the operation. Do you mind if I finish doing that?"

The man waved a hand at him. This was the hard part for Don. This was always going to be the hard part. He was accustomed to being treated with respect, and to his credibility and authority being unquestioned. Some of these people...

He shook his head and went on.

"The attack was two-pronged, something of a pincer movement. Agent Stone and the Chechen approached the docks by land, Agent Newsam and the Georgian in two separate speedboats. The initial attack by sea was a modified version of the October 2000 Sudanese and Al Qaeda attack on the USS *Cole*..."

Don shrugged and smiled just a touch. "Minus the suicide part, of course. I haven't spoken to my operatives yet, but it appears the attack was devastatingly effective. Not only did it severely damage the Russian freighter holding the submersible, it sowed confusion and chaos among the defenders, allowing Agent Stone and his partner to storm the front gate and overwhelm the defenders there."

Don looked around for any more challenges. None were immediately forthcoming.

"Within moments, Stone and his partner reached and freed the prisoners. Moments later, the second speedboat arrived, and under heavy fire, the prisoners were transferred to the speedboat, and the team made its escape.

"My understanding is that the freed prisoners are now in CIA custody, moving through a network of Georgian safe houses, and may in fact already be safely out of the country."

He stared at the CIA man. "Would you agree with that assessment, Vice Deputy whatever you are?"

The man looked up. His bland eyes met Don's. "The men are at a military hospital in Israel. We needed to get them somewhere friendly that was nearby and had top-quality medical care available. Between the three of them, they sustained nineteen gunshot wounds during the rescue. The civilian submersible pilot, Peter Bolger, appears to have suffered a heart attack of unknown severity."

"Will they pull through?" Don said.

The man looked at his paperwork. "All three men are considered in serious but stable condition. They will be debriefed when their conditions allow it."

Don looked at the president. "The prisoners were rescued. The high-tech submersible was scuttled. The three surviving members of the infiltration team all received gunshot injuries as well, but are expected to pull through. All of my SRT operatives are en route to the United States, on timetables and using methods that will safeguard their identities. The fact that this caused diplomatic trouble was baked in from the very beginning. If we want to avoid problems like this in the future, I'd suggest being more judicious about where we plant our submarines, and which operatives carrying sensitive information we put in the field."

Dick Stark was still standing. His face, stern before, seemed disappointed now. He turned to one of his aides. "Roger, can you give us a rundown of the most recent intelligence assessments so that Director Morris has a clearer idea…"

"Dick," Don began.

But the general put his hand up. "Don, you were a great soldier and you're a great American. But you need to hear this. It's not a rodeo out there. Frankly, this has been my concern about you from the start. And believe me when I say I've voiced my concerns to the FBI director, and to the president. You're a cowboy, Don, and you always have been. But the era of cowboys and Indians is over."

Don said nothing to that.

"Roger?"

The aide looked down at the papers in his hand. The paperwork had been passed to him from a runner who had come bustling in moments ago with a pile of printouts.

The aide cleared his throat.

"Intelligence analysts assessing the situation at the Port of Adler docks are calling the operation a bloodbath. American and allied forces appear to have taken the Russians completely by surprise and wiped out somewhere between twenty and forty Russian military, private security, police, and firefighting personnel."

He turned over a sheet of paper.

"At approximately eleven forty-five p.m. local time, three forty-five our time, less than ninety minutes ago, a Predator drone controlled by the United States National Security Agency made multiple strikes on the *Yuri Andropov II* freighter, docked at Port of Adler. To be clear, Port of Adler is located inside Russian Federation territory. This is thought to be the only direct act of aggression against Russian soil in American history. The attack circumvented normal chains of command. It was apparently requested by Agent Mark Swann of the FBI Special Response Team, and was carried out without authorization by an unnamed NSA drone pilot. Apparently, the two men are friends."

The aide looked up, allowing the full weight of what he had just said to sink in with his audience. Two guys, drinking buddies probably, working at different agencies, had gotten together over the phone and decided to attack Russia.

Don shook his head. Swann!

It was upsetting, of course, but at the same time, it was almost comical. He wanted his people to show initiative. But drone strikes on the Russian mainland took the initiative a little too far.

The aide went on:

"Immediately after the attack, American listening stations throughout the world began to pick up alarming Russian military chatter. Uh ... the Russians appear to be treating this as an unprovoked act of war. As of four p.m. Eastern Daylight Time, Russian Strategic Command has mobilized far-reaching military assets. Infantry units have sealed the major border crossings between Russia and Georgia, and additional infantry as well as heavy tank and artillery units have begun to mass along that border. More infantry units are moving to the border between Russia and Ukraine.

"Russian Navy units have seized the Crimean port of Sebastopol, and taken Ukrainian sentries there prisoner. A Russian naval strike force is moving into the Bosporus Strait, and we believe that very soon the strait will be closed to shipping traffic, cutting off trade to two dozen ports in Ukraine, Romania, and Bulgaria."

"They can't do that," someone said. "It's against every—"

"The Turkish government has already lodged complaints with the Russians themselves, the United Nations, and the NATO Supreme Headquarters Allied Powers Europe. However, there isn't much that can be done about it at this time. If the Russians want to take that strait, they're going to. For all intents and purposes, Russian naval assets operate virtually unchallenged in the Black Sea."

The aide turned another page over and continued.

"As of four fifteen p.m., the Russian natural gas pipelines delivering fuel supplies to the Czech Republic, Poland, and Germany have begun to shut down. Obviously, this is summer so these deliveries are not as crucial as they would be in winter. However, if this becomes a long-term standoff, each of these countries will face natural gas shortages within short timeframes. In particular, Poland has few reserves and at current usage rates will be out of gas, so to speak, in fourteen days or less.

"More concerning, Russian bombers and fighter planes have begun patrolling at the edge of American airspace in the Bering Strait, and have penetrated across the Arctic Ocean, testing British RAF response in the North Sea, and buzzing Canadian airspace over Newfoundland and Labrador. American fighter jets have made very dangerous visual contact—repeat, visual contact—with Russian fighters in the airspace between Iceland and Canada."

The aide turned over the next page and skimmed it before reading aloud. He was a young man, perhaps in his early thirties. He was obviously concerned about the things he was reading. He cleared his throat again and breathed deeply.

Despite the aide's deep concern, Don found himself somewhat comforted by the initial actions of the Russians. They were angry, and perhaps justifiably so. But the moves they had made were always at their fingertips. They could close the Black Sea to shipping, or turn off natural gas supplies to central Europe, any time they wanted.

Without American intervention, they should be able to run right over the Georgians and the Ukrainians. Hell, they could probably take Crimea without firing a shot. It was part of Ukraine, but most of the population was Russian.

They were rattling sabers a little bit.

And the fighter planes buzzing American airspace? That part was a dog and pony show. We knew it, and so did they. Those old Soviet MiG-29s were so much target practice for our advanced F/A-18s. The Russians weren't going to dogfight us with their Cold War leftovers. We would turn their Air Force into Swiss cheese.

"It's a measured response," Don said. "They haven't attacked anyone or anything. Not yet, anyway."

The aide coughed. Then he spoke again.

"Perhaps most worrisome, more than two hundred missile silos across the Russian heartland and Siberia are reporting states of combat readiness. These include launch silos for nuclear-equipped intercontinental ballistic missiles targeting the United States.

"Intelligence assessments suggest that the major danger here is not that the Russians will launch a massive first strike. The danger is that Russian command and control has degraded significantly in the years since the collapse of the Soviet Union. Our analysts are concerned that during an extended crisis, Russian Strategic Command could either lose contact with outlying silos or installations, or that communications could become unclear or misunderstood. According to the assessments we have, there is a very real danger of Russia launching a missile or missiles by mistake."

He took another deep breath.

"Our own missile defense system remains as robust as ever. Any nuclear missile attack launched by the Russians, whether on purpose or in error, will trigger a massive response from us. And we have to assume that such a response from us will in turn trigger a massive response from them."

The aide turned over the paper and looked at Dick Stark.

Stark looked at Don.

"Don, your explosive little foray into Russian territory has put on the verge of World War Three."

What do you want me to do?

David almost said it to them. He was sitting in the Oval Office with the group of them. The carpet beneath their feet had the Seal of the President. It was ringed with a quotation from Franklin Delano Roosevelt: *The only thing we have to fear, is fear itself.* The tall blue drapes were pulled, shutting out the natural daylight. Two big Secret Service men stood by the door.

The meeting was David Barrett, Vice President Mark Baylor, Richard Stark, and Stark's aide Roger. David had dismissed Don Morris back to his agency, and that made him sad. He would prefer if Don were here. He would prefer if this meeting was just him and Don, maybe having a light meal. He liked Don Morris, he liked his straight talking ways, his fearlessness, his leadership, and his tougher than leather exterior. If life had been different, he imagined that he and Don could have been friends.

"I know domestic issues are not my department," Richard Stark said. "But you should be aware that protests have cropped up in Russian expatriate communities in Brooklyn, in New Jersey, in Cleveland and Los Angeles. Also London. The ones in Brooklyn and London have turned violent, and our assessments suggest that the violence is being instigated by Russian intelligence assets embedded within those communities. This may call for a response from us."

He turned and looked at his aide. "Roger?"

The aide gazed down at the paperwork in his hand. "American naval strike forces are reporting high states of readiness across all theaters. Should it become necessary, we have nuclear-armed submarines operating in the Bering Sea, the North Sea, the Pacific, and the Arctic Ocean ready to deliver retaliatory strikes on our go. We have a dozen bomber wings currently flying with fighter escorts at the limits of international airspace. They are prepared to leave their holding patterns and make deep runs into Soviet, uh, Russian territory upon receiving the order from Strategic Command. American missile defense is reporting four hundred silos at combat readiness. Three hundred more will be brought to readiness within an hour."

Roger flipped the page over. The man was a master at recounting the statistics of mass murder with a complete lack of emotion.

"We've been in touch with the Chairman of the Joint Chiefs of Staff. At this time, the Pentagon leadership wants to elevate worldwide readiness, including Strategic Air Command, NORAD, and all branches of the military from DEFCON level 4, where we have been for the past eight months, to DEFCON level 3. This will mean the Air Force is ready to mobilize in fifteen minutes. Other critical assets will be combat ready within six to twenty-four hours. Naturally, the Russians will intercept these communications, and will understand we mean business. There is broad consensus that making the change is necessary and prudent in the current environment. We just await your orders, or the orders of the secretary of defense, to do so."

David Barrett was one just person, and these were gigantic, impersonal forces at work. If fully unleashed, they could destroy everyone and everything on earth. It was too much for one person to digest, never mind come to any meaningful decisions about.

Couldn't they see that?

"Mr. President?"

There were billions of people on earth. So many that no one really knew the actual number. There were hedge fund managers living in fifty-million-dollar penthouse apartments in Manhattan, private chefs cooking them dinner. There were Stone Age tribes living in thatched huts deep in the Amazon jungle, hunting their food with poison blow darts. The... *diversity*... There was almost something surreal about it.

There were hundreds of millions of people in the United States and Russia alone. They had massive armies and thousands of nuclear missiles. Tanks, airplanes, submarines, spy satellites. Secret agents silently stabbing each other to death in alleyways. What the hell was it all for?

"Mr. President," General Stark said. "I understand that your family is currently vacationing at your family's ranch in Texas. May I recommend that for the duration of the crisis, they immediately be evacuated to the Cheyenne Mountain Complex in Colorado? By plane, Cheyenne is very close to their location, and is the most secure nuclear bunker we have. It can withstand a nearly direct hit by a thirty-megaton warhead. The valve system there is the most advanced in terms of filtering radiological contaminants from the outside air. In the event of…"

The general paused, apparently looking for a word that might describe what he had in mind. Armageddon? The Apocalypse?

This was stupid talk, frankly. Plain stupid. It was better to have a barbecue with friends and family in the backyard than to talk about these things.

His daughter Elizabeth was *alive.* It was amazing to realize that. First she was gone and everyone was sure she was dead. Then she was alive, and home. But not well. After everything that had happened, she might never be well again. She was seeing a therapist twice a week. She wasn't going to school this fall.

He sighed. He felt like he might begin crying any minute. He felt like his mind was coming apart.

He wanted to tell these men that, he really did. *"I'm the president here, and my mind is coming apart."* But you couldn't say that.

Instead, he kept his mouth shut, and let General Richard Stark of the Joint Chiefs of Staff prattle on importantly from across the sitting area, with his aide preening in the chair next to him. It had taken David this long to grasp what the man reminded him of. This aide in dress greens, this Lieutenant Colonel Roger, whoever he was, looked an awful lot like a praying mantis.

To David's right, Vice President Mark Baylor sat upright with one leg crossed over the other. Baylor hadn't been at the briefing, and so far he hadn't said a word in this meeting, but it didn't matter. He was never far away these days. All of a sudden, he was David Barrett's right-hand man.

He was like a vulture sitting over a hospital bed, waiting for the patient to die. Baylor was a carnivore, and he had the instincts of a hyena. Late one night they would find him crouched on David Barrett's body, feasting on his flesh.

Baylor was tall, like David Barrett himself was. But he was also broad, getting broader and thicker all the time. The man liked donuts, that was well known. And he liked fried chicken. He was going to give himself a stroke if he wasn't careful.

Fact was, Baylor was a mess. He was growing fat. His teeth were too large. His hair was already white, and he did nothing to remedy that situation. David guessed that Baylor thought the white hair gave him gravitas.

He guessed wrong.

The man was a simpleton. His major claim to fame was that he came from a rich, blue-blood, old money family, but he went and fought in Vietnam anyway. Call it *noblesse oblige* run amok. The man had deferred his entry to Yale for a year, joined the Marine Corps, raced to the other side of the world, managed to engineer a couple of minor gunshot wounds in the leg, and was back in New Haven in time to ogle the co-eds at freshman orientation.

David Barrett, also from old money, had skipped Vietnam. It was optional for a young man from his background, and he had better things to do with his time. Boy, they never let that go, did they? If someone had told him that this decision would follow him the rest of his life …

But it didn't really matter, did it? He still became president of the United States. And the big-toothed American hero Mark Baylor got to be his understudy.

"Mr. President?" Richard Stark said. His eyes showed a look of concern. Was it concern for his president's well-being? Probably not. He was probably just worried that his boss was no longer listening to him.

"Let's take a break, guys," President David Barrett said. "Okay? Leave these assessments with me and I'll go over them this evening. I'm going to call my wife and my parents and see how they feel about this evacuation plan. In the meantime, with everything else, steady as she goes."

"We'd like your order to go to DEFCON level 3," Stark said.

Barrett raised a hand. "Richard, let's just hold our horses, stay where we are, and continue to monitor the situation."

The eyes of the three other men in the meeting told him that was the wrong answer. Those eyes seemed to dart back and forth, imparting information to each other that David couldn't understand.

A wave of unreality suddenly washed over him. It was almost as if these men were imposters. Those hostile, angry eyes seemed to be set deep inside rubber masks.

No. It was impossible.

"General, I appreciate all of your recommendations," David said. "And I will take them under advisement. But the end of the world can wait a few more hours."

Those few hours passed, and then a couple more.

The shadows outside the tall windows grew long, then dark began to settle in. David Barrett did not open the heavy drapes. He did not want to see the sun setting on a warm early summer night. He did not want to think about summer at all.

He did not want to think about the crowds gathering to watch the Nationals play baseball. He did not want to think about people at the Delaware beaches, or in boats on Chesapeake Bay, catching the glorious fire of the sun as day became night. He knew that the people were out there, doing these things. *He knew it.*

In here, we were supposedly having a crisis. We had done a bad thing, spying on the Russians. Then the Russians did a worse thing, taking our spies prisoner and stealing our little submarine. Then we topped it with an even worse thing. Now they were toying with doing very bad things. And if they did them, then we would have to…

"David?"

Were we children? Was that what it was? We had never graduated from childhood? It was sure beginning to seem that way.

"David, please."

He looked up and noticed he was sitting in the same tall-backed chair he had occupied during the meeting with General Stark and Mark Baylor. That meeting had happened hours ago. He had taken his dinner right here in the Oval Office, and had never moved from this chair.

He had dismissed his Secret Service men long ago, though he was sure there was at least one still standing out in the hallway. The truth was he had begun tracking their movements. And that was odd because his daughter, Elizabeth, must have been doing the exact same thing, in the days before she…

"David!"

He nodded. "Yes."

Sitting across from him was Kathy Grumman, his new chief of staff. David had hired her when he banished Lawrence Keller to Legislative Affairs after the crisis with Elizabeth's kidnapping had been resolved.

Kathy had come from the State Department, where she had been chief-bottle-washer or some such. David couldn't remember now. He knew she had come highly recommended. And when he met her, he liked her personally. In fact, he still did. He just didn't really care what she had to say anymore.

"We need to develop a strategy to deal with the events that are unfolding," Kathy said. "The Pentagon brass are very upset that they didn't get to move their little DEFCON needle one number to the right. The protest in Brighton Beach, Brooklyn, has devolved into a full-on riot, with looting of shops, arson, and shots fired. There are almost certainly agents provocateurs mixed in with the crowds there. The Russians have closed the Strait of Bosporus, against international maritime law, and we need to determine a response. The United Nations General Assembly is going to vote tomorrow morning to condemn our rescue action at Sochi.

"The Russians have ordered their embassy staff, right up to the ambassador, to leave for London as soon as possible, and have given our Moscow embassy personnel twenty-four hours to leave the country. None of this takes into account the troops massed at the borders of Georgia and Ukraine, the ramped up missile defense readiness on both sides of the fence, or the fact that our fighters and theirs continue to make repeated visual contact in various parts of the world."

David stared at Kathy. She was probably about forty-five years old, with blonde hair just going gray. She was well-preserved, attractive even. She had blue reading glasses that hung on a silver chain. She was wearing a dark blue skirt suit. The hemline was conservative, just above the knee.

She had never married, so he understood. Married to her work, he guessed. You almost had to be. These people around here, they were very ambitious. Jobs at the White House weren't handed out for free on street corners.

She was still speaking, her face serious. For a moment, he felt very sad for her. All that sacrifice, and where had she gotten herself? Here? With him? For what? Didn't she understand that there were baseball games and barbecues going on?

"At this point, I'm concerned that events are racing out ahead of us," she said now. "We haven't made any sort of statement acknowledging the gravity of the situation, nor have we come up with anything like a cogent plan of action. Respectfully, I'd like to request that you give me free rein to move forward on…"

David raised a hand. "Kathy, let me stop you for a minute. I've heard everything you said. Here are my answers. The guys at the Pentagon are always pining to go to DEFCON whatever. If there isn't a war, or the threat of one, then what are they supposed to do all day? I think we can safely ignore them for the time being.

"Meanwhile, a riot in Brighton Beach sounds like something for the New York City Police Department to worry about. If you want, feel free to call Mayor Dietz and tell him we're pulling for them over here. We're in their corner. I'll even do it, if you set up the call for me.

"Next, if the Russians have closed the Black Sea to international shipping traffic, that sounds like we need to lodge a complaint with someone."

Kathy nodded. "We already have. So have the Turks, the Romanians, the Bulgarians, the Ukrainians, the Greeks, and the Georgians. Once the General Assembly is finished condemning us tomorrow morning, it's likely they're going to condemn the Russians immediately afterward."

David shrugged. "See? There you go."

He and Kathy stared at each other for a long moment.

"David," she said, "I think you might not be fully grasping that with the possible exception of the Cuban Missile Crisis, the United States and Russia are as close to war as we've ever been. They are furious about what happened at Sochi, and are refusing to negotiate or even speak with us. Meanwhile, a shooting war could break out at any one of a dozen flashpoints at any time, and there are real concerns among our intelligence community about command and control of Russian missile defense. An errant nuclear launch is all it would take..."

He nodded. "Yeah. It's a big problem. I get that."

"Have you turned on the TV? The press is hammering us, and so far our response is that we are crafting a plan, which we will announce shortly. Things are dangerously close to being out of control. And at least as of this moment, we are not demonstrating the leadership needed to guide this situation to a positive outcome. It's not the mayor of New York's problem. It's not the UN's problem. We need to take the reins here, David."

He could see her point. Of course he could. He was the president. He didn't get here by not understanding things. He recognized that there was a crisis going on. He just didn't feel up to the job of managing it.

"Kathy, I think I may be going insane," he almost said.

But he didn't say that. The president of the United States didn't say things like that, even if they were true.

"Okay," he said. "Have me some remarks drafted. Hit all the right notes. Our fervent desire to work with the Russians to deescalate. Our absolute right to rescue American citizens who have been held incommunicado by a foreign power. How we stand firm with people of good will everywhere. Our willingness to work with the UN to broker some sort of deal. Whatever doesn't declare war, and makes sense to all of our stakeholders."

She took a sheet of paper from her stack and handed it to him. "Already done."

He gazed at the paper in his hand. "Thank you. I'll look this over and get back to you. We can do the statement first thing in the morning, a briefing format, no live reporters in the room."

Kathy shook her head. "David, I was thinking tonight. It's just about nine thirty. It's a short speech. If we do it now, a lot of networks will interrupt programming for it, and we'll get a lot of coverage on the eleven o'clock news. We can put surrogates to defend it on the late night cable shows."

David shook his head. "I haven't even read it yet."

"Tomorrow morning is too late, David. The Russians are eight hours ahead of us. We can't let this go on all night."

David finally felt something stirring within him. It was anger. She was drifting toward insubordination here.

"Kathy, I just gave you my answer. I'm tired. I'm going to review the speech, chew on it a bit, and then I'll probably go to bed. I suggest you go home, relax, enjoy yourself, then get back here bright and early tomorrow morning, ready to work."

He paused, wondering if he was going to say the next thing in his mind.

Yeah. He was.

"In other words, get out of my office."

Chapter Ten

10:15 p.m. Eastern Daylight Time
Georgetown
Washington, DC

It was getting late. Nearly time for bed.

That's when the telephone rang.

Lawrence Keller sat in the living room of his Georgetown brownstone, sipping a cup of hot hibiscus tea. CNN was on the TV, with the sound muted. They were covering the Russia crisis non-stop. All Russia, all the time.

Keller sighed. He was fifty-two years old, and had been a long distance runner his entire adult life. Recently, his doctor had told him his blood pressure had crept up into the hypertension range.

What did the man expect? After the past couple of months he'd had, anybody's blood pressure would be up. Unlike most people, however, Keller had resolved to do something about it. Something besides going on medication. It wasn't like he could start an exercise program. He already got more exercise than ninety percent of the population.

Hibiscus tea was his answer. If you drank it every day, supposedly over time it lowered your blood pressure. Well, the jury was still out on that. But in the meantime, it did have the benefit of making him sleepy.

He stared at the phone, still ringing, still insistent. It was after ten o'clock. Who would be calling him this time of night? The answering machine picked up, but whoever was on the other end hung up as soon as Keller's voice came on.

Wrong number.

Then the phone started ringing again. He picked it up but didn't answer. The caller ID was blocked.

Keller wasn't interested in speaking to anyone, especially not a drunk-dialing old friend or former military buddy. He had been divorced for ten years. His daughters were grown women who lived on the west coast, Seattle and San Jose, respectively. He spent much of his time alone these days, and he preferred it that way.

After his divorce, Keller had thrown himself into his work, and had clawed his way to become chief of staff to the president of the United States. That arrangement had lasted until six weeks ago.

When David Barrett had fallen apart after Elizabeth was kidnapped, Keller had become David's eyes and ears in the Situation Room. It was possible that Keller had saved the world from nuclear disaster—he was no longer quite sure. And after it was all over, how had Barrett thanked him? By showing him the door and kicking him downstairs to Legislative Affairs.

Well, Lawrence Keller would be dipped in brown sauce before he would work in Legislative Affairs. He had taken a leave of absence and was burning through the personal time he had accrued during decades of government service.

The phone started ringing again. Keller pressed the green button.

"Yes. Can I help you?"

He recognized the voice instantly. How could he forget the sound of the man who had been his boss for years?

"Lawrence, it's David. I need to speak with you."

Keller had been watching the news coverage for the past several hours. Once again, the world was on the brink. And he realized that in the back of his mind, he had almost been expecting this call. Not a sure thing, certainly not. But he wasn't surprised by it.

"David, I'm happy to talk anytime you like. I know it must feel like you have a lot on your plate right now."

Keller thought David would like that phrasing. The man was weak, and he often talked in terms of his feelings. In Keller's experience, the thinking David Barrett did was constantly being polluted by feelings. Often enough, his thoughts made no sense at all.

"I heard you left Legislative Affairs," Barrett said.

"I didn't leave. I never went there in the first place."

"So you're available?"

This was already going somewhere Keller enjoyed. Kathy Grumman was well meaning enough, and was reasonably effective as bureaucrats went. But chief of staff to the president? She was hardly made of that kind of material.

"Yes. I'm available. What do you have in mind, David?"

"I need to talk to you," Barrett said. "In confidence."

Keller smiled. David wasn't offering him his old job back. Not yet. And that was just fine. Keller's mind jumped a few moves ahead, looking for something he might get out of this that was even better than his old job.

"Fine. I can call tomorrow and schedule a meeting through your people, if you like, or you could put it on the schedule yourself."

"Not like that," Barrett said. For a split second, his voice sounded agitated.

It was a strange thing to say. Keller waited.

"Later tonight, I don't know what time, possibly quite late, you'll get a call from a number you don't recognize. When the call comes, pick it up."

"Okay, David."

"Thank you," Barrett said. "Speak with you later."

The line went dead.

Keller had a flashback to a moment when he was in the Oval Office with David. David had been standing behind the Resolute Desk, the great old mammoth nineteenth-century wooden desk that had been a gift from Great Britain.

He remembered thinking that David Barrett was too small for the desk. Not because David was a small man physically—he wasn't. In fact, he much larger than the average man, probably at least six feet five inches tall. He was dwarfed by that desk because he was too small for the job. Great men had stood at that desk, confronting gigantic problems. Old photos of JFK during the Cuban Missile Crisis often showed Kennedy and his advisors around the desk. David Barrett didn't belong at that desk.

Keller had always known this about him. Their relationship had been a marriage of convenience—David had stumbled into the presidency through a confluence of family connections, money, good looks, and grooming. Their own party had installed Keller as David's chief of staff, with the hope that Keller could guide the man through the minefield of his own lazy mind and awful instincts.

It hadn't worked, and now David had wandered into yet another disaster he had no idea how to handle. Without someone like Lawrence Keller around to do his thinking for him, David was like a homeless waif, the survivor of a shipwreck, clinging to a piece of flotsam and drifting wherever the currents took him.

The phone rang again. Keller picked it up at once.

"Grand Central Terminal," he said.

"Do you know who this is?" a voice said.

Of course he knew the voice. Getting a call from the president of the United States was not such a simple thing. They were monitoring David's phone. They had heard everything that was just said. It was a wonder they still hadn't figured out how to listen to people's thoughts. In any event:

"Yes," Keller said.

"My guess is you'd like to find your way back to relevance again."

Keller shrugged. "The thought had crossed my mind."

Maybe *this* was the opportunity that was better than returning to chief of staff. Then again, maybe it wasn't. He had done these people a favor not that long ago, was ushered into a room full of psychopathic warmongers, and quickly found himself out on the street.

"Our friend has been acting strangely, even for him. We're concerned that he won't be able to stomach the meal set before him."

"Does that surprise you?" Keller said.

The person at the other end of the line ignored the question. "Do you know where he plans to call you from?"

Keller shook his head. "The White House? Camp David? His family ranch in Texas? I have no idea. You would know better than I. This was the first time I've spoken with him in more than a month."

"Okay," the voice said. "Then here's what I need you to do…"

Chapter Eleven

June 27
3:35 a.m. Eastern Daylight Time
Headquarters of the Special Response Team
McLean, Virginia

"Sir?" someone said. "Sir, we're here."

Luke snapped awake. He sat up. It took him several seconds to figure out his surroundings.

He was inside the confines of a helicopter, riding in darkness. The chopper was new, and the interior was plush and comfortable. The seats were leather and hadn't even begun to scuff yet. He knew this chopper well. It was a beautiful bird, the sleek black Bell 430 that Don had acquired for the Special Response Team.

One of the pilots was looking back at him. He was a clean-shaven young guy in a helmet, cherub face, probably just out of the military. His helmet had a small microphone adjusted just above the chin strap. The kid was smiling.

"You dozed off, sir."

"Right," Luke said.

He blinked and looked out the tinted windows. Just to his right, north, were the bright lights of Washington, DC, and its close suburbs, Arlington, Alexandria, and the rest. He could see reflections on the water where the wide river emptied into the bay. To the south, there was less light as the suburbs did their slow fade into rural Virginia.

The chopper began to drop down, and Luke could see the helipad approaching. The SRT headquarters was a wide, squat, three-story building made of glass and steel. It had been a HUD building until recently, but they had given it a bit of a facelift when Don's team moved in. The windows sparkled in the lights of the approaching helicopter.

The bird was low now, the building, its parking lot, and the small green campus rising up to greet it. A signalman in a yellow vest and holding bright orange wands stood to the side of the helipad and guided the chopper in.

The pilot set the bird down perfectly in the middle of the pad. He killed the engine and the rotors immediately began to slow. There was a whine as they powered down.

"Thanks, guys," Luke shouted.

He climbed out of the passenger cabin with his bags, ducked low, and crossed the tarmac. He was inside a fenced-in security area, the fence topped with barbed wire. It was a cool, breezy night. The breeze felt good on his skin. He felt good. Tired, in some pain, but overall… okay. He knew there were problems waiting for him here, but he was confident they could be worked out.

What was it a wise man had once said? *You have to crack a few eggs to make an omelet.* Well, he and Ed had cracked a few eggs. A few dozen, in fact. And Swann had, you know, vaporized an entire egg factory, but…

Luke nearly laughed at the thought of it. Overkill. That was probably overkill.

A small, slim figure stood at the open security door to the building. As he approached, the figure resolved itself into Trudy Wellington. She wore a dark shirt and slacks. Her long hair was tied back into a bun.

She held the door wide for him. He walked through, a bag on his shoulder and one in his right hand.

"Any word on Ed?" he said to her without preamble.

She nodded. "He's okay. They took him to Baghdad. Turns out he got hit eight times. He had a bullet lodged in his thigh and needed emergency surgery to take it out. It was an inch from his femoral artery. He's lucky."

"He's lucky he has thighs as big as twenty-pound turkeys," Luke said. "How did he come through surgery?"

"Fine. He's stable. They have a cover story for him. He's a consultant who got hit during an ambush while coming in from the airport. He's going to be recuperating there for a few days."

Luke smiled. "His old stomping grounds. He's gonna love that."

"How was your trip?" Trudy said.

Luke shrugged. "I barely remember. They put me on painkillers, and a Georgian military doctor took the shrapnel out of my forearm and my calf right there on the plane. If you've never had gunshot wounds cleaned inside an eight-seat Lear jet flying above thunderstorms over Greece, I can't really say I recommend it."

He stopped and looked down at her. Behind her big round glasses, her eyes were tired. Her face looked drawn.

"You?" he said.

She nodded. "Fine. We left Turkey as soon as the mission was over." She shook her head. "I mean, when that dock blew, we just packed up everything in five minutes and got out of there. We landed about two hours ago. The trip was uneventful until we got home."

They were moving down the hall. All the office lights were out. The small cafeteria was closed and locked. There was no one around. Why would there be? It was nearly four in the morning. What was Trudy doing, lurking in this building by herself?

"Swann here?" Luke said.

"Don sent him home. Luke, Swann's been suspended, pending an investigation."

Luke's shoulders slumped. He shook his head and sighed. "Ah, man."

"Don's in his office, waiting to see you when you come in. There's trouble, Luke. There's been a lot of fallout."

Luke didn't have much to say to that. "Okay."

He turned left at the darkened foyer to Don's office. His door was open a crack and the light was on. Trudy lingered at the threshold of the foyer.

"Good luck," she said.

"Thank you. Hopefully I won't need it."

He went in. Don was sitting behind the wide expanse of his desk. The desk was like a football field. It was like the hood of an old Chevy muscle car. Outside of the office phone and a computer monitor, there was nothing on top of it.

Luke put his bags down.

"Don, I take full responsibility for the drone strike. Okay? One of the objectives of this mission was to scuttle that sub, and it wasn't going to happen. We were caught in a full-on shitstorm. That freighter was an ordnance dump, and we had no way of knowing that beforehand. Everything was blowing up. We didn't even have a visual on the sub. If we didn't get out when we did, everyone would have died. Swann calling in a drone strike didn't just kill the sub, it probably saved our necks."

Don looked at him and gestured at one of the chairs across from him. His eyes were flat and hard. "Sit down, son."

To Don's right, Luke's left, the flat-screen TV on the wall was on. It was CNN, showing reruns of news from earlier in the night. On the screen was video of a blonde-haired woman, maybe thirty-five years old, taken in what seemed like the late afternoon. She was astonishingly beautiful, in a bright blue blazer and white dress shirt. She was standing at a bank of microphones, holding some sort of press conference.

Senator Susan Hopkins (D)—California read the caption at the bottom left-hand side of the screen.

Luke raised his eyebrows. "Wow. That's the senator from California? I thought it was an old guy."

"There are two, as I'm sure you must know," Don said. "The other one is an old guy. This one is a freshman, just got elected last year. She was some kind of supermodel before this, cover of *Bimbette* magazine and all that. Her husband is a dotcom billionaire. This is who the people in their wisdom are voting for these days."

Don turned up the sound from a remote control in his hand.

"Once again," Senator Hopkins said sternly, "our military has blundered into a disaster of its own making, carrying out an unprovoked attack on a sleeping giant, the only other major nuclear-armed power in the world. Do they want to start a world war? I don't think I need to remind anyone that a nuclear confrontation between the United States and Russia has the potential to end all life on earth as we know it."

She paused, and turned over a page in front of her. The narrow black podium in front of her looked like something a musician would use for sheet music. She made eye contact with the cameras again.

"So-called black operations, black budgets with no Congressional oversight, black sites where prisoners are taken without due process and are routinely tortured. The American people are tired of the Pentagon giving this great country a black eye in the rest of the world. My office has strenuously requested that the details of this unprecedented attack be made public, but we are being stonewalled by the ..."

Don turned the sound down.

"They don't make it easy on us, do they?"

Luke smiled and shrugged. It was hard to peel his eyes away from the freshman senator. "She's cute, though."

Don nodded. "Plus the whole black theme of her remarks. Black this, black that, black eye. It kind of works, doesn't it?"

"It works," Luke said absently. He wasn't sure if it worked or not.

He turned to face Don again.

Don ran a big hand across his forehead. He yawned. It was late.

"She's right, you know. People are stonewalling. The Pentagon, the CIA, all the intelligence agencies, they're running interference for us on this. They're not happy about taking a bunch of arrows, but they see the need for group cohesion."

"They were all in on it," Luke said. "It's not like they can wash their hands. It was a CIA sub from a CIA front company. Big Daddy gave us the Chechen and the Georgian, and Big Daddy is CIA. One of the prisoners was a Navy SEAL. The drone was NSA. We don't even have any drones. The president himself requested that we do this. I sat in on a meeting with a general from the Joint Chiefs and a guy from Homeland Security. What did all these people think would happen when we went in there? That nobody would notice?"

"Luke..."

"Don, I don't remember anyone telling me to go into Russia, rescue the prisoners, kill the sub, but for God's sake, don't break anything."

"Son, you overstepped," Don said. "I don't blame you for that, but I'm not the one who gets the final say. I was called on the carpet at the White House this afternoon. It was a difficult mission. I explained that to them. Then I was called in by my direct boss, the FBI director. He understands, certainly better than some of the people at the White House, what goes into an operation like this, the risks involved, and the split-second decisions that need to be made. All the same, he's under pressure himself. The shit is running downhill, to coin a phrase."

"The operation was a success," Luke said. "We met both of the objectives, and we lost one man. A man who showed up wearing a suicide vest, by the way, in case anyone is wondering what his intentions were."

"The fallout is we are eye-to-eye with the Russians everywhere on earth," Don said. "Even if cooler heads do prevail in the near term, and there's no guarantee of that at the moment, you can bet they're going to pull some stunt to get us back. Meanwhile, the president has a public relations and diplomatic disaster on his hands."

"We saved his daughter's life less than two months ago," Luke said.

Don nodded. "I've met the president, he is a good man and has been a fan of this agency for obvious reasons. But just between the two of us, I don't think he is the toughest president we've had during my time on this planet. He isn't built for stormy weather."

"What are you saying, Don?"

Don sighed. "The director told me that the Bureau is going to conduct a full internal investigation of the operation, its design, the personnel involved, and their actions. He has also agreed to an objective third-party assessment, in all likelihood carried out by the office of the Judge Advocate General's Corps. I've engaged with a well-regarded firm of private defense attorneys, on the outside chance that criminal charges result against any of our people."

Luke stared at him. Things were going in a strange direction. "Why would JAG have any jurisdiction here? We're not in the military anymore. This was not a…"

Don shook his head. "It's for show, Luke. Try to understand that. This was a mission ordered by the president, and sanctioned by Homeland Defense, to rescue special operations personnel, including a Navy SEAL. They can make a case for JAG investigating it. They can make a case for Bozo the Clown investigating it, if they want to. It's all about looks right now."

He paused for a moment and took a breath.

"We're hanging by a thread, son. The legal firm is going to punch a whale of a hole in our budget. Eventually, it's going to come to light that we spearheaded this operation, no matter who else was involved." He gestured at the TV. An ad for Dodge Ram trucks played silently. "And people like your supermodel friend are going to start demanding our heads on a plate."

Luke opened his mouth as if to speak. But he couldn't think of a single thing to say. Instead, Don went on:

"I suggest you kids get your stories straight. So far you, Swann, and Trudy Wellington have all walked in here at different times and claimed responsibility for the drone strike. That's not going to hold water. Either Swann followed your orders, or he went rogue. It's really going to be that simple."

"Don…"

Don sighed heavily. "I hate to do this. I really do. And I want you to know that I am going to go to the mat for you, and for the entire team. Personally, I'm proud of what this unit accomplished. But in the meantime, you are suspended from duty, with full pay and benefits, pending the outcome of any and all investigations into your conduct during this mission. If you have your service weapon with you, I need you to surrender it now. Also, I need you to surrender your Special Response Team identification, FBI badge, and your access card to this facility."

Luke felt himself going numb. It was an odd sensation. He'd been in combat since he was eighteen years old. He'd experienced many disturbing things.

But this felt... It felt...

He didn't have the words to describe it.

Don eyed him. "I'm sorry, Luke. If it helps any, think of it as a paid vacation. You have a new baby boy. You have a beautiful wife. Spend some time with them. Relax a bit. Grow a beard. Let me worry about this."

Finally, Luke found his voice. It sounded small and weird to his own ears. "How long will the investigation take?"

Don shrugged. "They seem to want to move fast. A month? Six weeks?"

"And the outcome..." Luke said.

"We're in the civilian world now, son. Newspapers... politicians... bureaucrats... I couldn't even hazard a guess."

Chapter Twelve

11:45 a.m. Moscow Time (3:45 a.m. Eastern Daylight Time)
Strategic Command and Control Center
The Kremlin
Moscow, Russia

The young man walked briskly through the wide hallways of the control center, on his way to the large War Room.

His footsteps echoed along the empty corridor. He wore a dress uniform of the Russian Ground Forces. He carried himself with military bearing, his carriage erect, his eyes alert, his face calm, impassive, and serious.

Just ahead, a wide automatic door slid open. He passed through the doorway and into the swirling chaos of the command center's main room. The chatter of voices hit him like a wall as he entered.

At least two hundred people filled the space. There were at least forty workstations, some with two or three people sitting at five computer screens. On the big board up front, there were twenty different television screens.

Screens showed digital maps of Russia, Georgia, Ukraine, Turkey, and the wider Middle East. A series of screens showed location maps of American nuclear capabilities and missile sites spread out across North America, Asia, and Europe.

"Corporal Gregor," a female voice said to his right.

He turned and a secretary was standing near an open door. She was heavyset, perhaps in her fifties, with a stooped back. She gestured at the door with one open hand, as if welcoming him to a weekend dacha. "This way, please."

Gregor moved through the doorway and entered a smaller, oval-shaped room. A crew of men, some in uniform and a few in civilian clothes, sat around a conference table. They were mostly older men. Gregor came in and stood at parade rest, hands clasped behind his back, chest out, shoulders back.

The room was stark, mostly bare, and cigarette smoke lingered in the air. None of the technology from the larger room was in evidence in here. Instead, there were half a dozen ashtrays on the table.

A fat general, his nose red from decades of vodka, poked the table with a heavy index finger. His hands were large and thick.

"Twelve hours since their attack," he was saying. "It is unreasonable to wait any longer. We are ready, so take one of their pieces off the board. Without further delay."

The men looked up at Gregor.

One rose from his chair and came around the table. He was a colonel, in the uniform of the Strategic Air Command, another man in his fifties, but he was tall and trim, with white hair. "Ah, Gregor. Come in, come in."

He turned to the others. "Gentlemen, this is Corporal Gregor. He's a good man and an exceptional soldier. We've already discussed his valorous actions during the Second Chechen Campaign. How many confirmed enemy kills, Gregor?"

Gregor's face didn't change. Showing pride in one's actions was frowned upon. Also, he would not describe the emotions he felt about his time in Chechnya as pride. Nor did he look with pride on the weeks he spent at his mother's cold-water flat afterward, screaming into his pillow and drinking until he blacked out.

"Twenty-six, sir."

"Twenty-six confirmed kills," the man repeated. "Infantry kills?"

Could the man not tell from Gregor's uniform that he was infantry?

"Yes, sir. Of course."

"Hand-to-hand combat?" the man said.

"Yes sir, five confirmed kills in close quarters combat."

"How did you dispatch them?"

"Ah ... four with my knife, sir. In the case of the other one, I had lost my knife in the battle, and I killed him with ... with my hands, sir."

An image came to Gregor of a thick-bodied, short man with an auburn beard. His eyes were dark. The man wrestled Gregor in the burnt-out shell of a building in the Grozny city center. They were alone, and they grunted together like pigs. The man was strong, almost unbelievably strong. There was snow inside the building, blowing through the holes in the blasted out walls.

Through some dumb luck, he couldn't remember what, a fluke perhaps, Gregor ended up on top of the man. He choked him with both hands, his fingers pressing like talons deep into the man's flesh, while the man punched Gregor in the face again and again. Gregor leaned all his weight on the man's throat.

The man gurgled and slowly subsided. Gregor kept choking him. The man's eyes went blank and his face set, his mouth half open. Gregor continued to choke him. He choked him until his own fingers went numb. Finally, when he was sure the man was dead, he rolled off and vomited in the drifting snow.

Now, in the command center, the colonel smiled. "An excellent record, Gregor."

"Thank you, sir."

The colonel went to the corner of the room and came back with a large black leather suitcase. The case was old and battered, the leather itself torn through in a few places, giving a flash of silver steel beneath it.

"Do you know what this is, Gregor?"

Gregor thought he did know, but he also found it better not to speak.

"This is the Cheget," the colonel said, using the word for the nuclear suitcase. "One of only three in the entire country. Do you understand?"

"Yes, sir," Gregor said.

"Give me your wrist," the colonel said.

The suitcase had a handcuff attached to it. The colonel reached down and clamped the handcuff tight around Gregor's thick left wrist. The metal seemed bit into Gregor's flesh. He was right-handed, so at least he would retain the use of his dominant hand. He would need it in an emergency.

The colonel handed Gregor the suitcase.

"The suitcase contains the codes and mechanisms to launch nuclear missile strikes against the West, and especially the United States. You will carry it for the duration of the current crisis. You've been chosen for this honor because of your record of courage, level-headedness, and ability to act in the face of mortal danger."

"Yes sir."

"Do you know the defense minister?" He gestured to a man in a military uniform adorned with many medals and ribbons, but which did not indicate a rank. The man had hair so dark it appeared he must rub black shoe polish into it.

"I know of him, sir. Of course."

"You are not to leave his side until the Cheget is once again removed from your wrist. Accommodations will be made for you here at the command center. In the event of war, you will join the defense minister in the deep fallout shelter."

The colonel paused. He must have seen the look on Gregor's face. "Questions?"

"I have family, sir. My wife and young son. My mother. I have three siblings, and a close uncle …"

The colonel waved that away. "Of course, your family will be provided for."

Gregor didn't have to ask twice what the colonel meant by that. His family would die in the bombings and the radiation with the rest of the helpless millions.

The colonel turned back to the table, leaving Gregor standing alone with the infernal death machine strapped to his wrist.

"Back to business," the colonel said.

"An attack," the fat general said again, picking up right where he left off, as if there had been no interruption at all. "I want a show of resolve, and I want it now. This comes directly from the president. So give me an American piece we can take off the board. It could be a pawn, or it could be the king himself. I don't care."

His stubby finger hit the table three times. Thump. Thump. Thump.

"Give me something easily within our reach."

Chapter Thirteen

4:10 a.m. Eastern Daylight Time
The White House Residence
Washington, DC

David Barrett had a dog.

The dog's name was Mocha, and really she belonged to David's younger daughter, Caitlynn. But the whole family was at the ranch in Texas, recuperating and taking a long deep breath, just being together and appreciating each other and having fun after the near-disaster with Elizabeth.

All of them were there except David himself. He was stuck here in Washington with the dog. Mocha. Mocha was okay. A white and brownish little dog, a mixed breed, what people used to call a mutt.

She wasn't David's favorite dog ever, or the best dog in the world, or anything close to that. Caitlynn liked her (Mocha somehow inspired like rather than love), and she had been useful for photo ops. The First Family should have a dog. It wasn't the law, but it was something pretty close.

She was about to become even more useful.

David had taken to walking her on the White House grounds late at night. As time passed, he began to go later and later. There were Secret Service men lurking around this time of night, but not many, and not close.

As long as the grounds themselves were secure, as long as David stayed close to the house, and as long as he was back in five minutes, what was the worry? He was lulling them to sleep. About ten days ago, he had snapped at a big Secret Service guy he had encountered on his little walk.

"Can you back the hell up? Please? I don't mind if you can see me, but I don't want to see you. Understood? I'm just trying to walk my dog. I need a few minutes in this world to myself, don't I? Give me at least the illusion of privacy. Can you do that?"

After that, they had backed off quite a bit. But David didn't do anything alarming in response. He just quietly walked the dog. He didn't really extend the time he was gone. Seven minutes one night, eleven the next, nine the next. Nothing to see here. Everything was normal.

As far as he could tell, they had not the faintest inkling what he was up to. That was the most delicious part of all this. They had no idea what came next.

"Come on, Mocha. Let's go!"

The dog knew. Dogs were smart, much smarter than the scientists who studied animal intelligence gave them credit for. The sound of the leash, the time of night, the intonation of his voice...whatever it was that gave it away, the dog knew they were going to the do THE FUN THING. They were going outside.

She came running, waiting patiently while he strapped the harness leash on her. They went down the wide central stairs and over to the back door. He swiped the reader with his card and punched in the code.

At the nighttime guard station, they were now alerted to what he was doing. He had unlocked the security system which until a moment ago had him hermetically sealed inside the Residence, impossible for evildoers to reach.

He had voluntarily breached that level of security. Now Secret Service agents would converge on him, trying to remain out of his sight so he wouldn't throw a tantrum and try to get them reassigned. Oh yes. He knew what they thought of him.

Did he have a quick temper sometimes? Yes, he did. Did he throw tantrums, like a child? No, he did not.

For the moment, he was still probably the safest man on earth. After all, he was on the White House grounds, surrounded by high spiked fences, snipers in their aeries, and twenty-four-hour real-time video monitoring. Only crazy people ever tried to infiltrate the White House grounds.

But the security was primarily designed to keep people out. It was less robust in terms of keeping people in. That was his theory, anyway.

"Come on, Mocha! Let's run!"

Mocha loved to run. And she knew exactly what he was talking about when he said the word *run*. The two of them burst off as one down the gently sloping hillside. To their left was the fountain on the North Lawn, lit up in blue.

Mocha, as tiny as she was, was fast and stayed with David step for step. It was all very normal. The president ran with his dog every night.

They ran downhill into a small, dark copse of trees. Instantly, David stopped. He glanced around. Could they see him in here? He didn't think so.

There was a spot he'd had his eye on for some time. It was just ahead. There was a gap between the Northeast Gate and the road called East Executive Park. Just a stretch of tall fence there, nothing important, nothing to look at. On the other side of that fence was the wide pedestrian mall expanse of Pennsylvania Avenue. Directly across the street was the park called Lafayette Square. In fact, the statue of the Marquis de Lafayette was right there. He'd seen all of this on a map.

He was breathing heavily. So was Mocha. He kneeled down beside her and unfastened her harness. He didn't want her on the leash if he wasn't going to be holding it. Dogs got tangled up like that. Terrible things happened sometimes.

"Okay, girl," he said when she was free. "Go ahead! Go home!" He gestured up the hill with his arm. Mocha bounced in place and eyed him quizzically.

That wasn't going to work. No problem. Mocha could roam the grounds until they found her. She'd be fine.

David removed the dark blue windbreaker jacket he was wearing. He wrapped it tightly around his left hand and forearm. He looked out of the trees at the tall fence that surrounded the grounds. It was very high. A normal person couldn't hope to climb that thing. But David was not a normal person.

They'd forgotten that about him, or they had never known. He was tall, and he kept himself in excellent condition for a man in his mid-fifties. In his high school and college days, he was a competitive high jumper and pole vaulter.

During his time at Exeter, he had set a school pole vault record that lasted twenty-two years. It had been broken a little over a decade ago, in an era when everything was different. The equipment and the techniques were different, the shoes were different, the training and nutrition programs were different. Everything had been improved, and it still took them more than two decades to break his record. David was proud of that fact.

Suddenly, without thinking much about it, he ran for the fence.

He was only going to get one shot at this, and if he botched it, he was going to look like quite the fool.

Mocha ran at his feet.

Okay, that was okay. David put on a burst of real speed, dashing out in front of the dog. Then he was blazing, running faster than he had in decades. His body went into a gear he scarcely knew he had. He careened toward the fence like a kamikaze.

At the last second, he planted his feet and leapt, all the energy in his legs. He bounded high, just as he had imagined he would. Halfway up the fence, he seized the iron bars with his hands, his powerful arms driving his body even further, up, up, up…

He planted his left hand, thickly wrapped in his jacket, on top of one of the sharp spikes and gave one last frenzied push. He arched the rest of his body, worming his way over the rest of the spikes.

Then he was clear, coming down the other side and scrabbling madly to grab the fence and slow his fall. He got it and wedged his feet against it, the friction slowing him the tiniest amount. He hit the short grass with a thud and fell backward onto his butt.

His body rolled and he hit his head. It hurt. It surprised him how much.

But he was out. The president of the United States had jumped the fence. He gazed up at it from his spot on the ground. It was incredibly tall. No one would guess that a person could jump that thing. But he had guessed. And he had guessed correctly.

Mocha was on the other side of the fence from now, bouncing and yipping at him.

"It's okay, girl. Daddy's okay. Now go home."

He stood. He'd better get a move on. He had no idea if his little act had raised alarms in there, but if it didn't, it soon would.

He looked around.

Pennsylvania Avenue was blocked off from car traffic here. The park was across the street. There were small cardboard shanties lining the edges of the park, with signs erected everywhere. The signs were strident, in hand-painted capital letters.

NO NUKES!

MY BODY, MY CHOICE

IMPEACH BARRETT

Ha! That one got his attention. Impeach him for what? There were many others, but David Barrett stopped reading them.

People were living in this park. There were a lot of them. The people were dirty, in shabby clothes. Some were awake. Cigarette ends lit up brightly as smokers inhaled. They were staring at him. Eyes followed David's progress beneath crazy tangles of hair and above long, dense beards.

"Aqualung my friend," David said under his breath. "Don't you start away uneasy."

These people were living right across from the White House. Why didn't he know this? You'd think someone would have informed him. Talk about a security breach. They didn't show things like this on maps.

The street was deserted this time of night. Maybe a hundred yards down from him, to his right, a car was parked. It was just outside the concrete traffic barriers, and its lights were on. The car itself appeared to be yellow, and it had something on the roof. It could be a police car, he supposed, or a pizza delivery car, but he didn't think so.

He walked toward the car, almost dizzy with the sensation of being outside the fence, and outside his protective circle. He reminded himself that he could go back inside anytime he wanted.

He got a vague sense of being an animal who was domesticated, then suddenly released into the wild. Would the animal survive out there?

Slowly he unwrapped the jacket from his hand and his forearm. Ah! He knew it. His hand was bleeding, pretty badly. The spike at the top of the fence had stabbed right through the jacket and punched a hole in his palm.

The bloody hole in the middle of his hand looked like an all-seeing eye. Like the stigmata of Christ. The blood from it ran down his arm toward his elbow. It was a mess. He flexed his fingers and shook his head. He was going to have to get that cleaned up somehow. He didn't want to get an infection. Absently, he held the windbreaker to his hand, hoping that would stanch the blood a bit.

The sign on top of the car clearly said TAXI.

He had arrived at the car. It was a taxi, parked along the sidewalk, doing what? Waiting for a fare after four in the morning? He reached for the rear door and pulled the handle. It was locked. He tapped the window a few times.

The door made the sound of an automatic lock opening. Ca-thunk!

Suddenly, there came the sound of shoes running on pavement. David looked up and a man was running down the block toward him, coming from the David's right. He was moving very fast.

David stepped back, nearly frozen. Instantly, he understood his own foolishness. This was why he had protection. Outside the fence three minutes, and already he was under attack. Had Elizabeth felt this way when she realized…

"Hey, buddy, I need that cab!" the man said.

He was breathless, gasping for air. His eyes were wild. He was bearded, and his face was half-covered in blood. His shirt was torn. He grabbed the door and wrenched it open. He was going to take David Barrett's taxi.

But he stopped. He stared at David for a moment. His head craned gently to the side, his mouth hanging open. He was missing one of his front teeth. He glanced back the way he had come, apparently looking to see if anyone was in pursuit.

When he turned back, his eyes had lit up in a strange kind of wonder. He held the door to the taxi wide open.

"I'm sorry, Mr. President. That was rude. You take the cab. You were here first. I'll find another one."

"Thank you," David said. "Very kind of you."

The man held out his hand and David shook it.

"It's an honor to meet you, sir," the man said.

David slid into the car. The man closed the door behind him, made sure it was firmly shut, then took off running again.

The taxi driver turned around and looked at David. He was a young, dark-skinned man with a beard, wearing a green turban. He smiled broadly. They stared at each other for a moment. If anything, the smile strengthened. The man was grinning maniacally now. He was positively beaming. David didn't think he had ever seen a smile quite like it. Was the man insane? He could easily be mistaken for a suicide bomber.

"Sir!" the man said. "My name is Jahjeet, at your service! You may simply call me Jeet, if you prefer. That is my nickname."

"Are you Muslim?" David said.

The man shook his head. "Sikh. We are a religion of peace, and you have nothing to fear from me. I came here from Punjab, and this is the best moment of my life! I am so proud of this night. Wait until I inform my wife! The American president was in my taxicab. Where may I take you?"

The man's enthusiasm was endearing. It would be nice if some of the other people David dealt with demonstrated half this much fire.

"Well, Jeet," David said, "just drive. I'll tell you where we're going in a minute."

What he didn't want to add was: *As soon as I figure it out myself.*

"Of course! We can drive all night, if it pleases you. I will not even turn on the meter. This drive is free of charge."

The car lurched out from the curb and moved along the edge of the park. Briefly, David considered having the man drive around to the entrance of the White House grounds and take him back inside. There would be a strange scene at the guard station, but it would probably be the prudent thing to do.

Of course, he would spend the day trying to explain his escapade to a group of people who might not have his best interests at heart. They had already stripped him of the presidency once. He didn't relish the idea of defending his actions to the team of psychiatrists Mark Baylor had called in to assess David's mental stability.

He took the cell phone out of his pocket. It was a cheap, nondescript unit, a flip phone. It had prepaid minutes already loaded on it, and it had never been used before. Calling from it was a completely anonymous endeavor, as anonymous as anything could be in this age of spy satellites and communications data mining by supercomputer.

It was the kind of phone that Lawrence Keller used to refer to as a "burner."

He dialed Lawrence's number.

The phone rang once, two times, three…"

"Yes?" a voice said. It was Lawrence. He sounded tired, maybe a little irritated. But he was still awake, just like David had asked.

"Do you know who this is?" David said.

"Of course. I was waiting for your call."

David nodded. "I would like you to meet me at the Lincoln Memorial."

"Meet you at the…" There was a pause as Lawrence Keller digested the idea of meeting the president of the United States at such a very public place.

"When would you like me to meet you there?"

David Barrett smiled. "Now."

Chapter Fourteen

12:33 a.m. Alaska Daylight Time (4:33 a.m. Eastern Daylight Time)
The Skies Above the Bering Strait
Between Cape Dezhnev (Russia) and Cape Prince of Wales (Alaska)

"Almighty, Almighty, do you read me?"

The American F-18 Super Hornet screamed north across the sky, flying air patrol at the western edge of American airspace, just east of the International Date Line. To its right was Alaska and the good ol' USA. To its left was Siberia and Mother Russia.

Inside the cone of the fighter jet, the sky was wide open. It was dark out here tonight. The plane was traveling just under nine hundred miles per hour.

Captain Walter "Wildman" Caples glanced at his radar.

He was fitted with a helmet, a flight suit, a g-suit, and on top of that a parachute harness and a survival vest. The gear was bulky as hell, but he'd been at this so long it felt like a hug from the loving arms of God.

He was thirty-nine years old, married with three beautiful young daughters, and his wild man days were long past him. But people still called him Wildman and he did not mind. They had to call him something, didn't they? And "Walter" didn't seem to fit.

There was a lot of energy out here. That's how Wildman thought of it: energy. He hadn't seen it like this since his early days, back during the last years of the Cold War. The Russians were the wild men tonight.

He'd been catching visuals of MiG-29 fighter formations for hours, something he rarely did. Flight paths were usually announced and shared ahead of time, to limit the chance of surprise interactions. That was off the table. Now it was anything goes.

Wildman knew. He knew. Something had happened, some classified mission gone awry. The Russians had their blood up. It wasn't good. But to his mind, cooler heads would prevail. They always had before.

Now, up ahead and to his west, three MiG fighters had just crossed out of Russian airspace. His radar told him they were on an intercept course with him. If they wanted to do that, they were going to cross into American airspace.

He hoped they knew what they were doing. His plane was better than theirs. And he'd been at this a long time.

He radioed air control again.

"Almighty, this is Ninety-Nine, do you read?"

"Copy, Nine Nine."

"I've got three bogeys leaving Russian airspace and crossing International Date Line. Attack formation, and they appear to be on intercept heading."

"Distance?" the air controller said.

"I'm at thirty thousand feet," Wildman said. "Bearing fifteen degrees. Bogeys at twenty miles and closing. Bearing one forty-five. Looks like they want to give me a haircut."

"Nine Nine, hold your heading."

"Roger," Wildman said.

Wildman had been around the block a few times. He'd flown patrols everywhere on planet earth. The Persian Gulf. The South China Sea. The Barents Sea. The Arctic. When he was a kid, he'd done his time right along the edge of the Iron Curtain in Europe. Later, he did bombing runs over Iraq, and then Serbia. Cat and mouse didn't bother him. Chicken didn't bother him. Mock attacks by Syrians or Iranians didn't even get his pulse rate up. People played these games all the time.

But these guys were Russians. They were mad. And they were coming hard.

"Let's not start World War Three out here, boys," he said under his breath.

The Russian fighter jets had adjusted their headings slightly. They were coming directly toward him.

"Almighty, this is Ninety-Nine. Those bogeys have me on their noses, twelve miles out." He waited a moment and watched the approaching airplanes. They were going very fast, headed on a near collision course. "I'm at altitude, still thirty thousand, ten miles out now. Uh... nine miles."

"Hold your heading, Nine Nine."

"Eight miles, Almighty. Coming hard."

"Wildman, that's your airspace. Hold your heading."

"Roger that."

A moment passed. Wildman realized he was holding his breath and pushed the air out, forcing himself to breathe normally.

"Status, Nine Nine?"

"Six miles and closing," Wildman said. "This is going to be tight."

He paused.

"Four miles. Jesus. These guys have a bug up their ass tonight."

"Hold that heading, Wildman. That's our sky."

"I heard you the first time."

He glanced at the radar. The lead MiG was banking away to the south. But the other two were still on an intercept heading. What were they doing? Wildman didn't like that.

"Status?"

"Lead bogey has dropped off. New bearing to the south The other two have me right on their noses. Coming hard. Two miles."

Wildman took a deep breath. This was really going to happen.

"One mile. Here they come."

Wildman glanced to his left. Force of habit—it was black out there. A dark shadow, a blur, came almost too fast to see.

His heart pounded in his chest.

"Sons of bitches!"

The Russian fighter roared past, way too close. The shriek of its jet engines was loud in Wildman's cockpit. An instant later, the turbulence hit him and his plane shuddered. And an instant after that, the second jet passed.

Wildman screamed a bad word at them. He was a Christian, and it was not his habit to use foul language. But he hated those guys. He'd never had much use for Russians, and this just confirmed he was right all along.

Wildman let out a long breath. He felt his heart thumping steadily, thumping hard, but already almost like normal.

"Status, Nine Nine?"

"Still here, but I think those Russian boys are over America right now."

"We have a formation ninety miles out, en route to your location. Hold your heading, Wildman. The cavalry is on its way."

He glanced at his radar. The two Russians were behind him, to his southeast, making a deep run into American airspace. It was plain stupid, what they were doing. This area was sparsely populated, sure, but they were playing a dangerous game. At these speeds, that American fighter formation would be here in five minutes.

On his radar, he noticed the first bogey, the one that had peeled off, now approaching from the southwest. It was on an intercept heading again, this time from behind him.

"Ah hell," he said.

"Nine Nine?"

"The first one's back. He broke formation before, but he's got me on his nose again. He is to my southwest, very close, three miles, heading forty-five degrees."

"Steady, Nine Nine."

As he watched the radar, he saw something he would never have believed. Suddenly, the MiG-29 fired a missile.

"Almighty, he's firing!"

Wildman's heart skipped a beat in his chest. His hands moved automatically with no input from his conscious mind. His plane banked hard left and gained altitude. He over-steered and put himself nearly upside down. He rolled, still banking hard.

The missile flew by within a hundred meters. It zipped past and exploded in the air less than a mile away. The shockwave hit him and his plane shuddered again.

"Ninety-Nine? Ninety-Nine?"

"Copy," he said.

"Status?"

"Still here."

"Ninety-Nine, you are cleared to engage."

"Roger, Almighty."

Wildman knew his rules of engagement meant he could fire back when fired upon. It wasn't on his to-do list when he woke up today, but it was always a possibility. He banked the plane around to his left and back. He fell in behind the MiG, which was still running north. The other two MiGs were back on his radar, coming hard from the southeast.

"It's a party now," Wildman said. He felt eerily calm. "Bogeys have me on their nose from the southeast. Where's that cavalry?"

Wildman controlled his breathing and maintained his posture. These guys were trying to intimidate him, but he was operational, and he was free to engage. They had fired first. He was the good guy.

"Sixty miles," said the voice. Still pretty far away.

"I can take him anytime," he said.

"Take him," Almighty said.

"Bogeys on my tail."

"Shoot him, Nine Nine. Shoot him down."

Wildman locked on with a Sidewinder missile. "Fox Two," he said, using the brevity code for the Sidewinder. "Fox Two, Almighty. You better get that cavalry here. My ass is hanging in the wind."

"Roger."

Wildman launched the missile. "Fox Two away."

The missile shrieked across the sky between Wildman and the MiG, closing the distance in a few seconds. The MiG attempted evasive action, but it did no good. Wildman pulled up hard as the missile hit home. He saw a flash of white light, and the MiG spinning out of control.

"Nine Nine, status?"

Wildman glanced back and below. The Russian plane spiraled away and down into the darkness.

"Fox Two kill."

"Roger, Nine Nine," Almighty said. "Confirmed MiG-29 kill. Nice shooting."

"Thanks, but I still got problems."

"Hang in there, Nine Nine. Our boys are coming."

Wildman glanced at his readout again. They were right on his tail. If they attacked now, he was in deep trouble.

"Don't do it," he said.

He watched as both planes launched missiles simultaneously. It was the worst possible outcome. Dodging one would send him into the path of the other. He hesitated, costing himself a crucial second. Two seconds. Three. He realized, too late, that the thing to do was a steep, near-vertical dive.

For an instant, he saw an image of his three girls, in pretty summer dresses and Easter bonnets.

He stared at the image. It was as if he could reach out and…

"Status, Nine Nine?"

"Uh… I'm fired upon. Again."

"Take evasive action."

He saw a flash of light, blinding in its intensity. An instant later, there was another.

"I'm hit," he said, but he no longer felt much urgency.

"Abort! Abort!"

The plane was spinning. The night sky zoomed past in a kaleidoscopic frenzy. The forces were so powerful, so sickening, that he could barely keep his eyes open. Walter. His name was Walter. Suddenly, he could see why they named him that.

He was dizzy. He reached for the red lever that accessed the EJECT button. He pulled it, but nothing happened.

He could not speak.

"Wildman?" the radio said.

The plane was spinning, spinning, down into the black. There were lights above his head, the lights of a settlement somewhere far below. He was upside down.

He closed his eyes and saw his girls again. They smiled and waved. The youngest was missing her two front teeth.

"Wildman! Do you read?" someone said, but the voice meant nothing to him now.

"Wildman?"

He spun in darkness.

"Wildman?"

Chapter Fifteen

4:50 a.m. Eastern Daylight Time
The Lincoln Memorial
Washington, DC

The man had gone insane. That much was clear.

Whatever opportunity was here for Lawrence Keller, it was looking less and less like it was as chief of staff for President David Barrett.

The two men stood about twenty feet apart on the polished stone floor inside the Greek temple of the memorial. Lawrence had a brief flashback of running on that floor in bare socks as a child, then sliding along it. It was slippery.

Nearby, the marble likeness of the greatest president in American history loomed above them. Between the statue itself, and the platform it sat upon, the entire work stood nearly three stories high. Abraham Lincoln was bathed in an eerie white light, like a saint, or a god. He sat in his chair, a colossus, both in sheer physical size and in the space he occupied in the history books and the minds of the generations that had followed him.

Above his head was his epitaph:

IN THIS TEMPLE
AS IN THE HEARTS OF THE PEOPLE
FOR WHOM HE SAVED THE UNION
THE MEMORY OF ABRAHAM LINCOLN
IS ENSHRINED FOREVER

Lincoln gazed down upon his distant successor. A century and a half separated these two presidents, but the gulf was even wider than that. Lincoln could not be impressed by what he was seeing.

"Thank you for coming," David Barrett said. He was wearing a pair of jeans, sneakers, and a dark cotton V-neck T-shirt. He seemed to have some sort of jacket wrapped around the lower part of his left arm.

"David, I came because I'm your friend. I'm concerned about you. You must know this is terribly ill-advised."

Lawrence Keller was speaking as much for posterity as he was speaking to the president of the United States. Sewn inside the lining of his jacket was a tiny but very powerful digital listening device. All of this was being recorded to a computer chip.

Lawrence looked around again. What he was witnessing seemed impossible. He had never heard of anything remotely similar happening, certainly not in the modern era. How could it be?

"Are you really here without a security detail?"

David smiled. "I gave them the slip. It's easier than you might imagine."

Keller shook his head. "I think that's hardly the point, David. They're there for a reason. It's not a good idea to give them the slip. We found that out in a very painful way when Elizabeth did something similar to this. It wasn't that long ago."

"She might have been on to something," David said.

Keller raised his hands as if he was about to surrender. "Okay, David. I'm not going to argue with you about it. But I'm going to ask you one last time. Where is your Secret Service detail?"

"This isn't what I came here to talk about," David said.

"David, I will talk about anything you like. Just please answer my question first."

David took a deep breath. He rolled his eyes. Keller imagined he was watching this strange presidency coming to its end.

"I'm tired, Lawrence. Don't you understand that? I brought you out here tonight because I'm sick and tired. I need an out, a cover story. I need some time off. I need to go home and be with my family for a while."

Keller shook his head. "David, please just answer me. Where is your Secret Service detail? This is a very important question."

David Barrett, the president of the United States, began to cry.

"I can't take it anymore, Lawrence. I hate this job."

He closed his eyes and stood there before his former chief of staff, weeping like a small child. His broad shoulders shook with the force of his sobs.

"I can't take it."

A strange urge came to Keller then. It was the urge to go to this giant man-child and comfort him. He stifled it. People had been coddling David Barrett for far too long. That's how the country had come to this pass.

An overly privileged man, a man who had never graduated to adulthood, had wandered into the most important job in the land, and it was a job that he was manifestly unprepared to do. Now he was breaking down.

"David, where is your security detail?"

Barrett shook his head like a teenager learning he was grounded for a minor offense. "They're back at the White House, okay? I told you already. They're not here. I crossed the grounds, climbed the fence, and came here alone. As far as I know, no one is even aware that I'm gone. All right, Lawrence?"

Keller nodded. That was all he needed from David. It didn't matter what else David had come here to talk about. He wanted to go home. He wanted to quit. It didn't matter what David wanted. It was all going to be worked out, by adults, and probably without his input.

Four men materialized from the deep shadow recesses behind Abraham Lincoln's chair. They wore dark suits and earpieces. You could almost mistake them for Secret Service agents.

Although they didn't run, they moved with astonishing quickness. They didn't say a word and barely made a sound. They carried out their task with blank-faced, impassive professionalism.

Within a few seconds, they had surrounded David Barrett. They were all as tall as he was, but younger and broader and stronger.

"Lawren…" was all David managed to say.

One man stood behind him and covered his mouth with a big hand. Two others grabbed and held his arms on either side. David's eyes when wide as he attempted to struggle against them. It was no use.

The fourth man stood in front of David and ripped his shirt away, from the V-neck down. An instant later, he had a Taser device in his hand.

"Mmmmmm!" David Barrett said. "MMMMMMM!"

The Taser made a low humming noise as it powered up. Suddenly, the twin probes flew out and caught David on his bare chest just below the neck. Fifty thousand volts of electricity coursed into David's body. His nervous system overwhelmed, the president of the United States jittered and jived, his teeth clicking together. His eyes rolled back in his head. Drool formed at the corners of his mouth.

He went limp in the arms of the men holding him. They lowered him gently to the ground. Now four big men hovered over him. The man who had just Tasered him kneeled next to him.

"Mr. President?"

David Barrett's eyelids fluttered, and his eyes opened. After a moment, they focused on the man again. When David spoke, his voice was a rasp.

"You can't do this. I am the presi—"

The probes spent, the man used the Taser's touch stun feature to give the president another jolt. David's entire body thumped along the ground. His head banged off the same polished stone that Lawrence Keller had once gone sliding on.

His eyes opened again. He stared at the man. There was anger in those eyes. David Barrett was famous for his temper tantrums. He swallowed.

"You…" he said.

Then he rode the juice again.

A moment later, the four men lifted David Barrett's limp body and carried it carefully down the stairs. His head drooped.

Parked on the plaza at the bottom of the stairs was a large black SUV with smoked windows. It hadn't been there a moment ago. Its engine was running, just a bit of steam coming from its tail pipe. The men carried David Barrett to the car, loaded him in the back, and climbed in behind him.

The SUV's headlights came on and it pulled away slowly.

Lawrence Keller watched it go. A moment later, the sound of footsteps came up behind him. Keller didn't even turn around. He knew how these things went. Either they would reward him for his help, or they would kill him. Try as he might, there wouldn't be much he could do about either thing. It was out of his hands.

A man in a three-piece suit with slicked-back hair appeared next to him. He was a handsome man in a very generic way. Five minutes after meeting him, you would have trouble describing anything about his face. His shoes were polished to such a high sheen they almost seemed like patent leather.

He was a CIA agent whose specialty was domestic spying, misinformation, and psychological operations. He was a shock doctor. When bad news happened, something traumatizing, something that threw entire populations off balance, he probably wasn't far away. Some people called him the Dirty Trickster.

"Wallace Speck," Keller said. "Fancy meeting you here."

The man put a finger to his lips. Shhhhh.

"Hello, Lawrence."

"What happens now?" Keller said.

The man shrugged. "You wanted a return to relevance? You got it."

Keller gestured toward the SUV that was no longer there.

"What about David?"

"Oh, he'll be okay," Speck said. "We'll get him the help he needs. Anyway, you don't have to worry about that. Focus on you. Your country needs you. Expect a call, probably not today, but maybe tomorrow. There's always a place near the top for a proud American who's also a loyal servant."

"And who will I be serving?" Keller said.

Speck smiled. "Who else? The president of the United States."

"As chief of staff?"

Speck's shoulders slumped. "Come on, Lawrence. You know Mark has his own people in place. But there'll be something good on the table for you. I promise."

Suddenly, back toward the White House, there was a loud explosion. A rumble, a long rolling BOOM like thunder, came to them. The floor beneath their feet trembled the slightest amount. The sky lit up over there.

"Well, I see the fun has started," Wallace Speck said. "That's my cue to leave."

He looked at Keller. "Lawrence, if I were you, I'd go home, relax, and be ready for that call. Big things await you."

Speck turned to go, but then stopped.

"And Lawrence?"

Keller looked at him. Speck's eyes were hard. Worse than hard, they were blank. Keller had often heard policemen and FBI profilers talk about eyes like these, in a face like this. It wasn't a heartless face. It wasn't cruel. It was empty.

Lack of affect was what the cops called it. The face of someone for whom killing no longer meant anything, if it ever did. Keller didn't want to give that face even a drop of satisfaction. He also didn't want to give it any reason to become angry.

The sirens had started. Everywhere at once, sirens were approaching. A lot of them. A gunshot rang out. Then another. Then a burst of automatic fire.

Hue City, Lawrence thought. That place was never far from his memory.

"Yeah?" he said.

"Be a good boy and try not to rock the boat this time."

Chapter Sixteen

5:01 a.m. Eastern Daylight Time
Queen Anne's County, Maryland
Eastern Shore of Chesapeake Bay

Luke was beat.

"Beat" didn't even really get to the heart of the matter. He was beyond tired. Other than dozing on airplanes, he had barely slept in the past two days. He had driven here asleep with his eyes open. Thankfully, there was no one on the roads this time of night.

He got a piece of good news as he pulled into the gravel driveway of the house. Becca's beat-up Subaru station wagon was there in the glow of his headlights. Audrey's Mercedes sedan was nowhere to be seen.

Could it be? Luke almost didn't dare to hope.

Could Audrey have gone home?

He killed the engine and the headlights, and just sat in the dark for a long moment. It was still an hour before sunrise, a beautiful time of day. Lights shimmered on the water. On the other side of the bay, the lights of a larger community gave off a pale glow. He closed his eyes and allowed his body to relax.

Somewhere far away, there was a distant rumble of thunder.

The painkillers weren't really working anymore, but that was okay. Pain was something he had long ago learned to live with. It was almost comforting.

He was under suspension, but still on the payroll. He was hopeful he would be cleared of any wrongdoing, but according to Don, the case could take a month or more. A month! Or more!

A wave of elation washed over his exhausted body.

A month here at the cabin. On the water. In the middle of summertime. Just him, Becca, and the baby. Sunset on the patio. He could buy a little outboard motorboat. Hell, Swann was under suspension, and Big Ed was bound to be, whenever he got back. He could have them out here for barbecues. Ice cold beer.

It kept getting better.

No commute. He had surrendered a service weapon (he had others). More to the point, he no longer had his agency ID or his key card. He couldn't get into the SRT offices if he wanted to.

"Well, I guess I'm just stuck out here," he said under his breath, and smiled.

Okay. It was time to go inside. He left his bags in the car. He would deal with them tomorrow sometime. He walked silently to the door. Somewhere nearby, an owl was hooting.

"Hoo?" it said. "Hoo, hoo?"

Luke smiled again and let himself inside. He was careful not to let the screen door bang. He took his shoes off and moved around in the dark in his socks. He was careful not to let the floorboards creak. If Becca and baby Gunner were sleeping, he didn't want to do the slightest thing to disturb them. It was absolutely silent in here.

He navigated by the nightlight above the stove.

There was a piece of card stock paper folded like a tent on the kitchen table. On its face, in her big, capital letter, childlike scrawl, it said: *LUKE.*

He picked it up and read it in the dim light.

Babe, we decided to go to Mom and Dad's, to be closer to the doctors, and for more room, and so Dad could be with the baby. We all went in Mom's car. I miss you. I hope you are alive and okay. Let me know when you get in. Love you.

She had drawn a simple heart with an arrow through it at the bottom.

Luke grunted like he had been punched.

Becca's mother and father lived ten minutes from the SRT offices. Not that Luke could turn up there in the middle of the night, and not that he would want to. He didn't want to spend any more time at their house than was absolutely necessary.

Okay, no one was home here. He hadn't known that because his mission was classified and he couldn't be in touch while he was away. That was all right. He was home, he was safe, they were safe, and they were at Audrey and Lance's house.

Luke went to the refrigerator, less concerned about noise now. He pulled out a beer, went to the couch, and sat down. He cracked the beer and took a sip. Yikes, that was good. He simply sat for a few moments, sipping his beer and staring at nothing.

The exhaustion began to settle in again. Every time he stopped moving, it seemed to catch up with him.

There was an old wooden grandfather clock here in the living room. That thing was ancient, and with age came quirks. It ticked along, never quite on the right time. It tended to gong sometimes. There was no rhyme or reason to it, just whenever it was in the mood.

Luke put his beer down on the floor. He let himself lie across the couch. It was a great couch, comfortable and big enough to accommodate his body.

He realized he didn't want to be down here when that grandfather gong went off. He'd better get off this couch and force himself to go upstairs to bed.

It was a good idea, and he was going to do it.

Any minute.

He just wanted to get a few things straight in his mind.

He closed his eyes and was asleep in seconds.

CHAPTER SEVENTEEN

5:05 a.m. Eastern Daylight Time
Near the Northeast Gate
The White House
Washington, DC

"I'm down here, God damn it! Cease fire!"

Agent Ricky Saviello screamed into the mouthpiece of communications headset. He lay flat on his stomach thirty yards from the blown out remains of the fencing just to the right of the Northeast Gate.

Something was on fire on the other side of the fence, perhaps a van or a truck. Twisted, flaming metal lay strewn all over the lower lawn and on the nearby stretch of the Pennsylvania Avenue pedestrian mall.

That vehicle looked like it had been hit by a missile. If there was anybody inside there, they were roasted. Bright orange flames and black smoke towered into the sky.

Single gunshots and what sounded like heavy automatic weaponry still rang out, seemingly from behind him, back up toward the house. Live rounds were flying over his head. He kept his face to the grass.

"I'm down here! I'm down here! Stop shooting!"

Saviello was of Afro-Dominican descent. Wearing a navy blue suit, he was blending in well with the dark tonight, a little too well for comfort.

"Do you people see me?"

There'd been an attack of some kind. That's all he knew. When the explosions and the shootings started, he had raced downhill toward the action. But the situation was strange. There didn't seem to be any perpetrators. Just a lot of gunfire, coming *downhill*, from our side. Also, he had caught a glimpse of the president's tiny dog, running frantically through the firelight.

The gunfire died down.

Saviello waited. His service weapon was out, pointed toward that giant hole in the fence. He scanned the sloping hillside for unfriendlies, then focused on the fence again.

Suddenly, a man appeared there, a silhouette walking slowly out of the smoke and flame. His hands were at his sides.

"Don't shoot!" the man shouted. "Don't shoot! I have no gun!"

"Stop right there!" Saviello shouted from the ground. He had a perfect shot at the guy if he needed to take it. He put his sights right on the man's center mass. "Raise those hands where I can see them."

The man stood in place. "I cannot raise my hands."

The flames of the burning van crackled in the night.

"Raise those hands!"

"I cannot! They are tied!"

"You better raise those fu—"

A series of shots rang out. The man did a sputtering dance and fell to the ground right where he stood. Oh yeah. That guy was gonna be dead. Saviello had seen the spray of blood and bone as the kill shot took off the top of the man's head.

Saviello hadn't even touched his trigger.

"Cease fire," he said into his mic. "He's down."

There were no more gunshots. Saviello gave it an extra moment just to make sure. Then he climbed slowly to his feet and moved toward the body.

"Nobody shoot. I'm going to check the subject."

He moved down the slight incline to where the man had been standing. The grass was spongy and wet with early morning dew. The dead man lay on the wet grass, his body askew, his legs out at strange, unnatural angles. Just as Saviello expected, half of his head was gone, from the eyebrows up.

Strangely, the man's arms were still at his sides. Saviello looked closer. The man's wrists were shackled, secured to his sides with a thick chain that looped around his waist. The set-up reminded Saviello of the way corrections officers secured inmates for travel from one facility to another.

"Something odd here," he said into the mic.

He glanced uphill toward the White House. He felt the bullet pierce his chest before he heard the gunshot.

"Wait..."

There was another shot, then another. He heard them echoing across the White House grounds and the surrounding streets and parks. They were long rolling booms, like waves crashing at the beach late at night.

Three shots. He counted them.

Then he was on his back in the wet grass. He realized his life was ebbing away. How could it be?

Friendly fire. It happened sometimes.

But he told them not to shoot.

Chapter Eighteen

6:45 a.m. Eastern Daylight Time
The Oval Office
The White House
Washington, DC

Mark Baylor glanced around the office.

Three tall windows, with drapes pulled back, still looked out on the Rose Garden. Light was just beginning to fill the sky. Near the center of the office, a comfortable sitting area was situated on top of a lush carpet adorned with the Seal of the President. In the corner, the Resolute Desk was there in its customary spot.

Standing at the closed double doors were two Secret Service agents. Another dozen people, including more Secret Service, fanned out across the room.

Baylor loved everything about this office. *His* office.

Just in front of him, a man and a woman stood. Photographers snapped pictures of them. One of the men was short and bald. He wore a long dark robe. He was Clarence Warren, Chief Justice of the United States. At just sixty-four years old, he was expected to remain Chief Justice for a long time to come.

The woman's name was Kathy Grumman. She wore a dark blue suit and a frown on her face. She was holding a Bible open in her hands. She had been David Barrett's Chief of Staff, and might still be.

Everything was happening on the fly. The White House had been attacked in the night, and David had gone missing. The house and its grounds were now thought to be secure, but David still hadn't turned up. Maybe he would materialize later, or maybe he was dead. No one seemed to know.

Mark Baylor knew a bit about what was going on, who was involved, and where their allegiances lay. He knew much more than he let on. But even he didn't know if David Barrett was still among the living. Whoever had taken David Barrett, Mark Baylor was not sure of their plans.

In the meantime, someone had to be president, and quickly. That someone was Vice President Mark Baylor. The country was in crisis, and he was the perfect man for the job. He was decisive, an actor rather than a thinker. In that way, he and David couldn't be more different.

In the night, there had been a dogfight between American and Russian jets in the Bering Strait. No one knew who fired first. We claimed they did. They claimed we did. But we knew they had crossed into American airspace. And we knew that after our airplane had been shot down, a formation of five of our fighter jets had destroyed all three Russian planes in the vicinity.

And when Mark Baylor became president a moment from now, he was going to act instead of think. He was going to order the Pentagon to move to DEFCON 3 worldwide, as they had requested yesterday.

Truth was, he was going to give the military anything they wanted. They needed latitude to fight a war against a dangerous enemy, and they were going to get it. He breathed deeply at the thought. It was a proud time to be an American.

This would be the second time he'd taken this oath in less than two months. He thought it was a nice touch to have Kathy Grumman hold the Bible. He felt that it demonstrated his loyalty to his friend David. Also, with the early hour of the morning, the evacuation, and the sudden, unexpected need to administer the Oath of Office, there just weren't that many people around.

Baylor stood with his left hand on the Bible. His right hand was raised.

"I, Mark Twain Baylor," he said, "do solemnly swear that I will faithfully execute the Office of President of the United States."

"And will to the best of my ability," Judge Warren prompted.

"And will to the best of my ability," Baylor said.

"Preserve, protect, and defend the Constitution of the United States."

Baylor repeated the words. For his second go-round, and even more abruptly than before, he became president of the United States.

Don't come back this time, David.

Chapter Nineteen

7:25 a.m. Eastern Daylight Time
Georgetown
Washington, DC

Lawrence Keller awoke with a start.

In his dream, he and his squad of Marines had been camped down by the Perfume River in Hue City. It was February 1968. No one told him this, he just knew it. He knew that month like he knew his own name. Everything in the dream was sepia toned and old-timey, everything except the blood.

The blood was bright red, garish, like neon paint, like the wave of blood that flowed out of the elevator and onto the little boy in *The Shining*.

The whole squad was being sliced apart by something Keller could not see. It made no sound. His men were just... falling apart, disintegrating in great big foundations of electric red. And Keller was in a bathroom. He turned to look in the mirror, and he was bathed in the blood of dead men.

He opened his eyes.

"Okay," he said. "It's okay."

But he knew that wasn't true. It was most definitely not okay. He got up and padded into the living room in his boxer shorts and T-shirt. He hit the remote control and CNN came on. This was his morning ritual, no different today from any day.

He hated the news. He hated the voices of the talking heads. He hated the enthusiastic fake seriousness of the newscasters. But if you lived in Washington, and you wanted to be a player, you had to know what was going on and who was doing and saying what. Up to the minute was good. Before it happened was better, of course, but you couldn't always be that far ahead.

Sometimes, though ... you knew things before everyone else. It's what you did with that information that counted.

He rubbed his bald head, went into the kitchen, put the coffee on, then came back out with a banana and small glass of orange juice. He stood there, staring at the muted TV.

There was an image of fencing along the Pennsylvania Avenue pedestrian mall. A large chunk of the fence was ripped apart and thrown in the street like a broken toy. The charred skeleton of some kind of delivery van lay near the hole, burned to such an extent that it resembled a human skull.

LIVE it said at the top left. *White House ATTACK thwarted. Secret Service and DC Metro Police give all clear.*

Along the bottom scrolled more good news. *Dogfight in the Bering Strait. Three Russian MiG-29 fighter jets and one American F-18 have been confirmed destroyed over western Alaska. "We are as close to war as we have ever been," Pentagon general says.*

A mug shot appeared on the screen. It was the face of a hard young man, with glaring eyes and a crew cut. He was half-smiling, as if the fact of being in police custody, possibly facing jail time, was a joke to him.

Keller turned the volume on.

"Aleksander Rostov was the first man killed by the Secret Service," a female voice said. "The thirty-one-year-old native of Astrakhan, in southern Russia, had been living in Brighton Beach, Brooklyn, for the past several years. He has been arrested numerous times by the NYPD, and is thought to have been an associate of Russian mobsters operating in Brooklyn and in other East Coast cities."

Keller watched, not in disbelief, but in slowly mounting fear. A Russian mobster was killed at a White House gate by the Secret Service? For what? The president wasn't even there. At the time of the alleged attack, he was over at the Lincoln Memorial, being Tasered by agents of the ...

Another mug shot appeared on the screen. This man was older, heavier, balding with dark hair. He could use a shave. He stared straight at the camera, not smiling. He looked like he might kill the cameraman, or eat him.

"Viktor Bakhurin, forty-three, was an ethnic Russian raised in eastern Ukraine. He has long been associated with organized crime figures in both Kiev and Moscow, as well as Hungary and Bulgaria. He is thought to have been involved at the highest levels in a wide range of criminal enterprises, including drug smuggling, weapon sales, human trafficking, prostitution, and murder for hire. It is unknown how long he was in the United States. He was at the wheel of the getaway van when it exploded, and he died in the subsequent fire."

It wasn't true. Of course it wasn't true. The young guy, maybe. But this guy, this Bakhurin? There was no way a high-level mobster sends himself on a suicide mission, one that had no hope of success.

Attack the White House? And do what?

Kidnap the president, of course. This was the cover story. The president was gone. They apparently hadn't announced that yet or it would be the only thing on. And if the president never came back, then…

The Russians did it.

They must have had these Russian mobsters on ice, tucked away somewhere until they needed them. Mobsters disappear all the time. Their friends kill them and dispose of the bodies. They become government witnesses. They decide it's just a good idea to make themselves invisible for a while. No one even really looks for them.

The full horror of this reached Keller, and he began to go numb. They had taken David, and they weren't going to give him back.

Really?

Another image appeared. It was of a smiling young man in a green turban. It appeared to be the photo identity they posted on the back of the glass partition when you took a taxicab. The man's eyes were blacked out. The name on the ID was blurred.

"A taxi driver was found dead two blocks away, of a gunshot to the back of the head. His body was left on the sidewalk. Police believe he was the victim of a carjacking by an unknown number of the escaped White House attackers. CNN is not releasing the man's name pending notification of next of kin. His taxicab has not been recovered."

Keller stared at the man. A new feeling began to come over him. Terror.

David had taken a taxi to the Lincoln Memorial. It was the first thing he told Keller. He had been absurdly proud of himself for that. Apparently, he hadn't been inside a taxicab in close to three decades.

They killed his cab driver.

Keller felt his heart pumping, banging on the wall of his chest. If they would kill a cab driver, who knew little or nothing about what was going on, what would they do to the man who had set up the president in the first place?

Why hadn't they killed Keller last night? Because they were going to offer him a great job? He doubted it.

Because the missing president's former chief of staff lying dead on the steps of the Lincoln Memorial is bad optics? That seemed more likely.

Yet another image appeared on the screen. It was of a young smiling black man with wearing a formal Marine Corps "dress blues" uniform. His white peaked cap with gold device told Keller he was an enlisted man. His gold Naval Parachutist badge said he had made at least ten qualifying jumps. His red, white, blue, and gold Navy Combat Action Ribbon informed Keller that the man had seen combat.

Keller knew these things about the young man in the blink of an eye, almost before he was aware he was taking in the information. He hadn't studied the man. He had merely glanced at him. You left the Marine Corps, but it never left you.

"This just in. The Secret Service agent killed in the gun battle on the White House grounds has been identified as twenty-nine-year-old

Enrique Saviello of Union City, New Jersey. Agent Saviello was just a two-year veteran of the Secret Service. Previous to that, he served with the United States Marine Corps, performing one tour of service each in both Iraq and Afghanistan. He leaves a wife and an eighteen-month-old daughter behind."

Keller went into the bedroom and kneeled by the bed. There was a bunch of junk under here. Shoes he never wore anymore, an old laptop, a travel iron. He moved that stuff out of the way. Here was a flat box. He pulled that out.

He opened it. A Sig Sauer P226 semi-automatic handgun lay encased in protective foam. Next to it were three fifteen-round magazines, loaded with .40-caliber Smith & Wesson hollow-points, bullets designed for maximum penetration and maximum soft tissue damage. He had a license to carry this weapon.

Good Lord. He had made an audiotape of David's kidnapping.

That fact hit him with the weight of a thousand bricks. In ordinary circumstances, it might be a good thing. But these weren't ordinary circumstances. *They* knew his habits. They knew he taped conversations. He had provided them with tapes in the past.

He pictured Wallace Speck putting a finger to his lips and shushing him.

"Oh my God," he said out loud.

They already knew. They knew even then.

He had to get out of here. Just get in the car and drive somewhere far away. Keller was nothing if not a chess player. He had created false personas for himself in anticipation of this day, or a day just like it. There was money, identification, another car, a cabin, and another apartment waiting for him out there in the world.

It was enough to give him a head start. At some point, that head start would run out and he would have to improvise. But improvisation was another one of his skills.

Of course, there was nowhere on earth you could go where they couldn't find you. He'd just have to be ready for them when they did.

If they thought they were going to take him easily, then they didn't know Lawrence Keller very well.

Chapter Twenty

7:40 a.m. Eastern Daylight Time
Parkfair Apartments
Columbia Heights
Washington, DC

This should be the right apartment. 3B.

The man's large, hairy fist knocked on the heavy steel door again. He glanced at his partner, a tall, good-looking black man he'd been told to address as Roger Stevens. That wasn't the man's name. Or maybe it was. Impossible to say.

Stevens was dressed in the uniform of a DC Metro police officer. He certainly looked like a cop. Serious like a cop. He had a whole benevolent hard-case, up from a difficult childhood thing, happening around his eyes. The act was convincing.

"I don't know, Rog. It's early, you'd think someone would be home."

The man's name was Dell. Michael Dell. Call him Mike. That wasn't really his name, either. It would be nice if it was. He was dressed like a cop, too. Somehow, he felt like he didn't pull it off quite as well as Officer Stevens.

For one, he was bulkier than Roger Stevens, and the cop suit didn't fit him right. For another, he had tattoos. A lot of tattoos, to be frank. Mostly, they weren't showing right now. The cop suit hid them pretty well. All except for the ones on his knuckles.

The fingers on his left hand, if they were coming at you in a fist, spelled out the word BANG. The fingers on his right hand spelled out the word POW! He was right-handed, and tended to jab with his left. So: BANG, BANG, BANG. Then the right: POW!

Good night.

Most cops didn't have tattoos quite like these. Oh well. It probably wouldn't matter. The cop game only had to last a few minutes.

"I hear a rustling in there," Officer Stevens said. "I think she's coming."

They were in the third-floor hallway of a new, clean, well-kept building of low-income housing. The neighborhood outside was gentrifying, with the immigrants and minorities who had lived there for generations being joined by a steady influx of well-to-do young white people armed with college degrees and entry-level jobs on Capitol Hill. Restaurants and nightclubs and malls were opening to cater to them.

The neighborhood had been a dump not that long ago, and now it wasn't as bad. Officer Michael Dell thought that was all very nice. Heartwarming, even. An urban success story.

The door to 3B opened. A beautiful young woman stood there. She had straight black hair, dark coffee-colored skin, and she wore a loose, flowing garment of white and purple. Her brown eyes were tired, but wary. She looked like she just woke up.

"Yes?"

Officer Dell glanced at the card in his hand. He held the card out to his right, above and away from her. He was mindful of the POW! on his fingers.

"Are you Nisa Kuar Brar?" he said, nearly stumbling over the tongue-twister name. "Wife of Jahjeet Singh Brar?"

She looked from Dell to Stevens and back again, her eyes widening.

"Yes?" she said.

"Your husband drives a taxicab for On Time Taxi service?"

She nodded. "Yes."

Dell nodded. "I'm Officer Dell, and this is Officer Stevens, of the Washington, DC Metropolitan Police Department. May we come in a moment?"

"What's wrong?" she said, her eyes darting back and forth now, something like a panic starting. "Is it Jahjeet? Is he all right? Is he in trouble?"

"Please, ma'am. May we come in?"

She stood aside and allowed them to pass into the apartment. Dell heard the woman shut the door behind them, and—a small gift—she bolted the lock as well. The policemen were inside now, behind a door that was closed and locked. And that meant the game was over almost before it had begun.

Down a narrow hallway there was a living room. Morning light flowed in through two large windows. The floor in the hall was some kind of wood laminate, probably over concrete. It was the same in the living room.

These apartments were generic, built for efficiency and resistance to wear. The family had dressed the place up with too much furniture, and with photographs of family members, a colorful rug, and various religious totems on shelves. But the brute Stalinist form was still there beneath it all.

There were children in here. A small child, in a diaper and a pink shirt, crawled slowly across the rug. A larger child, a girl perhaps three or four years old, sat on the sofa in bare feet and Barney the Dinosaur pajamas. She was absorbed in some sort of hand-held electronic game. Her hair was long and black like her mom's. She was a pretty little girl, like her mom.

That was bad. Michael Dell didn't like the child aspect of all this. But a job was a job and it had to be done. He glanced at Officer Stevens. He barely knew the man. Stevens reached out and almost touched a plant on the windowsill with his hand. He didn't touch it, but it looked like he did. Very clever.

Maybe Stevens was one of these stone killers. That would make this go easier.

The woman, Nisa, came into the room. She was a head shorter than either of them. She didn't offer them something to eat or drink; didn't invite them to sit down. It was just as well. They weren't going to stay long.

"Is everything all right?" Nisa said.

"Mrs. Brar," Stevens said. It was the first time he had spoken since she opened the door. "When was the last time you spoke with your husband?"

"Is he in trouble?"

Stevens shrugged. "He's not in any trouble. He doesn't have to be. Just please tell me when you spoke with him. And please be honest. We'll know if you lie."

Now the look of panic on the woman's face began to transform. She looked like a rabbit about to take off running.

"This morning," she said. "Maybe ninety minutes ago. I was asleep when he called. I almost couldn't believe the things he was saying."

"What did he say?"

"It didn't seem to make sense. He said that he drove the president of the United States in his taxi. He said the president appeared out of the darkness late at night near the White House grounds, and requested to be driven to the Lincoln Memorial, which is not very far away. Jahjeet was very excited, and drove him there. He did not plan to charge the man for the ride, but the president insisted on giving him a fifty-dollar bill. So he accepted."

"Do you believe that the man he drove was the president?" Dell said.

Nisa shook her head. "I don't know. It's all very extraordinary. I would suppose that the president should have his own car service, and armed bodyguards with him."

"But he didn't?" Stevens said.

"Jahjeet said no. He was alone."

"Did Jahjeet see him again after he dropped him off?"

She was looking at the floor now. "He said no. He said the man told him someone else would drive him back home."

"Now Nisa," Stevens said. "I have to ask you a very important question. It's the most important question I'm going to ask you."

"Where is my husband?" Nisa said.

"We'll get to that in a moment. But first, and I want you to think carefully about this, who else have you told about your husband's little encounter?"

Dell moved to the window. He was relaxed about it, just a cop circulating around an apartment during an interview with a possible witness. He looked outside. Three stories below was a drab courtyard between buildings, concrete walkways with small squares of grass in between.

Very subtly, he gravitated to his left, moving in behind the woman. There was an open door a little further left. He glanced inside. He saw a double bed, with the covers kicked down near the bottom. The parents' room.

"I told no one. I was asleep. I just got out of bed a little while ago."

"You're sure about this? You didn't tell anyone?"

She nodded. "I told no one. You must understand. Jahjeet is a beautiful man. He is honest, and a good provider. But he is quick to believe. Too quick, sometimes. His story of driving the president..."

She shrugged. "I wouldn't tell anyone this story. I wouldn't want him to be embarrassed..." She trailed off.

"When it turned out not to be true?" Stevens said.

"Yes."

"Where did you say you folks are from again?" Stevens said.

"I didn't say. But we are from India. Punjab."

Stevens nodded sagely, as if this confirmed some piece of information he had already acquired.

Dell was directly behind her now, still near the window. He pulled the garrote from his pocket. It was nothing more than a length of wire, with small wooden grips fastened at either end. The wire was standard network cabling. Good for this kind of work. Dell had experimented in the past with more durable wires like steel and copper, and he'd had a couple of messy near-decapitations. That was not his cup of tea.

He nearly smiled. The woman was Indian. They grew tea in India.

"You're absolutely positive you didn't tell anyone?" Stevens said.

She shook her head. “Why would I lie? I told no one. I can promise you …”

That was enough confirmation. Dell stepped up from behind her and slipped the wire over her head and around her throat. She gasped as he crisscrossed his arms, tightening it. In almost the same move, he pulled her backward and into the bedroom, away from where the children might see. The whole thing happened in three seconds.

She was so small and light, her struggles were useless. He sat down on the bed and anchored his feet against the floor. Her hands were on the wire, fingers trying to pull it or move it. She didn’t try to hit Dell or attack him at all. She choked, sputtered, and wheezed. He held on a while longer.

Sounds came from out in the living room. They were furtive sounds, rustling, fast movements. Dell put those out of his mind.

When he was sure, completely sure, he let her body slide onto the floor. He put the garrote back into his pocket. He sat for a few moments, breathing deeply. He thought back through this interaction. Had he touched anything in the apartment with his fingers? Anything at all?

He didn’t think so.

He got up and went into the living room. He avoided looking at what was left of the children. Instead, he stared into his partner’s eyes. He was right about Stevens. The man was a stone killer. He was peeling off a pair of rubber gloves and stuffing them in his pocket.

“You ready?” Dell said.

Stevens shrugged. “Not much more to see here.”

Chapter Twenty One

8:45 a.m. Eastern Daylight Time
Queen Anne's County, Maryland
Eastern Shore of Chesapeake Bay

"Stone."

Luke's eyes opened slowly. He had trouble focusing. It was daytime now. He was sideways on the couch.

He took a deep breath. It seemed like someone had spoken his name.

"Stone. Are you awake?"

He pushed himself to a sitting position. He was tired. He glanced at the old grandfather clock, still ticking away, its gold-plated pendulum swinging back and forth. The arms pointed to 3:15. That couldn't be the time, could it? He shook his head. No. That thing was never right.

"Good morning, Stone."

A man sat in the flowered print chair across from him. He was dressed in a sort of business casual style, with khaki pants, a blue dress shirt with a pink collar, and brown leather shoes. His thin legs were crossed in an almost effeminate way. His fingers were long and thin, as if he had once played the piano. He was an elderly man with skin like wrinkled parchment, a rude shock of white hair, and piercing blue eyes.

Those eyes were staring at Luke Stone.

Luke recognized the man right away. He knew this man. He appeared to be old, and certainly he had piled up the years. But he also played at being old. Luke knew he tended to move slowly—he liked to give the impression that he was infirm, a vulnerable elder who was no threat to anyone. Sometimes he even put on a slight limp.

"Kent Philby," Luke said. "To what do I owe this... pleasure? Is that what someone would call it?"

Luke glanced to his right, and then to his left. A man was standing near the wide doorway to the kitchen. He was not particularly large. He was not particularly anything. He wore a light blue windbreaker jacket and black jeans. His dark hair was slicked back away from his face. His eyes were dark and hard and deep set. His face was narrow, like a ferret's face. His skin seemed splotchy, white and red, like the skin of an alcoholic.

He held a matte black Glock nine-millimeter in his right hand. The gun had a long sound suppressor attached to its barrel. He pointed the gun idly at Luke, almost informally. It wasn't that serious a thing. I'll kill you, or maybe I won't.

Across the living room from him, standing near the curtained window to the front of the house, was another man. He was a similar type of man, neither big nor small. Thin but probably well-conditioned. His face was broader, and his short hair was brown with streaks of gray and white. He might have been a little older than the other one.

He wore a uniform similar to his friend's—gray windbreaker with blue jeans. He also held a gun, something a little more exotic. At first glance, Luke wasn't quite sure what it was. It also had a silencer mounted on its snout. It was also pointed at Luke.

The faces of both men were blank. They were all business.

"I see that you're finally waking up to your circumstances," the old man said. "It's interesting to me that someone like Luke Stone could be caught so easily with his pants down. Fast asleep on the couch just after returning from a top secret mission. The kitchen door wasn't even locked. Meanwhile, the world is falling apart all around him, and while I won't say he was the cause of this, he was certainly one of the precipitating factors."

Luke rubbed his head. He ignored the man's little speech.

"Can I help you gentlemen?"

"Just to be clear," the old man said, "I'm going to talk, and you're going to listen. You're not going to like what you hear, which may give you the urge to shut me up. You will resist that urge. These men are killers. Remorselessly so. They have you in an awkward position. If you attempt anything at all, they can triangulate their ..."

"I know what triangulation of fire is, Kent. Tell me something that isn't the first thing I noticed."

The man sighed deeply and then smiled. It was smile that didn't reach his eyes. They were vastly intelligent eyes. Eyes that knew secrets. Eyes without pity.

"Kent," he said. "It's a name from a long time ago. Not one I'm comfortable with anymore. So let's try a different name, shall we?"

"Okay," Luke said. "What should I call you?"

"Wesley is good," the man said. "Wes for short."

That was funny. Wes, Steve, Jim, the man always went by some nondescript name. When Luke was young, the name had been Henry, or Hank. He was the man without a name, the man without a country. What could you say about someone who was a Cold War spy, who sold his own country's secrets to the Soviets, then turned around and sold the Soviets' secrets to the British and the Israelis? And that was the little Luke knew about. There was probably a lot more.

One thing you might say is the guy was lucky to be alive. Another thing is that it was amazing he could choose to live in the United States now, right under the very noses of people who would be happy to kill him or put him away forever. But perhaps betrayal had an expiration date. After a certain amount of time had passed, maybe no one cared anymore. Maybe all the people who once cared were retired. Or dead.

"Quite a little trip you went on," Wesley said.

Luke shrugged. "What do you know about it?"

A long sigh came from the old man. It sounded like the air going slowly out of a tire, all the way, until there was nothing left. He gestured to the gray-haired gunman by the window.

"We know everything," the man said. It was the first time he spoke, and Luke noticed his Russian accent immediately. Somehow it didn't even surprise him that Kent Philby had turned up here with a Russian agent. It was unexpected, like your kind aunt showing up at your door with a home-baked fruitcake. But it wasn't surprising.

Luke looked at Kent, or Wesley, or whoever. "Still working for the Russians, huh?"

Wesley shrugged.

"Do you think we do not see you?" the Russian said. "An atrocity is made on Russian soil by Americans, with help from the Islamist terrorists the Americans love so well. Then an airplane leaves Georgia, flies across Europe, and lands near Washington, DC. Are we blind? Do you think this?"

As the Russian spoke, the old man, Wesley, stared at Luke. There was a wild sort of light in the man's eyes. To Luke, he looked like a carnival barker, or a conman with the traveling medicine show. He smiled again, but this time he seemed delighted.

"You've been a very bad boy, Luke. But I do enjoy watching your career unfold. As you well know, I had you pegged as a major talent from an early age."

For a moment, Luke had been concerned about these men, and their presence here. That worry was beginning to fade. He had considered denying any role in the rescue operation, but why bother? These men already knew what he did. They had followed him home.

"Well, if you were going to kill me in retaliation, I doubt you would have gone to all the trouble of waking me up."

Wesley squinted just a touch. "You have no idea what's going on, do you?"

Luke shrugged. "I got in late last night and fell asleep as soon as I got here. I just woke up a minute ago. I have no idea what the right time is. It feels pretty early to me, but I'm not sure. Also, yes, I have no idea what you're doing here. That doesn't mean I don't like to see you. But it would be nice if you called ahead next time."

Wesley stared at Luke another moment, then looked at the other men. For a split second, Luke thought they all might just walk out the door.

"There was an attack on the White House early this morning. Two men were killed, seemingly after blowing a hole in the fence and trying to enter the grounds. Both were Russians, and both were associated with Russian mafias, here and abroad."

Luke looked back and forth between the men.

"It was false, of course," the man by the window said.

"The attack was staged," Wesley said. "I happen to know that the more senior of the two men involved has been in American custody, moving among CIA black sites, for more than a year."

None of it made any sense. Luke knew Wesley as an aggravating man, an irritant, like sand inside your clothes. Nothing had changed.

"Why would someone do that?" he said.

"They want a war," Wesley said. "It's that simple. Slowly, at a snail's pace, with two steps forward and one step back, Vladimir Putin is rebuilding the Russian industrial economy. He is rebuilding Russian society. And worst of all, he is rebuilding the Russian military. They want to nip this threat in the bud before it gets out of hand. The Russians were in the dead letter office even just a few years ago. Earlier this year, in fact. But they're trying to crawl out. So have the war now, and put them right back where they belong. That seems to be the reasoning."

"Have a major shooting war with the Russians?" Luke said. It went against all of his training. When he was in the Rangers, and in Delta, the unwritten (but oft spoken) rule was: *Don't engage Russians in a firefight.* Until this rescue mission had arisen, he would never have dreamed of…

"Of course," the man by the kitchen entryway said. It was the first time he had spoken. "Nothing works. Everything is rusted. The weapon systems are old. They were devised by better minds than we have now. There are no replacement parts, and no way to make them. The people are hungry and tired, and do not want to fight. The forests catch fire, and no one is there to put them out. We do not stand a chance against the Americans. You saw that yourself."

Luke had to admit he had seen it. Dozens of Russian soldiers, sailors, and first responders, not to mention whoever cooked up their strategy for them, had been caught flat-footed and ill-prepared to fend off him, Ed, and a couple of suicidal lunatics they'd never met before. Four determined men had sliced through the Russian defenses like they were made of butter.

He looked at Wesley. "So what are you doing here? You're on some kind of mercy mission to get this called off, so the Russians won't have to lose?"

A ghost of a smile passed over the man's lips. "I always enjoy our meetings."

"Tell me," Luke said.

"Putin will not allow us to lose," the man by the window said. "He lived through the humiliations of the 1990s. He will kill everyone before he will live them again. To save face, he will launch a nuclear war."

"You can't know that," Luke said.

The man nodded. "I *can* know this. I am SVR, what you once called KGB. We keep intelligence estimates on everyone, even our dear leader. We know what he says when he believes he is alone among his closest confidants. We know what he whispers to his mistresses in the night. We know what the man thinks. And I have seen the dossiers."

Luke shrugged. "So kill him."

The man grunted, laughed, and then shook his head.

"Here's something else we know," Wesley said. "And you won't see this on TV. Not yet, anyway. The president of the United States has gone missing. David Barrett is not up to the task. He does not want a major war. He lacks the intestinal fortitude, and he has consistently made that clear during his time in office. There've even been rumors that he's had some sort of psychological breakdown. Either way, they've disappeared him in favor of someone who can stomach a war with Russia. Mark Baylor secretly took the Oath of Office early this morning."

Luke was still trying to digest what he was being told.

"*They*... disappeared him?"

Wesley nodded. "Yes. The CIA, the Defense Intelligence Agency, the NSA, the Secret Service, all of them together, or rogue elements within each. It's alphabet soup. I don't really know who did it, and it doesn't matter who."

"But *they* made it look like the Russians did it?"

His smile broadened. "Now you're catching on. You're very clever, Luke. Not as quick-witted as I imagined you'd be when you were young, but..."

"Do you know where David Barrett is?" Luke said.

"We think we might, yes."

"And you want *me* to go get him back?"

Wesley nodded. "Rescuing David Barrett may be the only way to stave off a conventional war between the United States and Russia. And stopping that war may be the only way to save the world from nuclear annihilation."

Luke had no idea how much of this was true. Wesley was a professional liar. Wesley! It wasn't even the man's name. And he was here with Russian intelligence agents. How was Luke supposed to believe a word they said?

Last night, as he was drifting off, he remembered thinking how he would make himself some eggs and sausage and toast when he woke up. How he would also brew a pot of coffee, and how he would carry the whole mess out to the patio and slowly enjoy it while gazing out at Chesapeake Bay.

Then he would call Becca and negotiate her and Gunner's safe return here from her mom's house. And then they would do nothing for the next month except... very pleasurable things.

"I think you guys are barking up the wrong tree," he said. "I've been suspended from my job. The powers that be think I might have overstepped during that atrocity in Russia you mentioned.

I handed in my gun and my badge. I have no access to Special Response Team or FBI resources."

He paused. "I can't even get into my own office."

At his feet, his SRT cell phone began to ring. He must have put it on the floor when he fell asleep this morning.

The ringer itself was off, but the phone was set to vibrate. It was a dark blue flip phone with a tiny screen on the front that told you the time. It reminded him of the handheld communicator Captain Kirk used to carry on the old *Star Trek* show.

With each ring, the phone bounced across the wooden floorboards a tiny amount. MMMMMMM, came the sound of the vibration. MMMMMMMM.

Luke stared at it. It was insistent. It seemed to have a mind of its own, and right now it was bent on exposing everything he had just said as lies.

He looked up at Wesley.

Wesley gestured toward the phone with his head. He smiled. "Apparently, you've been reinstated."

Chapter Twenty Two

11:55 a.m. Eastern Daylight Time
Headquarters of the Special Response Team
McLean, Virginia

"Good morning, Luke," the receptionist said as he entered the building through the glass doors of the main entrance.

Her name was Ginger. She was a friendly, talkative middle-aged lady with reading glasses hanging from a chain around her neck. She was also ruthlessly efficient in the way that anyone who worked for Don Morris was, or came to be.

"How was your trip?"

Luke smiled despite himself. He was exhausted, running on painkillers, two cups of coffee, and a Dexedrine pill. He rarely popped Dexies when he wasn't on a mission, but today he made an exception. He couldn't have gotten off the couch otherwise.

"It was a whirlwind tour, I'll give it that much."

She handed him a page from a small pink MEMO pad.

"I'm glad it worked out. You got a call yesterday from a man, name of Kevin Murphy. He said call him whenever you can. Also, Don said to tell you he's on a conference call and he doesn't know how much longer it will last. He wants to schedule with you for about one p.m. You, Mark Swann, and Trudy Wellington."

Luke glanced at the clock on the lobby wall. Time was flying by as usual. They should be meeting *now*, not an hour from now. If what Kent Philby (or Wesley, or whatever he wanted to be called right now) had said was true, then they needed to move on it, and fast.

Unfortunately, Luke had no way to confirm the information. The SRT had the resources, but Luke couldn't just commandeer those resources in his current predicament. He needed Don's buy-in. And he needed it now, but Don was in a meeting.

So Luke would do what was in front of him. He glanced down at the page in his hand. Murph had given him a Virginia phone number to call.

"Is there any way we can get Don to move our meeting up?" he said. "I've got new intel that I really need to share with him."

Ginger nodded, but didn't commit. "I'll see what I can do."

"Thanks, Ginger."

"Thanks for being you," Ginger said.

Luke moved past Ginger's desk and into the atrium. There seemed to be swirl of activity going on that his mind had trouble making sense of. So many new employees coming on. Young guys in sports jackets and khaki pants. Women in business suits. Who were these people? They were sprouting out of the floor like mushrooms.

He saw a face he recognized.

"Swann."

Swann was talking to one of the sports jackets. He turned, saw Luke there, took his leave of the other guy, and came over. His long hair was pulled into a tight ponytail. He wore jeans, yellow-tinted wraparound sunglasses, and a vintage Herbie the Love Bug T-shirt. He looked ridiculous. Suspended or not, criminal charges pending or not, Mark Swann was going to go down swinging.

"Luke, we need to talk."

"I like your shirt," Luke said.

Swann smiled. "This old thing? Listen, about that drone strike..."

"Don't worry about it," Luke said. They were moving down the hall toward Luke's office. "We've got bigger fish to fry. I told Don I ordered the strike, and that we never would have made it out of there without it. Half true, half false, but that's the story I'm going to stick with. As far as I'm concerned, you saved our necks in there."

Swann shrugged and nodded at the same time. It was an odd gesture. "Thanks. I appreciate that."

Luke was on the verge of telling him about the president. It was on the tip of his tongue... but no. Luke felt like he was tiptoeing through land mines. Tell Swann, Swann starts to run with it, tries to confirm it, but he needs help from outside the agency. Who does he tell? Who does he bring in? Is any of this even real?

Kent Philby wasn't always right, and he wasn't always trustworthy. He was a man who followed his own agenda, and there was no way of knowing what that was.

"Don't mention it," Luke said. "In the meantime, I need some way to call out of here, totally encrypted, untraceable on either end. Can you do that?"

Swann nodded. "Sure. It's already set up. We've got our own communications satellite now. I can shoot a phone call from here into space, bounce it off black satellites all over orbit, and put it anywhere you want. Nobody will know where it came from, nobody will know where it went. That said, like always, keep it as brief as you can. The quicker the better. Where do you want to call?"

"Right here," Luke said. "Ten minutes away."

He saw the quizzical look on Swann's face. "Some people came to see me this morning. Luckily, they were friendlies. But it means I'm being followed, and I need to talk to my wife."

Luke held the phone pressed to his ear.

It was a digital phone, a landline that came with its own sort of mini-laptop. Swann had brought in and plugged it directly into the wall. He ran through a bunch of screens on the display, input some numbers, and then smiled at his own cleverness.

"It's ready to go. You are officially a clandestine caller. Try not to hurt this thing, though, okay?"

Now, after a delay while (to hear Swann tell it) the call bounced up to the moon, and across to Mars and the deep space Oort Cloud, then back again, Becca's cell phone rang and rang. Finally, it picked up. For the third time in a row, he got her voicemail.

Her voice was vibrant and bright. He pictured her: beautiful, smiling, optimistic, and energetic. "Hi, this is Becca. I can't answer your call right now. Please leave a message after the tone, and I'll call you back as soon as I can."

Aarrr. Frustrating. He hadn't wanted to leave her a message, but he would have to. *They* could hack into her voicemail account.

"Sweetheart," he said in a friendly, sing-songy voice. "This is Luke. Your husband. I love you very much. Everything here is fine. I am going to call you back again in a few minutes. Yes, it's a strange number. But now that you know it's me, please answer when I call."

He hung up.

He took a deep breath and held it for a moment. When he let it go, it flowed out, loose and jittery. He was pushing, probably too hard. He was due for a crash, he knew that. He had come through hellfire in Russia, had been burned and shot, flew back here to the United States, and was immediately suspended from his job.

He had driven home, slept for three hours, and was awakened by Russian spies pointing guns at him and telling him the president had been kidnapped. Now he had driven back here in morning traffic, suspended, not suspended, he had no idea. And he hadn't even talked to Becca yet.

He looked at the pink MEMO page again. Murphy. He dialed the number.

Murphy, unlike Becca, answered on the first ring.

"Yeah?"

"Murph. Stone."

"Oh, hey, Stone. Listen, about that fight..."

"Yeah, don't worry about it, Murph. It happens. I know where you're coming from."

"It was funny though, wasn't it?" Murphy said. Murphy's Bronx accent chopped his words down to almost nothing. *Funny doh, wadn it?*

"We had the tourists running for cover. I thought one of us was gonna catch on fire there for a minute."

Luke smiled. He pictured two guys, dressed for a funeral, rolling back and forth across John F. Kennedy's eternal flame. It must have been quite a scene.

"Yeah," he said. "They were moving."

"Did you mean what you told me?" Murphy said. "About coming on board? Okay if you didn't. I'm just checking. I wouldn't mind getting out of the rain."

"I meant every word," Luke said. "I've got a few problems here myself at the moment, but I'm hoping to get them cleared up today. How's tomorrow afternoon look for you? You could come in, take a look around, maybe make your case to the boss."

"Sounds good. Two o'clock?"

"Two o'clock," Luke said. "See you then. If I happen to get fired between now and then, I'll let you know."

He hung up. Okay. That was okay. The prospect of Murphy *maybe* coming on board, *maybe* getting a second chance ... that was a good thing. Luke needed good things right now.

He dialed Becca again.

She answered instantly. "Hello? Luke?"

"Hi, babe."

"Oh my God, it's so good to hear your voice. I saw the thing on television, and I didn't know what to think. I was so—"

Luke interrupted her. "What thing on television?"

It was the wrong question. In a split second, she was off to the races.

"On the news. They had a segment about an American attack in Russia. They said there weren't a lot of details because it was top secret. But it was a prisoner rescue and a lot of people were killed. I immediately thought of your mission. They called the rescue a bloodbath. And now there are all these ... I don't know what to call them. Provocations? There was a shootout with fighter jets over Alaska last night. A bunch of planes were shot down. They say we could be on the verge of World War Three. Oh, Luke, it's so—"

He raised his hand, although of course she couldn't see that. "Sweetheart? Sweetheart, it's okay. There isn't a war. Cooler heads are going to—"

"Were you there, Luke? Were you in Russia?" Her voice dropped to just above a whisper. "Did you start all this?"

"Becca, listen…"

"Did you? Did you kill all those people?"

He paused. The silence between them drew out.

Her voice was shaking. "They said it was a bloodbath. It's going to start a war."

"No," he said finally. And now that he had lied to her, he came down firmly on the side of lying. No more fudging. No more messing around. "I wasn't there. I never left Turkey. But I know about that mission, I was sent to monitor it and be part of the communications team, and I know what happened. If they said it was a bloodbath, they are blowing it out of proportion at best, and lying at worst. There was a shootout, yes, but it's not even clear if anyone was hurt. No one on our side was."

He almost couldn't believe he had just said these things. He glanced down at the bandages on his arm. There was another one on his calf, currently covered by his pants leg. He had been shot twice. He was in a lot of pain.

How was he supposed to cover this up?

The answer came to him as quickly as he asked the question: by avoiding her until he was mostly healed.

At some point, and soon, he was going to have to go out of town again. Oh, man. Maybe Don could send him on a mission to the beaches north of San Francisco.

"Why would they lie?" she said.

He shrugged. That was an easy one. "Television ratings. You know the old saying in TV news… if it bleeds, it leads."

"Where are you now?" she said.

Luke nearly sighed with relief. They were moving back toward mundane territory. His footing was firmer here. "I'm at the office. I got in late last night. I didn't call because I didn't want to wake you.

I drove home to the cabin, but you weren't there. Don gave me the morning off today, so I slept in. I just got here a little while ago."

"What is this number you're calling from? It was like twenty digits long."

Yeah. That.

"Becca, I want you to try to understand this the best you can. I was not involved in the cross border raid, but my part in the operation was, and is, still classified. It's possible that people might try to follow me, or learn more about me."

"Oh my God, Luke. It's true, isn't it? I can hear it in your voice, don't you know that? I know when you're lying to me. You were there, and it was a bloodbath. Right? Isn't that what you're telling me?"

"Becca…"

"Did you kill people, Luke?"

"No. I didn't even hold a weapon."

"Luke, we have a newborn baby! Can't you understand that? How can you be a father to our son? How can you murder all those people and expect to come home and be my husband?"

"Becca, I didn't murder anyone."

He looked at the ceiling and shook his head. He was digging himself deeper and deeper. Yes, he had. He had taken the mission and killed people. He couldn't even hazard a guess how many. And now he was lying about it. But he had killed people before, a lot of people, and she had never questioned him this closely.

Anyway, was it really murder? He was doing his job, and those men would have killed him if they could.

It was her mother. Audrey was putting her up to this. It had to be. She saw her opportunity, and was trying to drive a wedge between them while she had a chance.

"Am I in danger?" Becca said. "Is the baby in danger?"

"You're not in any danger," he said. "But I do think it's best, just for the next few days, until this blows over, that you stay close to the house. No one is looking for you. No one knows you're there. Your mom and dad are there. The servants are there. The house has a good security system."

"Oh God, Luke."

"Becca, if you were in danger, I'd be the first person—"

"I can't live like this, Luke. I can't do it. You're not in the Army anymore. You don't have to have a job like this. You don't have to kill people."

Her voice seemed to break up for a moment. When it came back on, it was deeper, as if she had a lump in her throat.

"You're putting your own baby in danger. I can't even speak to you right now."

"Sweetheart," he began, and at this point he had no idea what he was going to say next. But she saved him the trouble of thinking about it.

The line went dead.

Chapter Twenty Three

7:35 p.m. Arabian Standard Time (12:35 p.m. Eastern Daylight Time)
Ibn Sina Hospital
The International Zone (aka the Green Zone)
Karkh District
Baghdad, Iraq

"You all right, Bob?" Big Daddy Bill Cronin said.

Ed Newsam looked at him. As white boys went, he was a bear of a man. Tall, with a thick body, big shoulders and arms, a bushy red beard going a little gray. He wore khaki slacks, shiny black shoes and an open-throated dress shirt. The day was over, but he looked like he was just getting started.

Ed had met Big Daddy for the first time two months ago, when the SRT came here with one mission in mind, but then ended up rescuing the president's daughter. The man was CIA, no nonsense, about as hard as they came.

Ed had watched him do a little light torture on a couple of guys who were his prisoners. One of those guys was an American. Big Daddy had chambered a round in a .38 revolver, gave it a spin, and put it to the man's head. An old-fashioned game of Russian roulette, and he had pulled the trigger three times.

He had poured gasoline on the other guy and threatened to set his legs on fire.

Bad. Ass.

Ed was pretty sure you weren't supposed to do that stuff anymore.

"I'm all right," he said. "A little pain, but they're keeping it under control."

He was lying in a bed at the hospital in the Green Zone in Baghdad. The place was stark and unpleasant. Once upon a time, it had been Saddam Hussein's personal hospital, the place where his family and friends were treated. But by American standards…

Eh. Who knows? Ed tried to steer clear of hospitals.

The bed he was in was uncomfortable and too small for his body. He could feel the steel frame digging into his back through the mattress. They'd done surgery on his right thigh at some point last night or early this morning, to clear out a round that had nearly penetrated his femoral artery. If that thing had hit…

He shook his head. He would have died on the boat ride to Georgia. He didn't even like to think about it.

His roommate was a big white kid with tubes running in and out of him, including an oxygen mask and a tube down his throat. He was hooked to all kinds of machines, beeping, monitoring his vital signs. The kid had been shredded by machine gun fire. He was a lump of meat.

Ed had seen a lot of war zone injuries. That kid was a goner. Ed had slept most of the day, but he would wake up sometimes and look at the kid. He hadn't been conscious all day, and Ed would bet he'd never be conscious again.

The kid was four feet away from Ed's cot. It was like lying down next to the Grim Reaper. Bill Cronin didn't seem to notice the kid at all.

"How did I come to be here?" Ed said. He honestly didn't remember.

Big Daddy shrugged. "You're a private military contractor named Bob Zydeco. You were on your way out to the airport last night and your convoy got shot up. They brought you back in here by helicopter."

An Army nurse came in. She wore combat fatigues, boots, and blue surgical scrubs. The scrubs had a logo on the left breast, a silver cross with a tree inside of it, and a deep red ribbon across the bottom. The word *Evacuare* was stenciled on the ribbon. It was the insignia of the 115th Combat Support Hospital, an Army medic unit with roots going all the way back to World War I in France.

She looked at Ed's chart. "How are you feeling, Mr.... Zydeco?"

The name seemed to throw her. Ed wondered about that himself. Had they run out of cover names? Was anyone on earth really named Zydeco?

Ed nodded and smiled, glossing the problem over. "I feel okay. You guys have been great. I'm thinking about when my discharge might be. I'm ready when you are."

She was smiling, but shook her head. "Believe me, we move people in and out of here as fast as we can. We need the beds. But you've got at least twenty-four hours before you're cleared for travel to Germany."

"Can I take him for a walk?" Big Daddy said.

The nurse shrugged. "If he feels up to it. But I wouldn't take him too far in case he gets weak. Mr. Zydeco is a big man. I'm not sure you'll be able to hold him up."

Big Daddy smiled. "I'll do my best." He looked at Ed. "What do you say, big man? You want to try to take a little walk?"

"Maybe you should carry me," Ed said.

It felt good to move around a bit.

They walked slowly through the crowded halls of the hospital. Ed wore blue scrubs. He limped along grasping his IV drip pole in one hand. It had wheels on the bottom and rolled easily across the stone floors. He had a small black clicker in that hand as well, through which he could administer small doses of morphine if he needed it. In his other hand, he carried a silver metal cane.

Ed was surprised at the amount of effort he was expending just walking.

"I'm really out of gas," he said. "That's great."

"It's to be expected," Big Daddy said.

They shuffled through the lobby of the building, then they were out on the grounds in the heat of early evening. They turned left from the front doors and walked between two tall rows of upright rectangular ten-foot-high concrete slabs—blast walls, in case anyone decided to make a suicide attack.

They passed under the green awning of the checkpoint. There was a concrete guard post here. Big Daddy waved at the guards on duty. No one tried to stop them.

Then they were out on the street and walking along a sidewalk, another large concrete blast wall to their left. A couple of Humvees moved along the roadway. Pedestrians were out for evening strolls.

The Green Zone was always a strange place to be.

"Okay, here's the deal," Big Daddy said. They were away from the hospital grounds now. There was traffic on the street, and no one could hear them.

"Hit me," Ed said.

"You were shot up the worst of the bunch. I had to get you out of there. Georgia is a nest of spies. It's crawling with Russians. This whole game was supposedly so we'd have a heads-up if the Russians decide to invade. It's a joke. The Russians will run right over the whole country in two days, heads-up or not.

"Anyway, I didn't want you in a hospital in Tbilisi, drugged up and vulnerable after surgery, just to have some Russian spy come in and pinch your tubes. So I had them get you stable and we brought you down here to God's country. It's perfectly safe in the Zone here, and we've got better much medical personnel."

Ed nodded. "And Stone?"

"He was roughed up, but not as bad. We put him on a plane and shot him right back to DC. They cleaned up his wounds on the flight."

"Ouch," Ed said.

Big Daddy laughed. "I'm sure it was real pretty."

"The prisoners?"

Big Daddy shrugged. "Classified. But alive and well, so I hear."

"The newlyweds?" Ed said.

"You know how young kids like that are," Big Daddy said. "Fickle. They abruptly decided that Turkey wasn't really a great place for a honeymoon, so they packed up and headed home."

Ed smiled at the thought of Swann and Trudy pretending to be a married couple.

"My friend Garry?"

"He got clipped in the arm, took a nice chunk, but I hear he was drunk as a lord an hour after the boat hit the beach."

Ed nodded. "So mission accomplished and things are good."

"No," Big Daddy said. "Nothing is good. The whole group of you were suspended last night. The Russians are pissed and there's been a lot of saber rattling. There was a dogfight in the Bering Strait maybe eight hours ago. We lost one plane, they lost three. Normally, I'd say that coolers heads are going to prevail, but..."

"We got suspended?" Ed said.

"Ed, listen to me. There's a lot going on. I know you were looking forward to a little holiday in Iraq, but you need to go back. I've known Stone for years. He's going to be right in the middle of things. I can tell, even from here. But he hits a lot harder with you on his wing. And he's going to need to hit very hard indeed."

"You heard the lady," Ed said. "They're planning to hold me another..."

"Never mind that," Big Daddy said. "I'm going to get you out of here tomorrow morning, first light. With a little luck and a good connection in Germany, you'll be back in the USA early afternoon, DC time."

"What's going on?" Ed said.

Big Daddy shook his head. "Loose lips sink ships, my friend."

"So let me get this straight," Ed said. "You want me to race home against doctor's orders, but you're not going to tell me why?"

"Yes," Big Daddy said. "Exactly right. I don't know you well enough to give you information like this. But let's put it this way. Very few people know about it at this moment, it's big, and you're going to want to be there."

He paused and took a breath. "Stone will be very glad when you show up."

Chapter Twenty Four

1:20 p.m. Eastern Daylight Time
Headquarters of the Special Response Team
McLean, Virginia

"I might know where the president is."

Luke spoke before Don Morris had even started the meeting. The three of them, Luke, Trudy, and Swann, had all filed in just a minute before, and had taken seats facing Don's desk like a group of unruly students in the principal's office.

Steel-eyed, salt and pepper Don, looking both impeccable and formidable in a tight-fitting white dress shirt, sat back in his leather office chair. He half-smiled and shook his head. He made a grunting sound that was almost, but not quite, a laugh. It was more like an exhalation of air that a hydraulic system might make. Luke translated its meaning easily. He was fluent in Don Morris by now:

It figures.

Don looked at Trudy and Swann, scanning their eyes to see what they might know. They both turned to Luke.

"I'll go with the White House," Swann said. "Or maybe Camp David, considering the White House came under attack last night."

"The president is missing," Don said. "This hasn't been made public for fear of starting a widespread panic. Officially, he's in seclusion at an undisclosed location for his own safety in the aftermath of the attack. He'll be made available when the Secret Service decides it's safe to do so. But the media is already asking uncomfortable questions about that, and it's only a matter of time before the less responsible among them start spitballing off the wall conspiracy theories.

"The entire security apparatus of the United States has circled the wagons. To be clear, although we've been included in the circle, we are very tangential to this. No one is asking us to do or contribute anything. But I have just spent the past ninety minutes listening to high-level intelligence estimates of where the president might be, so he can be retrieved before things get out of hand."

He stared hard at Luke now. "Only I guess that cat is already out of the bag."

"The president is missing?" Trudy said. Her eyes became wide for a brief moment, then settled down again as her brain started to process the startling information. "What does that even mean? How does a person surrounded by security at all times go missing? The Russian attack on the White House …"

"I don't know," Don said. "No one seems to know. At least, no one is willing to admit they know. Or almost no one. Care to enlighten us, Agent Stone?"

"I can't say how I found out," Luke said.

"You can't say?" Don said. "Don't you work here? Aren't I your employer?"

Luke shrugged. "I don't know. You tell me. I got a call telling me to come in. Not a call telling me I wasn't suspended anymore."

Don waved a hand. "Fair enough. Tell us what you know."

Luke looked at Swann. "How is this room?"

Swann nodded. "Good. We sweep the whole place for bugs once a week. We sweep the offices of key personnel every two days. So far, we've been clean as a whistle. No one even seems to be trying to infiltrate."

Now Luke nodded. He looked at Don. "He might be at a safe house in the Allegheny Mountains, near a town called Cheat Bridge, West Virginia. It's in the middle of nowhere, and there's something about that region making the house hard to hit."

Trudy had already pulled a small laptop out of her bag and opened it.

"In your opinion, how did he end up there?" Don said.

Luke shook his head. "I don't know. But I do have an exact address, in case we need it. It's one of these no name rural routes."

"Cheat Bridge isn't really a town," Trudy said. She was typing fast and scrolling through screens, her eyes staring into the screen and darting back and forth, her super-sharp brain absorbing information at a fast clip.

"It's an unincorporated area around an old Civil War–era covered bridge that crosses the Cheat River. It's in the Monongahela National Forest. Besides the remote location, the reason it would be a hard place to hit is it's located right in the middle of the National Radio Quiet Zone. Most radio and cell phone communications are blocked there. Wi-Fi is blocked. Even microwave ovens are against the law. All other forms of communications, such as landlines and satellite, are monitored constantly."

Everyone looked at Trudy now.

She shrugged. "Now you're gonna say you didn't know there was a National Radio Quiet Zone, right? And you're gonna ask me why it's there."

Don gestured to her with one hand. "Enthrall us."

"There's not much to it," Trudy said. "There are two major facilities out there. The Green Bank Radio Telescope Observatory at Green Bank, West Virginia, and the National Security Agency listening station at Sugar Grove, West Virginia. The two places are about forty miles apart. Cheat Bridge is very close to the telescope observatory. But Sugar Grove is the far more important facility. The NSA runs a top secret ECHELON station there.

"If you believe the hype, they intercept all international communications entering the East Coast from there. If you believe the conspiracy theorists, they intercept *all* communications, both international and domestic. Email, telephone, satellite, radio, anything and everything. NSA wouldn't even admit the place existed until a report released by the European Union in 2001 outed them. Whatever they're doing, that whole region is a communications dead zone. And the communications that are allowed—for example, radio contact by local police and fire departments—NSA listens in on."

Don looked at Luke.

"Why do you suppose the Russians would steal the president of the United States and bring him to a far-flung, blacked-out place, nestled right in the bosom of the American intelligence networks?"

Luke shrugged. "I didn't say I think the Russians did it."

An hour had passed.

They had moved to the conference room. It was Don, Luke, Trudy, and Swann. The door to the room was closed.

Swann had three laptops open across the long conference table. He had pulled generic satellite imagery of the overall region, then zoomed in on the areas in question. On one screen, there was a wide-angle image of the Allegheny Mountains, from the border of Virginia to central West Virginia.

On another screen was a close-up of two large circular clearings cut into the forest, with white buildings, parking lots, satellite dishes, and radomes. The third screen was a split image. One half was an aerial shot of an area of dense woodland, with a dirt road leading to a large house. The other half was a close aerial shot of the house itself, large and white with New England–style gables and a wide stone chimney, perched on a steep escarpment overlooking a valley between two low mountains.

Trudy spoke. "The house and the surrounding land are registered to a Russian immigrant named Maxim Kletka. His address of record is a P.O. box in New Jersey."

"Who is he?" Luke said.

Trudy shook her head. "No one. As far as I can tell, he doesn't exist. Kletka is not a typical surname in Russia, or in any eastern countries. It's a joke. In Russian and Serbian, the word *kletka* means cage or cell, like a jail cell. It's also commonly used as part of the phrase for bird cage."

Luke looked at Swann. "How old are these images?"

"Three months. It's just generic data from a mapping satellite."

Luke's shoulders slumped.

Swann raised a finger. "Don't start, Stone. You want me to get you rich satellite data on that house from yesterday, or today? I can do it. I can practically look in those windows for you. But that's going to raise alarms with the people you seem to think are in there."

"Who do I think is in there?" Luke said. He didn't even know the answer himself.

"Well, you don't think it's the Russians, and I tend to agree with you. The place is in a communications blackout zone controlled by the NSA. There's a cone of silence around that entire region. If I dial up a little custom peek on those coordinates, our friends are going to know about it."

Trudy jumped in again. "There isn't a town or city of any size within fifty miles of that spot. There isn't a legitimate police force, fire department, hospital, or EMS dispatch center anywhere near there. Professional first-responder services are provided at the county level, if that. If you want a real police intervention, you're going to be relying on the West Virginia state police."

Don looked at Trudy now.

"What are you suggesting, Wellington?"

She shrugged. "As a safe house location, or as a site to take prisoners, it's almost insidiously well-placed. Outsiders can't have radio communications there. You'd have to request them beforehand. *Why do you want them? Well, we want to kick the door in at this house.* Which means you can't have any sort of command and control over an operation without letting NSA know ahead of time.

"Airspace isn't restricted per se, but if you do a drone flyover, they're going to know about it at Sugar Grove. You can't have real time satellite data without them knowing. You can't make a phone call. If you request support from state or local law enforcement, where do you think their loyalty lies? With you, or with the federal agency that dominates that region? Do you think NSA doesn't have moles at the state police?"

"So you're saying you think the National Security Agency of the United States stole the president?" Don said.

Trudy shook her head. "I'm not saying anything. I'm not saying the president is even there. To me, that part doesn't add up. It could just be a big empty house on a mountainside for all we know. We could get there and find a man grilling steaks and drinking beer on the porch. But if we are going to go there, then I think we'll need to do it in total secrecy."

"And total secrecy won't even be possible," Swann said. "There is a fence around the perimeter of that property, and a long dirt road leading up to it. My guess is you'll hit an electronic gate when you reach the fence, and there are probably cameras on that road. Whoever is in that house will know you're coming."

"Helicopter?" Luke said.

Swann shrugged. "Possible. But it's all mountainside and there's nowhere to land. So you're going to have to hover and fast rope down into the front yard."

He pointed at the wide area image of the region.

"If you looped around the outside of the entire area and came in from the west, that would be your best look. You'll be coming in from the West Virginia side, and the Sugar Grove listening station is well to your east, near the Virginia border. They might not pay you any heed right away."

Now Trudy pointed. "If the chopper came in along this corridor from the northwest, following US Route 250, you could be a very early morning traffic helicopter or highway cops monitoring the roads for speeders. The highway passes five miles north of the house. You could cut off at the last second, and I'll bet the SRT chopper can cross that remaining territory in two or three minutes."

Swann nodded. "Two minutes before you hit the house, you could call me on the sat phone. I could be ready to pull up real-time imagery, so you wouldn't be going in completely blind. Yeah, that would alert NSA, but if they're really in cahoots with whoever's in that house, they'd have almost no time to relay the warning."

Luke looked at Don.

Don sat back. He laced his hands across his head, tamping down his salt and pepper hair. He nodded.

"We've been ramping up, as you know. We've got guys on board now with SWAT experience. The chopper seats six, with gear stowed. I can give you five good people, you round it out at six. Can you do it with six?"

Luke stared at the house and the surrounding grounds.

"The SRT chopper's a passenger bird. It's not configured for a fast rope exit."

"No. I could pull a few strings and get a Black Hawk or a Little Bird here for a training exercise, but it'll raise eyebrows if I say I need it before first light."

Luke nodded. "We can make our bird work. And six? Yeah, I think we can do it with six. We just took out half the Russian empire with four. All we're doing here is knocking on a door."

"Ding-dong," Swann said. "Avon calling."

"Except the president might be in there," Trudy said.

Don shook his head. He grunted. "They're gonna say I'm a crazy old coot. Probably put me out to pasture after this. I just suspended my best people because of pressure from above, then I unilaterally unsuspended them, and now we're going to hit what's probably a US intelligence safe house without giving anyone a heads-up. Because based on no evidence whatsoever, we think the president might be there."

Luke looked at him. "Does that mean we're going in?"

Don's eyes were hard and serious. "If you think this agency is hanging by a thread right now, just wait until tomorrow. We'll be hanging by our necks instead. But yes, we're going in."

He paused and took a breath.

"I don't see any other choice."

Chapter Twenty Five

4:45 p.m. Eastern Daylight Time
Just south of the Canadian border
Newport, Vermont

The place was falling to hell.

Lawrence Keller was working quickly, going in and out of the house, and he could barely get himself to glance at it. His old summer house. He'd been driving all day, he was damn near exhausted, and the place was bumming him out. If he focused too much attention on it, there was the possibility that he might start crying.

The house was tiny, 700 square feet, one bedroom, one full bathroom, plus a glorified closet with a toilet and a sink. It was over a hundred years old. The cedar shingle siding, decades past its expiration date, had turned gray and yellow and brown. Some of it was rotting out. The rain gutters were plugged with leaves from last fall. Some sort of moss was growing between the asphalt shingles on the roof. The winters here were long and cold, but that moss was tenacious.

It looked awful.

Moreover, the house was *slumping*. It was tired and had forgotten how to stand up tall. It seemed like it could fall in on itself at any minute. He really needed to take better care of it. Truth was, he hardly got up here anymore.

There were two good things about his old Vermont vacation house. One, and by far the less important of the two, given the circumstances, was that the house was situated on a small peninsula of land called Lake Park, which stuck out into Lake Memphremagog a few miles north of Newport. The house was right on the giant lake, and its back deck looked out on the water and the surrounding countryside.

The most important thing about the house was it sat just a couple miles south of the Canadian border, in a quiet, somewhat forgotten corner of the state. People here were poor. They didn't get out much. They were not curious about you. Keller had seen a statistic somewhere that fully one-third of the townspeople of Newport could be considered obese. Time had passed this area by. Now there was little to do but sit around and eat.

The house was owned by a man named Kevin Lawrence. Kevin Lawrence looked an awful lot like Lawrence Keller. In fact, they were identical in every way. Kevin also had a Vermont driver's license, and a tan 1995 Oldsmobile Cutlass Ciera sedan with Vermont license plates. The car's registration was up to date.

Right now, the car was parked inside the small garage in the back yard, along with a canoe, a bicycle, some deck chairs, and bunch of other summer stuff he hadn't taken out, or even looked at, in years. The garage windows were blocked with nailed-on wood. You couldn't see inside. There was no reason for anyone to look in there anyway. The nondescript car in there was one of the most reliable sets of wheels that Kevin Lawrence and Lawrence Keller had ever owned.

In a few moments, he was going to go in there, start up the Ciera, and pull it out. Then he was going to back Lawrence Keller's fancy Audi Quattro in there. Soon after Keller left his apartment in DC, he had switched his BMW with the Quattro, which he kept in an underground parking garage in Silver Spring, Maryland.

As he moved through the yard, Keller caught a glimpse of the lake. It was a gorgeous early summer day and some kids were water skiing from a little motorboat out there. The lake was beautiful.

"Man oh man," he said.

He really should have done more with this place. It wouldn't have taken much to make it a very nice place to spend time. But he had let himself get caught up in the excitement of life in DC. He'd been so important! The chief of staff to the president! Then the president had unceremoniously kicked him to the curb. And now the president...

He shook that thought away.

A short time later, he was behind the wheel of the Oldsmobile. The Audi was locked away. The little house was locked up. And Kevin Lawrence had all his papers and his luggage together (including his gun), along with seven thousand Canadian dollars. He was leaving the country.

There was no sense waiting. A real war could break out at any time. If that happened, they might suddenly decide to seal the border. Also, at some point, someone in the public was going to realize that the president was missing. When that happened, all bets were off.

He took North Derby Road headed east right along the border. At the end of the road, he turned left on Beebe Road. The post office was on the corner on his left.

There was a Canada Border Service Agency facility, right at the border, where Beebe Road linked up with Canada Route 247. The offices were in a couple of small buildings, set back from the road. One of them looked like it used to be a bank, with a little drive-through window under a canopy out front. You didn't even really need to stop there.

This entrance to Canada was an open secret. For the locals who crossed back and forth between countries all day, often running minor errands, it was a matter of course. There was no United States Customs station here.

A few miles to the east, there was a more stringent border control marking the line between Derby Line, Vermont, and Rock Island, Quebec. But even over there, crossing was no big deal. The border control was right on Main Street. And Lawrence knew that in the little town, there were people living in the United States on one side of the street, while their neighbors across the street lived in Canada.

At one time, there was even one post office in the town, the only international post office in the world. Canadians entered through one door, Americans through another. There was a line down the middle of the floor they weren't supposed to step over.

Just to the east of that was the real customs and border control station on Interstate 91. Thousands of tourists on the highway stopped and did their border crossing there. Sometimes their cars were searched for contraband. Sometimes they got hassled. And little did they know, crossing over there was entirely voluntary.

Kevin Lawrence chose to cross over here. One day they might put concrete barriers here and fences with razor wire, but in the Year of Our Lord 2005, the crossing was still wide open. And that was the way he liked it.

A white and green SUV of the Canadian Border Patrol was parked under the canopy at the little pull-in area. As he passed, Kevin Lawrence raised a hand and waved at the Canadian border officer leaning against the SUV. The man waved back.

And just like that Lawrence Keller and his doppelganger, Kevin Lawrence, were across the border and in a different country.

He was in a car that was nearly invisible, with Vermont plates, and with a Vermont driver's license. He was two hours from Montreal, a major city with 1.8 million people in the city, and 3.5 million in the metropolitan area. Montreal was a great city, and a great place to be anonymous, maybe even to disappear.

Kevin Lawrence kept a little apartment in town, a *pied-à-terre,* a "foot on the ground," as the French might say. And Kevin Lawrence did speak a little French left over from his high school and college days.

Lawrence Keller took a deep breath as he drove north. He had ditched his cell phone this morning, tossing it out the window near the border between Maryland and Delaware. Let them trace it to that location if they could, some grassy terrain along the side of I-95, hundreds of miles south of here.

Ah. All the trouble was behind him now.

He was going to be okay.

Chapter Twenty Six

8:15 p.m. Eastern Daylight Time
Potomac Towers
Arlington, Virginia

"A little more wine?" she said.

Luke nodded. "A splash. Why not?"

He was at Trudy Wellington's one-bedroom apartment on the eighth floor of a high-rise development across the water from downtown DC. There was no access to the outside from here, but the tall windows almost made it seem like there was.

From where he stood, he could see a panoramic sweep of the Potomac River heading down to Reagan National. One after another, ceaselessly, the fat-bellied commercial jet planes came upriver and made their slow descents to the runway. Luke could see a line of them glinting in the fading sunlight, all the way out to the horizon, waiting their turn to land. It was a busy airport.

Beyond the airport was the raging torrent of traffic on the eastern loop of the Beltway, where it linked with Interstate 95 on the south side of the city. The day was ending and people had their lights on. From here, the red taillights of the northbound traffic looked like lava flowing.

She came in from the tiny kitchen with a bottle of chilled German white wine. Liebfraumilch. He had enough German to translate: *mother's milk*. Luke had never tasted it before, but it was good. Zesty, fruity, but not so sweet as to taste like juice. It went down easy.

Trudy had changed into a pair of pink sweatpants and a flimsy blue T-shirt. She must have had that shirt since junior high school. It had been worn and washed so many times it was starting to become see-through. It had a peeling iron-on decal of Betty Boop on the front. Betty was bending over to smell a rose, and showing a lot of leg.

So nice read the caption at the bottom.

Trudy's hair was down. She poured another splash of the wine into his glass. Luke was in trouble.

"Thank you," he said. "You're a very good host."

She smiled and poured some more into her own glass.

He was here. It had happened. There wasn't any way around it right now. He was due back in the SRT offices at one a.m. for a final briefing with his team, gear up, and then on the chopper by three a.m. They were going to hit the target in the sleepy hours before dawn. There was no real surprise involved. It was just circadian rhythms. Even professionals, trained to expect and defend against an assault, often couldn't stay alert through the middle of the night.

But in the late afternoon, he had found himself so tired that there was no way he was going to make the long drive back out to the Eastern Shore. Could he have gotten a hotel room and expensed it? Sure, he probably could have. But he was exhausted and he was no longer thinking straight. So he went down to the SRT locker room, turned off the lights and fell asleep on one of the benches.

Sometime later, she had come in and woke him up. His eyes opened to her standing over him. He was in pain again, the pills having worn off while he was asleep.

"What are you doing, silly?" she said.

He shook his head. "I don't know. Taking a nap?"

"You can't sleep here," she said. "It's no good. You won't get any rest, and you have a mission in the morning."

"I know. But I can't go all the way home. It's a three-hour round trip."

"You can come to my place," she said. "You can sleep on the couch. It'll be a lot more comfortable than this. Better yet, I'll let you have the bed."

It was reasonable, of course. And it was the entryway to a very slippery slope. Now he was sliding down, headed for the bottom, no way to stop or even slow down. He was still beyond tired. The wine was going to his head. Becca wasn't speaking to him. Worse than that, Becca had accused him of murder. He was lying to her about his missions. She was forcing him to do this. It was hard to swallow.

Meanwhile, Trudy knew everything about the missions. She didn't judge them. And Trudy was beautiful. More than beautiful, she looked…

Delicious.

He knew this was wrong. He was making excuses for his behavior. He had a new baby. He should just go. Go anywhere, to a hotel, sleep in the car, an alleyway, wherever. He had carried out missions where he was even more exhausted than this. That's what they made Dexedrine for.

He focused on her TV set. It was a large flat-screen mounted on a faux brick wall. The brick was a nice touch somehow. The apartment was well-designed. He had to admit that. For what it was, he liked it. There wasn't much to it, but it was modern, spare, very hip. He liked her taste in furniture, and the long red splotch of a painting hanging on one wall. For an instant, he wondered if the place came furnished or if Trudy had picked all this stuff out.

CNN was showing on the TV. A man was on there, of indeterminate age. He had a beard, long hair, and bruises on his face. He wore a loose-fitting button-up short-sleeve shirt, almost like a Hawaiian shirt. The shirt was dirty, as though he had been wearing it for weeks. He was in a grassy place, and people behind him were staring at him. He was shouting something and waving his arms.

Earlier Today the caption at the bottom read, *Washington, DC.*

A smooth female voice spoke over the video. "This was the scene this afternoon at Lafayette Park in Washington, DC, just across Pennsylvania Avenue from the White House grounds."

"David Barrett is dead!" the man shouted. "The president is dead! They took him! I saw it. His cab driver is dead. I gave him the cab!"

"This man, thought to be homeless and identified only as Crazy Joe by long-term denizens of the park, claims to have seen President David Barrett get into a taxicab late last night, just before the mysterious attack on the White House. In fact, he claims he was going to take the taxi, but let President Barrett have it as a gesture of respect. He also claims the taxi was driven by Jahjeet Brar, the cab driver found murdered near the White House early this morning. President Barrett has not been seen in public for two days, but White House officials have been clear that he is alive and well."

On the screen, video appeared of three large men in suits walking Crazy Joe through the park toward a waiting black SUV. Crazy Joe tried to shake their grip on his arms, but they held him tight. They put him in the open back seat and pushed his head down so it wouldn't hit the roof of the car.

The female voice continued. "The man called Crazy Joe was later seen accompanied by what are believed to be plainclothes officers of the DC Metropolitan or perhaps the Capitol police."

Now a new image appeared. It was of a middle-aged white woman with long dreadlocked hair. She wore a tie-dyed T-shirt in bright colors. She held a small sign that said IMPEACH BARRETT.

"Joe is a very nice man," she said. "He has never hurt a soul, and is sometimes targeted and victimized by others. He is always welcome here in the park. Obviously, we prefer him when he's on his medication, but we love him and put our arms around him however he chooses to be."

Luke gestured at the TV. Trudy was standing very close to him now.

"While I'm out getting killed tomorrow, I think you should find that guy. Looks like DC Metro has him."

Gently, she took the wine glass out of his hand.

"Crazy Joe? Why would I want to find him?"

Luke was looking down into her eyes now. He was much taller than she was. The slippery slope just got steeper and even more slippery. And he was falling.

"He might know something we don't."

She smiled and licked her lips. "I doubt it. There are a lot of crazy people out there. There's going to be a lot of crackpot conspiracy theories."

Their bodies were nearly pressing together now. He felt the animal heat coming from her. He wanted to rip her threadbare shirt apart. Alarm bells rang in his head.

Red alert! Red alert! Red alert!

He leaned in for a kiss.

And stopped.

"I can't do this," he said. "I've got a wife. We have a new baby."

Trudy smiled, but her eyes were hard.

"You don't have to do anything you don't want to do. You're not my prisoner."

He nodded and took a deep breath. Suddenly, the full weight of his exhaustion hit him. "Okay. I really should get some sleep."

She gestured at the long couch.

"I'll get you a couple of pillows."

Chapter Twenty Seven

June 28
4:05 a.m. Eastern Daylight Time
Above US Route 250
Inside the National Radio Quiet Zone
Cheat Bridge, West Virginia

"ETA six minutes, gentlemen," the pilot said.

Luke glanced out the window. It was dark, black, the deepest part of the night.

The roadway snaked below them like a ribbon, cutting through the dense forest on either side. The mountains undulated away into the distance.

He felt that old trickle of fear, of adrenaline, of excitement. He felt alive and alert. Jazzed. The Dexedrine he had popped twenty minutes ago didn't hurt.

He knew the drug's effects. His heart rate was up. His pupils were dilating, letting in more light and making his vision better. His hearing was more acute. He had more energy, more stamina, and he could remain awake for a long time. Dexies were old friends of his. But it was more than that.

He turned to his team. They were helmeted, visors up, with black SRT fatigues covering light body armor. Flashbang stun grenades hung from chests. Sawed-off shotguns ready. MP5 submachine guns ready. A heavy two-person battering ram stood upright against one of the seats. They looked out of place in the well-appointed interior of a new executive helicopter.

Their eyes were on him, a couple sharp, but relaxed, a couple wide open and nervous. He barely knew any of these people. Don Morris had acquired them all from somewhere in recent weeks, but knowing Don, they were very good at what they did. They were four men and a woman. He had been formally introduced to them for the first time at the briefing a couple of hours ago. He knew them by the names sewn on their uniforms.

"Okay kids," he said. "You know the deal. We're going in short-staffed and partially blind. So we hit hard and fast. We're going to be vulnerable getting out of this bird, so the shorter amount of time that takes, the more likely you and your partner walk out of here alive. Clear on that?"

They all nodded.

"What?"

"Clear," they said, almost in unison.

"Fast rope, we go over the falls two at a time. One on each side, sequence reverse order, C-Team, B-Team, then A-Team. Hit the ground, get out of the way, and be ready to lay down covering fire as needed. Move to the house fast and disperse. Spread out. If there are shooters down there, we want to make it hard on them."

He paused. "Clear?"

"Clear!"

"C-Team?"

The blonde-haired woman and a young dark-haired guy raised their hands. He glanced at the names. Paige was the woman. Deckers was the man.

"I need you guys behind that house, covering rear exits *before* the ram hits. Be ready to triangulate fire on anyone coming out. Stay out of each other's way. You have one rule: Do NOT shoot the president."

C-Team smiled at that, but Luke wasn't being funny.

"B-Team?"

Two hands went up. Luke glanced at the names. Hokens and Lofthouse. Who were these people? The faces looked at him.

Luke raised one finger.

"One hit with the ram. That's what I need. Make it the best you've ever done. Get on that porch five seconds before…"

Luke looked at his partner. He was a tall guy with a heavy beard and steely eyes. His black uniform was the wife-beater version—no sleeves. His thick, muscled arms had a mad intaglio of tattoos all over them. There were a couple of scars that could have come from bullets. The guy had special ops written all over him. Just looking at him made Luke miss Ed Newsam. *Kerry* was the name stitched on the man's jumpsuit.

"Five seconds before me and Kerry. Hit that door, toss your flashbangs, then fall back hard. We are coming through at full speed. As soon as we pass, guns ready and in the door behind us. Careful, though. We may take fire going in."

He looked at Kerry.

"It's you and me, buddy. I sense you've done this before."

The guy smiled. He was missing a front tooth. "Oh yeah."

"We don't tolerate resistance," Luke said. "We don't want a gunfight, but we stop anybody who does. Someone shoots, someone so much as shows a weapon, they're out of the game. That said, we're not here to kill the president of the United States. Cool?"

"What if the people in there are Americans?" Kerry said.

"If they're Americans, they see us coming and they surrender," Luke said.

"Three minutes ETA," the pilot's voice said over the intercom.

Luke took out his satellite phone and speed-dialed Swann's number. The signal did its dance from earth to space, and back again.

"I see a flaw in this whole operation," Kerry said.

"Now's a good time to bring that up," Luke said. "We're going to hit in two minutes." What was it about this guy that reminded him of Ed again?

The man shrugged. "I've been thinking about it. It became clear to me just now."

Luke glanced out the window. They were flying low and moving fast through the darkness. The hillsides below them were blanketed with dense forests. They were just above the treetops. "Okay. I'm all ears."

"Suppose you're the Secret Service, and you evacuated the president here to keep him safe after the attack on the White House? Then a handful of SWAT-looking lunatics come falling out of the sky and crashing through your doors in the early hours before dawn? Are you just gonna surrender? Or are you gonna fight to the death?"

Swann's voice came over the phone. "Luke?" His voice was on speaker. Everyone in the passenger cabin of the chopper could hear him.

"Yeah, Swann."

"Okay," Swann said. "Clock is ticking. They're gonna know we're coming any second. I just pulled up real-time imagery."

"How's it look?"

"It seems like no one is there," Swann said. "There are no personnel apparent on the grounds. There are no shooters in the high gables. There are no cars parked near the house. There's no one on the porch. There are a couple of lights on inside, but they could be on a timer. The place looks completely empty."

That was odd.

"Okay. No one is home. I hope that turns out to be true. Don't go anywhere. We might need you."

"I'm right here." The phone went dead.

Luke looked at Kerry.

"Suppose you're the Secret Service," he said. "And you're protecting the president of the United States. You've probably got a couple of armored SUVs parked out front, and a few guys walking around with guns, don't you? You've got snipers in the high places. Maybe a Black Hawk hovering around with heavy weapons poking out of its snout?"

Kerry smirked.

Luke looked at the rest of them. "Okay, SRT. Eyes sharp, heads on a swivel. It could just be practice today, but if so, let's make it a good one. Are we clear?"

"Clear," they said as one.

Luke looked at Kerry. "Clear?"

Kerry shrugged. "Clear."

"Thirty seconds ETA," the pilot said. "We have a visual on the target. Cabin door locks are disengaged. Prepare for disembark."

"Go!" Luke shouted. "Go! Go! Go!"

A thick rope depended from either open doorway of the helicopter. The chopper was in a low hover over the dirt driveway leading to the house. It was a vulnerable position to be in. If they were attacked, the chopper had no weapons with which to fight back.

Luke could easily see the big white house from here, sitting over a steep drop-off to dense foliage far below. Except for a bleak yellow light on the first floor, the windows were like dark eyes in a skull.

C-Team went out on either side. Luke looked at his watch. 4:12 a.m. He tapped the green START button on his stopwatch function. He waited three seconds.

"Out!" he shouted. "Let's go! Let's go!"

The next two, the battering ram team, dropped over the sides.

Luke poked his head out the doorway and glanced below him. All was clear. He looked at Kerry, across from the cabin from him.

"A-Team!" he shouted. "Out!"

He went over the side. A second later, maybe two, he touched down onto the dirt road. He looked around, getting his bearings. The first four to drop were ahead of him, running up the short hill toward the house, moving fast.

He unslung his shotgun and started running. Across from him, spread out about twenty yards, Kerry ran, keeping pace.

Up ahead, C-Team split up, the woman taking the left side of the house, the man taking the right. B-Team sprinted up the stairs to the big wraparound porch. Firewood was neatly stacked on a pair of runners along the wall.

The two men stepped to the front door with the heavy battering ram. It was a swing-type ram, each man holding the handle on each side. They didn't make a sound.

Luke sprinted up the stairs one second ahead of Kerry. To his right, the world dropped away down the dark mountainside. He caught a glimpse of the sleek black SRT chopper circling out.

Just ahead, the two men reared back and swung the ram.

BAM!

The door exploded inward and came apart. The rammers tossed their flashbangs and ducked back.

Three…

Two…

One…

BANG! BANG!

The timing was perfect. Luke saw the flash of light and heard the stun explosions. The floorboards shook under his feet. He burst into the open doorway an instant later. Smoke lingered in the air and he plowed through it.

"Down!" he shrieked. "Down! Get DOWN!"

An instant later, Kerry was behind him, screaming the same thing.

Their voices echoed through the house. Luke moved through a wide open space. The ceiling in the atrium was two stories high, with a double bank of stacked windows granting a view across the steep stark valley. There were lights in the distance, perhaps a small village or a camp of some kind.

Luke passed through some white Greek-style columns. He moved quickly, taking cover behind the wall. He was just outside the wide doorway to a great room. Across from him was a large stone fireplace. The floors were polished marble. A tall lamp in the corner was on, giving off a circle of yellow light.

Behind him, he could hear the electronic lock on the shattered door.

Beep… beep… beep… beep… beep… beep…

Then the men with the battering ram. They had entered the house.

"Down!" they screamed. "Police! Get down!"

Luke stopped. He kept his gun up and ready, but he stepped slowly into the room. Four men were here. Three men were on the floor, blood spread out around their heads, congealed, tacky. Two of the men wore light windbreaker jackets and jeans. One wore a blue tracksuit.

Luke barely saw them.

There was another man here. He sat in a blue and white flower-patterned oversized armchair. He was very tall, slim, with salt and pepper hair. He wore a pair of jeans, white sneakers, and a dark cotton V-neck T-shirt. It was incongruous to see him dressed that way. Luke was accustomed to seeing him in suits.

He had a dark gag in his mouth and a blindfold over his eyes. His wrists appeared to be bound behind his back. His head was slumped to one side. He had the unmistakably boneless body posture of a dead man, just as dead as the men on the floor. His face was pale, with a tinge of green. In the gloom, Luke could see blood on the chair, and he could see the darker stain on the man's dark shirt. Even so, he couldn't get a sense of the cause of death. Was he shot? Was he stabbed?

Behind Luke, Kerry had just entered the room.

"Oh my God," he said under his breath.

"Search the house," Luke said. "Right now. Tell C-Team to establish a defensive line facing the road as best they can. Then take B-Team and search this entire goddamned house. Who's the medic on this operation?"

Kerry was still standing there, staring at the body.

"Paige."

"The woman?"

Kerry nodded. His eyes never moved from the body in the chair. He spoke absently. "She was an emergency room RN at some point. Before that she was a field combat medic with the 10th Mountain Division, something along those lines. I don't know. I just met her a week ago."

Luke glanced behind Kerry. B-Team was already here, also staring. There were three men with Luke in this room, highly trained, experienced, but also slack-jawed, as if in shock from a particularly gruesome battle.

"Okay, never mind the defensive perimeter for the moment. Get Paige in here."

Luke looked at the other two men. "The two of you," he said. "Search the rest of the house! Go!"

Their feet began to shuffle, and their eyes began to pull away from the sight in front of them.

"Now!"

The men snapped out of their reveries. Their body language became alert, and suddenly, they were professionals again. They lifted their shotguns, turned, and disappeared. A few seconds later, he could hear them kicking down doors and moving through rooms. He heard a pair of boots pounding up a staircase.

Luke pulled out his satellite phone. He pressed the speed dial for Swann again. He waited while the phone did its thing.

Swann picked up. "Number one best Chinese food."

"Swann, we got big problems," Luke said.

"Tell me about it," Swann said. "Where are you?"

"We're in the house."

"Meet any resistance?"

Luke shook his head. "No. Not so far."

"Okay, look. I'm guessing you guys tripped an alarm on your way in. There's a line of SUVs that just disgorged from the NSA station at Sugar Grove. They're going hell bent for leather, but it's going to take them a while to get there. Worse news is there are two Apache helicopter gunships headed your way from the south. Beats me where they came from, but they'll be on top of you in five minutes. Don told the SRT chopper to find a place to land and surrender to whoever pulls guns on them first. No sense making a run for it and getting shot down."

"Swann ..."

"There are flashing lights much closer than the SUVs, moving your way. I'm guessing local sheriffs or maybe state police. Ah, wait a second. I just lost my feed…"

"Swann, I'm gonna need…"

"Okay, somebody kicked me off the satellite. We're blind again."

"Swann, shut up a second."

Swann stopped. When he came back on again, he sounded a tad petulant. "Okay, Stone. How can I help you?"

"I need media attention. Tell Trudy to go big. Doesn't matter who gets here first, CNN, Fox, local news outlets, the *National Enquirer*, I don't care. But we need them here, on the ground, at this house, before this place gets overrun by government spooks. We're gonna hold it as long as we can, but if they come with force, eventually we'll have to surrender. Something's been happening here, and I'm afraid our own people, American intelligence assets, were in on it."

He took a deep breath. He was about to continue, but Swann was already talking.

"Uh, media's not our department, Stone. I know what Don's going to say without even having to ask. All inquiries are dealt with by the media liaison office at Bureau headquarters downtown. I mean, there's a very clear delineation of tasks. We really are a subagency of a much…"

Swann was saying something more, but there was a sound behind Luke that caught his attention.

He turned and Paige was there. Out of the helicopter and with her helmet off she was a small blonde, pretty, her hair tied in a bun. Her face said she was older than she had appeared earlier, certainly older than Luke.

That made sense. An Army medic, a hospital nurse, and now dropping out of helicopters and kicking down doors with the SRT. She had done a lot. Not for the first time, Luke felt a burst of admiration for Don's acumen. He had a knack for finding and deploying the right people.

Paige's mouth was half-open as her blue eyes darted from body to body. She seemed surprised, but not shocked. She was keeping her emotions in check. She had seen this before.

"Can you give me an estimated time of death on these bodies, without stepping all over this crime scene?" Luke said to her.

She shrugged and nodded. "I can estimate based on rigor mortis. I can also cut one man's pants open and take a rectal temperature. I can do that without moving the body or touching any wounds. Should be very minimally disturbing to the scene. That's only one body, but I'd say it'll give us a ballpark idea for all of them."

Luke pointed at one of the men on the floor, the one furthest from the center of the room. He was already lying on his side.

"That one," he said. "Nobody cares about him."

Swann's voice over the phone was growing irritated. "Luke, what are you…"

"Swann, I need a forensics team," Luke said. "I've got bodies here. I'm about to get an estimated time of death, but I need real forensics, a medical examiner, the whole nine yards. I need someone in authority to come in here and shut this site down. Someone we can trust. Tell Don I'm requesting the Bureau to send a team here, ASAP. I feel certain the FBI was not in on this, and I think we can trust in that. I need them fast, though. Preferably from a field office that's near here."

"Luke…"

"The president is dead, Swann. Okay? Did you hear me? The president is here, and he's dead. So get me what I asked for, all right? Yesterday, if you don't mind."

Luke hung up the phone. His heart was racing.

"Full rigor mortis, including arms and legs," Paige said from the floor behind him. "No evidence that rigor has begun to decline. Body temperature 74.3, roughly the same as room temperature. A good guess is this guy has been dead between twenty and twenty-four hours. Lividity suggests he died right here where we found him."

Luke checked his watch. Four twenty a.m. According to the stopwatch, C-Team had jumped from the chopper eight and a half minutes ago.

He tried to get his mind straight, think of the many things he was probably forgetting. He knew he had to start preparing to hold off all comers, but he couldn't take his eyes off the scene in front of him.

The dead man in the chair was President David Barrett.

"Be cool," Luke said. "Don't shoot anybody just yet."

He stood on the wide porch of the house, at the top of the steps. He was speaking to Kerry, his partner in A Team. Kerry stood just behind him, cradling his MP5. The man made for good theater—big and brawny. With his thick beard and tattoos, he looked like a movie tough guy.

It was still dark, but faint light was just beginning to appear below the horizon to the east. There was nothing but forest and mountains out there. That and a hovering Apache helicopter, the guns on its snout pointed directly at the house. Even from this distance, the rumble of its engines and the beat of its rotors made the porch vibrate the tiniest amount.

Luke cast a wary eye at the chopper. If it wanted, it could take this place down to the foundation in a matter of minutes. It could turn Luke and Kerry to liquid in seconds.

A group of men, as many as a dozen, walked toward the steps. The lead man was big and thick. He wore a gray and brown uniform and a tall cowboy hat. He carried a shotgun. He was just a little paunchy, like he enjoyed a few drinks after work. He might have been in his forties, or maybe his fifties. It was hard to say.

Behind him and his group were several police cars with flashing lights. They also had a Bearcat armored assault truck.

When the man had come within ten feet of the stairs, Luke called out to him.

"Okay. That's far enough."

The man looked up at Stone.

"Sir, I'm Inspector Reggie Harris, with the Randolph County Division of Emergency Management. We are also the local extension of the Department of Homeland Security."

His voice had a slight hillbilly lilt to it, polished enough to tell you this man was a professional, but noticeable enough to let you know he had emerged out of the backwoods and was keeping it real. He had nailed it. It must have taken some work to perfect that accent.

"Pleased to meet you," Luke said. "I'm Agent Luke Stone, with the FBI Special Response Team."

"Well, Agent Stone, I'm here to relieve you and your men. I have elements from my department with me, as well as units from the Randolph County and Pocahontas County police forces. We're all empowered as regional deputies of the National Security Agency. You're in good hands with us."

Luke shook his head. He almost smiled.

"Inspector Harris, my team are here for the duration. This is a federal crime scene, and we've been ordered to hold our position and secure this site until—"

"Sir, my orders are to remove your team by force, if need be."

Luke paused, then started again.

"Until FBI forensics teams and backup agents arrive here from Washington, and from Wheeling. I'm told the first units will be here within the hour."

The man suddenly began to walk toward the stairs again.

"Sir, I'll have to ask you and your team to stand down. We are the duly authorized representatives of the National Security Agency in this region. You can remove yourselves from that building, or we will remove you."

Luke spoke fast and loud.

"Inspector Harris! Look to your left if you don't mind."

To Harris's left, and Luke's right, was a large window facing the stairs. In the dim early light, the details of that window hadn't been obvious. But Harris looked at it now, and its lines became clear.

The window was open halfway, and Paige was there, kneeling on the other side. Her gun poked out at Harris and his men. Paige and the gun were mostly silhouettes.

"That's Agent Paige," Luke said. "She's a highly trained special operator with experience in two combat theaters. Can you see what she's holding?"

Harris had stopped. "It's a gun."

Now Luke did smile. "Oh, it's more than a gun. It's an MP5 machine gun, fully automatic. It's a very nice weapon. Paige is a crack shot, she's got forty rounds in the magazine, and I've seen her swap mags in just a couple of seconds."

Of course he was bluffing. He had just met Paige this morning. She was holding Luke's gun. He had never seen her swap magazines. He had no idea if she had ever shot one of those things in her life.

"She's got the drop on you, wouldn't you say? She could put eighty rounds into you guys with barely a pause."

Luke took a deep breath, letting his chest rise and fall.

"You've ordered a gun to be pointed at brother officers," Harris said. "I'll have your badge for this."

Luke nodded. "Maybe, but first that woman will turn you and your men into Swiss cheese. And she'll do it on my go."

There was a long moment of silence, no sound except the Apache helicopter, somewhere out there in space. Luke didn't take his eyes off Harris.

"What I suggest you guys do is go back down to the gate and establish a security perimeter around this place. I'm told to expect a team from Alcohol, Tobacco and Firearms shortly. Those men will help you."

Luke watched Harris's eyes. Those angry eyes were becoming clearer in the gathering daylight. They darted from Luke to Paige, and back to Luke.

"Until they arrive, do yourself a favor and stay out of my hair."

Chapter Twenty Eight

6:55 a.m. Eastern Daylight Time
Special Activities Center, Directorate of Operations
Central Intelligence Agency
Langley, Virginia

"I feel like you may be losing control over this situation."

The old man warbled in that unspeakable voice of his. There was driveway gravel lodged deep in his throat. He had just finished smoking a cigarette down to the nub, and now he was using his trembling yellow fingers to light a new one with the dying embers of the old.

He took a deep suck on the fresh cigarette, as if the heinous thing emitted life-giving oxygen, instead of so many toxic poisons it was impossible to analyze or even accurately quantify them all.

"Of course I disagree," Wallace Speck said.

"Oh?" the old man said. "I'd love to understand your position. You see, because what I've heard is the man's body has been found by the FBI in a rather…"

The old man interrupted himself with a brief but violent fit of coughing.

"… compromising position, right in the bosom of a communications dead zone hosted by certain friends of ours. Not only is there the embarrassment of the discovery itself, there's the little matter of an armed standoff between two secretive federal agencies, ongoing as of a few minutes ago, and broadcast on national TV."

Speck sighed. He hated coming down here to talk to this man. Once upon a time, he had thought of the man as his mentor. But as the years passed, he came to think of the man a monster, a dark fiend who lurked in closets and lingered under bridges.

Even this office the man had. It was below ground level. There were no windows. The ceiling was high, but the smoke from the man's cigarettes never seemed to find its way out. There was no airflow somehow. It smelled in here, and there was always a pall of blue and gray smoke.

"You should have died twenty years ago," Speck almost said, but didn't.

He sat across the wide steel desk from the old man. The desk was like a flat metallic desert. Speck could almost picture tiny Mongol hordes riding across its endless expanse. Usually the desk was empty except for the man's overflowing ashtray. But today there was something new. A small TV monitor sat there, facing the old man.

Speck could see it from an angle. Right now it was on CNN, showing helicopter footage of a large white house perched on a forested mountainside. Numerous emergency vehicles were parked outside of the house. Men in SWAT uniforms and carrying rifles stood sentry on the porch. The sound was muted.

LIVE said the words across the bottom of the screen. *Cheat Bridge, West Virginia.*

"Please do explain," the old man said.

Speck was tired, but there was no rest for the weary. Until this morning, he'd been congratulating himself, thinking that the loose ends were nearly tied off, with only Lawrence Keller left to go. He had even imagined he could afford to go home and catch a few hours' sleep ... a very foolish idea.

"There is no standoff," he said. "I can see the TV set as clearly as you can. There was some initial confusion in the aftermath of the first agents arriving on the scene and discovering the president. Why wouldn't there be? The men are professionals, but they were traumatized by what they found in that house. At this point, not even an hour into the crisis, there are representatives of the FBI, the NSA, the ATF, as well as local and state law enforcement agencies on the scene, all cooperating and working together."

"Go on," the old man said.

"The dead men in the house with the president are all Russians, men with long-term and well-known ties to Russian and other Eastern European mafias operating both here and abroad, and also with ties to Russian and Serbian intelligence agencies. One of those men stood accused of crimes against humanity during the Yugoslavian Civil War. Proper justice will never be served in his case."

The old man nodded and took a long, nearly obscene drag on his lifeline.

"More."

"The house is owned by a shadowy Russian businessman. The site was clearly chosen as an ingenious place to hide. Who would think to look for a Russian safe house inside an American intelligence security zone?"

"Why is the president dead?" the old man said.

Speck shrugged. "The president's death hasn't been announced yet. When it is, it will be announced by the White House, perhaps after a brief word from the director of the FBI. Everyone's going to be on the same page, reading from the same script. Now, we don't know yet what happened in that house, but we're investigating. Maybe it was a sudden dispute among the kidnappers? Or perhaps the plan was to kill him all along, and the men who abducted him. Maybe Russian intelligence agents killed everyone in the house and then left by car. Tire treads in the dirt road will confirm that a vehicle was there as recently as yesterday."

The old man seemed to be thinking. He became very still.

"And why did we deny the president was missing?"

"It's obvious, isn't it?" Speck said. "We wanted to prevent a widespread panic. We were trying to avoid a war with the Russians, and were attempting to negotiate his safe return. But the Russians were acting in bad faith."

The old man looked at Wallace Speck. His cunning eyes were gleaming, almost glowing in the strange half light of this room. He smiled, and as he spoke his long teeth did that clicking thing which bothered Speck so much.

It was like the old man was a giant piranha. "Now there's no way to avoid a war," he said. "Is there?"

Speck shook his head. "No, I don't think there is."

"And the people of America tend to become very patriotic and unquestioning when war arrives, don't they?"

Now Speck nodded. "Yes sir, I believe they do."

"Then it would seem," the old man said, and paused to allow a rumble of tiny jagged rocks to settle at the bottom of his throat, "that the sooner a war breaks out, the better."

"Yes," Speck said. "I couldn't agree more."

"Can we do that? Expedite the start of the war?"

"We can do," Speck said, "anything we like."

Chapter Twenty Nine

7:30 a.m. Eastern Daylight Time
Headquarters of the Special Response Team
McLean, Virginia

"Ah, hell," Don Morris said.

The phone hadn't stopped ringing in the past hour. The front desk receptionist wasn't in yet, and they were taking more phone calls in one morning than they normally took in a week.

For some reason known only to the office telephone system, the calls were ringing here to Don's office.

He picked up the latest call on the first go.

"Don Morris," he said.

"Don, you made a mess in your pants this time," a male voice said.

"Oh?" Don said. "How so?"

"You're a cowboy, everybody knows that. And that has its place. But this isn't the rodeo, old man. This is a team sport. You don't invade Russia one day, and then two days later stick your knife in the backs of your friends."

Don let the voice wash over him, trying to place it. The voice had some sort of encryption that turned it into something like a robot voice. Even so, there was a lingering remnant of an actual voice in there. He needed to get the man to talk a little more.

"Who are my friends?"

"I think you know who your friends are, Don. But you're losing them pretty fast since you hung your little shingle out. You need to stand down, Don. Your head is in the guillotine right now. You could lose everything you have there, the SRT, all of it. What you did today…there are people who don't appreciate it. I'm one of them."

"I gather that," Don said. "But I'm afraid you have me at a bit of a disadvantage. You know who I am. You even know where to reach me. But I don't know who you are…" Don glanced at the readout on the desk phone. "…and it seems your number is blocked."

"I intend to keep it that way," the voice said. "But while I have you on the phone, let me put things to you very clearly. Your team is on the bench for the rest of this game. There are things going on here that you don't know about, and you don't need to know."

"Like the assassination of David Barrett?" Don said.

"Funny. I haven't seen anything on the news about that. What I'm getting is an unfolding crime scene in West Virginia. It's still a mystery what's going on there."

Don shook his head. "What do you want?"

"I want you to bring your team home," the voice said. "And as I already indicated, I want you to sit out the rest of the game. Just stay on the bench and keep your mouth shut. Things are going to move very fast now, and you don't have an opinion about it."

Don shrugged. Stone and his team were already en route back here. FBI forensics agents had taken over the crime scene. But about this "rest of the game" stuff…

"Suppose I do have an opinion about it," Don said.

"Don, you're a family man. You have a wife and two lovely grown daughters. I don't really need to…"

Don felt his heart skip a beat. Until now, he had felt nothing about the person on the other end of the line. There wasn't a man alive on earth who frightened Don Morris. This anonymous, vaguely sinister call could have been a prank by a scrawny teenager.

Frankly, Don had even been willing to believe that the Russians had abducted David Barrett and murdered him. Certainly, there was no real evidence otherwise.

But now some coward was going to threaten Don's family? And this was because the SRT had found Barrett's body? For one thing, it seemed to confirm everything Stone had suggested about Americans being in on this. For another, it pressed the BIG RED BUTTON inside Don's psyche.

"Listen, you punk. I will cut your head off. Then I will reach down your throat and pull your lungs out the top. Test me on this. Do you think I'm not going to be able to find you? Think again. We trace every call that comes in here, and I will kill you for the things you've already said. Do you have any idea what I'm going to ..."

"If you'd like to make a call," a woman's recorded voice said, "please hang up and try again."

Don looked at the phone in his hand. He glanced up and Trudy Wellington was standing in the doorway.

"Everything okay, Don?"

He sighed. "Sweetheart, can you please tell Swann to reroute these calls anywhere else but my telephone?"

Chapter Thirty

9:15 a.m. Montreal Daylight Time (9:15 a.m. Eastern Daylight Time)
Old Montreal
Ville-Marie
Montreal, Quebec, Canada

Different country, same life.

Lawrence Keller followed nearly identical rituals almost every morning. First, he awoke from a series of nightmares he could barely remember.

He climbed out of the low to the ground, modern queen-sized bed in his Montreal flat and padded into the living room in a pair of boxer shorts and a T-shirt. He hit the remote control and CNN came on. Ah, news from America.

The flat was smaller than his Georgetown apartment, by a lot. It was on the third floor, one floor below the roof, of a two-hundred-year-old building in the oldest section of the city, just a few blocks from the St. Lawrence River.

Unlike the cabin in Vermont, Keller didn't neglect this place. He liked it to appear lived in, so he never turned off the electricity, the water, or the cable TV. He paid a local woman to come in twice a month, clean the flat, and give it a once-over. And he flew up here once in a while and stayed for a few days.

It was convenient that everything was on. It meant he didn't have to worry about turning it on when he got here. Which meant he didn't have to interact with anyone. This was good. Keller had survived a long career in Washington, DC, largely by being paranoid.

As it did every morning, it occurred to him that he hated the news. He hated the voices of the talking heads. He hated how often their conversations devolved into talking over and shouting at one another. He hated the enthusiastic fake seriousness of the newscasters. Did anyone like this stuff?

Keller watched it because for a long time, it had been crucial to his work that he knew what was going on. This morning he watched it because his life was in danger, and he was hiding out from powerful people.

There might be clues as to...

Who was he kidding? He watched it by force of habit. He pressed the MUTE button as the advertisements came to an end.

The image on the screen showed a woman and a man sitting behind a news desk, both impeccably dressed and groomed, both of indeterminate age and even indeterminate race. These two were not just indicative of the melting pot nature of American society—they had actually been dropped into the pot, and had melted to such an extent you could no longer tell what they once were.

Had their forebears been slaves working the cotton fields in South Carolina? Or had they come in steerage from Europe and been processed and quarantined at Ellis Island? Had they come across the Pacific from China and built the railroads that drove the great westward expansion? It was impossible to guess.

Now there was a helicopter image of a large white house perched on a green mountainside. The place was surrounded by emergency vehicles with flashing lights. Men with rifles and wearing black uniforms stood guard near the front porch.

PRESIDENT BARRETT FOUND DEAD scrolled along the bottom.

For a long moment, Keller stared at the screen. He could not bring himself to turn the sound back on. He didn't want to hear what the TV wanted to tell him. Suddenly, he felt lightheaded, as if his head was a helium balloon attached to his body by a string. The balloon floated, up, up, up and away.

Keller stepped backward, thinking he would sit in an armchair. He missed and slid to the bare wooden floor instead.

"Oh God," he said.

He sat quietly for a long moment.

"They're going to kill me." He realized the truth of it. They were out there, right now, looking for him. And there was no way they weren't going to find him. Maybe not today or tomorrow, but soon. There was no way to hide from these people.

Suddenly, it occurred to him that he had gotten David Barrett killed. In his mind, he saw David's eyes bulging in terror as the men grabbed him, covered his mouth, and shot him with the Taser.

Keller had become dismissive of David over the years. It would be hard not to become that way. But on some level, they had been more than just the president and his chief of staff. They had been friends.

When Barrett decided, driven by whatever fevered imaginings, that it was a good idea to escape the White House grounds, who did he call to come and meet him? He called Lawrence Keller.

"He trusted me," Keller said now.

Keller didn't care that he was taking to himself. He barely realized it. He felt a great lump welling up in his throat. He had played the Washington game for so long that unspeakable betrayal was just another day at the office.

He had gotten his friend killed, and now the killers would come for him.

Across from him, the image on the TV changed. It showed the press briefing room at the White House. The podium was there. Currently standing in front of the microphones was Nathan Morgan, David Barrett's press secretary. His face was flat and grim. He was waiting for the cue to begin.

Next to him was a man Keller recognized, but had never met—FBI Director Christopher Dunkin. Dunkin was tall, with silver hair. Keller happened to know that Dunkin was an ex-Marine with combat experience, just like himself. He was a Yale-educated lawyer, and he'd had a thirty-year career in law enforcement, including two decades with the FBI. There was hardly a man who had more credibility with the great mass of American people than Christopher Dunkin.

Keller looked down at his hand and realized it was still holding the remote control. He unmuted the TV.

"Good morning," Nathan Morgan said. "I will start by confirming what has already been reported widely. President David Barrett has been murdered. I want to assure you that the country is in good hands. Our new president, Mark Baylor, has already taken the Oath of Office."

Suddenly the lump in Lawrence Keller's throat was so thick he almost couldn't breathe. He closed his eyes so he didn't have to see the screen.

And a moment later, he started to cry.

Chapter Thirty One

11:20 a.m. Eastern Daylight Time
Headquarters of the Special Response Team
McLean, Virginia

"I thought it was bad, frankly."

Luke was sitting at his desk, back at the office. He was going to have to invent a new word for exhausted. Swann was bustling around, setting up another encrypted satellite call for him. Luke was going to try Becca again.

It was crazy, considering everything that had been said, and everything Luke had done. There was no way to undo the Russian operation. More details were leaking from it, and there seemed to be no way to stop the world events that were in motion.

Don Morris was standing in the doorway, impassive, big arms folded.

"Bad," he said. "How so?"

"You saw the press conference, Don. We kept the operation secret because of the possibility that rogue elements within American intelligence had kidnapped the president, and to me that seems more likely now than ever. Not only did they kidnap him, they killed him. Within minutes of us hitting that house, the NSA and Pentagon were throwing assets in our direction. They knew exactly where to go."

"I agree with you," Don said. "More than you can possibly know."

Luke shrugged. "Well, then you know what I'm talking about. The press conference was a lie. The Bureau director got up there with the White House press secretary and made it seem like it was somehow *their idea* that we hit that house. They didn't mention once that the house is in the middle of an NSA security zone. They didn't—"

"Would you expect them to?" Don said.

Luke sighed. "I don't know what I'd expect. A little honesty, maybe."

A little honesty.

Luke didn't want to think too much about that phrase.

"Now we have to have World War Three so people don't ask too many questions about what happened to the president of the United States? We just saved his daughter two months ago. I mean ..."

Luke was tired. He needed to go home and sleep for a solid day. Suddenly he realized that if he kept talking he was going to start to cry. He didn't want to do that, not in front of Don, and for some reason, especially not in front of Swann.

"Maybe they're going to need us to ask the questions," Don said.

"That's going to be hard," Swann said from the floor. "Considering the director just cut our legs off."

Swann stood, apparently oblivious to the scowl on Don's face. The phone he just installed was a digital device. It came with a small laptop computer, complete with fold-up screen. Swann ran through the screens on his display and input a long code.

"It's ready," he said.

"Maybe you should just leave that thing here," Luke said.

Swann shook his head. "We only have two of them. There can't be one for Luke Stone, and one for everybody else."

"Carry on, fellas," Don said. "Stone, excellent job this morning. You did this agency proud in a trying circumstance. I'm going to want a full report of the action sequence, and an assessment on your team's performance, as soon as you can. It doesn't have to be today. But don't forget we do have a meeting with your friend Murphy this afternoon."

"Oh, man," Luke said.

"No rest for the weary," Don said, and then was gone.

Luke looked at Swann.

"Nice job today, Swann. You got me what I needed, when I needed it. That's all we can do, right?"

Swann shook his head. "The things that go on ... people would never believe it."

Now Swann went out.

Luke held the phone pressed to his ear. He waited while the call bounced to Pluto, across the solar system and into the heart of the sun, then back to earth. He was not looking forward to this conversation, but it had to be done.

Becca's telephone began to ring. Her voice came on right away.

"Luke?"

"Hi, babe."

"Oh Luke. I am so glad to hear your voice. I was waiting for your call. I saw you on the TV news."

That couldn't be right. At least, he hoped not. His mind went to the Russia operation, the alleged bloodbath ... "You saw me?"

"In West Virginia. The news helicopters were zooming in on the house. I saw you come out with a group of your people. Everyone had SRT on their backs. They didn't identify you, but I saw you. They said the FBI Special Response Team found the president's body. You were there, weren't you?"

"It was my team that found the body," Luke said. He took a deep breath and sighed it back out. "We acted on a tip and went in by helicopter at dawn. Me and another guy were the first ones in the door."

"Oh my God, sweetheart," she said. "I am so sorry."

Luke nodded. "I am, too."

"Are they providing you trauma counselors?"

Luke smiled. He nearly laughed. Talk about a question flying in out of left field. This wasn't sophomore year in high school. They were not providing trauma counselors. He pictured himself walking into Don's office and asking to see a trauma counselor. His smile broadened into a great big grin.

Suddenly, he loved her all over again. He loved her so much his heart nearly broke. He wanted her to never know what went on in his life, the things he'd seen and done. He wanted to shield her from that information forever, and he never wanted his son to know, either. He wanted them protected, and far away from any of this.

"Luke?"

"Um, things have been moving pretty fast, hon. We just got back here a little while ago. I think, uh... the whole country's going to be in mourning. Plus we have this whole confrontation going on with—"

"But you saw the body," Becca said.

"Yes, I did. And I'm going to have to process that, I know."

The bodies he'd seen! David Barrett had been a pretty inoffensive corpse. At least he was more or less in one piece. Luke had seen bodies that looked more like linked sausage meat than people. He'd seen faces lying on the ground like rubber masks, utterly divorced from the person to whom they'd once been attached. He blinked to clear his mind of these images.

"You're my hero, Luke. I realize what you're doing is very important."

"Thank you, sweetheart. You're my hero."

"When can I see you?" she said. "I miss you so much. I want you to be here with the baby."

"Well, yesterday it looked like I was going to get a few weeks off. I'm not sure that's on the table anymore. But my dream is to be out at the cabin with you and Gunner, just the three of us..."

"Just the three of us," Becca said. "That sounds so nice."

"It's nothing against your mom..."

"I understand, Luke. It's better when we're alone. It's just with you being gone so much, and the depression..."

"I know," Luke said. "And we're going to work it out. I'm going to be in meetings this afternoon, but then I'm going to ask Don if time off is still in the cards..."

"Whatever happens," she said, "just know that I love you. I'm sorry that we fought. I love you more than life itself."

"I love you too," Luke said. "I love you so much."

Chapter Thirty Two

12:30 p.m. Montreal Daylight Time (12:30 p.m. Eastern Daylight Time)
Old Montreal
Ville-Marie
Montreal, Quebec, Canada

At some point, Lawrence Keller was going to need food.

There was a tiny grocery store just around the corner. This being Montreal, they were fanatics about fresh bread. Also, they had wine and nice cheeses. The stall out front on the sidewalk was usually piled with attractive fruits and vegetables.

Keller could climb down the narrow stairway here in his building, four stories, exit onto the charming old cobblestone street, turn left, and the store was probably no more than two hundred feet away.

It spoke volumes about his state of mind that he could not bring himself to do it. He had brought in a few things when he arrived last night. Cream for coffee. A loaf of bread, and a stick of butter. Half a dozen eggs. Oranges and bananas. It wasn't enough. It was not going to last.

He sat on the couch with his Sig Sauer in his hand. He hadn't gotten dressed. He had barely moved all day. He had looked out the window a few times, down at the street. It was early summer and the neighborhood was crowded with tourists. The crowds would give Keller's killers perfect cover. Keller could get knifed in the back just walking down the block.

If he went out into the street, he was an easy target. If he ordered food in, the assassins could push their way past the delivery man when Keller buzzed the front door open for him.

Keller understood. He was all the way gone in paranoia now, but he had every reason to be. These people were heartless killers. Wallace Speck, the dark lord himself, commanded them. They had murdered the president. There wasn't much to stop them from murdering Lawrence Keller.

An observer seeing him on the couch would probably think that Keller had sunk into a depression so deep he was nearly comatose. He seemed to be staring into space. But inside, his mind was alert and active.

It raced through his memories, like a computer searching its own data banks. If there was a solution to this problem, it was stored inside Keller's mind. He was in Canada, a two-hour flight from DC. They were going to find him here, that much was certain.

He had taken care to hide this place, but everyone made mistakes. In this day and age, it would be almost impossible not to. The new technologies, programs like ECHELON, meant that *they* could harvest Keller's communications. *They* could run algorithms that looked for matches, through IP addresses, GPS locations of cell phones, credit card transactions…

He had heard ECHELON referred to as an "eavesdropping program." It wasn't an eavesdropping program. It was a monstrous vacuum cleaner. It was a giant fishing trawler that cleared out the ocean of life. ECHELON ate everything.

Had he always kept Lawrence Keller and Kevin Lawrence's communications completely segregated? Had he never sent a Kevin Lawrence email from a Lawrence Keller IP address? He couldn't guarantee it. Once they matched the two men's identities, it wouldn't take long for them to find this flat. Indeed, they might have already found it.

Maybe he could leave the country. Assuming he made it to the airport, from here he could fly almost anywhere. He could go to a country that had no extradition treaty with the United

States—Cuba, maybe, or Venezuela. But Kevin Lawrence didn't have a passport. Which meant that Lawrence Keller would have to do the traveling. Which meant credit card transactions, itineraries, security checks...

That was out of the question. If they knew he was there, they could reach him in Havana or Caracas almost as easily as they could reach him here.

Across from him, the TV set was still on.

Mark Baylor, the new president of the United States, stood in front of a camera in the Oval Office. His hair was white, much whiter than you might expect for a man his age. His face was serious, saddened, but also determined.

Behind him and to his right a large American flag was draped. To his left was the Resolute Desk. These were nice subtle touches, of course, the kind of thing Keller himself would do.

Mark Baylor was president now. The Oval Office, the flag, the desk, these were timeless symbols of America. They were the trappings of power. They almost made it seem as if Mark Baylor had always been president.

Baylor was tall, like David Barrett himself had been. But he was much broader. He looked like a man who had played the linebacker position in high school, became sedentary, but never stopped eating like an athlete. The cut of his suit covered it pretty well, but he was not a thin man.

Lawrence Keller, who had been a long distance runner for most of his adult life, did not like fat people. He was not a racist. He was not a sexist. He had no opinions about anyone's religion or personal habits (within reason), but he had a real prejudice against fat people. All that excess meat made him uncomfortable.

"My fellow Americans," Baylor said.

David Barrett was dead. He was gone. And this man had played some role in his death, just as Lawrence Keller had, just as Wallace Speck and God knew who else had. It shouldn't be allowed to stand.

"This has been a painful day for all of us," Baylor said. "I stand before you humbled by the enormity of the tasks ahead of us, as well as angry and grief-stricken at the death of my good friend and predecessor, David Barrett. I have struggled since this morning to make sense of this terrible tragedy, and to find words to express my feelings to you about this great man, and about the difficult steps we must take to honor his memory."

Keller was only half listening. David Barrett. He was a long way from a great man. He was mostly a self-centered but well-meaning bumbler, who had somehow parlayed family wealth, connections, and good looks into a stint in the most important job on earth. He could have kept the job, but he was undone by his own fatal flaws.

The things that David gotten up to. He had an embarrassing man crush on the old Special Forces colonel whose operatives had saved his daughter. Did it make sense to feel indebted to the man? Of course it did. But Barrett was like a teenage girl with the man's poster on her bedroom wall.

Colonel Donald Morris, one of the original pioneers of Delta Force. That's who the man was. And he was a legend. Keller could picture him well enough. Steely blue eyes, flattop haircut, square jaw. He should play himself in a movie. In fact, he should play a caricature of himself in an absurd comedy.

Morris had retired from the Army and ran a sub-agency of the FBI now. He called it the Special Response Team. A handful of his operatives had crashed a helicopter in the rugged upper peaks of the Sinjar Mountains, wiped out a group of Al Qaeda in a firefight, and somehow brought Barrett's daughter Elizabeth back alive.

They must be madmen. Killers. And they would have nothing to do with the likes of Wallace Speck.

"As you know," Baylor said on the TV, "David Barrett was kidnapped during an attack on the White House carried about by Russian nationals with links to organized crime. For more than twenty-four hours, we engaged in increasingly fruitless conversations with the Russian government, in an attempt to secure the former president's safe return. Our attempts at a diplomatic solution were with an eye at preserving peace between our two countries.

"You will note that the nature of the attack makes it obvious that it was deliberately planned many days, weeks, or even months in advance. And the president was kept prisoner at a house purchased more than two years ago by a Russian operative. I am now at liberty to tell you that the corpses of three men other than the president were found at the house. All of the men were Russian nationals, all of them with ties to organized crime or Russian intelligence."

Baylor paused, looking directly into the eyes of the American people. Lawrence Keller sighed. They were really going to sell this as a Russian assassination, and then they were going to sell the war they had wanted all along.

He was angry. Of course he was. But he was also helpless, and he thought he might start to cry again.

"It seems nearly certain that Russia has undertaken a surprise offensive on American soil. We are still investigating, but the facts of yesterday and today speak for themselves. I'm sure the people of the United States have already formed their opinions and well understand the implications of this offensive."

Baylor raised a hand.

"I ask for your patience while we conclude our investigation. In due time, soon, all of the facts will be revealed. I have directed our security personnel to expel the Russian ambassador and all of his embassy staff here in Washington. I have also directed that the Russian ambassador to the United Nations, and all of her embassy staff, be expelled from New York. That will happen shortly.

"We are still in contact with the Russian government, and we have requested a reasonable and transparent accounting of their actions in recent days. If we do not receive one, and their response thus far does not inspire confidence, as Commander in Chief I will be forced to direct all branches of our armed forces to prepare for war."

He paused again. Despite the horror of what was unfolding, Keller had to admit that Baylor was doing well. He was convincing. The man had probably been rehearsing his entire life for just this moment—the day he could threaten the Russians with annihilation.

"I have complete confidence that we have the best military in the world. If it comes to war, no matter how long it takes, I know the American people will win through to absolute victory. I believe that I interpret the will of the people when I assert that we will not only defend ourselves to the utmost, but will make it certain that treachery like this never takes place again.

"We will discover the perpetrators of this terrible crime, and we will punish them with fire. If those perpetrators are found to be the Russian government, their intelligence operatives, and the organized crime figures they use as their pawns, then so be it."

Baylor's gaze was steel now. To Keller's mind, it was almost as if he was doing his best Don Morris imitation.

"So be it," he said again. "We do not shrink from a challenge. We are the greatest country on earth. The determination of our people will overcome the obstacles set before us, and we will gain the inevitable victory, so help us God."

Keller muted the TV again.

A moment later, the image switched from the Oval Office back to the newsroom. The talking heads were ready to begin. They would parse Baylor's every word. Keller could practically recite their lines for them.

President Baylor had been strong. He had been decisive.

He was waffling. He seemed in shock.

He seemed ready to carry the weight on his broad shoulders.

He's rattling the sabers.

Did he declare war or didn't he?

He toed the line perfectly.

He should have done more.

What the pundits didn't know, or would refuse to say, was that Mark Baylor was an amoral crazy person who would love nothing more than to give the generals exactly what they wanted—free rein to blast the Russians back to medieval times. Baylor was paying lip service to the idea of an investigation, to the idea of being patient.

The war would be declared soon, maybe after it had already started.

Keller's life was in danger, and all day he could think of almost nothing else. But now he was confronted by a larger, more terrifying fear.

He had been in the Situation Room with this president, and the advisors that he favored and kept close to him. Keller had seen it before, up close and personal.

Mark Baylor was capable of starting World War III.

Chapter Thirty Three

1:55 p.m. Eastern Daylight Time
Headquarters of the Special Response Team
McLean, Virginia

Three cups of coffee hadn't done anything.

He moved through the bustling hallways in a near daze. A hand reached out and touched his arm. He turned to look and it was Trudy.

Her hair hung down in soft curls. Her pretty eyes were behind her crazy red librarian glasses. She wore a blue blazer and dress pants.

They stared at each other for a long moment. Neither one spoke. To Luke, it wasn't necessarily awkward. He wasn't sure what it was. The office activity swirled around them. It was a hectic day. This morning's raid had returned the SRT to the glare of the national spotlight. All of these people were working as quickly as possible to put that glare elsewhere. Thankfully, it wasn't going to take much.

Russia and the United States were on the precipice of war.

He thought of Becca and Gunner. He had just talked to her... when? Whenever it was, the new president hadn't spoken yet. She must be having a freak-out at this moment. He didn't blame her. If he wasn't so tired, he'd probably be ready for one himself.

He needed to call her again.

In front of him, Trudy smiled, but her smile was tentative. She looked at him closely. "Are you okay?"

He smiled in return. "I am very, very tired."

"You seemed to have gotten some sleep."

He shook his head. "I did. Thank you. You saved my neck. But between the trip to Russia, the operation this morning, the dead president we found, and the world on the verge of—"

"I have something to tell you," she said.

Above all words, those were the ones he dreaded hearing.

"About us?"

She shook her head. "No, silly. About the job. I ran a search on this man they call Crazy Joe. Like I told you I would. His real name is Joseph Earl Pattinson. He's forty-four years old, and has a long history of mental illness, apparently schizophrenia combined with bipolar disorder. He's a long-time denizen of Lafayette Park. He's been arrested many times, but it's always been for minor infractions. Public drunkenness. Disturbing the peace. That sort of thing. As far as anyone can tell, he's never hurt a fly.

"But here's the strange part. I checked with DC Metro Police. I checked with Capitol Police. I checked with National Parks security. I checked with the Secret Service. None of them have any record of arresting him, detaining him, or even interacting with him yesterday. I rewatched the video of him being led away. The men with him have no identifying markers on their clothes, and there is nothing on the SUV they drove to identify it, either."

"Well, someone took him," Luke said.

Trudy nodded. "That's right. Someone did. It's almost like he saw the president of the United States getting in a taxicab, and someone didn't like him talking about that. Personally, I'd like to believe he's back in the park today, yelling about ham sandwiches, but I have a hunch he isn't."

Luke started to move down the hall again. "I'd go with your gut on that."

She made a move as if to kick him. Suddenly, Luke felt as if he was back in the fifth grade. "Don't try to run away from me, Luke Stone."

"Never," he said, and laughed.

"What do you want me to do about Crazy Joe?"

He shook his head. "I don't know. Find him. If he's got a mental illness like schizophrenia, any testimony he gives will be suspect. But he might be able to point us in a direction."

And as he said those words, Luke realized that he hadn't given up on this case. Someone wanted to make the country believe that the Russians killed David Barrett. He had no idea if it was possible, but Luke wanted to stop that person.

"I'll tell you what I'm willing to do," Don Morris said. "Then I'll tell you what I need you to do for me."

Sitting across the desk from him were Luke Stone and Kevin Murphy. It was a little like being a school principal, with two juvenile delinquents in front of him. Both of their faces were still lumped and bruised from the fight they'd had.

Stone looked exhausted. Don was going to need to send him home after this. He might even need to hire him a car on the company dime. He didn't look like he was going to make it home.

Other than his bruises, Murphy looked fine. He was dressed in a sports jacket, tie, and slacks. He almost looked like he already worked here. You might even say that Murphy looked relaxed, well-rested, and like he was keeping himself in good condition. A life of crime seemed to agree with him.

And Murphy had been a decent soldier. Competent, professional, generally calm under fire. He'd seen a lot of combat. He was fearless instead of courageous. Like many Delta guys, he didn't need courage—he lacked whatever genetic material made people afraid in the first place.

Murphy was not the top Delta Force operator Don had ever seen under his command, but he was nowhere near the bottom, either.

Murphy nodded. "Okay. Thank you."

"Don't thank me yet," Don said. "Here's what I'm ready to do. And bear in mind that this is entirely because Stone is vouching for you. You had an excellent military record, Murphy, but you screwed the pooch by walking away. Even so, I'll take you on, as soon as today if you're ready. We'll call you a consultant, and we'll pay you by the hour, or by the operation. It depends on the work you're doing."

"That sounds good, Don," Murphy said. "Really. I'm just happy to…"

Don raised a finger. "Wait a minute. We'll do this for a month. At the end of that month, we'll reassess. If I'm happy with what you're doing, I'll offer you a real job here. But I don't like how you left Delta. In the old days, we used to call that desertion. Times have changed a bit, I understand that.

"But while you're here working for me, I'm going to contact your final commanding officer and try to negotiate an exit for you from the Army. I imagine that's going to include a punishment of some kind. I've thought about this a bit, and I think that given your performance, six months at Leavenworth is a fair trade for an honorable discharge. And I think they'll go for it."

He and Murphy looked at each other for a long minute. Murphy was a good poker player. His face didn't give Don much to go on.

Stone said nothing.

"Will you do that?" Don said. "Will you do some time to clean up this military record? Because I'll be honest with you. I hate that you walked away. We've got a lot of vets coming on board here, and not a single dishonorable discharge among them. I don't plan to break that pattern, no matter what Luke Stone says."

Murphy smiled. "Don, I think I'm in the best shape of my life right now. Better than when I was in Delta. I feel like a million bucks. And I want to get my life back on track. If you're willing to go to bat for me like that, I'll do six months at Leavenworth standing on my head."

Don nodded. "Good. That's what I wanted to hear from you."

After they left, Don sat quietly for a little while. He was in a reflective mood. He thought of everything that had happened in the past twenty-four hours. He thought of the things Mark Baylor had said. This was a dangerous time, and it was possible that Baylor had been installed to push that danger to the limit.

But Don had seen world events pushed to the limit before, and they had never gone past it. That fact alone made him hopeful.

He thought of Murphy, and the second chance the man was getting. He thought of Stone, and his counterintuitive instincts. He swam upstream more than made sense, but it worked. Despite the heat it brought down, this morning's raid could ultimately become a feather in the SRT's cap. It showed an agency that had obtained inside information and had acted on it in decisive fashion.

His phone rang. He hit the button on the console, putting the call on speakerphone. A female voice spoke.

"Don?"

"Yeah, hi, Ginger, what's up?"

"You've got a call from a man who wouldn't reveal his name to me, but says you're going to want to talk to him."

"Terrific," Don said.

"Do you want the call?" Ginger said.

Don shrugged. "Sure, why not? It's been a crazy day. Let's make it a little crazier."

"Okay, here he is."

The phone beeped, indicating an open line.

"How can I help you?" Don said.

"Colonel Morris?" a male voice said.

"Yes." For a brief second, Don was concerned about a repeat performance of this morning's crank call, or whatever that had been. But this man's voice was not encrypted.

"Sir, my name is Lawrence Keller. Until recently, I was President David Barrett's chief of staff."

"Yes," Don said. "I remember you. My condolences. President Barrett was a good man. This has been a tragic day."

"Sir," Keller said, "I served in the United States Marine Corps, 2nd Battalion, 5th Marines, from 1967 to 1971, with two combat tours of Vietnam. I tell you that so you know where I'm coming from. You can access my service record, if you like."

Don shrugged. "I doubt that'll be necessary."

"I'm calling to tell you that I met with David Barrett after he left the White House grounds two nights ago. We met at the Lincoln Memorial. It was late. Believe it or not, he had run away from his security detail. I didn't think he was in his right mind. I handed him over to American intelligence agents, at least one of whom I can identify by name, and by agency. At the time I thought they were going to see to it that the president received the care he needed. I also thought they would... cover up the situation, let's say, so the American people didn't find out about it."

There was a brief pause over the line.

"But now I believe they killed him. I know they did."

Don sat and listened to the man's voice. He couldn't think of a single thing to say.

"I made a digital recording of the entire event," the man said now. "I've listened to it, and it's of exceptional quality."

This was a rare moment in Don's life. He was still looking for words.

"I want to give it to you," Keller said.

Chapter Thirty Four

2:40 p.m. Eastern Daylight Time
The Situation Room
The White House, Washington, DC

"Come to order, please," someone said. "Order, everyone!"

It did no good. The chatter went right on.

The room was packed. Coffee cups, empty food trays, and discarded sandwich wraps littered the conference table. Staffers huddled with decision makers, talking, looking at printouts, pointing at data on BlackBerries.

The seats along the walls—smaller red linen chairs with lower backs—were filled with young aides and even younger assistants, most of them slurping from Styrofoam coffee cups or murmuring into telephones.

Mark Baylor took a seat in a leather chair at the closest end of the oblong table. The seats around the table were all full.

At the head of the room, Richard Stark of the Joint Chiefs of Staff stood near a video screen. His face was jagged and hard. He was thin and he was very fit, but he was beginning to look his age. It had been a stressful couple of days. An aide was whispering in his ear.

"General Stark," Baylor said.

Stark looked up. He nodded when he saw Baylor.

"Order!" he shouted. He stood erect. "Order! The president is here."

The room went quiet nearly instantly. A few people continued to murmur, but that died out quickly.

Baylor was impressed. He liked the way Stark could seize command of a room. The man projected authority, as he should.

"Mr. President," Stark said, "I was proud to watch your speech on television today. And I want to tell you…"

Baylor raised a hand. What he didn't want was a speech from Stark. He didn't want a standing ovation from the people in this room. He didn't want well wishes. He didn't want smoke blown up his ass. He wanted to get on with it.

"Okay, Richard," he said. "Never mind the preliminaries. We all know what's happening. We all know what has happened. We know the risks in front of us. I want to send the Russians a message. Give me a message to send them."

Stark slipped a pair of black reading glasses onto his face. He looked down at the sheets of paper in his hand. He took a breath.

On screens around the room, a satellite photo of a body of water appeared. Baylor recognized it instantly as the place where all of this had started just a few days ago.

"What you're seeing on the screens is the Black Sea," the general said. "Pan up, please. I want Crimea and Tuzla Island."

On the screen, the image moved to the north. It showed a large landmass on the left side of the screen, and another large landmass to the right. The two landmasses were nearly kissing. There was a narrow sliver of water between them, connecting two larger bodies of water.

Stark used a long black pointer. Baylor liked that about him, too. Mark Baylor had been around the block a few times. He didn't like laser pointers. He didn't like PowerPoint presentations. He didn't like BlackBerries or Motorola Razrs. None of this new technology impressed him. As far as he was concerned, it was so many fancy gadgets for the toddlers to play with.

"The Black Sea has another sea which sits on top of it," Stark said. "The Sea of Azov. The Kerch Strait is this very narrow body of water that connects them. To the west of the strait you see the Crimean Peninsula, part of Ukraine. To the east you see Krasnodar Krai, part of Russia."

He looked at someone along the wall. "Zoom in, please. Right on the strait, right on Tuzla Island."

The image zoomed in, focusing on a long, narrow spit of land.

"Tuzla Island, which you see here, is in the middle of the strait. It is technically part of Ukraine, and is administered by the Crimean city of Kerch. However, it is in a strategic position, and is a constant source of dispute.

"The island is basically a strip of sand, and there is currently no permanent settlement. There were two small holiday resorts on the island, reachable only by boat, during the time of the Soviet Union. Those have closed.

"There are basic dock facilities with diesel-generated electric power, and both Russian and Ukrainian fishing boats stop there. There is an old, unused helicopter pad and a few paved roads now in disrepair. One road runs the length of the island."

An aerial shot of the island appeared. It showed a triangle of land in the foreground, with what appeared to be a few buildings and a couple of vehicles. A dusty road ran the length of the triangle, and at the top of the image where the triangle narrowed to a point, the road disappeared into the distance. To the right of the triangle was bright blue water. To the left was dark green and brown water. There seemed to be some sea grass and low scrub bushes, but not a single spot of shade.

Baylor found this island frustrating. He wanted to punch the Russians in the eye. He didn't want to split hairs about a little piece of nowhere.

"Get to the point please, General."

Stark nodded. "Of course, Mr. President."

A square of images appeared on the screen. The first, in the upper left-hand corner, was of a tank, painted in sandy brown camouflage, splashing through a muddy bog. The next image, moving clockwise, was of two similar tanks, on pallets and trussed with netting, being pushed out of the open rear hold of a large cargo plane. The third image showed a drawing of the same tank from the side, with arrows pointing to various features of it. The fourth and final image showed a missile standing upright, and next to it some typewritten specifications.

"In recent weeks, we've come to suspect that the Russians have airdropped an unknown number of BMD-1 amphibious armored assault vehicles onto the island, along with airborne infantry troops to man and support them. The BMD-1 is Soviet-era technology, essentially a light tank, armed with the Malyutka guided missile system. The tank also has two heavy machine guns, mounted in the front on both sides. Each tank takes a crew of four men."

Stark paused. "Tanks such as these can threaten any ships in the strait, as well as the city of Kerch, directly across the strait from there. Kerch is a city of regional importance with a population of a hundred fifty thousand people."

"Are the tanks there?" Baylor said. "Do we know that for a fact?"

Stark nodded. "Last night, a two-man team from the Naval Special Warfare Development Group, often called DEVGRU or SEAL Team Six, did a dangerous high-altitude skydive onto the island. The plane they jumped from never left Ukrainian airspace.

"The men are from the highly professional Black Squadron, and they were able to confirm the presence of at least six BMD-1 vehicles, and perhaps thirty Russian troops. Our guys took cover in sea grass on the dunes on a distant part of the island during daylight hours, but it is now nearly ten p.m., and they can be on the move and operational again."

Baylor wasn't sure he understood what Stark was saying. A fight like that seemed a mismatch, hardly the message he wanted to send. "Are you recommending that our men engage the Russian tanks, General?"

Stark shook his head. "No sir. They are in touch with their support personnel through satellite communications. Their mission is reconnaissance. I'm recommending they pinpoint the exact location of those tanks, and we take the tanks out with drone strikes. All of them, the vehicles and the crews. The Russians have nothing like our drone technology, and we gave them a small taste of it during the rescue operation in Adler. This time we give them a bigger taste."

Baylor nodded. It was good. He had been hoping for something more, maybe a small invasion of some kind, or a missile attack on a base somewhere. But this was certainly an ice breaker.

"What are the odds of success?" he said.

"Very high, sir. Quite frankly, those tanks are sitting ducks."

"And how do our men escape?"

Stark nodded. "Good question, sir. Those men are Navy SEALs. They're expert swimmers. Once they call in the strikes, they'll swim across the strait to the Ukrainian side, and link up with deep cover intelligence agents along the Crimean coast. From there, we'll evacuate them to neutral territory using standard protocols. They'll likely be back home within twenty-four hours."

Baylor looked around the room. It was very quiet. Everyone was carefully following this conversation between him and General Stark. No one was daydreaming. Everyone appeared alert. This was good.

"What," Baylor said, "do we anticipate as the Russian response?"

"We anticipate a feeble response, well short of nuclear war, sir. We know that hundreds of Russian ICBM silos across their heartland are reporting combat readiness. We know that their Strategic Air Command has nuclear-equipped bombers patrolling at the edges of their airspace, especially in the Arctic. But we've assessed this eight ways to Sunday. They are not going to launch Armageddon over a handful of tanks in the Kerch Strait, especially when the presence of those tanks constitutes an encroachment on sovereign Ukrainian territory.

"Failing the outbreak of nuclear war, we are in a very good position. In any conventional scenario, we hold clear dominance. We control the skies. We've shown that. Our infantry is modern, high-tech, mobile, and largely unstoppable. Theirs is static, moribund, and more suited to set-piece battles during World War Two. Their equipment is mostly obsolete Cold War relics. And there's really no sense in even comparing navies. Their navy barely exists anymore."

"What do you see as the end game here, General?"

"We hit them with repeated jabs, sir, ones they have no obvious or easy response to. The rescue operation at Port of Adler was a grave embarrassment to them. The dogfight in the Bering Sea was a black eye. They lost three jets to our one, and they're the ones who attacked first, without warning.

"So we just keep hitting them, over and over, upping the ante each time, demonstrating our superiority and tearing at their morale. We'll seize assets as we see fit. And eventually, after discussion with you of course, we'll go for a knockout punch, something that will leave them reeling and humiliated in the eyes of the world. When it comes time for that, we have a list of attractive options to present."

Baylor smiled. He liked it. He liked the way Stark put it on the table. It was concise and to the point. It was long on punch, short on bullet points. Mark Baylor didn't like it when people loaded him up with too much detail.

"Given the circumstances," he said, "I think the American people could use a victory right now. And maybe a little bit of revenge."

Stark nodded. "Yes sir. I agree. A sense of revenge is what's needed, and I'm confident we can deliver that."

Baylor looked around the room again. All eyes were on him.

"Do it," he said.

Chapter Thirty Five

10:01 p.m. Crimean Daylight Time (3:01 p.m. Eastern Daylight Time)
Tuzla Island
Strait of Kerch
Crimea, Ukraine

"This place is kind of a disgrace, isn't it?" Zimmerman said.

The men moved quickly along the wet sand of the beach, staying low. It was a dark night, and they wore night vision goggles. The goggles cast everything in an eerie green light.

"Shut up," Gruen said. This wasn't a time for talking. But he could see Zimmerman's point. The currents had turned the beach into a garbage dump.

All along the water's edge, there was the detritus of a throwaway seafaring culture—empty bottles, rusty beer cans, ripped plastic bags, broken plastic bait buckets, copper wiring and rubber tubing of all kinds, a steel-belted radial tire, various pieces of clothing and shoes, a metal weathervane, the entire fiberglass bow of a sailboat violently sundered from the rest of itself, and countless other bits of flotsam and jetsam.

The tiny strip of sand and grass was like a net, catching whatever happened to be floating by on the current. Walk ten yards and here was another ugly conglomeration of garbage—nets and ropes and bottles, cracked plastic toys, a bright reflector.

A line of scrub grasses and dunes bordered the beach. Right here, the island was about fifty yards across. Just to their left, not very far at all, it opened up to water again on the other side.

Further up, where they were last night, the island widened out into a broad triangle. That's where the Russians were, on the grounds of an old hotel or resort that looked like it had been out of business a long time. There were cinderblock bungalows falling to seed along the waterfront, and the Russian tank crews had taken up residence.

The lights of Kerch were directly across the strait from there. If you wanted to bombard the city, you probably couldn't find a better spot.

The tanks themselves were covered with sand-colored tarps, making them hard to see from the air. They were armored amphibious assault vehicles, with heavy weaponry and tracks underneath, making them able to move through shallow water and across sand and mud. He and Zimmerman had counted six of them last night.

Just before they reached the hotel compound, Gruen and Zimmerman got down on their stomachs and crawled like snakes the rest of the way. They came to the top of a dune, the tall sea grass all around them. The Russians were three hundred meters away.

Zimmerman broke out his night vision binoculars. He pulled down his goggles and put the binoculars to his eyes.

"What do you see?" Gruen said, his voice barely above a whisper.

"We've got movement. A few personnel around the tanks. No evidence of anything added since last night. Same as before. I'd say six tanks, plus crews, plus maybe a half dozen support personnel."

"Same location?" Gruen said.

"Same location. Nothing has moved."

Gruen pulled out his satellite phone. This would have to happen quickly. He pressed a button and waited. The phone shook hands with a satellite, the signal bounced around, and then:

"Little darlings, do you read?"

Gruen smiled at the code name. "Affirmative. Valhalla, this is little darlings."

"Little darlings, we are green light. Repeat, we are green light."

An electric thrill shot through Gruen's body. It was a sudden, unexpected surge of adrenaline, and it almost made him sick to his stomach. He and Zimmerman had dropped in here late last night, then hid in the weeds and the muck all day, and he figured it would all be for nothing. Usually, these things were exercises.

But not this time.

"Little darlings?"

"Copy, Valhalla. In that case, drop the hammer. Repeat, drop the hammer."

"Coordinates?" the voice said.

"Same as before. No change. Erase that triangle, and you'll get it all."

"Copy, little darlings. Fly away home now. Godspeed."

Gruen clicked off. He looked at Zimmerman. "It's real. It's a go."

Zimmerman took his binoculars down. He looked at Gruen with wide eyes as the realization came to him: this place was going to be an inferno a few minutes from now.

"Uh-oh," he said. Then he smiled.

The two men crouched low and ran down the beach the way they had just come.

CHAPTER THIRTY SIX

3:25 p.m. Eastern Daylight Time
Headquarters of the Special Response Team
McLean, Virginia

"It's on the TV right now," Becca said.

"I understand," Luke said. And he did understand. He had called her to tamp down her fears about war with the Russians. Only he had the poor timing of calling five minutes after they started showing footage of an air strike somewhere in Crimea. Becca didn't seem to grasp the details of it.

"Someone took a video of it with their own camera, then put it on the internet. Then the TV stations picked it up. They're saying it happened in the past half an hour."

"What does it look like?" Luke said.

"I don't know. Just darkness and then massive explosions. A whole series of them, again and again. And it sounds like thunder in the distance. I can't tell what I'm looking at. But then it's burning. It's still burning now. It's a giant fire on the horizon."

"Are they saying who did the bombing?" Luke said.

"They don't seem to know. It's an island in Crimea that was bombed, or maybe the island *of* Crimea. Which side would bomb Crimea? What is Crimea anyway? Are we really going to have a war because of Crimea?"

"*Ours is not to reason why,*" Luke almost said, but didn't.

"I don't know, sweetheart. I don't think so."

He would like to tell her to take Gunner, go back out to the cabin, and keep the television off. He'd like to tell her she and the baby would be safer there, away from the city. But he couldn't tell her that. It wasn't true, for one thing. If the Russians launched nukes, all bets were off. She'd be no safer on the Eastern Shore than she was here.

Also, he had awakened at the cabin yesterday morning to find Kent Philby and two Russians in his living room.

He looked up and Trudy was in his doorway. He cupped the mouthpiece of the phone.

"Don's calling a meeting right now. You, me, Swann, and Ed. He said it's important."

Luke stared at her. "Ed is back?"

"He just walked in half an hour ago. Well, walked is a strong word."

"Okay. I'll be there in two minutes."

"Luke?" Becca said inside his ear.

"Yeah, sweetheart. Look, I gotta run. I have a meeting. There's a lot going on here. I just suggest that for the time being, you turn the TV off, and don't worry about it. Okay? It's a nice day. Take Gunner outside in the backyard and get a little sun."

"Gunner is asleep. I don't want to wake him."

"Well, that's good news, anyway."

"Luke..."

Luke put up a hand. She couldn't see a hand, though. "Babe, I understand you're worried. But we've never had a nuclear war before, so..."

"Is that really what you believe?" she said.

Luke stopped. He didn't know what he believed at this point. He was beyond belief. The president was dead, and he had found the body. A couple of Russian spies and an old Cold War traitor had told him where to find it. And the world's two major nuclear powers were playing a dangerous game of chicken.

He shook his head.

"Becca, I love you. I have to go."

⚜ ⚜ ⚜

"Man, you look terrible," Ed said.

Luke had just walked into the SRT conference room. He sat down. Two young guys in dress shirts were taking the light fixtures apart, sweeping for listening devices. Another young guy was under the conference table.

Luke looked at Ed. He wore jeans with one leg cut off at the thigh because of the swelling. That leg was wrapped in heavy bandaging. His left arm was also dressed and wrapped. He wore a bright and colorful short-sleeve button-up shirt, as though he were on vacation in Hawaii. The left sleeve of the shirt was also cut off to make it easier to get the dressing in and out of it.

A metallic silver cane rested against the table where he sat. He hadn't shaved in a couple of days and his beard was coming in uneven. His eyes were bloodshot and tired.

"But you look beautiful," Luke said.

"Guys, come to order," Don said.

He and Trudy were already in here. A second later, Swann came darting in and slid into a chair.

"Mr. Swann, glad you could join us," Don said. He looked at the guys picking through the internal workings of the lamps.

"How does it look, fellas?"

"Clean," one of them said. His eyes never wavered from what he was doing. "I don't see evidence that anyone has touched this place since we last swept it three days ago."

Don nodded. "Okay, let's call it good then."

The young guys started packing up their equipment. It occurred to Luke that Don was becoming increasingly paranoid. How many times did they really need to sweep the conference room? The bug sweepers shut the door as they left the room.

Don looked at Luke. "Where's Murphy?"

Luke shrugged. "I don't know. He, uh..."

"He took a tour of the facility," Trudy said. "He ran into a former Naval Intelligence analyst he knew from somewhere, Michaels, so he was chatting with him for a bit. Now he's up in human resources with Helen filling out some paperwork. She drafted a month-long contract for him."

Don nodded. "Thank you." He turned to Luke again. "Do you trust him? Is he as good as you say?"

Luke nodded. "He's good. Right away he'll be among the best we have. That doesn't mean he's not a jerk. But he's good. He's tough. He's good in a firefight. He bides his time. He doesn't lose his head. He's calculating."

Luke thought back to that cold morning on the hillside in eastern Afghanistan. Murphy sat on an outcropping of rock, put an empty pistol to his own head, and pulled the trigger half a dozen times.

"Out," he said, and tossed the gun down the hill.

"And you've worked well with him before?"

"I've been in combat with him a dozen times," Luke said. "He can be a pain in the ass and damn near insubordinate. But he goes at the bad guys like a pit bull. Why?"

"We might need him," Don said now. "Tonight."

"What's going on?" Ed said.

"I got a call a little while ago," Don said. He lowered his voice, as if the room hadn't just been swept. "Lawrence Keller was David Barrett's chief of staff until two months ago. He remained friends with Barrett, or something. He told me that he met with Barrett at the Lincoln Memorial two nights ago. Barrett was out in public on his own. He had ditched his security detail.

"Keller says he was concerned about Barrett's welfare and handed him over to intelligence operatives. One of those operatives was a CIA agent named Wallace Speck. He works for SAC, inside the Directorate of Operations. Black ops. Keller thinks Speck had Barrett killed. He also thinks NSA operatives were involved, and possibly some others. Maybe some Secret Service."

There was a long moment of silence. Trudy broke it.

"Some friend," she said. "Handing him over to Special Activities."

"He says he has a digital recording of the hand-off," Don said. "His own voice, Barrett's, and Speck's are all clearly audible and identifiable. Also, he calls both Barrett and Speck by name."

"Have you heard it?" Luke said.

Don shook his head. "No. He won't send it to me. He wants to hand deliver it. He wants to make an announcement of it, with media attention, so it can't be swept under the rug. He wants to testify in a court of law, and he wants immunity from prosecution. Then he wants to go into the Witness Protection Program."

"Can we give him all that?" Swann said.

"We can't give him anything until we hear that tape," Don said. "We can't even consider it until then."

"Does he realize the absurdity of trying to hide from CIA operatives in the Witness Protection Program?" Trudy said.

"He's upset," Don said. "It was a brief conversation. I'm not sure he realizes anything. I think we need to bring him in, hear his story, listen to the tape, and make about a hundred copies of it. We can worry about the details of his survival later. Frankly, if he really did hand the president over to rogue black ops agents, the man's survival after all this is over is the least of my worries."

"Where is he?" Luke said.

In his mind, he thought: *Please don't say Bangladesh.*

"He's in Montreal." Don looked at Luke and Ed. "I want to fly you guys up there tonight, maybe with Murphy doing a ride-along. You both look like the walking wounded right now, so you might need a little added muscle. You go up late, take a ride into the city after the traffic is gone, and pick him up at his flat. Night is best. Swann can watch you from the sky, and he'll spot anything that might roll up on you. Once you have Keller, we fly him back down here. No one knows we have him, so we hold him for a few days and do a debrief. We'll see what's what."

"Where do we hold him?" Ed said. "We don't even have a—"

"I've acquired an old fallow tobacco farm northwest of Richmond," Don said. "It's the first SRT safe house. About two hundred acres. Couple of old storage barns on there where you can hide cars from prying eyes. The main house is in okay shape. Could use a paint job and some updates, but it's comfortable enough. It's a good spot."

Ed smiled. "Coming up in the world. I didn't know we had that."

"It's need to know," Swann said.

Ed glared at him. "You knew?"

Swann shrugged.

"Look," Luke said. "I'll be honest, Don. I'm tired. I haven't had a full night's sleep since before we hit the port in Russia. I don't know if I can do this and be sharp. I need to get at least a couple of hours in. Then, after that, maybe a Dexie and—"

"Why don't you take a nap in your office?" Don said.

"Where? On my desk?"

Don shook his head. "Son, where is your brain at? You don't keep a fold-out cot in your office? There's no better napping surface on this planet than a standard United States Army–issue cot. I've had one in my office, no matter where I've been stationed, for the past two decades."

Luke just looked at him. "I've never had an office before."

Don grunted, then laughed.

"You can borrow mine."

CHAPTER THIRTY SEVEN

3:40 p.m. Eastern Daylight Time
The Oval Office
The White House
Washington, DC

Wallace Speck stood away from the group. He glanced around the Oval Office.

In front of him, three tall windows, with drapes pulled back, looked out on the Rose Garden. Outside, it was a sunny day.

There were a dozen people in the room, men in suits, men in military dress greens, Secret Service agents. Mark Baylor sat in a high-backed chair in the sitting area. Beneath his feet was the Seal of the President of the United States. All of the people were in Baylor's orbit.

A large flat-screen TV was mounted on the far wall. Everyone stared at it. On the screen, Speaker of the House Clement Dixon stood at a sturdy wooden podium on the steps of the Capitol Building. There was a bank of microphones in front of him, and bulletproof plastic shields all around him.

He was older than dirt now, but in his prime Dixon had been known as a fiery speaker. White hair and wrinkles aside, he was doing his best to maintain that reputation.

He pounded on the podium.

"What evidence have we been shown that the Russians murdered our president?"

A large group of people flanked Dixon on either side. To Wallace Speck, they were the usual suspects, the loony left, the liberal wing of the party currently in power. Who was among them? He spotted a few he recognized.

Thomas Hayes, the current governor of Pennsylvania, had come down from Harrisburg for the festivities. No surprise there. Everyone knew Hayes had designs on the presidency. You couldn't miss his beak from a mile away. Susan Hopkins, the silly super-model turned senator from California, stood next to Hayes. She barely came up to his waist. Two dozen others, ready to hold hands up there and sing a campfire song.

The group murmured something in answer to Dixon's question.

"Here we go, call and response," someone here in the office said.

"No evidence!" Dixon said. "What reason have we been given to risk war with the world's other nuclear power?"

Dixon's cheerleaders were catching on. "No reason!" they said.

Dixon hammered the podium with his fist.

"What reason have we been given to risk the lives of our children and grandchildren?"

"No reason!"

"It's too bad they gave him that big podium to pound on," someone said. "Next time they should give him a sheet music stand."

There were a few chuckles in the room. People here were in a jovial mood. The Pentagon, in the person of General Richard Stark, had predicted America could hit the Russians with impunity, and so far that assessment was holding up very nicely. In the past half an hour or so, a drone strike had incinerated a formation of Russian tanks, and the Russians hadn't even attempted a response.

So far.

"Correct me if I'm wrong, but does Thomas Hayes look like he has a pickle attached to his face?"

"I wasn't thinking pickle," someone else said.

"Mr. Baylor," Clement Dixon said, directly addressing the President of the United States through the TV. "Stand down from this insane course of action. Show us one shred of proof that the Russians were involved in our president's murder."

"Mr. Baylor," Mark Baylor said. "That's nice."

"Disrespectful," someone said.

"This guy's gall knows no bounds."

"He's sticking his neck all the way out, and this time we're going to chop it off. Wait until we release the identities of the kidnappers. People are going to run Clement Dixon out of this town on a rail."

Speck nodded at the truth of that, but didn't speak. It wasn't his job to speak at meetings such as these. His job was to hover, to listen, to collect information. The less obvious his presence, the better.

He well knew the identities of the men who died as the house in Cheat Bridge. Of course he did. He had put the men there. All three of them were Eastern European mobsters with long-term ties to Russian intelligence agencies.

The Russians just loved to use mobsters to do their dirty work. Mobsters were violent. They didn't need any training. They were amoral and didn't try to fit their actions into neat political ideologies. And they were oh-so-expendable. Speck liked using them for the exact same reasons.

On the television screen, the next speaker had moved to the podium. The little TV party here in the Oval Office was starting to break up. That was Speck's cue to make a quiet exit. He moved toward the wide double doors, but a woman stepped in front of him. He took in her contours. Middle-aged, dressed conservatively in a blue pantsuit, beginning to suffer the spread that afflicted so many as they aged.

Her eyes said she was stressed out. It was Kathy Grumman, until very recently, David Barrett's harried and put upon chief of staff. Now that David was dead and gone, Kathy didn't fit the suit around here. Her days were numbered.

"Wallace," she said.

"Hi, Kathy. I am so sorry about David. I just…I don't have words."

She shook her head. "I know. It's terrible. We're all just trying to soldier on. Mark told me he wants to bring Lawrence Keller back on board in an informal role as an advisor. Maybe we can find a permanent place for him. He's got the most continuity as a David person. And I have no problem with that."

Her eyes said she was lying. Her eyes said Lawrence Keller coming back threatened her to the core of her being.

Lawrence Keller…

"I think Lawrence is great," Speck said.

Kathy nodded. "We're having trouble reaching him. Mark said you might know how to get in touch with him."

Speck put a hand to his chin as if thinking about it. "I might. Let me see if I can get hold of him. If I can, you'll be the first to know."

Chapter Thirty Eight

11:55 p.m. Moscow Daylight Time (3:55 p.m. Eastern Daylight Time)
Strategic Command and Control Center
The Kremlin
Moscow, Russia

A fight broke out in the War Room.

"It's murder!" a man screamed. "Mass murder! The end of the world has come!"

Corporal Gregor couldn't tell what was going on. It was happening at the other side of the large open space. Chairs and tables overturned as desk workers scrambled to get away from it. A computer fell to the floor and its screen shattered. People shouted, as people often did.

Several men seemed to be throwing fists over there. Military police moved from the edges of the fray into the middle of it.

Fistfights made very little impression on Gregor. He had seen and done much worse. He looked at the video screens mounted above everyone's heads. There must be a clue as to what had disturbed the man. Several of the screens were showing a map of the American territory of Alaska, specifically focused on the coastal city of Nome.

Gregor shrugged. It meant nothing to him.

He was growing fatigued. He was a big strong man, still young, but the Cheget was heavy. It pulled constantly on his arm, causing a dull ache in his shoulder and sharp pains in his elbow and wrist.

It seemed insane to have this monstrous thing attached to him. He'd heard that the Americans had similar suitcases, with their own nuclear codes inside. They called such a case a nuclear "football." The idea made him smile. If this thing were a ball, he would kick it as far away as he could. He wouldn't try to kick it into the opposing team's goal. He would kick it into the stands... no, over the stands and out of the stadium.

"Gregor."

The soldiers were beating someone with the butts of their rifles now, but Gregor turned away from the fight. The defense minister had come out of the small conference room. His eyes were tired. He reeked of cigarettes and alcohol. The top buttons of his shirt were undone and his tie pulled askew. He could use a shave. The gray and white of his eight-hour beard stood in marked contrast to the black shoe polish tone of his head hair. He could be the star of an absurd television comedy. But his face was stern.

"Come. We must leave."

Gregor followed the man. They left the War Room and walked down the wide corridor. There were two other soldiers with them, the defense minister's personal bodyguards. The footsteps echoed along the empty corridor. Even with the heavy damnable football case weighing him down, Gregor sped up and quickly came even with the minister.

"What is happening, sir?"

"Terrible news, Gregor. Terrible news. We must evacuate. In case of war, this facility will be utterly destroyed."

The minister's answer was mostly a non-answer.

"What is happening?" Gregor said again. He said it more fiercely than he intended.

He was already tired of the defense minister. The man frustrated him. Gregor reflected that he may have been a poor choice to carry the Cheget. He was a trained killer with battlefield experience. Life was no longer as meaningful to him as it might be to others. It was not out of the question that he would become violent with the defense minister before this crisis ended.

The minister looked at him. Perhaps he saw the anger in Gregor's eyes, perhaps he didn't. Either way, he was willing to talk.

"It is secret information, but I will tell you. Strategic Air Command and Missile Defense have gone to the Dead Hand protocol. Command and control are becoming decentralized. In the event communications with Moscow are cut off, commanders in the field are empowered to make their own choices. This extends to the launch of nuclear weapons. It is a dangerous decision. Communications are not as robust as they once were. It will be easy to make a mistake from now on."

Gregor walked quickly, keeping pace, trying to digest what he heard. He thought of possible things to say to this. His mind was very close to blank.

"Why?" was all he could muster.

The defense minister shrugged. "The Americans have attacked again, as you know. A tank patrol was destroyed. We are not prepared for skirmishes such as these. Their technology is much newer. Unfortunately, the realization has been reached that we cannot defend ourselves from these attacks."

The older man seemed like he was ready to weep. Weep that the hated enemy had reached such a staggering position of superiority. Weep at the humiliation of the lost Cold War. Weep at the crushed dreams of a once great civilization. Weep at the futility of a thousand years of Russian history.

"As soon as their next attack, we will immediately wipe one of their cities off the map. The small city of Nome, Alaska. Three thousand five hundred people. It will be gone within a few minutes. We will destroy it with conventional missiles launched from Siberia, but we must assume the Americans will not refrain from the use of nuclear weapons when they respond. History will show that we were not the first to launch, but if they do, then we will."

The men walked along in silence, footfalls echoing. They turned right down another hallway. They were headed toward the helipad.

"It's a cold comfort, I'm afraid," said the defense minister.

"Where are we going now?" Gregor said.

"A helicopter will take us to a military airfield outside the city. Then we will fly to a deep fallout shelter high in the Caucasus Mountains, near the Georgian border. Its existence is highly classified. It will be one of the few safe places left on earth. The president himself will be there."

The defense minister took a deep breath, but didn't slow down at all.

"Pray that we make it there in time."

They approached the entrance to the helipad. Two soldiers stood at attention at either side of the automatic doors. Outside the doors, it was night.

Three beautiful young women, dressed expensively in the uniform of high-class Moscow prostitutes, waited by the doors. High heels, form-fitting minidresses, fur shawls, painted faces. The doors opened and without a word the women joined the procession.

"Sir," Gregor said. "My family..."

The defense minister waved a hand. "Your family will be provided for, Gregor. Don't worry."

The big blades of the chopper slowly began to spin as soon as the group reached the tarmac.

Gregor felt nothing toward the prostitutes. They were little more than girls. They had their own troubles. He could not blame them for saving their own lives, at a cost they had paid many times before for a much smaller return.

But this callous decision for apocalyptic war was beyond the pale. And this defense minister was beyond the pale. He could dismiss the lives of Gregor's entire family without a thought, just as long as the fallout shelter was stocked with whores, and cigars, and (Gregor was certain) the best vodka and caviar.

How could these inhuman decisions be made?

The service pistol was in Gregor's free hand almost before he was aware of it. He drew the gun across his body, from the holster on the left side of his waist.

"Sir?"

The man glanced back at him and Gregor shot him in the face.

BANG!

The defense minister's guards began to turn at the sound of the gunshot, but they were too slow. Gregor shot them both in turn.

The girls threw up their hands and ran on their awkward shoes back toward the cover of the building.

Three bodies lay on the tarmac, blood flowing from each of their heads.

Gregor looked down at the defense minister.

"Twenty-nine," he said to the man's ruined face.

There was a rush of activity behind Gregor. He didn't bother to see what it was.

"Twenty-nine confirmed kills."

Chapter Thirty Nine

6:15 p.m. Eastern Daylight Time
Georgetown
Washington, DC

When you were Wallace Speck, the long days never ended. They just got longer.

He sat in the living room of Lawrence Keller's apartment in Georgetown, half-awake on the man's couch. In his right hand, he held a 9mm Beretta, with a long sound suppressor attached. It was a good one, as silencers went. He liked to think of it as the Sound of One Hand Clapping.

He glanced around the apartment. It really was a charming place. Victorian-era rooms, polished hardwood floors, high ceilings, very tall windows. An old, ornate radiator in the corner. The furniture was mid-century Design Within Reach. Speck recognized a few of the pieces from the catalog. He was a fan.

The bathroom was a well-done encounter between the old and new. There was a clawfoot tub in the center of the bathroom, with a drugstore tiled floor from the 1800s. But there was also a five-foot sink and vanity, and a glass cube rain shower. Somehow, it all worked.

Speck was wearing rubber gloves, so he felt free to touch whatever interested him. Keller had a Bose sound system with embedded speakers in every room. The whole thing could be controlled from the same remote that controlled the heating and the lights. Just sitting here, Speck realized that he *liked* Keller. Keller really was a clever man.

"Where are you, Lawrence?" he said to the empty room.

He was also beginning to understand, with a growing sense of frustration, that he had badly misjudged Keller. Obviously, the man wasn't here. His sporty BMW was not in the narrow driveway between this brownstone and the one next door. Moreover, his cell phone had just been traced to a copse of woodland and weeds along Interstate 95 outside Elkton, Maryland.

It appeared Keller got cold feet and had run away.

Maybe he killed himself.

Maybe he did, maybe he didn't. It wasn't helpful to speculate at this moment. Wherever Lawrence Keller had gone, whatever he was doing, it had to be confirmed. You didn't pull off an operation like this one and then leave a loose end like Keller just dangling out there.

The damnable thing was Keller wasn't supposed to be a loose end! Keller had been integral to the entire plot. He was the one who had sold out David Barrett. As his reward, and as a nifty little sub-narrative to better sell the overall story, he was now supposed to reemerge as a White House character. Not chief of staff, certainly, but as a trusted aide, a wise and steady *consigliere* with decades of experience and public evidence of the bridge between Barrett and Mark Baylor.

But he had disappeared instead.

Speck had been diligently tying up loose ends like crazy, and except for a few bumps, it was going pretty well. He'd been so focused on this that he had tucked Keller away in the back of his mind for a couple of days.

He'd like nothing more than if Keller suddenly walked in here with a bag of groceries in his arm and a perfectly reasonable explanation. If that happened, he would shoot Keller in the head for causing him this inconvenience, then move on with his life.

But that wasn't going to happen, was it?

As if to answer the question, his cell phone rang. He stared at it for a moment. It was a number he didn't recognize. Normally, he would let his voicemail answer it, but Wallace Speck was a believer in omens.

"Can I help you?" he said.

"Wallace Speck," a voice said.

"Go on," Speck said. "Tell me more."

"How are you enjoying the inside of that brownstone?" the voice said. "Did you find what you were looking for in there? I tend to doubt it."

Speck shrugged. So what? If you wanted to frighten Wallace Speck, you had to bring more than that.

"How are you enjoying following me around?" he said. "Is it exciting? Drinking a lot of coffee, are you? How's the food? Where do you take your bathroom breaks? Or do you keep plastic bottles in the car for that?"

"Speck, you and I are friends."

Speck didn't recognize the voice. And Speck rarely forgot people. Therefore: "Refresh my memory, if you don't mind."

"I worked on loan from the military, under Joint Special Operations Command, taking care of a little problem in Colombia, round about early 2001. We didn't meet, but you were on that project. Later, there was the small matter of an airplane crash. It was a private plane. You know how those things go down all the time. A guy from Missouri, a member of the loyal opposition—"

"Enough," Speck said. There were things in this world that should never be mentioned.

"Okay. But you see that we've worked together. I was a mechanic, under deep cover. You never learned my name."

"I assure you," Speck said. "I always learn the names."

"If that was true, you wouldn't be alive now."

Speck took a deep breath. "How can I help you? I'd love to reminisce with you about bygone days at some point, but right now I'm pretty busy."

"You're looking for someone," said the voice.

Speck nodded. "Indeed I am. I'm always looking for someone."

"I know where he is. He left the country, but I'm going to meet him later tonight, and collect him with some friends of mine. Friends of mine, but not really friends of yours. The man you're looking for owns a rare recording taken at the Lincoln Memorial, of all places. Says it's good quality, but that remains to be seen. Could be a little embarrassing, considering the things that were said and the people who were there."

Suddenly Speck was wide awake and alert. His heart began to beat against the wall of his chest. He could feel it in there, galloping along.

What was Keller doing?

"Do you want," Speck said, "to tell me where he is?"

"No, I don't."

"Then why are you calling?"

"I have a number in mind. I've been thinking about this number for the past hour or so. It's a good number, I think. Not too much, not too little, but just about right. Considering the stakes here, I think you might even consider it a bargain."

"What's the number?" Speck said.

"Five."

"Five?"

"Yes, five. For whatever reason, it's always been one of my favorite numbers."

Speck looked at the white ceiling above his head. The man was asking for five million dollars. Things just got deeper and deeper, didn't they? He shook his head. The mystery man was shrewd, though. It wasn't an outrageous figure, given the situation. Supply and demand. Five million was a little bit of pain, for a lot of gain.

"Half up front," Speck said. "Half on delivery."

"Of course. I'll give you the numbers of my anonymous account. You know how things are these days. Everything is at the touch of a button. When I see the first half appear, I'll turn on a GPS unit that I'll bring with me to the pickup. Then you guys follow me there. It'll be like I'm dropping bread crumbs. But be forewarned. I'm not going to be alone, and you're not going to be the only one watching from the sky. So whatever you put in place, you'd better be able to camouflage it, then hit very hard."

Speck didn't speak. He let the silence draw out between them.

It sounded ... fine. He could put a dozen men on this problem at short notice. They would be hard hitters, all right—merciless, fast, the kind who attacked without warning or hesitation. And Speck could move the money. Two and a half million was a lot of cash, of course. But in big picture terms, it really was a bargain.

Besides, the man would never live to see the other half.

"Speck?"

"You've made a reasonable request," Speck said. "But I need to talk to a couple of people, and a couple of hours to put it together. You know, making bank transfers with that kind of—"

"Come on, Speck. This isn't Citibank. You know as well as I do how fast that money can move. This is all happening tonight. I can tell you where it's going down, or I don't have to. You could be hanging from your belt by tomorrow morning."

Speck grunted. The man seemed impatient, and possibly as if he had anger management problems. There might be a way to use that against him.

"Consider it done," he said.

"That's better," the voice said. "The man you're looking for is in Montreal. We're going there tonight. There will be three of us. I'm the driver. Have your people ready to pick up my signal as soon as we land. But I want you to understand something. I've been at this a long time. In all my years, I've never taken a bullet. I'm hard to kill. Don't even dream of double-crossing me."

Speck smiled. It made sense. Of course it did. The man was a special operator who'd probably been in combat many times. And he claimed he'd never once been shot.

But there was always a first time.

"If you're concerned about that, why don't you just give me the man's exact location, stay home and out of harm's way, and I'll take care of everything?"

"Believe me," the voice said, "I would do that if I could. The man is being clever. He won't tell us where to meet him until we arrive in the city. I imagine he wants to get a look at us first. He requested special couriers to collect and deliver him, so he probably wants to make sure he's getting what he ordered."

"Tedious," Speck said.

"You know how some people are," the voice said. "They make everything harder than it needs to be."

"Suppose he's not there," Speck said. "Suppose he leaves you waiting at the altar. What about my money in that case?"

"That's just a chance you'll have to take," the voice said. "And the chance I'm taking is that one of your goons accidentally decides to shoot me. I can promise you if that happens, I won't be happy."

"My friend, you have nothing to worry about," Speck said.

Chapter Forty

June 29
12:05 a.m. Eastern Daylight Time
Montreal-Saint Hubert Airport
Longueuil, Quebec
Canada

The guy from Executive Armor met them with the car.

"That's a beautiful thing," Ed Newsam said.

Luke couldn't agree more. It was a big black gleaming Mercedes SUV. The front grille looked like a malevolent smile. All four doors were open.

Murphy, making himself useful, placed an SRT gym bag full of guns and loaded magazines on the floor behind the driver's seat.

Luke was in a good mood. The three-hour nap on Don's cot was the best sleep he'd gotten in a long time. The plane ride had been easy and quick. For the first time in days, things were looking up. He had taken a painkiller, plus half a Dexie to even out the sedative effects. He felt pretty sharp.

They were at a tiny private airport ten miles east of Montreal. The place was little more than a runway, a taxiway, some hangars, and a small terminal building, currently closed for the night. The SRT plane was parked behind them, lights blinking, reflecting off the ground. The tarmac was wet and slick. It must have rained here at some point.

"Excellent," the rep from Executive Armor said. He was a young guy with dark hair. He was broad with gym muscles and wore a tight-fitting dress shirt and jeans, as though he planned to hit the nightclubs as soon as this delivery was complete.

"Very good car," he said and made a circle with his thumb and forefinger. As he spoke, his French accent became obvious. English was not his first language, and whoever taught him to speak it had forgotten to mention verbs.

The guy gestured at the car with both hands.

"Entire cabin armored, ballistic plate. Very heavy, rated high-power rifle, armor-piercing bullets. Entire roof, same. Entire floor, stronger, withstand roadside bombs. All windows, multi-layer ballistic glass. Can't open. Always closed."

He raised a finger in the air. "Windows very strong, but not forever. Many shots coming..." He shrugged. "Drive away."

Luke laughed. That was the best piece of advice he'd heard in some time. If people keep shooting your car, what are you sitting around for? Just drive away. It made perfect sense. Also, he really liked the car. He enjoyed hearing about the specs, but he hoped they weren't going to need any of this. Was this what the world had come to? You could rent your own armored car, and they'd bring it right to you.

The man waved at the tires. "Run flats. Shot full of holes, keep going. Gas tank armored. Battery, armored. Radiator protected, behind hood."

He nodded, as if to himself. "Best car we have."

Luke, Ed, and Murphy stood around the guy in a rough semicircle.

"All right, Murph," Luke said. "Looks like you're driving."

"So you like?" the guy said.

"We love it," Ed said. "We wish we were buying it."

The guy smiled.

"You buy, I get you very good price."

CHAPTER FORTY ONE

12:25 a.m. Eastern Daylight Time
Kondiaronk Belvedere, Mont Royal Park
Montreal, Quebec
Canada

"What's the story?" Lawrence Keller said into the phone.

He was nervous. This meeting was supposed to take place at midnight. They were late, and he'd already been here nearly an hour. He was at the top of Mont Royal, standing on the broad concrete patio overlooking the tall buildings of downtown Montreal and the Old Port behind them. It was an astonishing view. The city was lit up like Las Vegas.

It was a good spot to meet. The plaza wasn't crowded, but there were still plenty of people up here, mostly groups of young people and couples, some walking around, some sitting along the wall, chatting, laughing, holding hands. If you wanted to murder someone, this wasn't the first spot you'd pick.

"Don?" he said. "I'm hanging out here with my ass in the breeze."

"Let me check the status," Don Morris said into his ear. Keller could hear him talking to another person. "Swann, what's the status?"

A deep male voice said something in the background. Then Morris came back on.

"They're coming up the hill now. A couple of delays with the landing, a little delay with the armored car, now they're there. Where exactly are you?"

"I'm at Kondiaronk Belvedere. It's a little plaza that—"

"I know the place," Morris said. "I'll tell them."

"There will be signs for it on the park road," Keller said, but Morris didn't respond.

A long moment passed. Keller's eyes scanned the kids, the young guys with their thick beards, white girls wearing dreadlocks, tattoos, book bags and long skateboards in evidence, the smell of clove cigarettes and marijuana on the air…

None of these people were a threat. But threats could walk up out of nowhere.

"They've just arrived," Don Morris said. "Be cool, relax, let them do their thing, okay? Everything they do is for your safety."

"Is it the same men?" Keller said. "The men that saved David's daughter?"

"It is. Their names are Stone and Newsam. Newsam is the black guy. He's as big as the mountain you're standing on. Stone is the other one."

Across the way, a black SUV with high intensity xenon headlights drove slowly up one of the walking paths. It bumped over the curb and pulled onto the stone plaza. Its appearance caused the buzz of conversation to increase in volume a few notches. Did the young lovers and pot smokers and dreamers approve, disapprove, or think that the cops had suddenly come? It was impossible to tell.

Three men got out of the car. Two of the men made an immediate line for Keller. There was something disconcerting about that. They moved quickly, like sharks converging on a hunk of meat. Behind them, Keller saw the third man take up a position near the open rear door of the SUV. Keller caught the flash of a gun in the man's hand, something bigger than a pistol, a machinegun, maybe an Uzi or an MP5.

Then the other two were nearly on top of him. The black man walked with a silver cane and a pronounced limp. His pant leg was cut off below the thigh. His thigh and knee were dressed in heavy bandages, making it impossible for him to bend that leg. He came in like a thunderstorm, or a tornado. It was hard to take your eyes off him. His face was surprisingly youthful. He could be one of these kids on the plaza himself.

"Mr. Keller?" the other one said. He had materialized right in front of Keller's eyes. He was tall, with short blond hair and the beginnings of a beard. He might have been in his thirties. He was ruggedly handsome, in the way of a model for a cigarette ad. His face said he was tired, but his eyes looked alert, almost on fire. It was an odd combination.

"Yes?"

"I'm Agent Stone, this is Agent Newsam. Don Morris sent us to get you. I'm going to frisk you, and I'm going to confiscate any weapons you have on you. Is that understood?"

"I need—"

"No you don't," the big one, Newsam, said.

"Listen, I was in the Marines," Keller said.

"*Was* is the operative word," Newsam said. "When was that, before I was born?"

Keller shrugged. "Probably."

"I'm going to guess your training has gone a little stale."

Stone was already frisking him. He found the Sig Sauer more or less instantly. He took the magazine out, pocketed it, and checked the round for a chamber. "Nice gun. Is this the only weapon?"

Keller nodded. "Yes."

Stone continued to search him, his hands expertly roaming Keller's body.

"I just told you yes."

He nodded. "I know. This is how we establish some trust. We've got a car ride, a plane ride, and a helicopter ride ahead of us. You told me that's the only weapon. If it turns out to be true, already I feel a little better about you."

"Okay," Keller said.

Stone finished searching him. "Who do you have on the phone there?"

"Uh, it's your boss."

Stone took the phone. "Don Morris, the living legend," he said. He listened and smiled. "We're here, we have acquired the subject, and good Lord willing, we'll be on our way home very soon. Please tell Swann to keep his eyes on us."

He listened again.

"Okay, signing off."

He looked at Keller. Then he looked at the phone in his hand.

"Is this a burner?"

Keller nodded. "Yes."

"Good man. You won't need it anymore." He dropped it to the stone pavement, stomped on it several times, and kicked the remnants of it apart.

Keller looked at the two men. Newsam was scanning the crowd for threats. He wore a large Hawaiian shirt with one sleeve cut away to accommodate what looked like more wound dressings. His free hand was inside the shirt.

"Where's your car?" Stone said.

"I left it at my flat," Keller said. "I took the bus up here. Nobody gets murdered on the city bus."

Stone nodded. "Good. Then we can just leave it there."

"But I do need to go home first," Keller said.

Stone's shoulders slumped.

"No you don't," the big man said.

Keller nodded and looked at them both. "Yes, I do. I don't have any of my stuff with me. I didn't want to be a pack mule up here, weighed down and exposed. I need a few things. Most important, I don't have the recording with me. I thought it best if I left it at the flat."

"How far is your flat?" Stone said.

Keller shrugged. "Five minutes. It's in Old Montreal, right down at the bottom of the hill. I live two blocks from all the nightlife."

He could have killed them all.

Stone, Newsam, and Keller had been standing in a little group on the plaza. Stone and Newsam even had their backs to him. With the MP5, Murphy could have easily mowed the three of them down in a couple of seconds.

That would have done Wallace Speck's dirty work, but it would have left Kevin Murphy with a conundrum. How to escape?

He sighed. The night was full of conundrums.

He eased the Mercedes down the winding park road and back onto the Montreal city streets. They were on Peel Street, a wide avenue right in the heart of McGill University and a busy bar scene. There were swarms of people out on the boulevard, doing summer night pub crawls. There were a lot of cars headed in each direction.

"Swann, how are we looking?" Stone said from the back seat. He and Ed had given Keller the front passenger seat so they could keep an eye on him. Any false moves from Keller, and they could incapacitate him very quickly from behind.

Swann was the eye in the sky. He was watching via real time satellite, and he was talking on a satellite phone. Stone had him on the speaker phone feature.

"There's so much traffic on the streets, it's impossible to say for sure. I don't see anything moving in a pattern, I don't see anything shadowing you. I don't see anyone leapfrogging. But with hundreds of cars to choose from, I just don't know."

They moved slowly along with the night traffic.

"Murph?" Stone said. "Anything?"

Murphy shrugged. "Nothing jumps out at me. Just all these kids going to bars. I think we're good."

For Murphy, opportunity had knocked today. He had decided to join Stone at the Special Response Team not because he liked Stone. He didn't. And he hadn't joined because he liked the idea of police work. Frankly, crime was more appealing. All he had wanted was to come in from the cold for a little while, get a steady paycheck, get some health insurance, and maybe obtain access to inside information. Government spooks always knew where the big scores were.

And just like that, a very big score, the biggest of his life, had landed in his lap. This guy Keller was worth a mint. The trick was to make sure he fell into the hands of Speck's people, or died, and yet still walk away as a hero of sorts, or at least someone above suspicion. He had checked his account, and Speck had been as good as his word. As of this moment, Murphy was $2.5 million wealthier than he had been this afternoon.

The thought nearly made him lose his breath.

Give them Keller, collect the second half of the money, and disappear. That was the entire game right now.

"You know," Swann said. "You guys must have a GPS transponder in that car. You're giving off a signal that I'm picking up. I don't even need to watch you. I could plot your location on a map just by tracking the signal."

Murphy nodded. He *was* the signal, but he wasn't going to tell *them* that.

"It makes sense, Swann," he said. "This thing is an expensive ride to start with. It's loaded with probably a hundred grand in armor upgrades. I'd say the company tracks it because they don't want to lose it."

"Yeah," Swann said. "It does make sense."

"Turn left up ahead," Keller said. "There at the end of this block."

Murphy made the turn down a narrow one-way street. They were out of the university and moving down toward the river, into the Old City. More bars down here, more pedestrians, streets crazy with drunk people. He drove along for a few blocks.

"Okay, now a right."

Murphy turned down an even narrower street, this one made of cobblestones. The tires were hard, and the stones made a low bass rumble under the car. Two-hundred-year-old three- and four-story buildings hemmed them in on either side. Cars were parked along the curbside, making the street even narrower.

When were Speck's people going to hit? They had to be closing in by now, no matter what Swann said. Murphy was driving barely faster than a crawl. He seemed like he was nosing the car through busy nighttime traffic, being prudent, and he was doing that. He was also giving Speck all the time in the world to set up the hit.

"Come on, Speck," he wanted to say, but didn't. "Let's get this over with."

"This is it," Keller said. "The white building with the red door in front. My place is on the third floor. I can be in and out of there in five minutes."

Murphy pulled up in front of the building. It was an old brick construction, painted bright white. There was some sort of boutique house wares store on the street level, large glass display windows facing the street.

This street, man…It was very narrow, like a slot canyon. Murphy almost couldn't get over it. It was the perfect spot for an ambush.

He unlocked the doors.

"Murph," Stone said. "Do me a favor and keep the motor running, okay? I think we're fine, but let's run it like the real thing."

Murphy nodded. "You got it, chief. But don't be long up there or you might find me in one of these bars talking to the French girls."

"You got your radio on?"

Murphy took his little two-way radio out of the armrest compartment to his right. He pressed the TALK button. "Stone, you read me?"

"Stone, you read me?" said Stone's radio in the back seat.

Murphy let go of the button. "On," he said.

"In and out, five minutes," Stone said.

Murphy glanced up and down the street. It was quieter here than on other blocks, certainly, but there were people walking in the shadows. Lovers, drinkers, people coming home to their flats after a night out.

"See you in a bit," Murphy said.

Or in the next life.

⚜ ⚜ ⚜

"A little tight in here," Ed said.

They climbed the narrow stairs in single file, Luke leading, Keller in the middle, and Ed bringing up the rear. It was a small building, with just one apartment on each floor. They reached the third-floor landing, moved along the hall to the door at the end, and Keller used his key to open it.

Inside, the apartment was small, with tall windows and exposed brick. Luke supposed it was charming. It was the kind of place that would turn up in one of the home décor magazines Becca liked to read.

Keller turned up the lights from a round knob on the wall. They came up gradually, three lamps hanging from the ceiling in a row gaining brightness as one.

"Watch the windows," Luke said. "Don't get too close to them."

Keller responded as if Luke had told him to go directly to the windows. Just below the nearest one, there was a laptop computer on a small desk. He leaned over the desk and pressed a button on the laptop.

"I've got the audio on here," he said. "I was making another copy of it before—"

Just then, the window shattered near Keller's bald head. It exploded inward, sending flying shards of glass across the room. The glass sprayed all over Keller's face. Instantly Luke dropped to the floor, at least as fast as Keller's body did.

"Ed! Kill the lights, man!"

Almost before he said it, the room went black.

The windows above their heads kept shattering, glass crashing inward. Luke could hear the gunshots from outside. It could be a prankster lighting off firecrackers. Someone was firing from a silenced gun.

"Is he dead?" Ed said.

"I don't know. Keller? Keller!"

Luke's mind played the event over from the beginning. Keller leaned toward the computer. Suddenly, the spray of glass. Also, a spatter of blood.

"I'm alive," Keller said. "But I'm hit. My face is bleeding."

"Okay," Luke said. "We'll deal with that in a second. Are you in pain?"

"No. But I'm bleeding. My heart is pounding. I have adrenaline racing through my system. I've seen guys die almost before they realized they were hit."

"Thanks for the biology lesson," Luke said. "Ed, did you see where those shots came from?"

"I saw a shot knock a chunk of plaster off the ceiling. The angle tells me the shot came from street level."

Luke crawled to Keller. He rolled him over roughly. Keller didn't resist at all. His face was awash in blood. Wonderful. Keller himself was breathing heavily. Luke ran his hands over face and head, looking for an entry wound. Nothing, just cuts. He ran his hands over Keller's chest and neck. Nothing at all.

"You got lucky," he said. "Your face got cut by flying glass. You didn't get shot."

Keller didn't speak. He just kept breathing.

"Keller, are you all right? You have to answer me."

"I'm okay."

Luke went into the pockets of his cargo pants. He took out Keller's Sig Sauer and the magazine that went with it. The mag was loaded. Luke pushed it into the gun and drove it home. He handed it to Keller.

"Here. You might need this."

Luke looked back at Ed. Ed was sprawled on the floor. He had his pistol out.

"How you doing, Ed?"

"I'm fine, man. You know, with my leg how it is, I can't exactly pop up and down. It hurts, even with the painkillers. I can't crouch. I can't run. I don't have much leverage. The truth is, I agreed to come on this trip because I never been to Montreal before. Thought it would be easy. What are we even doing, picking up some guy? I figured while we're passing through, I might scope out the city a touch."

"Yeah?" Luke said. "What do you think so far?"

"I'm ready to go home."

Another burst of gunfire ricocheted through the apartment. More glass flew. There was an automatic weapon out there somewhere. It was keeping them on the floor. That was trouble. If Luke was the bad guys, he'd keep firing that gun while an assault team hit the building.

Murphy.

Where was he in all this?

Luke took out his two-way radio. He pressed the TALK button. "Murphy, we are under attack. Do you read me? Murphy, come in. Do you read?"

Nothing. Silence on the other end.

"Murphy!"

Murphy had watched the whole thing unfolding.

He pulled the car about fifty yards up the block while the hit squad came together. There was no sense getting in their way. They appeared like dark ghosts emerging from the shadows. An SUV drove up and stopped at the end of the street, blocking any escape that way. In his rearview mirror, Murphy watched another one do the same thing at the top of the street.

A man placed a tripod on the hood of a car, then mounted a heavy gun on top of it. From this distance, its profile suggested an M240 machinegun. It had a sound suppressor so large, it was nearly as long the barrel of the gun itself.

Oh boy. The guy was going to try to take the kill shot from ground level? Was that a good idea?

Maybe they had another thought in mind.

Murphy saw the light go inside the third-floor apartment. A few seconds later, he saw the muzzle flashes from the machine gun. That sound suppressor really worked. The flashes told Murphy that the guy was lighting up Keller's apartment. But all Murphy could hear was the snap of small firecrackers and the Christmas jingles of the spent cartridges ejected and hitting the pavement.

The two-way radio suddenly barked to life.

Stone's voice came through. "Murphy, we are under attack. Do you read me? Murphy, come in. Do you read?"

Murphy stared at the radio. His mind worked through scenarios. He could ignore the call. Stone and Newsam and Keller could all die. Then no one would ever know Stone made that call.

But what if one of them lived?

And even if they all died, what was he going to say, that he didn't hear it or see it happening? That wasn't going to wash.

"Murphy!" Stone shouted.

Murphy glanced out the window to his left. A man stood about fifteen feet away, out in the street. Murphy didn't get a good look at his face. Instead, he saw the snout of the gun in his hand. It was a little semi-automatic, with another large silencer.

The muzzle flashed and the gun bucked in the man's hands. Murphy flinched as high-velocity rounds struck the window an inch from his face.

And bounced off.

"Double cross! I knew it!"

The man kept firing. The window cracked and splintered, but held. Murphy slammed the car in gear. He glanced to his right. Another man was there, on the passenger side, just behind him. Murphy caught a glimpse of a bigger gun, an Uzi or Tec-9. The man sprayed the car with bullets.

Dunk-dunk-dunk-dunk-dunk!

Murphy stomped on the gas. The car went peeling out into the street. The man to Murphy's left ran alongside it, still firing into the driver's side window.

No way was that window going to hold up.

Murphy slammed the brakes. The running man's momentum carried him another several feet. He turned and began firing into the windshield. Murphy veered hard left and crashed into the man. THUMP as the man's hands flew up into the air and he went under the driver's side of the car.

Murphy crashed into a small white car across the street. It was a Toyota or some subcompact. Heavy metal crunched as the armored Mercedes demolished the car and drove right into and through its frame. Murphy's head wrenched forward and banged off the steering wheel. That rang his bell.

No airbags. They must have removed them to make way for all the armor.

Murphy shook his head, trying to clear it.

He reached behind his seat. His hand found the MP5 and brought it back around in front. His mouth hung open as he stared down at it, caressed it. No sound suppressor on this thing. This was gonna be LOUD. He was going to rip up the night.

The second guy had come around to the right side of the car. He fired burst after burst at the front passenger side window. The window spiderwebbed, flecks of it flying inward. It began to sag. It was almost a goner. The man was on the other side of it, ten feet away, pumping automatic bursts into it.

Suddenly, the guy stopped. Murphy could almost hear his thought: *Out.* He could see the guy's silhouette eject the spent magazine and reach to pop another one in.

Well, that window was gonna go anyway.

Murphy opened up with the MP5, the ugly blat of automatic fire deafening him. The window, badly abused from the outside, compromised, wasn't expecting more abuse from the inside. It shattered outward.

Murphy ripped it with the MP5, drilling rounds into the attacker, shredding him. The man did a death dance, his gun flying into the air. Then he dropped to the ground, disappearing from view.

"Two down," he said.

Murphy sat back for a few seconds and took a breath. His ears were ringing. The edges of his eyesight were darkening. He had face-planted right into that steering wheel. He put his left hand to his face. It came away bloody. He slapped himself hard across the cheek.

"Wake up!"

The MP5 was loud. Speck's men had been hoping to do this quietly. In a crowded neighborhood like this one, that was the right approach. But the plan was ruined now. Between the car crash and the rattle of the MP5, the neighbors were awake.

"Speck!" he shouted in frustration, before he was even aware he was going to do it.

The thing could have worked out in everybody's favor. Instead, Speck tried to kill him. Murphy had specifically warned him not to do that.

A thought began to form. He couldn't quite articulate it yet. Speck had double-crossed him. And yet, he had sent Murphy a lot of money earlier today. Murphy was already rich from this deal, and it was clear that Speck wasn't planning to pay him the rest of the money anyway. Murphy didn't owe Speck anything.

And Speck didn't even know his name.

Five million bucks and I walk away from everything. Two point five million and… I keep my job?

The two-way radio had fallen to the floor by his feet. He reached down and picked it up. As he rose back up, he fought a wave of dizziness. He pressed TALK.

"Stone?"

There was a moment of quiet.

He looked to his right. Two men were creeping toward him from the SUV that was blocking the bottom of the street. They had guns out, pistols, but they hadn't taken a shot yet. They were leery, maybe. They had just watched Murphy kill two men.

Murphy fired a blast out the missing passenger side window. The men split up, each taking one side of the street, flanking him. They were going to try a pincer move.

"Stone, do you read me?"

Stone's voice squawked over the airwaves. "Murphy!"

"Yeah."

"What the hell is going on out there?"

Murphy looked to his left. The man with the machine gun was still there, still sending bursts into the apartment. Four guys were going up the fire escape of the building. As Murphy watched, three more guys smashed the windows of the street-level store. They lit gasoline bombs and tossed them inside. Within seconds, the store was on fire, the flames dancing in the night.

Somewhere, sirens had begun howling, and were coming this way.

One of the bombers kicked in the red front door of the building. The three men disappeared inside. They were running out of time, and they knew it. They were pulling out all the stops.

"Murphy! Status!"

"Bad," Murphy said. "We got problems out here. I had to kill a couple of guys. You've got what looks like a standard tripod-mounted M240 with a really high-tech suppressor on it trained on your windows. I wouldn't stand up if I were you. You've got some guys coming up the fire escape, and some more coming up the stairs. And they're giving you a hotfoot. The whole first floor of the building is now burning nicely."

"Murphy, what are you doing?"

Murphy looked in front of him. Now the windshield was cracking and splintering. One of the men from the SUV was directly in front of him, on the sidewalk between the ruined Toyota and another brick building. He was using the wrecked car for cover and was firing into Murphy's armored windshield.

"Hold on a second," Murphy said. He put the walkie-talkie down on the seat and slid it under his left leg. He put the car in gear again and stomped on the gas.

The Mercedes peeled out on the street. The tires shrieked and burned on cobblestone, then caught. The big armored SUV lurched forward, driving the Toyota in front of it. The Toyota slid a foot—something was caught—but then the resistance snapped and broke. The man with the gun made a wide-eyed look of surprise.

Murphy pushed the Toyota at high speed into the brick wall.

He rode the impact. His body wrenched forward, but he didn't hit his head this time. The guy with the gun was gone, caught between a car and a hard place.

Murphy picked up the radio.

"Stone?"

"Yeah, Murphy."

"Hold tight. Watch your windows and doors. They're coming in. I'm gonna try to work my way back to you. Listen, I hope you picked the optional insurance coverages on this car. I think I put a couple of dings in it."

Murphy pushed his door open and rolled out onto the cobblestone street.

Luke looked at Ed in the semi-darkness.

Luke was crouched low. Both Ed and Keller were sprawled on the floor. Luke had a hand on Keller's chest to keep him there. Keller wasn't really trying to get up.

"We got guests coming."

Ed nodded. "I heard him as well as you did. Up the stairs and up the fire escape. And the building is on fire. What do you want to do?"

Luke shook his head. "I don't know. Keller, where's the fire escape in this place?"

"It's a little platform outside the bedroom windows."

"This place is a one-bedroom?"

"Yes."

They were squeezed. The hallway came to that door at the front of the apartment. The fire escape came to the windows in the back. Men were about to burst in from both directions. There was a shooter with a machine gun. He had stopped firing through the windows, but he was still out there, shooting at something. And fire would be coming up through the floor soon enough. Luke shook his head.

"It's about to get hot in here."

"Yeah," Ed said. "Listen to the gunner out there. He's shooting the walls now. He's probably trying to punch a hole through the brickwork. That's what I would do."

Luke listened. Ed was right. The automatic rounds were hitting the outside of the building, more or less exactly where he was crouched. If that guy managed to open up the wall…And really, it wasn't a matter of if, but of when.

Luke didn't want to think about that right now.

"Okay, this is what we do," he said to Ed. "I'll get the bedroom, you get the front door. Kill anything that comes in. Sound okay?"

"Fine."

"Keller, you stay low, maybe crawl behind some furniture. You're the reason for this party, so stay out of sight."

"What about the fire?" Keller said.

Luke shrugged. "Pray for rain."

The man at the machine gun was focused on his job. He pumped rounds into the brick just below the third-floor window. His gun ate the ammunition belt, but he had three more stacked after that one.

Murphy gazed up there. That wall was coming apart. The guy would knock a nice hole in it any second. After that first hole opened up, he could make Swiss cheese out of that thing.

What a scene. Between the machine gun and the fire, they were turning that building into something out of Beirut, circa 1982.

Murphy's MP5 was spent. He was out of extra magazines for it, so he tossed it. He was down to his Glock pistol now. It was fine. He liked the Glock.

Murphy looked at the machine gun. It was an M240, just as he had guessed.

He walked right up to the man wielding it. The guy was so riveted by the action across the street, he forgot to pay attention to his surroundings. Murphy sighed.

Situational awareness. It was the key to everything. A lot of people didn't seem to know that.

The guy must have heard Murphy's footsteps. Too late. He looked up at Murphy and was surprised to see him there. His eyes went wide.

"Hi," Murphy said. "Nice gun. Mind if I try it?"

He shot the guy in the face, then pushed his thick corpse out of the way.

He got in behind the machine gun. He put his eye to the scope. VERY nice. There was only one man left on the fire escape. The first three had already gone in through the window. This last one looked like he was either waiting to go in, or trying to obtain a shot through the window.

Murphy squeezed the trigger and squirted the guy. The guy's body folded and went flying through the window and into the apartment.

Murphy looked up. That was it. That was the only shot he had.

Sirens were everywhere now, close, closer still, and far away. They were bringing everything they had.

Somewhere above his head was the heavy beat of a helicopter.

He'd better get off the street before someone got overzealous and decided he'd make a good target. He took the remaining ammo belts from the M240, draped them over his shoulder, and crossed the street. He looked both ways before he crossed.

The storefront was an inferno, flames pouring out and licking the side of the building. The front door to the stairwell was kicked in.

Murphy tossed the ammo belts into the fire and went up the stairs.

⚜ ⚜ ⚜

Luke crept to the bedroom door, staying low.

He stayed behind the wall and pushed the door open a crack.

It squeaked. The door squeaked.

Dammit, Keller! Oil your hinges!

Three men stood in the bedroom, just on the window side of Keller's wide bed. They were big guys, almost identical in bearing. They were in a tight circle, whispering together. One man, the one in the center, seemed to be in charge. He was diagramming the play. They all looked up when the door opened.

All three men raised guns.

Luke swung his gun around and fired it before the men got off a shot. One shot—he put a bullet right between the eyes of the boss. A red dot of blood appeared on the guy's forehead. He stood still for one second, then dropped bonelessly to the floor, dead before he hit the carpet.

All of a sudden, another man came flying through the window. He crashed through what remained of the glass and landed in a heap on the floor.

Luke didn't even question it. He fired at the other guys, BANG, BANG, BANG, but they had already dived for cover. He missed all three shots. He ducked back into the living room.

A second later, a volley of return fire splintered the walls at the threshold. Luke backed away, waited a beat, then wrapped his gun hand around the doorway. He fired three more times, then dropped back.

A new volley of shots came, ripping up the doorway again. Luke rolled up on one knee, ten feet away from the door. The shooting went on for a long time. Finally, it stopped.

A man darted through the doorway, gun out.

BANG! BANG! BANG!

Luke put three bullets in him, all in the center body mass. The guy fell over, holding his guts.

By Luke's count, one more guy was in there.

He kept his gun trained on the door.

"Come on! Come on!"

Behind him, at the other end of the small apartment, the front door blew apart. It came flying inward, ripped to pieces. Luke hit the ground and covered up.

He rolled over just in time to see a big man burst through the doorway. The man had a sawed-off shotgun for close quarters fighting.

Guns fired from the floor, coming from two directions. Ed was shooting from the kitchen floor, Keller from the living room.

The man with the shotgun did a crazy dance, hit from two sides.

Two more men were right behind him. The second man also had a shotgun. He fired, hitting the first man through the door in the back, cutting him to ribbons.

Bullets from the floor hit the second man.

He tossed something silver in the air.

"Grenade!" Keller screamed.

"No."

The third guy wasn't hit. He ducked back into the hallway and threw in another grenade. Luke watched it bounce into the living room and roll on the hardwood floor.

For a second, Keller seemed like he would crawl toward it.

"Keller!"

BOOOM! Luke got hit with a wave of light and sound.

He opened his eyes.

For a moment, he didn't know where he was. He didn't know how much time had passed. There was darkness, but there was also sound, and flickering light.

He sat up. His head was pounding. The room was on fire. All around him, flames were licking up through the floor. The place was starting to fill with smoke.

He touched the wooden floor with his left hand. The floorboards were hot. He looked at his right hand. It was holding a gun.

He was Luke Stone, and he was in Montreal.

"Flashbangs," he said. "They were just flashbangs."

The men had thrown stun grenades into the room. They were designed to disorient your targets and put them in a state of shock. It worked.

Luke climbed to his feet. He glanced at the windows. Forgot about that. There was a man out there with a machine gun. Well, if he had still been there, Luke would be dead now. Luke was alive, so...

A man came running in through the front door.

Luke raised his gun to shoot him.

The man raised his hands.

"Stone! Don't shoot."

In the orange gloom, the man resolved into a familiar shape. Tall, thin, with short blond hair. A narrow, arrogant face.

"Murphy. There was a guy out in the hall."

Murphy nodded. "Yeah. I saw him. I killed him."

Luke looked down at the floor. "We need to get out of here."

"I know. This place is gonna go any second."

Ed was on the kitchen floor, sitting with his big arms wrapped around one knee, his wounded leg extended out.

"You alive, Ed?" Luke said.

"Yeah. I'm alive."

"You hurt?"

Ed shook his head slowly, like a man with a migraine.

"Only my feelings."

Bald-headed Keller was curled in a ball on the living room floor.

"Keller, you alive?"

Keller didn't move. "Barely."

"Do you have the recording?"

"I have two copies on disk in my pocket. There's also one on my laptop. We should bring it just in case."

Luke nodded. The motion made him dizzy. "Okay. That should be good enough."

Murphy moved further into the apartment. "It's lovely chatting, but we have to go. The stairs are toast, so we need to take the fire escape. Where is it in here?"

He passed Luke headed for the bedroom.

"Murph, there's another guy in there. Murph!"

Murphy's gun was out. He didn't hesitate. He went right through the door. For a second, he was just gone. Luke turned, moving in slow motion like he was underwater, the residue of the stun grenade. He expected to hear a gunshot.

Murphy's head poked back out.

"The guy's gone. He must have made a run for it."

The narrow street outside was a mob scene.

In the background, the building burned out of control. Teams of firemen hosed it down, and hosed the neighboring buildings down, trying to half the spread. Half-asleep people were being evacuated by policemen.

Bodies littered the ground, now covered by sheets. Halfway down the block, the Mercedes was on the sidewalk, a small white car sandwiched between it and a brick building.

Crowds of people loitered on the other side of the yellow police cordon. Luke walked slowly up the street toward the cordon, one hand on Lawrence Keller's arm. He had this strange idea that after all of that, Keller might try to run. Murphy walked in front of them. Ed brought up the rear.

They were protecting him with their bodies now.

A French language newscast was at the edge of the police line—a cameraman with shaggy black hair and a young woman. They were the first news team on the scene. Suddenly Keller made a beeline for them.

"Keller!"

Luke let him go.

"*Parlez vous Anglais?*" he said to the woman.

She nodded. "*Oui*. Of course."

And just like that, the frightened rabbit of earlier tonight, bloody-faced, ripped-clothes Lawrence Keller, was authoritative and in command.

"My name is Lawrence Keller. I'm the former chief of staff of the American President David Barrett. You're going to want to interview me. This will be the biggest scoop of your career. Shoot it now, and confirm my identity later. If you do this, I promise the segment will go around the world. I have evidence that the president was murdered by American intelligence operatives."

The young woman stared at him. She glanced at the cameraman. He was older than she was, and probably in charge. He shrugged and nodded.

Luke stood and watched, the flames crackling behind him. A moment later, they were filming.

CHAPTER FORTY TWO

4:05 a.m. Eastern Daylight Time
Newington
Fairfax County, Virginia

He couldn't do it.

Wallace Speck had seen a lot of death, and he had brought much of it about. He had become rather nonchalant about it over the years. But when push came to shove, it was harder than it looked.

"How did it come to this?" he whispered to no one.

He was standing in the big country kitchen of his house on a suburban cul-de-sac. In the daytime, the view out the back was of woodland, but now it was dark as pitch. He lived here alone. His kids were grown and didn't speak to him. His wife had left him years ago.

The gun was on the granite countertop.

He knew what he had to do. But he couldn't even pick the damn thing up.

They were coming for him. He knew that. The game was over. When they arrested him, they were going to pressure him to talk.

They might offer him a deal—three hundred years in prison instead of the death penalty. They might even offer him something better than that. Whatever they offered him, there were people in this world who would prefer if he didn't talk. They would do what they could to see to it that he didn't get that chance.

The honorable thing would be to end it now. Because he was going to talk. He knew that about himself. He even knew exactly how it was going to go. They were going to give him a guy, an interrogator, who was going to be his friend. His buddy. His pal. That guy was going to get him little breaks. His own cell, maybe. In a quiet POD away from the maniacs. With some outside time.

These things could be his, if only he would tell them what they wanted to hear. And if he didn't? Other things could be his, too. Supermax could be his. Solitary confinement could be his. Arbitrary restrictions on books, pens and pencils, paper, contact with the outside world—they could all be his.

But he was going to talk, wasn't he? Yes, he was. He wanted to talk. He'd been very clever, and there were many, many things he knew about, not just David Barrett. He could blow people's minds, the things he might talk about. It could be very entertaining.

Which was why he shouldn't do it. You couldn't expect to give away the Agency's secrets and come to a happy ending.

Without thinking about it, he reached and picked up the gun. It was loaded, he needn't bother to look. He put the barrel to his head. One quick pull, and he could slip the noose, escape responsibility for his actions once again.

One quick pull.

Suddenly, there was a commotion at the front of the house. He couldn't see it back here in the kitchen, but he could hear. The front door exploded inward. Someone had hit it with a battering ram. One hit had done it.

Now heavy footsteps ran through the house.

"DOWN! Get DOWN!"

They were here. They were in. It was now or never.

He closed his eyes.

His finger caressed the trigger.

Behind him, the glass windows lining the back deck crashed inward. Speck didn't look. He didn't even flinch. He could imagine the big bodies tumbling through the windows well enough.

Do it! Do it now!

He grimaced, skating on the edge between life and death.

"Freeze!" someone screamed. "Drop that gun!"

Pull it. Pull the trigger.

A heavy body hit him chest high. He opened his eyes, flying through space. The gun was out of his hand. He wanted to scream. "No!"

Then he was on the kitchen's stone tile floor. Two men in black jumpsuits were on top of him, wrestling, undulating over him like snakes. They turned him over onto his face. A second later, they had his arms pinned behind his back. He could hear the cuffs clicking on. An instant later, he could feel the metal biting his wrists.

Rough hands roamed his body, searching for weapons.

"Wallace Speck? You have the right to remain silent..."

He tuned out the words that he knew by heart. The men pulled him to his feet. Now he was standing again in the kitchen, helpless, in their custody. He couldn't kill himself, and now he belonged to them. For the rest of his life, he would belong to them, or people just like them.

A group of these cop types milled around him, all wearing identical black uniforms. One of them turned around to go into the living room. There were three large white letters stenciled on the back of the man's black jumpsuit: SRT.

Chapter Forty Three

7:45 a.m. Eastern Daylight Time
Special Activities Center, Directorate of Operations
Central Intelligence Agency
Langley, Virginia

The end had come.

The old man reflected that it didn't bother him much. He was eighty-three years old. He had lived a long time, and he had done many things. There was no shame in endings.

His body had betrayed him years ago. Although his mind was still sharp, he lived with physical indignities now that he would never have dreamed of as a young man. Indeed, if someone had told him of the things to come in his last years, he would have answered them with two words:

"Shoot me."

He laughed at the thought. And his eyes fell upon the carved wooden box sitting on the wide expanse of his desk. He liked to keep the desk clear as a general rule, but today he was making an exception. The box was there, as were two small sheets of paper.

He lit a cigarette from the embers of the dying one. He inhaled deeply, exhaled, and watched the blue smoke rise toward the ceiling of this strangely cavernous office to which he'd been exiled. He smiled. He wished he'd be around to see the looks on the faces of the young lions who ran the Agency these days.

Well, middle-aged lions. They tended to treat the old man as something quaint, a pet or a mascot, or maybe one of those Norman

Rockwell paintings of a soda jerk leaning across the counter to accept a nickel from a young girl. Would these men be surprised to learn of his actions, of the things he'd still been capable of?

It was impossible to know. He didn't understand the thinking of modern men.

He gave a brief thought to Wallace Speck. The name alone could strike fear into the hearts of certain people. And yet, in the end Speck was a coward. Yes, the old man already knew that Speck had been captured. He even knew the circumstances of his capture, with Speck sitting on the fence, perched perfectly between honor on the one side, and disgrace on the other. And Speck had chosen disgrace.

Somehow, the old man was not surprised. Speck had gone about things with a sort of grim determination, an almost mechanical efficiency. He didn't seem to like his work. He brought no joy to it.

He was trying to get somewhere, to prove something, to realize some ambition that he quietly harbored. And that was his undoing. You did this work for the passion of it, the awe of it, the sheer spectacle.

"Try to enjoy prison instead," the old man said to Wallace Speck.

With the Keller man providing evidence, the Baylor government brought low, and Speck in custody and probably already talking a mile a minute, the next stop on the whistle stop tour was likely to be right in this office.

And that meant it was time to go.

He reached and opened the box. For a second, he allowed his ancient hands to caress the carved and polished wood. It was really a beautiful box. He'd had it custom made. Nestled inside was a Walther P38 pistol. This one was manufactured in 1942. The gun was even more beautiful than the box. The Germans really did make wonderful things.

The old man picked up the gun and got the feel of it in his hand. There was already a round in the chamber.

He had taken the gun from a Wehrmacht colonel. The old man had been a young man in those days, and he'd been a spy for the OSS, the Office of Strategic Services, which later became his beloved Agency.

The old man arrived in Paris two weeks before Patton's Third Army. German morale was disintegrating. On August nineteenth, the night of the French uprising—God, he remembered it like it was yesterday—he'd been in a bar where this German colonel was drunk, loud, obnoxious, and clearly terrified.

The big, balding, frightened German had slapped a young French woman in the face and knocked her to the ground. Then he threatened to execute her family.

A few moments later, the old man (who was still a young man) had followed him into the bathroom and shot him in the head while he was urinating. He remembered how the colonel swayed unsteadily, bracing himself with one hand on the wall.

Then: BANG.

Afterward, he looted the body and took the man's gun.

This lovely gun.

The old man took one last drag from his cigarette, then placed it on the ashtray. He didn't stub it out. Might as well let it enjoy its last few moments.

Slowly, he placed the barrel of the Walther in his mouth. He pointed it directly upward, against the top of his mouth, toward his brain. This was the most certain way to do it. Many people did it incorrectly, pointing the gun at the side of their head from the outside. Sometimes that resulted in unpleasant accidents, like a certain ex-Marine he once knew who ended up still alive with half his face missing.

None of that for this old man.

He took a deep breath. He didn't feel afraid in the least. He wondered if perhaps he should count to a certain number. Five, maybe. Or even three.

He eyes fell upon the two pieces of paper on his desk. On each piece, he had scrawled a message using a ballpoint pen. He thought they were clever enough to serve as his epitaphs.

Never get old, read one message.

He gently pulled the trigger of the P38. The gun used double-action operation, so the first pull cocked the hammer. Now he was ready.

Should he count? He still couldn't decide.

He glanced at the other paper, his second and last message to posterity.

Messy, isn't it?

Nah, forget the counting.

He pulled the trigger again.

Chapter Forty Four

8:15 a.m. Eastern Daylight Time
The West Wing
The White House
Washington, DC

"Mr. President, do you understand what I'm telling you?"

A dozen men moved quickly down a wide hall lined with Greek-style columns. Their footsteps echoed on the marble floor. They were headed for the main entrance of the building. Secret Service were among the men, flanking them in the front and rear.

Mark Baylor had gone numb. He had cut himself shaving this morning. He never did that. He was having trouble focusing. He glanced down at the man speaking to him. It was a small bearded man in a three-piece suit. His name was Ronald Griffin, and he was the head of the White House legal team.

"Tell me again," Baylor said.

"Everything is okay," Griffin said. "The interview will take place at FBI headquarters. You are a person of interest and not a suspect. Keep that at the top of your mind. Also, your entire legal team, including myself, will remain with you throughout the interview."

"Okay," Baylor said.

"And your Secret Service detail will remain with you at all times, even if you are arrested."

"If I'm *arrested*?"

"Mark, I'm going to be very frank with you."

Baylor didn't like that. A second ago, Griffin had been calling him Mr. President. Now he was calling him Mark. That was a rather sudden downgrade.

"I consider this a hostile interview," Griffin said. "We requested a transcript of the questions from the FBI nearly an hour ago, and they've refused to provide it. I'll caution you now that they've taken Wallace Speck into custody, and we believe he's going to become a cooperating witness. We know Lawrence Keller is already a cooperating witness."

Baylor tripped over his own feet, and a hand steadied him from behind. Wallace Speck was cooperating with the FBI? *Wallace Speck?* Wallace Speck was as guilty as the day was long. He was a one-man crime wave.

The thought of Speck testifying...

Griffin went on. "Whatever the nature of your relationship with those two men, I urge you not to discuss it with the FBI at this time. This is an informational interview, and you have no information to provide about them. You are merely a person of interest. Remember that you are not under arrest."

"And what if I am..." Baylor said. He could barely get the words out. "What if I'm arrested?" He felt like he might start crying at any second. He had never been arrested in his life. He was a Baylor. Baylors didn't get arrested.

"If you happen to be arrested, your situation actually improves," Griffin said. "There is an immediate protocol that goes into effect. We terminate any further questioning, and we drop the façade of cooperation. You are no threat to anyone, and you're too prominent to be a flight risk. A reasonable bail will be set, and we will post it immediately. You'll be back out within an hour or two. And as I indicated, your Secret Service detail will remain with you throughout the process."

Griffin paused.

"Also, keep in mind that it's an open constitutional question if a president can even be arrested, or charged with a crime. If they arrest you, they'll be treading on very shaky ground. That's why I'm confident that—"

"Oh God, Ronald," Baylor said. "Is this what we're reduced to? Shaky constitutional questions?"

Griffin nodded. "I'm the first to admit it's a minefield. But we're going to navigate it, and we're going to come out the other side."

"That's very comforting," Baylor said.

"I'm not your security blanket, Mark. I'm your lawyer."

Baylor stumbled along. There was no feeling in his legs now. He had no idea what Wallace Speck did or didn't do. He hadn't known that David Barrett was going to be murdered. How could he know a thing like that? He wasn't in on any of this.

The FBI probably wouldn't arrest him. That was good, he supposed. On the other hand, how did you remain president when the FBI questioned you as a person of interest in the murder of the previous president?

Simple answer: you didn't. There were too many forces aligned against it. The media, the public, the Congress. The opposing party would never stop calling for your head. Your own party would race for the exits. The liberal wing had already been questioning his legitimacy yesterday afternoon, before any of this had happened.

From now on, and forever, Mark Baylor was radioactive.

The group was approaching the main doors. Outside, there was a line of waiting SUVs. The sky was bright out there. Somewhere, in a different reality, it was a sunny summer morning.

As the doors opened, tall men in dark suits reached to take Mark Baylor by the arms and guide him to the open rear doors of an SUV.

He let himself go limp and allowed strong hands to lead him toward his new life, whatever that may be.

Chapter Forty Five

5:30 p.m. Moscow Daylight Time (9:30 a.m. Eastern Daylight Time)
Strategic Command and Control Center The Kremlin Moscow, Russia

The place was mostly empty now.

A small crew continued to run operations here in the War Room, monitoring events in far-flung places. But everything was quiet. There were no flashpoints. Dead Hand had been rescinded. The order to destroy Nome had been cancelled.

Colonel Viktor Chevsky stood looking at the big open space and smoking a cigarette. He breathed deeply. Several janitors were sweeping the floors and cleaning food packages and soft drink cans from the computer stations.

The American Speaker of the House, next in line for the presidency, had apparently called as soon as the recently departed president had been taken into custody. He had ordered a unilateral military stand-down, and he hoped the Russian Federation would join him in this.

Chevsky shook his head. The Americans! So superior in so many ways, yet they couldn't seem to decide who their president was and whether or not they wanted to fight. They might never know how close they came to the end of everything.

And the Russians? Their response to all of this had been yet another disaster. The military was completely unprepared for conventional war with a major power. There was confusion and infighting at all levels of command. The evacuated defense minister had been murdered on the helipad by the man tasked with carrying the nuclear codes.

It was black comedy.

And that humorous little murder would probably spell the end of Chevsky's career. After all, he had handpicked Gregor for the assignment. Even so, he might as well try to slip his own neck out of the noose. There were other, perhaps better, necks to blame.

"Let the record show," he said, speaking to the aide standing behind him, who instantly scrawled his words on a notepad in shorthand, "that Corporal Gregor was suffering from undiagnosed combat stress stemming from his experiences in the Second Chechen Campaign. Gregor was failed, and the state was failed, by the military medical authorities whose job it is to detect the symptoms of this very serious ailment. A reassessment of the processes by which troops are evaluated for psychiatric illnesses when returning from combat is in order."

He stopped. He looked at the young aide.

"*Is in order*," Chevsky said. "That sounds weak."

"Yes sir," the aide said. "Perhaps something stronger. *Must be undertaken*?"

Chevsky nearly laughed. What did it matter? In the military, out of the military? Reassessments that were in order, or that must be undertaken?

Chevsky had picked Gregor because Gregor's record showed he was good at killing. It was a bad decision. He should have picked someone who was good at carrying a suitcase. He might lose his rank, but the days when he could be shot for incompetence were long over.

He smiled at the aide. "It nice to be alive, isn't it?"

The aide nodded. "Yes sir. It is."

Chapter Forty Six

July 4
6:45 p.m. Eastern Daylight Time
Queen Anne's County, Maryland
Eastern Shore of Chesapeake Bay

"Stone, you call this rare?"

Luke looked at Don Morris. Don's appearance was beyond strange. He was wearing a pink Polo shirt and blue madras shorts. He had deck shoes on his feet with no socks. The clothes fit his muscular body well. He could be on an ocean sailing team. He could be in an L.L. Bean catalog, the idealized version of someone's outdoorsy granddad. But Luke had never seen him like this before.

Don had a can of beer in one hand. And one of Luke's hamburgers in the other.

Luke was standing at the big double grill, masterfully grilling burgers, hot dogs, sausages, and vegetable shish-ka-bobs for the guests, of which Don was a prominent one.

Luke shrugged and smiled. He took a chug of his own beer. "It's not alive anymore, if that's what you mean."

"I like my burgers with a heartbeat, son. I might have to show you how to do it on the next one."

Luke shook his head. Nobody was taking over his grill. "Un-unh. On the next one, I'll just wave the raw meat over the fire for a few seconds."

"That'll do it," Don said. "All right, Stone. I'm not supposed to fraternize with the help, but here I go anyway."

Luke watched as Don headed downhill to the patio. Was Don a little drunk? It seemed so. And why not? It was a day to celebrate. The SRT was on its way up. Wallace Speck was singing like a bird. The FBI had rolled up his entire operation.

In the end, Mark Baylor hadn't been charged with a crime, at least not yet. There didn't seem to be any evidence that he knew anything. But his presidency was so thoroughly compromised in the eyes of the public, there was such a shadow over him, that he'd had to resign. Now the liberal wing was coming. Luke didn't know how he felt about that, but he knew the SRT had been responsible for taking Baylor down, and everyone else knew it as well.

Down on the patio, Don did a little jig. Yeah, he was drunk. Don's wife, Margaret, was here, but Becca's parents kept attaching themselves to him. Luke smiled.

Audrey and Lance were nothing if not social climbers, and Don was the founder of the Special Response Team, the legendary pioneer of the very concept of special operations, and one of the founders of Delta Force. He could picture the two of them at a dinner party with their rich friends:

"Well, we were chatting with Don Morris the other day. You know, *the* Don Morris..." Like chatting with him at a barbecue meant they owned him.

Either way, they were on their best behavior today, and Luke would take it.

Who else was here? Ed had come with his new girlfriend, Cassandra. At first, Luke thought Ed had showed up with the supermodel Naomi Campbell. That's how beautiful Cassandra was. Swann was here, solo, as was Trudy. The whole group was standing, talking with Becca, who was holding...

No, Trudy was holding Gunner. She and Becca were chatting and laughing about something.

Luke took a deep breath. It was hard to...

"Stone."

Luke turned and Murphy was standing there. He must have just come out of the house. He wore jeans and a plain blue T-shirt. He was tall and thin and unassuming, drinking his beer. You would never guess in a million years the kind of fighting skills this man was harboring.

"Murph ... ready for another one?"

Murphy nodded. "Yeah."

Luke gave Murphy a hamburger, well-done.

"Thank you."

They stood for a moment, the silence stretching out between them. Murphy was quiet, Luke knew, not a conversationalist. In fact, he was an enigma. A mystery. It was impossible to guess what went on inside his mind, and Luke sensed that he liked it that way. Luke wondered if Murphy had ever found a way to enjoy his life, even a little bit. It didn't really seem that way.

Luke looked out at the water of Chesapeake Bay. Tonight at sunset, there would be fireworks out there. Luke's body was healing, and he felt really good for a change. Don had given him several days off, and he was sleeping a lot. This morning was the first time since the Russian operation where he had awakened and wasn't in a great deal of pain. The pain was still there, but not enough to immediately take a pill.

Becca hadn't even pressed him about his injuries. She must have assumed they happened during the Montreal operation. She was busy with the baby and happy for this time together, and the fact that her husband's gunshot wounds were healing nicely didn't even seem to be on her radar.

"How did they know?" Murphy said. "That's what I keep coming back to. How did they know?"

"In Montreal?" Luke said.

"Yeah."

Luke shrugged. "They were probably following Keller. They were planning to hit him when the time was right, then we stepped in, so they moved on it. That's about all I can think of. Don is clearing the SRT headquarters of bugs pretty much constantly."

Murphy nodded, but didn't commit to anything. If he agreed with Luke's assessment, he wasn't going to say it. If he thought the

SRT was riddled with CIA spies, or the offices were contaminated with bugs, he wasn't going to say that either.

"Well, it was a hell of an operation anyway."

Luke lifted his beer and they clinked cans.

"Cheers to that, brother."

"I enjoyed it," Murphy said, and finally he cracked a smile. "I have to thank you for that. It's nice to be one of the good guys again."

Luke watched Murphy walk down to the group on the patio.

One of the good guys.

Bad guys over there, good guys over here. Ours is not to wonder why. Ours is but to do and die. It was easy to believe these things once, but getting harder all the time. He stared up at the sky for a long moment. It was a big world and people were constantly trying to carve it up to their own advantage. There were sinister forces always at work, and the next dark mission was always right around the corner.

He gazed past the patio and out at the waters of Chesapeake Bay again. Today was the Fourth of July. And it was a beautiful day for a barbecue.

NOW AVAILABLE FOR PRE-ORDER!

PRIMARY THREAT
(The Forging of Luke Stone—Book #3)

"One of the best thrillers I have read this year."
–Books and Movie Reviews (re Any Means Necessary)

In PRIMARY THREAT (The Forging of Luke Stone–Book #3), a ground-breaking action thriller by #1 bestseller Jack Mars, elite Delta Force veteran Luke Stone, 29, leads the FBI's Special Response Team as they respond to a hostage situation on an oil rig in the remote Arctic.

Yet what at first seems like a simple terrorist event may, it turns out, be much more.

With a Russian master plan unfolding rapidly in the Arctic, Luke may have arrived at the precipice of the next world war.

And Luke Stone may just be the only man standing in its way.

PRIMARY THREAT is a standalone, un-putdownable military thriller, a wild action ride that will leave you turning pages late into the night. The precursor to the #1 bestselling LUKE STONE THRILLER SERIES, this series takes us back to how it all began, a riveting series by bestseller Jack Mars, dubbed "one of the best thriller authors" out there.

"Thriller writing at its best."
—Midwest Book Review (re *Any Means Necessary*)

Also available is Jack Mars' #1 bestselling LUKE STONE THRILLER series (7 books), which begins with Any Means Necessary (Book #1), a free download with over 800 five star reviews!

PRIMARY THREAT
(The Forging of Luke Stone—Book #3)

Made in the USA
Las Vegas, NV
21 November 2020